A KISS TO DREAM ON

Passion swept through him as his hands roamed her back. He wanted her, he realized, like a dying man wants time. With little encouragement, she could become an obsession. He could need her. Desperately and dangerously.

In the dark places, where memory haunted him, Cammy lit him up. She brought life where he'd begun to wonder if he'd ever feel again. He drank at that fountain like a man dying of thirst. His hands tightened on her upper arms. His mouth demanded. Blissfully, hers yielded. He pulled her closer, as close as he could get her. And still it wasn't enough.

Other Avon Contemporary Romances by
Neesa Hart

HALFWAY TO PARADISE

Neesa Hart

a Kiss to Dream on

AVON BOOKS  NEW YORK

This is a work of fiction. Names, characters, places, and incidents either are the product of the author's imagination or are used fictitiously. Any resemblance to actual events, locales, organizations, or persons, living or dead, is entirely coincidental and beyond the intent of either the author or the publisher.

AVON BOOKS, INC.
1350 Avenue of the Americas
New York, New York 10019

Copyright © 1999 by Moneesa Hart
Published by arrangement with the author
Library of Congress Catalog Card Number: 99-94461
ISBN: 0-380-80787-4
www.avonbooks.com/romance

First Avon Books Printing: December 1999

AVON TRADEMARK REG. U.S. PAT. OFF. AND IN OTHER COUNTRIES, MARCA REGIS-TRADA, HECHO EN U.S.A.

Printed in the U.S.A.

WCD   10 9 8 7 6 5 4 3 2 1

a
Kiss to
Dream
on

✿❤ one

If Cammy Glynn had learned one thing growing up in the shadow of the media, she'd learned that every media debacle started because someone had good intentions.

Cammy's eyes drifted shut in frustration. "Look, Mike, I know you thought you were helping."

Dr. Mike Costas, Cammy's longtime friend and business partner, leaned back in his chair. The soft creak of leather and slightly oiled springs signaled his lapse into informality.

Cammy opened her eyes in time to see him prop his pricey Italian loafers on the mirrorlike surface of his cherry desk. Mike did nothing without flair. "Cammy," he said, his voice the same butterlike sound that calmed so many of his patients, "you have got to think this over."

"I have thought it over." Agitated, she surged from the chair to pace to the window. This was unusual for her; in the six years she'd shared office space and a practice with Mike, they'd never had a major disagreement. She liked him, personally and professionally, but this time he'd pushed her too far. "I know you feel the publicity will benefit Wishing Star."

"It will."

She ignored his interruption. "I also know you were doing me a favor by talking to your friend at Associated Wire."

"Cammy—"

"But I don't want Jackson Puller disrupting my work with the children." She shot Mike a dry look. "Or disrupting my life."

"This press aversion you have is—"

"Phobic. I know. You've told me. Spare me the professional rhetoric."

"Look." Mike sat up straight. "It's time to face facts, Cam. You know I support what you're doing with the Wishing Star Foundation, but you've got to be realistic. You're scraping by on private donations. You're spending so much of your professional time doing charity work, you've barely got a paying patient left in the bunch."

"I do my share of the billing."

"But not the collecting." He exhaled a long breath. "Truth is, you're not the only one that needs the publicity. Five years ago, everyone in this town wanted to see a shrink. Neurosis was in vogue. That's not how it is anymore. It's getting harder to make ends meet."

"Mike, if the practice is in trouble—"

"We're not in trouble. Not yet."

"You could consider another partner."

"I don't *want* another partner. I like the blend we

have, and our rapport. I like having a child psychiatrist down the hall. Despite my reputation for avarice"—he flashed her his million-dollar grin—"I actually like to help people. Besides, Bess would kill me if I dumped you."

Cammy laughed. Mike's oft professed fear of his wife's supposed bad temper was a standing joke between them. "I wasn't suggesting that you dump me, Costas. I was merely pointing out that we could expand a bit."

"No. I think we have an excellent balance here, and I don't want to screw around with it."

"Fear of change—"

He held up a hand. "It's not a joke, Cam." His expression turned uncharacteristically serious. "You and I have both known for some time that your heart's with Wishing Star—*not* in private practice. You don't want to spend your hours treating the overindulged neurotic kids of public officials any more than I want to spend my days volunteering at the homeless shelter. All I'm trying to do here is help you out."

He was undeniably, frustratingly correct, and she knew it. "I know."

"A little positive media attention is just the thing you need to get Wishing Star firmly established. You'll pick up some decent corporate funding, a few big private donors, and then you can spend all the time you want working with those children. If nobody ever pays you a dime, it won't matter. Besides," he said, indicating the window with a wave of his hand, "you can't beat the view from the office."

She didn't need to look. Mike's Sixth Street office

suite overlooked the U.S. Capitol on one side and the Washington Monument on the other. Cammy studied him for a minute. "You're right."

"I know I'm right. So what if I pulled a few strings? So what? It's not a criminal offense, you know. This is Washington, D.C. The city doesn't turn without somebody pulling somebody else's strings."

"But why Jackson Puller?"

Mike's white eyebrows lifted. "That was pure luck. When I talked to Chris, he was going to send some junior hack over here. He agreed to the series of articles only because he owed me. He wasn't going to give you anybody prominent."

"Lucky me."

He ignored her dry comment. "Then Puller came back from Bosnia with a Pulitzer prize in his hip pocket. And it seems the bureau chief down there is afraid that his wonder-boy is going to burn out."

No doubt, she thought. Jackson Puller, star reporter of the Associated Wire Service, had more stickers on his passport than the president of the United States. He'd made a name for himself with human angle stories—generally stories featuring children—in just about every political hot spot in the world. "That last series from Bosnia was incredible," she admitted.

"When he wrote about that kid dying in that car bomb explosion, the response from the public was amazing. But that's what Chris says won him some downtime."

"Great. I'm downtime."

"Don't take it personally. Look at it as providential. Puller was pretty shaken up, from what I understand, by seeing that kid die. He's got a real thing for kids. When he got back, his bosses decided he needed a break. Your story came up, and the work of Wishing Star seemed like the perfect decompression assignment for their ace reporter.''

Visibly exasperated, he waved his hands in front of him. ''Look. The benefits of this are immeasurable. Because Puller's column is syndicated, they give each installment of a series a full week to run its course. He'll do three installments on you, four if he likes the subject. That means you get at least a month of *national* attention, and all you have to do is answer a few questions and act polite.''

''I understand that, Mike.'' At his skeptical look, Cammy nodded. ''I do. That's not the point. It's just that in my experience, reporters like Jackson Puller are extremely disruptive. He'll show up with an agenda and a preconceived idea of what he will find here. Next thing you know, he'll be pressing me for a certain kind of story. And then he'll want an interview with one of my kids who has a particularly wretched home life, because that's what sells papers.''

She turned to face the window again. ''Whatever I come up with won't be enough. Never mind that I'm trying to make Wishing Star a haven for deaf children. Never mind that they already face enough challenges just trying to survive in a world that's hostile to their disability. Puller's going to insist that he needs something sensational. If he can, he'll take one of my kids, exploit their story by dragging their family history through the mud of public opinion, and then he'll just walk away. It's not a plum assignment for him, so what does he care? I know the type, Mike. He's nothing more than a vulture who feeds on the carnage of broken reputations and wounded lives.''

''Then I guess we'd better shoot him before he does any more damage,'' came the strange voice from the doorway.

Cammy froze. The rush of adrenaline she'd felt from her passionate outburst drained from her body like water through a burst dam. Mistake number one, she thought wryly. Nothing like insulting the press to get them on your side. Her father was probably twirling in his grave. No choice now but to tough it out. She placed a hand on the windowsill to stabilize herself.

Mike's chair creaked again. She heard him round his desk. ''You must be Mr. Puller.'' His voice had lost none of its buttery quality. Cammy alone knew him well enough to hear the slight edge.

''Jackson,'' he answered. She watched his reflection turn to look at her. ''I'm here for Dr. Cameo Glynn.'' Undisguised curiosity tinged his voice.

''We're delighted,'' Mike assured him. ''I'm sure you're going to enjoy working on this story.''

Jackson shook his hand, then seated himself in one of the leather chairs. Costas's office looked much as he'd expected. It was the woman at the window who had surprised him. ''I spoke with Chris Harris this morning,'' he told Mike. ''I understand you know him.''

If Costas detected the slight note of censure in Jackson's comment, he didn't show it. ''Chris and I go way back.''

"So he tells me."

Costas propped one hip on the side of his desk. "You know, Wishing Star's work with deaf children is really quite groundbreaking. Cammy's done an incredible job working with these kids. The results are fantastic."

Jackson nodded, not bothering to take his gaze from the woman whose back remained stubbornly to him. "I've heard that. They meet here?" he prompted Costas, while he continued to study Cammy. Her hair, a fascinating shade between red and gold, was caught in some kind of trap thing that looked like it wanted to explode.

"Once a week," Costas answered. "She's got two different groups with ten to twelve kids each. Wishing Star has also funded a number of encounter sessions with other experts on hearing impairment."

"Oh?" The breeze from the air-conditioning vent played with several wispy strands of her soft-looking hair. The occasional lift of the tendrils near her right ear gave him glimpses of a tiny electronic device. Hooked to the ear frame of her glasses, it looked like a miniature microphone. Cameo seemed unperturbed by the current dancing across the nape of her neck. Jackson wasn't sure he'd ever met a woman who ignored her hair. "That often?"

As expected, the question sent Costas into a long discourse on Wishing Star's activities. Jackson settled in to contemplate Dr. Glynn. He had to admit, the coolness of her reception surprised him. She hadn't even faced him yet. In the window, he could see the tension in her face. It was a good face, he decided.

All the basic equipment was there to make it an attractive face. Even an honest one.

He'd built a career on reading faces. Long ago, he'd decided there were few honest adult faces left—and none of them lived in Washington. It was just one of the reasons he preferred working with kids on stories. He always got straight answers. Having spent the first part of his career covering the political world, he'd learned, quickly, just how devious adults could be.

Like Costas, he thought, who was gushing about a Wishing Star fund-raiser set for later that month. "That's quite impressive," Jackson supplied.

"It is." Costas took off on another verbal detour. Jackson tuned him out again. He'd been mad as hell when Chris had sent him over here. After ten years in the field, he no longer had to cover feel-good assignments. It wasn't that he didn't find the doctor's efforts admirable, or even that he didn't find them interesting—what had torqued him was Chris's insistence that he'd been handpicked by the bosses at AW for this particular assignment.

Jackson had to suppress an irritated snort. That was a joke. He'd lay down real money that what had happened was that a phone call from Costas had sent Chris scrambling for options. Since the suits—as the field journalists called the mostly useless group of executives who signed their paychecks—had decided that Jackson was on the verge of cracking up, Chris had seized the opportunity to give Costas what he wanted. They'd put him on this mostly useless filler assignment while they decided whether or not he was going to crash and burn—and what in the hell they'd do if it happened.

The fact that Costas specialized in two kinds of cases—rich divorcées and grief-stricken patients on the verge of a breakdown—had tipped Chris's hand. Not only could he and his bosses at AW use the flimsy excuse of this story to keep Jackson from returning to the field for a while, but they were also holding out hope that he'd use the opportunity to spill his guts to Costas. Costas, they imagined, could slap a psychiatric bandage on the pain he felt and send him blissfully on his way.

No one had bothered to ask Jackson's opinion. They wouldn't have liked his answer if they had.

After a heated argument with Chris, he'd taken a cab over here, expecting to find Doctor Glynn ready to gush over him—at least tell him how delighted she was that he'd been assigned to her story. If she'd gotten Costas to pull the strings for her, she couldn't possibly have dreamed he'd land such a big fish.

It sounded arrogant, but Jackson frequently quipped, "False humility is for morons." He said the phrase so often, in fact, that one of his copy editors had it mocked up as a headline and article, and framed it for him. It hung over his desk in the AW office on Twelfth Street—the office from which he'd built a world-class reputation for his stories on kids and their problems. A story, not to mention a *series*, under his byline would put Cameo's charity on the map. He knew it, and, unless she was a complete idiot, she knew it, too.

That's why she'd thrown him. Surprises rarely

came his way, but unless he missed his guess she wasn't exactly pleased with his presence. The square set of her shoulders beneath her loose-fitting clothes betrayed her tension.

"So," Costas was saying, "where would you like to start?"

"I'd like to sit in on one of Dr. Glynn's sessions," Jackson announced.

Cammy finally turned from the window. The impact of intelligent gray eyes steadily watching him through tortoiseshell glasses made him miss a breath. There was a world of mistrust in that gaze—mistrust he hadn't expected. He'd been right about the face, though. Honest. Not very pleased, granted, but honest. Something about her expression made him feel absurdly curious about what lay beneath her facade. For the first time that day, he found something appealing about this assignment. He'd settle his issues with Chris later. For now, he'd enjoy the challenge of deciphering the enigma of Doctor Cameo Glynn.

Cammy gave him a measured look as she took a firm hold of her nerves. Despite her objections, she knew Mike was right. Jackson Puller could do a lot for Wishing Star. The images she'd seen of him blinking from her television screen, staring up from a grainy newspaper photo, splayed in color on the pages of a news magazine, didn't begin to do him justice. *Charisma* was the only word she had for him. He embodied it, with his dark hair, broodingly byronic features, and large, solid build. Even the simplicity of his clothes—a collarless denim shirt, well-worn khaki trousers, and navy blue suspenders—raised images of another age, but of an age when decency and honesty mattered. She mentally shook herself. An age that had no place in the tactics of the modern media.

Thrown slightly off-balance by the direction of her thoughts, Cammy took a quick assessment of the man and his possible motives. His shrewd expression told her many things. First, he hadn't listened to a word Mike had said. As the daughter of a former U.S. senator, she'd seen too many reporters try to mask boredom. She could spot it across a room of three thousand high-dollar donors, much less in the confines of Mike's office. Jackson had spent the last few minutes studying *her*, forming opinions, building strategy.

And second, he wasn't any happier about this than she was. That, at least, didn't surprise her. This assignment wasn't his usual style. It wasn't flashy, or dangerous, or high profile. He wasn't likely to break new ground or win awards simply by writing a few articles on the deaf kids she was trying to help. The public was just as guilty as the media for the general downward spiral into sleaze and muckraking. Honest journalism, she'd learned the hard way, had gone the way of the Hula Hoop and the station wagon. Still, if Jackson Puller considered this particular assignment so beneath his great journalistic reputation, then he could take his notepad and go back to Bosnia.

At the protracted silence, Mike cleared his throat. "I'm sure Cammy would be glad to have you evaluate a session. It'll give you a chance to see the foundation's work in action," he assured Jackson.

Cammy extended a hand to Jackson, but she held

her ground by the window. The air between them seemed oddly heavy. "I've seen your work," she told him. "Very impressive."

His expression turned quizzical as he regarded her hand. "So is yours," he told her. He levered out of his chair, then took three smooth strides to where she stood. For the first time, she noticed the white bandage on his palm. It felt harsh when his hand grasped hers. When he slid his fingers away, the scrape of it left a searing impression she feared might linger for days. "I glanced through some of your PR material before I took a cab over here. You've pulled together an eclectic group of supporters."

He had charm, too. In her experience, most reporters had all the charm of rattlesnakes. She felt a twitch of amusement play across her lips. "Bargain from a position of strength," her father would say. "I understand congratulations are in order for your Pulitzer."

When a faint shadow passed over his blue-green gaze, the string that had seemed to sit taut between them snapped. He lifted one broad shoulder in a casual shrug that belied what she sensed was an internal struggle. "People found Leo hard to resist." His voice had taken on a gentle quality that handily unnerved her.

"That's the child from your series." She didn't need to ask. She, like the rest of the country, had been enthralled by Leo's life through Jackson's series of articles. When the child had died, she'd taken it personally.

"Yes."

The soft admission reached her like nothing else could. This was a man who understood pain. She found herself quickly reassessing, reevaluating her opinion of him, and she felt ashamed to realize she'd committed the same crime against him that she'd silently accused him of committing against her. She'd formed her opinion based on the most cursory of information, filtered through the screen of her own personal bias.

In a thousand lifetimes she wouldn't have expected that sharp look of grief at the mention of Leo. She couldn't ignore it. Grief, and the way it manifested itself in others, had always been her weak spot. He stood looking at her with that sorrow unmasked in his expression, and Cammy felt her resistance crumbling. Professionally, she recognized the symptoms. Personally, she shared them. She saw that Jackson Puller represented a worthy risk. "I'm very sorry for your loss," she told him.

She understood.

He seemed to know it.

And he smiled. That clinched it. That damned charming, mischievous world-on-a-string smile sucked her in. It failed to completely chase away the shadows, but it did wonders for the sharp lines of his face. In Cammy's experience, reporters never smiled— at least, not genuinely.

Jackson Puller's smile had charmed cameras, graced millions of television screens, and been splashed on hundreds of thousands of newspapers. She'd seen it dozens of times, but nothing compared to seeing it in person. It was impossible, she decided, to thoroughly dislike a man with that kind of smile. When she caught herself staring at his lips, she forced her gaze to his eyes. That was worse. He knew exactly what she was thinking.

Jackson watched curiously as she pulled herself together. "It's nice to meet you, too."

The remark, she knew, was meant to tell her he hadn't missed the frostiness of her reception, nor the implied warning in her cool gaze. The slight twitch at the corner of his mouth did not escape her notice. Smart, too, she marveled. Would wonders never cease? "I'm afraid, Mr. Puller—"

He held up a hand. Strong-looking and slightly callused, it was an incredibly appealing hand. "We'll be together a lot in the next couple of weeks. I'd prefer if you'd call me Jackson."

The subtle challenge was unmistakable. He'd sensed the change in her position and had moved quickly to capitalize on it. Cammy felt the tug of a conceding smile. "All right. I was just about to say, though, that I don't think I'll be able to let you observe one of my sessions with the children."

"Now, Cammy—" Mike advanced toward her.

She ignored his interruption. "The balance of trust, of understanding, is crucial." She continued to watch the play of emotions across Jackson's face. Lines of amusement at the edges of his eyes softened his features and made him downright irresistible. Blast him. "I think the children would be uncomfortable around a stranger."

"I'm very good," he said, leaning slightly in her

direction, "at making children feel comfortable."

"True, true." Mike nodded vigorously. "You must admit, Cammy, he's got a point there."

She gave Mike a scathing look but stubbornly held her ground. "I've worked hard to develop a rapport with these kids. They trust me."

"Then surely they will trust you if you introduce me as one of your friends."

"I've never brought a stranger to a session before."

"Then this should give you a chance to try something new."

He'd won another point, and he knew it. Cammy struggled for tactical ground. To her surprise, she found herself enjoying the verbal sparring. She wasn't quite sure just what it was about Jackson Puller's devil-may-care expression that almost demanded a challenge, but she was powerless to resist it. "I'd like to start with something a little less intimidating than a world-famous, award-winning reporter."

"The children will have no idea who I am when they come here."

"They'll be intimidated once they find out."

"Or fascinated."

She was fascinated by the way his lips formed the word. "They won't be. Besides, most of them speak only with sign language. You won't be able to communicate."

"You'll be there to interpret for me."

"It's not the same."

"But it could work."

"It won't."

"It could."

She felt herself losing ground. If he didn't look so devilishly pleased with himself, she might manage to feel annoyed. "I don't want to regress. They're just starting to really open up to me."

Instantly, his expression turned from merriment to concern. "Are you genuinely afraid that might happen?"

Was she? Belatedly, she realized that she'd been so immersed in challenging him that she'd gotten conversationally reckless. She *never* wasted words. Anyone who knew her knew that to be true. Yet within ten minutes of meeting her, Jackson Puller had reduced her to a chatterbox. "Maybe."

"I'm here to write a story, not to jeopardize your work."

Cammy blinked at the obvious integrity in his expression. The argument, she sensed, was over. "I know."

His gaze turned curious. "Sure about that?"

"Yes. Unless I miss my guess, you're not any happier with this situation than I am."

"It's not my usual kind of story," he admitted, "but that doesn't mean I don't see its merit." The honesty of the statement shocked him. Less than an hour ago, he'd been practically accusing Chris Harris of tabloid sensationalism.

"My top concern has to be the children."

He actually *liked* this woman That had to be the most surprising turn of the day. For the first time in his life, he'd found a political activist he didn't immediately think of as pond scum. She lacked the high polish and hard edges he'd expected. In the few minutes she'd spent evaluating him, he'd felt an odd sense of connection with her that had him reeling. Even now, what should have sounded like a well-rehearsed line to impress him felt more like a mother tiger warning him away from her brood. He nodded, seeking to reassure her. "Then we can find something to agree on. I completely understand."

"But would you still push me for a certain story angle?"

Cammy Glynn was a straight shooter. He hadn't met a straight shooter over twelve years old in longer than he could remember. He tilted his head to the side as he studied her. "Dr. Glynn, why don't you let me concentrate on the angles? You worry about your kids. That way, you'll keep me in check."

Beneath the smooth texture of her skin, the color heightened. She wasn't blushing. Instinct told him that Cammy couldn't be baited into blushing. Yet something about the cause of that slight flush taunted him. Was it passion? The thought made his flesh tingle.

"Does anyone ever keep you in check?"

Exhilarated, that's how he felt. The simple pleasure of sharpening his wits was making him feel alive for the first time in weeks. "Sometimes."

"But not usually?"

He didn't even try to hide his amused smile. "No. Not usually. Don't you think you're up to the challenge?"

"Don't you?"

The question delighted him so thoroughly that he almost laughed out loud. He had to remember to apologize to Chris Harris for the rotten things he'd said that morning. Chris had been right. A few weeks with Cammy Glynn might turn out to be just the thing to help him rebuild his sanity. "Definitely."

She watched him for a long moment, then nodded. "All right. We'll try it."

Mike Costas exhaled a long breath. "Excellent."

"But," Cammy's gaze turned serious once more, "you're going to have to follow my lead. If I think your presence is even remotely disruptive, I'll put a stop to this. Agreed?"

"Absolutely. I'll just be there to observe."

"And I don't want you to interview any of my children without me present."

"No problem."

"If you want a photographer present, I'll need to meet with him. He needs to understand some ground rules I have."

"It's a her. I'll talk to her myself. You'll like Krista. She's great with a camera, and great at her job. I'll have her set up a meeting with you. I'll also guarantee you photo approval. Nothing gets printed without your okay."

"But she's photographed children for you?"

"Yes. Krista's got an excellent eye for a shot. You'll be pleased."

Cammy nodded. "All right. I'll give you some guidelines for a typical session, and you can tell me how you want to proceed, but I'm serious when I tell you I won't have my children upset or disrupted."

"Not to worry, Doctor." His gaze was pure mischief. "I'll blend into the wall. You'll never even know I'm there."

✧✧✧♡ two

He created utter chaos.

When Jackson entered the room, her children fell head over heels in love with him. Cammy had already told the children he was coming, and one flash of that charming smile was all it took. He seated himself cross-legged in the center of the small group. Less than twenty seconds later, he had one of them in his lap. If he hadn't looked so completely at ease amid the group of swarming bodies, she might have felt annoyed at the way he took over her session. Instead, she stood to the side, marveling at the way he communicated with the children when he couldn't speak their language. She interpreted when necessary, but she mostly allowed him to find his own way—cursing the gall of the man for looking so damn appealing.

After the first half hour, she gave up trying to recapture the kids' attention. Jackson's charisma held them hostage. From the edges of the room, vaguely noticeable in the overwhelming shadow of Jackson's presence, Krista Swenlin, a young, owlish-looking woman, snapped silent photos.

As the session drew to a close, and the sponsors and volunteers began rounding up the children, Jackson stayed among them, drawing out his encounter until the last possible moment.

Cammy told the children good-bye as they fed through the door, until an insistent tugging on her trousers demanded her attention. She turned to concentrate on the tow-headed child in front of her. "Yes, Amy?" she signed.

Fingers flying, Amy asked, "Can he come back?"

Cammy's lips twitched. "Do you want him to?" she signed.

"Yes." Amy's blue eyes widened expressively. "He almost knows how to spell his name."

"Almost?"

"He can't tell K from P." She demonstrated the two similar signs. "I promised I'd show him next time."

From the doorway, the sponsor who shuttled the children from their resident school to Cammy's office waved a hand to signal she was ready to leave. Cammy nodded to her, then signed to Amy, "I'll ask him if he wants to come back. You'd better go. Don't want the van to leave without you."

Amy threw her arms around Cammy's legs with typical affection. Seconds later, she raced across the room, giving Jackson a universally understood thumbs-up on her way out the door. Jackson waved to her, and the room fell quiet for the first time in hours.

Jackson unfolded himself from the floor with a groan. "I'm getting too old for this. My butt's asleep from sitting on the floor so long."

She resisted the urge to look, again, at that portion of his anatomy, which was showcased in his jeans. "Occupational hazard," she assured him. "After the first couple of weeks I worked with these kids, I had trouble walking properly. It might be days before you get all the feeling back."

He stretched, arching his back, linking his hands over his head so his body pulled into a lean bow of muscled perfection. "I still haven't figured out how a room full of deaf kids can be so noisy."

Cammy laughed. "Some things are universal to the childhood experience."

"They're amazing."

"I think so."

The photographer finished packing her gear. She approached Jackson with an easy familiarity that Cammy envied. How long, she wondered, would a person have to know him before his presence failed to daunt? It had taken her children about twenty seconds, and here she was, still struggling a full twenty-four hours after she'd first laid eyes on him.

The photographer patted the top of her camera bag. "I got some great photos, Jack. Nice stuff."

"Great," Jackson said.

"Listen, I'm meeting Rory at Dirksen at three to cover Senator Goss's press conference. I'm going to head over to the office and get these developed for you. You should have something to look at this afternoon." She straightened her camera bag on her shoulder and looked at Cammy. "Nice meeting you, Dr. Glynn."

"Nice to meet you, too," Cammy answered.

Krista looked at Jackson. "See you later, Jack," she called as she hurried from the room.

In the late morning sunlight, he looked, Cammy decided, every bit as intriguing as he had the day before. Today, he'd worn jeans and a faded blue Henley that heightened the color of his eyes and did nothing to lessen the impact of his presence. "You were right," Cammy told him. "I like her."

"I'm usually right," he joked. "How did you feel about this morning?"

"I felt like I didn't get done what I wanted to." She studied his expression. Why couldn't she label the shifting emotions she read in his gaze?

He nodded. "We were late. It was my fault."

She looked at him in amazement. "How very impressive, Mr. Puller. I don't think I've met many men who are willing to accept blame."

He laughed, but she still sensed his tension. "In your line of work, I guess not. Anyway, I want to apologize. I'm still a little jet-lagged, and I just didn't get moving as quickly this morning as I would have liked. I know you wanted us here before you started." He took a step in her direction that carried him across the invisible line of her personal space.

Cammy drew a deep breath and forced herself not to retreat. "It probably would have been less disruptive if the children could have met you as they arrived."

He winced. "I know. I promised you I wouldn't disturb your work, and I have a bad feeling I failed."

"Miserably."

Another step brought him close. "You mean your sessions don't normally look like this?"

"Like a melee, you mean?"

"You're not swinging at me. I'm going to take that as a good sign."

"It's all right. I wouldn't want this to happen every time, but the kids had fun today. There should always be room for fun."

He touched the sleeve of her sweatshirt with a large hand. The heat of him seeped through to her skin. "I like them."

She studied him through narrowed eyes. Something lurked beneath the surface of his easy calm. She felt it simmering, waiting. "They liked you," she told him carefully.

His fingers moved absently over her fleecy sleeve. "So am I off the hook?"

Cammy held his gaze, determined not to glance at his hand. "Not exactly."

"There's hell to pay, isn't there?"

Was it her imagination, or did that sound more like a proposition than a question? She shook her head, then used the opportunity to move away from him. "I don't think the price is quite that high. I would like you to have a clearer picture of what generally goes on here, though." Cammy began to pick up the scattered toys and books.

"I read the materials you gave me yesterday. I know you normally work on their language skills."

"It'll be easier for them in the long run if they learn how to speak the language of the world they live in."

"That's a controversial position, isn't it?" He accepted a stack of books from her, then turned to shelve them deftly on the bookcase.

She exhaled a long breath. "Very. There are members of the deaf community who feel that lip-reading and audible language are concessions to the hearing world. They don't feel that deafness is a disability, and shouldn't be treated as something to overcome. For them, speaking sign language is like speaking Spanish or French." She dropped an armload of toys into a bin. "It's just another way of communicating."

"You don't agree." Jackson finished restoring the pieces of a puzzle before he glanced at her.

"I'm practical, I suppose." And would do well to remember it, she chided herself. She straightened her glasses. "American Sign Language is an incredible liberator—one of the best things that ever happened for the deaf community. If deaf Americans lived together in a cloistered environment, where only ASL was spoken, then yes, I'd have to agree there's no reason to go through the process of trying to learn audible speech." She tidied a shelf. "But the reality is, these children live in a world that speaks and understands English, not ASL. In my opinion, and it's not necessarily a popular one, they'll have more opportunities and better chances in life if they learn to function in that environment."

"According to the material you gave me to read, it can take several years for a deaf child to learn audible speech and lip-reading."

"Think of it as teaching a blind person how to paint a tree. Not only are they unable to see the canvas or the paints, but they have no frame of reference for what the tree looks like. If it were art, it wouldn't matter. Your tree may look different than my tree. But with speech, it's not valid if it isn't understood."

"It's an incredibly arduous process, isn't it?"

"Almost as hard as recapturing their attention after you walked in the room today."

He covered his heart with his bandaged hand. "Ouch. Point well-taken, Doctor."

Cammy glanced at her watch. "Let's grab lunch, and I'll fill you in on your penance."

He attempted to sign OK. With a shake of her head, Cammy tipped his hand into the proper position for the K. "Amy told me you had trouble with that one."

Jackson mentally thrust aside the remnants of a sour mood as he watched Cammy thread her way through the dense crowd at the Tune-In. The morning had exacted a high price. He should have known that being around Cammy's kids was going to batter the walls that closed off his painful memories of Leo. No matter what Chris or the rest of those morons he worked for at AW thought, he was completely in control.

Of course, it hadn't helped matters that he'd seen Leo in the faces of Cammy's children. What he needed was enough solitude to work Leo, and the memory of his death, methodically out of his mind. This ploy to have him spill his guts to some shrink— he watched Cammy stop to talk to someone she knew—no matter *how* attractive the package, wasn't going to work. Leo was his struggle and his alone. No one else could go there with him. He wrestled with the ghosts for another few minutes. Finally, he mastered them by forcing aside his grim thoughts and concentrating on Cammy.

When she'd suggested the greasy Capitol Hill hamburger joint, he'd had to add another twist to his evolving opinion of her complex personality. He'd have pegged her for the falafel/humus type.

Over the blare of the jukebox, she shouted her name to the waitress. The woman signaled her, then headed back into the dark recesses of the booth-lined restaurant.

Cammy reached his side after dodging two waiters and a delivery driver. "Five minutes," she assured him. "Most of this crowd is here to pick up takeout."

Jackson nodded, silently using the excuse of the noisy atmosphere to study her rather than make conversation. He decided he liked the way the exertion of reaching the waitress had heightened her skin color. When he'd first met her the day before, he hadn't been able to suppress a healthy male, if politically incorrect, twinge of regret that her loose-fitting clothes had generally concealed her figure. Today, however, she wore slim-fitting jeans and a yellow sweatshirt that looked incredibly feminine.

He'd been acutely aware of her that morning. As she'd moved around the edges of the room, interpreting for him when necessary, interacting with the children when needed, her gray gaze had stayed fixed on him. She had watched and assessed—evaluating him as often as she evaluated her kids. Her scrutiny had almost unnerved him, and with his equilibrium gone haywire, he hadn't been able to resist moving in on her after the children had left.

He was an expert at reading faces, and Cammy's had been clear when he'd rubbed his fingers on her sleeve. In the back of his brain, he'd filed her startled look of awareness for further consideration.

The waitress signaled them over the heads of the crowd. Jackson let Cammy take the lead. When they were finally seated, blissfully away from the noise in a dark corner booth, Jackson leaned against the vinyl seat and waited.

Cammy's eyes lifted from the menu to meet his gaze across the table. "Have you ever eaten here?"

He nodded. "Great hamburgers. A little loud."

She fingered the little microphone by her right ear as she studied the laminated card. "The ambiance leaves a little to be desired, but they've got some of the best food in the city. Besides, I like noise."

The waitress approached their table. "What'll you have?"

Jackson suppressed a smile. The tiny restaurant was also renowned for the less than hospitable attitude of its waitstaff. He gave his order without comment.

Cammy stuffed the menu card into the wire condiment rack. "I'll have the same."

The waitress hurried off. Jackson met Cammy's gaze. "So," he said, "are you going to tell me how much trouble I'm in, or are you going to make me sweat?"

She released a slow breath. Inwardly, she knew she'd been trying to avoid this. He was too engaging, and, she had the feeling, too observant. She sensed a barely leashed frustration in him, however, something he'd effortlessly hidden from her kids but couldn't quite keep from his expression when he looked at her. She saw no reason not to ask him to show his hand. "I want you to answer a question for me first."

"Shoot."

"What have you got to be so irritable about?"

Something unreadable flickered in his gaze. He leaned back in his seat with a slight grunt. "Look, I'm not going to lie to you. Coming off that assignment in Bosnia, my nerves are a little raw. I'm tired as hell, and not exactly in top form."

"That's understandable."

"Yeah, well, my boss, and his bosses, seem to think that all I need is a few hours of psychotherapy to tune up my mental engine."

"Mike mentioned that."

His frown turned to a scowl. "Is everyone in on the joke?"

"I don't think—"

He bit off a curse. "I've handled thousands of assignments, in thousands of places. I've won those bastards at AW a hell of a lot of awards, and the financial benefits to go with them."

"No one's arguing—"

"And now, they concoct this charade to send me scuttling off to your office in hopes that I'll choke out my life story to your business partner."

"Jackson—"

"What happened in Bosnia—" He shrugged, and uttered something harsh and foul. "Look, I've been in worse places. Nobody ever decided that I needed a shrink before.''

"No one ever died before.''

His gaze narrowed. "Succinctly put, Doctor. You use that kind of method on all your patients?''

She drew a calming breath. "I was afraid you weren't going to let me get a word in edgewise.''

"Maybe I didn't want to hear what you had to say.''

Cammy's eyes drifted momentarily shut. Story of her life, she thought. When she opened them again, he was watching her with that probing gaze she found so unsettling. "Did it occur to you that maybe they want to help you?''

His laugh was humorless. "Let me give you a little lesson in how journalism works, Doc. Nobody helps anybody. Everybody runs for the next story, the next hot item that'll sell more papers and earn more money. When you develop a reputation for getting that story, for outmaneuvering the competition, people notice. And they want you to keep on doing it.''

"You're very good at what you do.''

"I'm excellent at what I do.''

"And you think that Chris Harris's only motivation in sending you to me was to make sure you weren't going to quit on him.''

"Chris was under pressure.''

She watched him for several seconds. He was struggling. He showed all the signs. His fingers gripped the edge of the table. His eyes had narrowed to glittering slits. She sensed the anger, the reluctance in him to reveal anything deeper. His anger radiated toward her in the close confines of the booth.

She found herself wanting to help him, wanting to reach inside his mind and find the place where that anger had taken root. His expression made it clear, however, that he wouldn't be pushed. There would be time, she reminded herself, later. Cammy relaxed against the padded seat. "Thank you for telling me."

He watched her, his gaze wary. "That's all you want to know?"

"That's not half of what I want to know. But you don't want me to push, do you?"

He hesitated, then shook his head. "No."

With a slight shrug, she said, "So I won't ask."

"You'd make a rotten reporter."

"And you'd probably make a rotten psychiatrist."

The corner of his mouth twitched, banishing his mask of anger. "So we're even?"

"Not quite. You were still late to my session this morning—after you promised you wouldn't be disruptive."

"How long are you going to make me pay for that?"

"Not long." She toyed with her spoon. "I thought the children interacted with you quite well."

"They did, didn't they?"

She liked the sudden gleam in his gaze. He'd enjoyed himself that morning, that much was obvious. Even though she sensed a certain reticence about him as he'd interacted with her kids, something she'd bet real money had to do with his memories of Leo, she'd also seen him settle naturally into the dynamics of the group. "Amy wants you to come back next time."

"She's trying to teach me to sign my name." He used the index and middle fingers of each hand to form the sign for *name*.

"She doesn't usually open up to people that quickly. It took me weeks to get her to talk to me."

"She's obviously come a long way since you started working with her."

Cammy studied him curiously. "You don't think she just responded to your natural magnetism?"

His eyebrows lifted slightly. Something she couldn't quite define flickered in his gaze. He leaned across the table so his face was inches from hers. "Do I have natural magnetism?"

His anger, she realized, was completely gone now, replaced by the teasing banter he liked to use as a shield. She refused to take the bait. "You know what I mean."

"Tell me?"

"You're very dynamic," she told him, deciding to be honest. "You have a talent for talking to kids, and you've been able to use that gift to communicate with children all over the world."

With his hands splayed on the table, he looked almost predatorial. His eyes searched hers with unnerving intensity. "Or, maybe," he said, "you've helped those kids see that not everyone in the world is their enemy. They trust you. Consequently, they know you wouldn't have introduced me into their midst if you thought I couldn't connect with them." He narrowed his gaze. "Did you ever worry there'd be a language barrier between the children and me?"

"No. Once you had a chance to familiarize yourself with sign language, I knew you could reach them. You've formed relationships with kids in dozens of foreign countries whether you spoke their language or not."

"You'd be surprised how far a guy can get on a pack of American bubble gum and an instant camera."

"True, but I still didn't see any reason why the kids in my focus group would present different challenges from the kids you meet anywhere else in the world."

"But you weren't sure?" he guessed.

She raised her eyebrows. "What makes you think so?"

Jackson leaned back in his seat again. She told herself she was relieved. "You're the doctor," he told her. "Why don't you tell me?"

Cammy drummed her fingers on top of the table. "Am I going to see this in the morning paper?"

Momentarily he pursed his lips. She couldn't decipher the expression. He withdrew the notepad from his hip pocket and dropped it on the table. "No. I want to know what makes these kids tick. What brings them to you? How do you reach them? I want to know because I like them." He paused. "Because I like you, and not because I think they'll make a good story."

"Are you sure?"

"You don't trust me." It wasn't a question.

"Don't take it personally."

"So it's just the media establishment in general, and not me in particular?"

"Something like that."

"That's encouraging."

"You think so?"

"Sure. If it's just all of us who fall in your lower-than-pond-scum category, I have a better chance of distinguishing myself from the pack. If you had a bad impression of me, I'd have to work harder." He shrugged. "I could still do it, you understand. It would just be harder."

A slight laugh escaped before she could stop it. "You're very sure of yourself."

"You have no idea."

"Don't bet on it. I'm a professional shrink, you know. It's my job to assess people."

"I'll watch my step." He tilted his head to one side. "You want to tell me about this gripe you have with my species, or do you want me to torture it out of you?"

She eyed the notebook. "What about that?"

He studied her a minute. "Okay, I'll level with you. You're a smart woman. And you were right. This story isn't my usual style."

"I know that."

"You also know that Chris Harris, my bureau chief, and Mike Costas are old friends. We talked about that when I met you."

"Yes."

"Did Costas also tell you that he pulled strings to get Harris to do the story?"

"I'm not sure he phrased it like that, but I got the idea."

He stared at her for long seconds. "I hate string pullers."

"Maybe you should take that up with Mike."

He shrugged. "Chris was going to send you some rookie just to get Mike out of his hair."

"But, lucky you, you got stuck with me instead."

"I told you, that's because my bosses are concerned about my mental state. They think I might be headed toward burnout."

Her gaze dropped to the bandage on his palm. "Are you?"

"Is that a professional question or a personal one?"

She flinched. "I didn't mean—"

"Cammy, you try to second-guess my motives in every conversation. Why shouldn't I second-guess yours?"

The question was valid, and she knew it. She met his gaze again. "All right. What if I tell you it's both personal and professional, but mostly more of the former? I'd like to help you."

"Why?"

"Beats me," she admitted.

"You're very direct."

"I've been told."

"I like it. You don't meet very many direct people in this city."

The corner of her mouth lifted in a slight smile. "You must really make waves, then."

He laughed. "Why do you think the bosses at AW are always so anxious to get me out of town?"

"Until now?"

"Until now."

"I read you right, I see. You weren't just adverse to Chris Harris sending you off for some therapy. You didn't like the idea of this whole story."

"No. I didn't. And you didn't want me to do it either, which only made things worse."

Cammy shook her head. "You're right. I didn't."

"But we're stuck. I'm going to write a series on you, and your kids, and on Wishing Star. It's my assignment."

"Is that the only reason?"

"No. I could have refused. It wouldn't have been easy, but I could have done it."

"You didn't."

"Because I promised Chris I'd meet you first."

Their waitress plunked their plates in front of them. "Anything else?"

Jackson shook his head, but didn't take his gaze off Cammy. Cammy glanced at the waitress. "No, we're fine."

The waitress dropped the check on the table before she hurried away. Jackson reached for the check the instant Cammy's fingers closed on it. His hand stayed on hers. "I'll let you buy my lunch under one condition."

She managed a slight smile. "I can see you're new to this bribing business."

"You have every intention of picking up the bill. I can spot a determined woman a mile away."

"And you're going to fight me over it unless I tell you what you want to know?"

"You bet."

"What if I just give you the bill?"

"You won't. Your pride's involved."

"I'm supposed to be the expert on psychiatry, here."

"Call it gut instinct."

She hesitated. "What do you want from me, Jackson?"

"Your story." His gaze held her in a place where their conversation had very little to do with the check for a couple of hamburgers. "Right now, I'll settle for some answers. I want to know why you distrust me so much."

"I thought your story was on my kids and on Wishing Star."

"Technically, it is." He glanced at the notebook, where it still lay on the table. "But now I'm curious. You weren't what I expected, and I want to know why. It's ingrained. I can't help it."

"And I'm direct, but wary. Sounds to me like we've got a serious problem."

"Not serious. Not yet, anyway. Potentially serious, I'll grant you. So what do you say we make a deal?"

"What kind of deal?" It was her turn to lift her eyebrows.

Jackson indicated the notebook again. "It if doesn't go in there, it doesn't go in my story. Anything you tell me when I'm not taking notes is strictly off the record."

"If I trust you?"

His fingers tightened on hers. "I hope you will. I'd like to know more about you, Cammy, but I'd rather hear it from you. You know, I deliberately avoided the temptation to look through the file on you I got from my research assistant."

"That was noble."

"Most people would call it dumb."

The amusement in his gaze affected her like nothing else could. This would have been much easier on her, she thought, if he weren't so damned hard to dislike. Cammy carefully extracted her hand—and the check—from his. She tucked the small piece of paper into her shirt pocket. "What do you want to know?" she asked him.

His expression relaxed. "Where do you want to start?"

Jackson leaned back in his chair and studied the black-and-white photo of Cammy. As promised, Krista had left the developed pictures on his desk. He'd found them when he'd returned to the office that afternoon. He still wasn't sure how Cammy had managed to talk through lunch and leave him feeling even more baffled than when they'd started.

Enigma didn't even begin to describe her. She'd skated deftly around his questions about her personal life, and told him all the scientific and social data he'd wanted to know about the challenges, causes, and treatments of childhood deafness. She'd explained in vivid detail the experimental cochlear implant that had restored her hearing. He'd held the processor, about the size of a pager, and examined the microphone and transmitter she wore.

With a sweep of her elegant fingers, she'd shown him the scar in her hairline where a receiver had been implanted in the bone behind her ear. Electrodes, sur-

gically implanted in her cochlea, completed the circuit
and gave Cammy something she hadn't known since
birth—eighty percent hearing.

He'd been interested in what she had to say, but
even more caught up in what she didn't say. The long,
technical discourse lacked most of the passion he'd
seen in her that morning. More than journalistic instinct had him craving answers to the contradiction.
Once or twice, he'd seen a glimpse of something
deeper, some reservoir of sadness she guarded behind
her carefully cultivated civility.

His gaze left the photo to rest on the background
file on his desk. Sheer obstinancy was keeping him
from opening it. In that file were all the details he
might want about the public aspects of Cammy's life.
Yet, somehow, he sensed she'd resent him for reading
it. One of the things that made him good at his job
was reading people. Practice had honed his intuition
until he rarely missed. There were more layers to
Cammy Glynn than met the eye—he was willing
to bank on that, but, for reasons he couldn't begin to
fathom, he resisted the urge, strong as it was, to indulge his curiosity by studying her background file.
Something told him that he'd find a lot of public facts
and not much of what he was looking for.

Instead, he studied the pictures Krista had left for
his perusal. In the photo, Cammy looked more at ease
than he'd ever seen her. Krista had captured her deep
in conversation with little Amy Patterson. Cammy's
face reflected unabashed affection. Her normal air of
reserve was conspicuously absent. She loved that
child, that much was obvious. At lunch that afternoon,

Cammy had told him that Amy, abandoned by both parents, lived in a center for special needs children. Her mother's addiction to crack had most likely caused the birth defect that had stolen Amy's hearing. She'd come to live at the center as a two-year-old. No one knew where and how she'd spent the first years of her life.

That she'd evolved into such a loving child was miraculous. Even before he'd heard her story, Jackson had been impressed with Amy's intelligence and warmth. Her feelings, he noted as he looked at the picture, weren't directed at him alone. Amy's expressive eyes watched Cammy with adoration. The black-and-white picture filtered out unnecessary elements of the scene and showed, instead, the clear affection between the two. Cammy was "listening" intently as Amy's small fingers formed the signs that allowed her to communicate. Jackson had consulted the reference book on American Sign Language he'd ordered from the library and learned that Amy's hands formed the sign for *speak*.

Krista, he decided, had unwittingly done it again. He put a check mark at the top of the photo, then sifted idly through the rest of the pile. The first one was undoubtedly the best. It perfectly captured the essence of the morning.

One more caught his eye. It showed him watching Cammy as she helped a child form a W with his lips by blowing bubbles through a wand. Jackson knew himself well, and he knew that the expression on his face betrayed more than casual curiosity. Cammy Glynn had captivated him.

"How's it going, Jack?" Chris Harris leaned through the door of Jackson's office.

Jackson surreptitiously slid the photo into his desk drawer. "All right. I spent the morning watching one of Doctor Glynn's sessions."

"I heard. I just spoke with Mike Costas."

"Are you two going to spy on me until I finish writing this series?"

Chris didn't bother to deny it. "Mike is a grief specialist, you know?"

Jackson calmly stacked the rest of the photos on his desk. "You don't say?"

"Just thought I'd mention it." He looked pointedly at Jackson's hand. The burn scar had begun to tighten the skin, and he'd taken to flexing it to ease the sting. "How's the hand, by the way?"

"Fine." He laid his palm flat on his desk. "The bandage comes off next week."

Chris visibly wavered for an instant, then dropped the subject with a brief nod. "Listen, I talked to Sheila. She wants to have Costas and his wife, and you and Doctor Glynn over for dinner. How's next Friday for you?"

"Don't tell me you're falling into one of your wife's matchmaking schemes, Chris. I thought you were a better man than that."

"She's not matchmaking. She hasn't seen Mike and Bess in a while, and thought this would be a pleasant, low-key kind of evening. Give everyone a chance to socialize a little."

"Where Mike Costas can casually evaluate me, and where I spend time with Doctor Glynn?"

"Don't be so suspicious."

"Don't be so transparent. You want me to talk to Costas. That's why you put me on this story."

"I think maybe you could use some help coping with what happened in Bosnia."

"Have you seen anything—have I done anything— to make you think I'm not coping?"

"You want to talk about why you're so bristly lately?"

"No." He glared at Chris.

Chris glared back. "I didn't think so."

"Hell, that doesn't mean I need a shrink."

"It's not a weakness, you know. That kid died. Anyone would have been rattled by that."

Inside him, in the place he never looked, something was threatening to explode. He wrestled the door shut, but it took more effort this time. "Of course I'm rattled. But I also know that the best thing for me to do is to go back to work."

Chris exhaled a long breath. "You're not yourself, Jack."

"I don't normally have my boss trying to force me into psychotherapy. When did you start doubting my mental stability?"

"I'm not doubting it."

"Then why are we having this conversation?"

"Because no one can stand to be around you lately. Irene in copy told me you ripped her head off about a misspelled caption."

"They're not supposed to make mistakes like that."

"And you're not supposed to send people fleeing the building in tears."

"That's your job," Jackson shot back.

Chris swore. "That's what I mean. Krista's the only person who can get along with you lately."

"Krista's competent."

"And you're a real pain in the ass."

"That's not the first time I've heard that today."

"So when are you going to take it to heart?"

Jackson leaned back in his chair. He forced himself to get rid of his irrational anger. It had no identifiable source, and Chris Harris was his friend. He didn't deserve this. "Now, I guess. You sure Sheila wants me in my present state of mind?"

"Are you going to rip her a new one if the mashed potatoes have lumps?"

He accepted the quip as a peace offering. "Considering I haven't had a decent meal since I got back, I'll probably get over it."

"Is six-thirty okay?"

"All right. Should I bring anything?"

"Doctor Glynn?" Chris suggested. "Why don't you pick her up on your way."

Jackson gave his friend a dirty look. "I'll call her." When Chris didn't budge from his post at the door he added, "Now. I'll call her now."

✿☆
☆ ♡ *three*

He had the kind of dark good looks that made girls swoon. And even at five years old, he knew it. Cammy shook her head at Trevor Blackfort as he flashed his beautiful smile and signed his invitation. "No, Trevor," she prompted. "*Say* it."

He rolled his eyes but capitulated. "My dance recital is tonight."

"I know." One of her colleagues from Gallaudet University, the Washington College for the Deaf, had approached Cammy two years ago with the idea for the dance troupe. Using progressive teaching methods and a combination of skill, naiveté, and pure fearlessness, Lynette had founded the Washington Foot Notes—a dance company comprised of both hearing and deaf children. With a grant from the Wishing Star Foundation and a studio that let them practice rent-free, the group had begun as an experiment and blossomed into a valuable learning environment. Several of Cammy's patients participated in the program. After two years, Lynette finally had the children ready for a recital. "I got an invitation in the mail," she told Trevor.

"Are you going to come see it?"

Cammy nodded. "Since you asked, I'll come." He wrinkled his nose as he stared at her mouth, unable to read the more complex sentence on her lips. She signed her response to him.

Trevor immediately followed her lead. With flying fingers he began telling her the details of his tap solo in the evening's performance. He was midsentence when his mother cracked open the door. "May I come in?"

Cammy greeted Macon Stratton-Blackfort with a warm smile. She held up a hand to interrupt Trevor, then pointed behind him. "Look who's here."

He swiveled in his chair and said, "Hi, Mom."

At the perfectly enunciated sentence, Cammy saw Macon's expression turn misty. "Hi, buddy boy." She set down her briefcase and held out her arms to him. Trevor raced across the room to fling himself into her embrace. Cammy watched the exchange with a familiar feeling of wistfulness. Every child should have the kind of love and support Trevor enjoyed from his parents.

Macon released him to sign, "Did you have fun?"

"Yes. Cammy's coming to see me dance tonight." His hands moved in an ever-widening range as he warmed to his topic. "I told her she should bring Mr. Puller."

Macon met Cammy's gaze with a lifted eyebrow. "You did?"

"Yeah. He was here at the group session last week.

He's writing stuff about Cammy and us for the news-paper.''

"*Jackson* Puller?'' Macon asked Cammy. Cammy stifled a groan.

Trevor pulled on Macon's sleeve. "Mom?'' He said the word out loud to grab her attention.

She brushed his nose with her index finger, then signed, "I'm listening. What did Cammy say?''

Trevor shook his head. "You came in before she answered.''

Macon pressed a quarter into his hand. "Why don't you go play the video game,'' she said, indicating the machine in the corner, "and I'll see if I can talk her into it.''

Trevor gave her a smacking kiss before he hurried off to fight interplanetary invaders. Macon pinned Cammy with a curious look. "Jackson Puller? Cam, you've been holding out on me.''

"Don't look at me like that.''

Macon eased across the room to seat herself across from Cammy's desk. "How do you expect me to look? I have to find out from my five-year-old that one of my best friends is keeping time with Washington's stud of the year.''

"We are *not* keeping time. He's doing a series of articles on Wishing Star.''

"A series.'' Macon grinned. "So it's a protracted kind of thing.''

Cammy laughed. "You're incorrigible.''

"And insatiable. Spill your guts, kid.'' She glanced at her watch. "I've got a meeting in an hour and I want details before I leave.''

"Well, I've got another appointment in ten minutes, so you're out of luck. We're going to talk about Trevor instead."

Macon's expression turned suddenly serious. "Why? Is something wrong?"

"No, of course not. He's doing great."

Macon glanced across the room to where Trevor sat with videogame controls defending the future of the universe. "He loves his dance class."

"I'm glad. He talks about it a lot. I'm just a little concerned about school."

Macon's breath came out in a long sigh. "Me too. He doesn't mention it often, but I can tell he's stressed."

"It's normal. He's worried he won't fit in, or the kids will pick on him, or he'll spill his milk on his shirt the first day."

"I've talked to his teacher—"

Cammy held up a hand. "Macon, every kid in America worries before the first day of kindergarten. It's normal."

"It's really hard not to fight his battles for him."

"I know. But that's got Trevor worried. He wants the chance to fit in on his own. He's afraid you're going to be overprotective."

"Who me?" She frowned. "The original Smother Mother?"

Cammy laughed. "You and Jacob should be really proud of yourselves. A lot of kids in Trevor's position would be terrified. He knows his family adores him, so he's a little more secure about taking chances."

"I just hope we're doing the right thing. Jacob felt

really strongly about sending Trev to public school.''

The couple, Cammy knew, had spent months making the choice between public school kindergarten, where Trevor would need an interpreter, and a private school for deaf children. ''There's not a right or wrong answer, Macon. You made the choice you felt was right for your child. If it doesn't work out, you can always change your mind. Trevor is very gregarious, and he's a natural leader. Give him two weeks, and he'll be class president.''

''Do you think so?''

Cammy nodded. ''I think so.''

She watched as Macon struggled visibly with her doubts. For all Macon's professional and personal accomplishments in the fast-paced world of Washington politics, she still had a healthy share of maternal insecurities. As a media consultant, she'd managed countless political clients with award-winning confidence and success. But when it came to Trevor, she showed a rare vulnerability. She and Cammy had become fast friends the moment Macon and her husband had brought their son into her office. Cammy considered herself privileged to know a side of Macon that few others had ever seen.

Macon was watching her dubiously. ''You're sure?''

Cammy assured her. ''He'll do great. Just give him a little space to grow.''

Macon's eyes drifted momentarily shut. ''If he comes home in tears, I'm going to die.''

''Before or after you swat the kid who upset him?''

When Macon opened her eyes, amusement sparkled

in their depths. "Swatting is Jacob's department. I just sit in the corner and wither."

Cammy gave her a wry look. "Am I seriously supposed to believe that?"

"Okay, maybe I don't exactly *wither*."

"Uh-huh."

"All right, all right. I confess. Usually, Jacob has to peel me off someone before I inflict mortal wounds."

"That I believe."

Macon glanced at Trevor once more. "You're sure he's doing okay?"

"He's great. We talked a little about the possibility of a cochlear implant." She tapped the receiver behind her ear. "He's not sure he wants one."

"We're still struggling with that. It's hard to think about subjecting your five-year-old to a four-hour operation that may not even work."

"I'm sure it is."

"But you think we should do it?"

"No. Not necessarily. Just because I had it done, and it worked for me, doesn't mean I think every deaf child needs an implant. It may not be right for Trevor. You and Jacob and Trevor are the only ones who know that."

"But you think he'd take to it?"

Cammy shrugged. "I think his personality is well-suited to the risk." At Macon's frown, she laughed. "Okay, in laymen's terms, I think that Trevor is a very secure and happy little boy. He's doing very well with his verbal skills, but the longer his brain goes without auditory stimulation, the more you run the risk of deterioration to his auditory nerve. His brain may, or may not, be able to effectively process the information he hears. Unfortunately, it's not an exact science. No one can make you a guarantee.''

"The more research we do, the more confused I get.''

"I know. It's frustrating. How does Jacob feel?''

"Like I do. We want to give Trevor every chance we can, but we don't want to take unnecessary risks either. I'm worried that Trevor will put too much pressure on himself. If he has the operation, we're afraid that he'll think he'll have to set some record in language development just to please us.''

"He might.''

"But he might not.'' Macon looked at Cammy for confirmation.

"The more you affirm him, the more time you spend with him, the more likely he is to take the adjustment in stride. If he knows you and Jacob aren't disappointed with whatever progress he happens to be making, he won't feel as frustrated.''

Macon's expression turned plaintive. "You know, I have made million-dollar campaign decisions that weren't this complicated.''

"I know.''

"And Trev's doctor keeps pressuring us. He's convinced we should move ahead immediately.''

"It's a big decision, Macon. You and Jacob and Trevor need to be committed to it before you proceed.''

"You don't think we'll do irreparable damage if we wait to see how he makes out in kindergarten?''

"I think you'd do worse damage if you all rushed into this." She glanced at Trevor. "It should happen sooner rather than later, but he needs to be sure about it, too."

"You're right." Macon gave her a grateful look. "As usual." She glanced at her watch. "You didn't know you were going to get to conduct two therapy sessions today, did you?"

Cammy smiled. "My pleasure."

"I'm sure it was. You were delighted to distract me from interrogating you about Jackson Puller."

"I see I failed."

"Dismally. You didn't think I'd drop something like that, did you?"

"A girl can always hope."

"No way. You've still got three minutes until your next appointment. Just hit the highlights for me."

"There's nothing to tell." At Macon's speculative look, she shook her head. "I swear. Mike pulled some strings at AW to get the story, and they sent Jackson Puller."

"Lucky you."

"If you say so."

Macon tapped her fingers on the arms of the chair. "Just tell me one thing. I met him about three years ago at a press corps event. Has he still got sizzle?"

"Is that a technical term?"

Macon laughed. "No. In media land, we'd call it camera-friendly charisma. 'Sizzle' is girl-talk."

"Okay," Cammy relented. "Yes. He's got it."

"Really?" Macon's eyes sparkled. "And exactly how long is this series of articles he's doing on you?"

"The articles are on Wishing Star, not on me. Get that speculative look out of your eyes."

"Too late. You've got my imagination dancing through all kinds of schemes."

"I'm doomed."

"Face up to it, kiddo. There's nothing like a media mogul on the move. Besides, it's not even an election year. I'm in my slow season."

"Lucky me."

"You have no idea. So are you bringing him to the dance recital tonight?"

"I hadn't thought about it."

"You should."

"So you can ogle him?"

"So I can check out how the two of you look as a couple."

"We are not a couple."

"Sure, sure. I have a pretty good idea, but there's nothing like the visual impact of the real thing. Besides, Jacob will be there, and he's always good for a second opinion on things like this."

"Terrific. I've always dreamed of having my love life be a topic of after–dinner conversation."

"So it's a love life now?"

"It's a figure of speech. You know I'm not going to get involved with him."

Macon's expression turned suddenly serious. "Cammy—"

Cammy held up a hand. "It's okay, Macon." At Macon's skeptical look, Cammy nodded. "It is. Really."

"I just don't think you're being reasonable about

this,'' Macon frowned. ''Your parents may have done some number on you about the fact that you can't have children, but that doesn't mean you have to let it govern your life.'' She exhaled an exasperated breath. ''I know this sounds easy for me to say—but there are worse fates than infertility. I'm not trying to be insensitive.''

''I know.''

''I just don't think you should take your father's opinion that this makes you less of a person as gospel truth. It's just ridiculous. And archaic.'' She frowned. ''It was a lousy thing to do to tell you that, and if the bastard weren't dead, I'd kill him myself.''

Cammy managed a smile. ''If he weren't dead, he'd probably be one of your clients.''

Macon snorted. ''Don't bet on it. I have a definite policy against taking clients who punch all my buttons. Look, you're one of the smartest people I know, Cam. You don't have to live by his rules anymore.''

''I'm not. I paid $165,000 for a psychology degree to learn how to make my own decisions. It's my decision.''

Frustration flared in Macon's gaze. ''If I had time, I'd argue with you.''

''I've learned to count on that.''

''But I don't, so I'll save it for later.''

Cammy laughed. ''Okay. We'll have lunch one day soon.''

Macon stood and began to make her way across the room toward Trevor. ''I'm not letting you off the hook.''

''I'd be disappointed if you did.''

"So are you bringing him or not?"

"You're relentless, aren't you?"

"Absolutely. Let's not forget that I built a career on it." She tapped Trevor on the shoulder. "Is the world safe for another day?" she signed to him.

He grinned at her as he explained the outcome of his video battle. "Can I play one more game?"

"*May* I," Macon corrected.

Trevor frowned, but adjusted the question. Macon shook her head. "We've got to go." She indicated Cammy with a wave of her hand. "Cammy's got another appointment, and she has to call Mr. Puller to invite him to your recital."

Trevor beamed at her. "Is he coming?"

Cammy gave Macon a wry look. "You knew I couldn't resist that smile, didn't you?"

"Slays them every time. Just like his father."

Turning to Trevor, Cammy shook her head. "Your mother is completely crazy."

"That's why she likes my dad," Trevor informed her gravely. "He's crazy, too."

Cammy laughed. "Do you think so?"

Trevor nodded. "Are you going to ask Mr. Puller?" he persisted, then executed an intricate series of tap steps. "He'll like it."

"Why do you think so?"

Trevor shrugged. "Because he likes me."

Hard to argue with that line of reasoning, Cammy thought. "Yes, he does."

"And he likes you."

Macon gave her a smug look. "See?"

Cammy groaned. "Oh, Lord."

"Just ask him," Trevor insisted. "You'll see."

She sensed his presence before she saw him.

At seven that evening, in the lobby area of the rented auditorium, a large group of families and friends and the merely curious milled about in an effort to calm nervous jitters. The children had already made their way backstage for last-minute instructions and costume checks. A Broadway premier, Cammy knew, wouldn't have created a greater sense of excitement.

Cammy was in the middle of explaining to Macon that she'd had the invitation to the recital couriered to Jackson's office when she felt a tingling sensation at her nape. It might have been precipitated by the sudden stillness in the room. She might even have blamed it on the knowing look Macon gave her. She feared, however, that the electricity racing through her blood had little to do with crowd dynamics and far too much to do with the arrival of Jackson Puller.

She turned to find him standing by the door. He looked tired, she noted.

And disarmingly attractive.

And he was looking for her.

Somehow, the effect of that moment notched her temperature up a couple of degrees. In a crisp white shirt with wide blue suspenders and navy trousers, he managed to look simultaneously elegant and relaxed. One day, she thought, she must remember to ask him how he did that. For now, she was too interested in the effect he was having on the large group. When a member of the press, especially one of Jackson's stature, arrived at events in Washington, D.C. like this, the crowd reaction was sometimes antagonistic, but, more often, merely blasé. She'd seen it happen countless times. Public officials who maintained a symbiotic relationship with the media generally preferred to ignore reporters who haunted their social lives.

But when Jackson entered the room, it felt like a bomb had exploded. He drew attention, Cammy noted, like red clover drew bees. Well-wishers, fans, and the ever-hopeful began to press in his direction. Macon sent a silent signal to her husband, who threaded his way through the circle of women rapidly closing in on Jackson. Cammy suspected that her sigh of relief was audible when she saw Jacob Blackfort's hand reach through the throng like a rescue worker scooping a victim from a deadly current.

Jackson sent Cammy a wry look that felt oddly intimate across the breadth of the room. Macon's hand looped around her elbow. "Let's go meet your guest."

Cammy continued to study Jackson's dark head as he conversed with Jacob Blackfort. "I thought you said you already knew him."

"You know what I mean." Macon guided her neatly through several would-be obstacles of inquiring eyes and prying questions. In an effortless move that won Cammy's unending admiration, Macon somehow managed to maneuver through the curious ring of women who surrounded Jackson and her husband and ease themselves into position by the two men.

Jackson smiled at her. "Cammy, hi." He bent to

kiss her cheek in greeting. It should have seemed the most natural thing in the world, but when his hand settled at her waist, and his clear eyes met her gaze with something far too warm to be called casual, her heart missed a beat.

"I'm glad you made it," she told him.

"I'm glad you invited me." His expression told her he had more to say, but he merely watched her as she smoothed a hand over her loose green dress.

Macon delicately cleared her throat. Cammy pulled her gaze from Jackson's face to make the necessary introductions. "Jackson, I believe you've met Macon Stratton-Blackfort."

Jackson extended his hand. "It's nice to see you again. I met your son, Trevor, the other day at Cammy's office. Is he dancing tonight?"

Macon nodded. "A tap solo, a duet, and a couple of chorus numbers. He's quite the showman."

Beside her, Jacob Blackfort laughed. "He gets that from his mother."

Macon planted an elbow in his ribs. "Liar. Trevor's got your genes, and Natalie has mine."

"Is that why she had a tantrum when we left her with the baby-sitter tonight?"

"You bet. You know us Stratton women. We like to get our way." Macon turned back to Jackson. "So I understand you're doing a story on Cammy."

"It's on Wishing Star," Cammy insisted.

Jackson's fingers tightened on her waist. "It's a series on the work Cammy's doing, and the success she's having with the foundation."

"How does it feel to be grounded back in Washington for a change?" Jacob asked.

From the corner of her eye, Cammy noted the slight tightening of Jackson's lips. Just as quickly, it passed. "I didn't think I'd like it, but I'm warming to the idea."

If the heated imprint his hand was leaving on her skin was any indication, that had to be the understatement of the year. Cammy listened to the quiet rumble of Jackson's voice while he told the couple the details of his current assignment. No one, she noticed, mentioned what had happened in Bosnia. Despite the overwhelming tide of publicity Jackson's story and subsequent Pulitzer nomination had received, Leo's death stayed firmly out of the ring of conversation. She noted this omission carefully, and would have suggested they move to find seats in the auditorium when a disturbance by the door arrested her attention.

Amy Patterson, looking perilously close to tears, and wringing her hands in the folds of a black-and-white pinafore, was frantically searching the crowd. Distress marred her usually bright face. The harried-looking woman behind her shook rain from an umbrella as she frowned her displeasure.

Cammy mumbled a slight apology to Jackson as she eased her way past him to the door. "Amy." She tapped the child on the shoulders. "What's wrong?"

Amy's small face crumpled as she threw her arms around Cammy's legs.

"We got caught in traffic," the older woman reported. "No one told me I was supposed to drive her over here until thirty minutes ago. There was no one else to do it, or I never would have agreed to come out in this rain. I hate driving in the city at night, and the rain makes it worse.''

Cammy decided against losing her patience with the volunteer in favor of comforting Amy. She tipped the child away from her and signed, ''It's okay, sweetheart. You're not too late. They haven't started yet.''

''My costume's all wet. We couldn't find a place to park.''

Cammy straightened the dress with a few wipes of her hands. ''It'll dry before you have to dance. Your part is in the middle of the show.'' She flipped open her program and pointed to Amy's name. ''See. You still have plenty of time.''

Some of the worry began to ease from the child's face. ''Is Miss Lynette mad at me?''

Cammy shook her head. ''No. She knew you'd be here in time for your part.''

The volunteer grunted. ''Barely. You should have seen the traffic on Pennsylvania Avenue.''

Cammy mustered a sympathetic look. ''I'm sure it was terrible, but Amy's here now. That's what matters.''

The volunteer wouldn't be deterred. ''I've got to stay for this whole thing, I suppose. How else is she going to get home? Then we'll have to drive back late at night, and us with nowhere to park. It's not safe to be out in this city that late, you know?''

Jackson, who had skirted the edges of the room to where wet coats and umbrellas hung in a tangle on the temporary racks, appeared at her side once again. "Hi, Amy. I'm glad you made it."

Cammy interpreted for him. Amy greeted him with a bright smile that chased away the lingering threat of tears in her eyes. Cammy was tempted to kiss him in gratitude. He squatted in front of the child so his face was on eye level with her. "I brought you something." He presented her with a paper-wrapped bundle of roses he'd retrieved from the sleeve of his trench coat. "Break a leg."

She cradled the roses close to her chest and looked at Jackson in adoration. Cammy couldn't blame her. She was thinking he looked pretty darned adorable at that particular moment herself. He glanced at the still flustered volunteer. "Thanks for bringing her, Ms., ah—"

"George. Edith George."

"Ms. George. Thanks for driving her over here. Would you like us to give her a ride home?"

The volunteer looked from Cammy to Jackson to Amy, then back at Cammy. "Oh, well, I don't know. I'm not supposed—"

"Amy is one of my patients, Ms. George," Cammy interjected. "I think you've brought her to my office before."

Recognition dawned. "Oh. You're the therapist."

"Yes."

"Well, then I suppose it would be all right. I'd really rather not wait and have to drive back in this rain."

"I understand," Jackson assured her. "Driving in

the city at night is never pleasant. We'll be glad to do it for you.''

Amy was looking at Cammy expectantly. Cammy quickly interpreted the gist of the conversation for her, then asked, ''Would you like to ride home with us tonight?''

She nodded vigorously enough to reassure Edith George. The older woman began pulling on her plastic rain bonnet. ''Well, then, I thank you. I'm going to head on back before the rain gets worse. I wish they'd told me about this yesterday so I could have gotten another driver. You're sure you don't mind bringing her home?''

Cammy watched in relief as the woman pushed open the door. ''Not at all. We're glad to do it.''

Beside her, Jackson and Amy were having a jumbled conversation of lip-reading and mixed signs and muffled laughter. By the time Cammy had Edith George firmly out the door, a slightly rushed Lynette had joined them. ''Amy, we've been waiting for you. I'm glad you made it.''

Amy apologized for her wet costume. Lynette assured her it would dry in plenty of time. Jackson rose next to Cammy, who was feeling perilously close to throwing her arms around him when Lynette said, ''What beautiful roses.''

Amy beamed at Jackson, then slid her hand into Lynette's. The two hurried away to the backstage door. Macon and Jacob, Cammy noticed for the first time, had stood quietly watching the scene. Cammy glanced at Jackson, who was looking almost embarrassed. ''How did you know?'' she asked.

"About giving her a ride home?"

"No. About the flowers." She heard her voice catch.

"My sisters had dance recitals. I remembered that there were always flowers."

"But you bought those for Amy. How did you know she'd need them?"

He shrugged. "I had a hunch. I figured if I didn't use them by the time the night was over, I'd give them to you."

"It was a very nice thing to do."

"Sometimes, I'm a very nice guy."

Cammy laid her hand on his sleeve. "Leo was lucky to have had you for a friend."

His expression darkened momentarily as he tilted his head to one side. "Do you make a habit of that?"

"What?"

"Saying exactly the right thing at exactly the right moment."

"Words mean a lot to me." She squeezed his arm. "I just thought you should know that I think Leo couldn't have asked for more."

"You know, if I'd known a couple of roses was all it would take, I'd have done it days ago."

"What do you mean?"

"I've been wondering what I'd have to do to get you to look at me with that expression in your eyes."

"What expression?"

"The one that says you think I'm maybe not such a bad guy after all."

She suspected that her expression said a good deal more than that, but she didn't say so. "Now you know my secret. I'm a sucker for men who rescue damsels in distress. Even if the damsels are only six years old."

He reached for her hand. "So you're weakening?"

She almost choked. He had no idea. "A little."

"Enough that if I tell you I read your background file today you're not going to start frowning at me?" He rubbed his thumb on the back of her hand.

Cammy stifled a laugh. "Did you learn anything juicy?"

"You're not angry." It wasn't a question.

"It's just a file, Jackson. Newspaper clippings and stuff, am I right?"

"Yes." His grip tightened as he pulled her hand to his chest. With their linked fingers lying against his heart, she felt its steady thrum.

"It's not like you called the CIA and asked them to put together a dossier." She gave him a narrow look. "Is it?"

"Cammy—"

"I'm kidding." She tried not to notice the way his hand shifted so he could caress her palm with his fingertips. There was something blatantly seductive in the action. "Of course I'm not angry. You needed the background material to do your story. Why should I be angry?"

"Your father was a real bastard."

"He was a very powerful man. Some people even thought he was a hero."

She saw the frustration on his face. "People have weird ideas about what makes a man a hero."

"Do they?"

"Some people think all it takes is a public office and some positive press."

"And some people think a man can make himself a hero with three roses and a ride home." She squeezed his hand. "Heroes, in my experience, know exactly what to do with sensitive information. I'm safe with you."

A spark darkened his eyes to near black as he visually consumed her features. "Where did you get a lamebrained idea like that?"

Cammy would have responded, except the lights blinked, signaling the beginning of the recital. Jacob slipped his arm around Macon's shoulder. "That's our cue."

Jackson nodded. "We'd better find seats. I don't want to miss anything."

Cammy felt a slight tug on her sleeve and turned to find Macon studying her with avid interest. "Tomorrow," Macon hissed. "You and I are having lunch *tomorrow*. We have a *lot* to talk about."

✨♡ *four*

"Good morning, Mother."

Laura Glynn didn't bother to turn her head. Propped against the white pillows, her bed framed by the grayish green walls of the psychiatric hospital, she stared avidly at the water pitcher on her nightstand.

Cameo drew a deep breath. "Do you want some water?"

"No."

"Are you going to look at me today?"

"I don't know."

They lapsed into silence. Cameo searched her mother's profile for signs of change. Hard lines of disillusionment still etched her face. Her hair, perfectly coifed as always, seemed at odds with the confusion in her eyes. "I'm sorry I didn't get by to see you earlier this week."

She'd been busy trying to pretend that Jackson Puller wasn't having a serious effect on her equilibrium. She turned her thoughts instead to his behavior at the dance recital. As the children had danced, performed miracles on a stage where deafness didn't prohibit them from keeping time and rhythm, she'd sensed a storm brewing inside him. His casual good mood had given way to something more emotionally profound during the course of the recital. The fleeting dark look she'd seen when she'd mentioned Leo had taken up permanent residence on his face. By the end of the evening, ghosts had lived in his gaze.

Concerned, she'd pressed him slightly during the intermission. He'd responded with distracted answers and a hollow tone in his voice that told her his mind had returned to Bosnia. Frustrated at her own inability to reach him, she'd offered to drive Amy home for him after the show. He'd seized the opportunity with a mumbled apology about his deadline and left before the finale.

Cammy wasn't normally prone to panic, but then Jackson Puller represented an unusual set of circumstances. Forcibly, she set the image of his haunted look aside and dragged herself back to the sterile room. "I've had a lot to do," she told her mother. "What with the fund-raiser for Wishing Star coming up, and my usual appointments. I'm very busy."

"Aren't you always busy?"

The bitter statement explained much. "Generally, yes." Cameo leaned back in her chair as she reminded herself of her mother's emotional immaturity. Oddly, years of professional psychiatric training never seemed to prepare her for facing the grim reality in this room. Nor, evidently, the worry she'd battled through the night about Jackson's peace of mind. "But that doesn't mean I don't have time for you."

"You don't know what it's like, Cameo. Sitting here, day after day, wondering if your only child forgot you."

"You know I won't forget you."

"If you'd had children, you'd understand."

Long ago, the barb had lost its ability to hurt her. She'd come to terms with the birth defect that had caused her infertility, just as she'd come to terms with her deafness. When puberty had failed to bring the usual changes to her body and her system, her mother had dragged her to an endless stream of specialists. With her fear and confusion amplified by her deafness, Cammy had withdrawn even further into her shell. The night her mother had confronted her father with the news of Cammy's infertility, he'd been on his way to a speaking event. He'd taken the news in stride and casually dismissed it as a "blessing in disguise." No chance, he'd informed her mother, that Cammy's deafness could be genetically transferred. Cammy had sat on the steps of their town house and read the brutal words as they'd tumbled from his lips. He'd offered her a forced smile on his way out the door.

She hadn't realized she'd lapsed into the memory until her mother finally looked at her. A hint of wildness flitted across her gaze. "Where's your father?"

She always asked. Cammy always gave her the same answer. "He's out of town." For years, Laura Glynn had refused to accept the reality of her late husband's death. Cammy had eventually found the evasion easier than the truth. "I don't know when he'll be back."

"He was supposed to take me to the ball this week."

"Really?" This was a new development.

Laura nodded. She raised a weathered hand to pat her graying curls. "I've had my hair done."

"Which ball, Mother?"

"Ivan and Nadeja Korsinski are in town for the summit. Hadn't you heard?"

Cammy's brows lifted slightly. Of course she'd heard. Traffic jams, news reports, and tightened security had surrounded the Russian president's state visit for the past several days. "I didn't know you had."

"I read the papers," her mother snapped. "There's a ball tonight. At the embassy. Your father is supposed to take me."

The fantasy, Cammy admitted, was not completely beyond the realm of reason. During her father's reign as chairman of the U.S. Senate Foreign Affairs Committee, he often attended state functions. "Did he tell you he would?" Cammy prompted.

Laura nodded. "Last week. He stopped by." Cool gray eyes registered a look of triumph. "He's getting rid of her, you know. I knew he would."

"Her?"

"That woman. Don't be so naive, Cameo. You know about her. Everyone knows about her."

Everyone had. Cameo had first learned of her father's infidelity in precisely this fashion. She'd been seven, then, and wholly unprepared for the harsh truth. Time had taught her that her mother's psychological deterioration, not deliberate insensitivity, had

triggered those early bouts of rage and near hysteria.
Time had not, however, completely healed the
wounds. Cammy briefly closed her eyes. "Yes,
Mother. I know."

"He won't get away with it."

"Won't he?"

"The press will destroy him. He hates them, you
know. Just like he hates me."

"He doesn't hate you." The response was auto-
matic. Years ago, she'd decided to play the role of
daughter, not doctor. "I'm sure that's not true."

"Yes, he does. He hates me. And he hates you. It's
not my fault you can't hear, you know?"

Cammy nodded. This was familiar territory. Her
mother had never seemed to comprehend that surgery
had corrected most of Cammy's deafness. Instead,
she'd continued to remind her that Durstan had little
use for either of them. "I know."

"Deafness runs in your father's family. Not mine."

"I know that, too."

"Then you can't blame me for it."

"I don't."

"Your father does." She pressed her lips together
in a thin line of dislike. "Don't ever forget it either,
Cameo. No matter what he tells you, he can't stand
the fact that you're deaf. He likes to drag you out in
public to make himself look charitable, but he hates
it. There's nothing Durstan hates more than imperfection."

Fifteen minutes later, Cammy stepped out onto the
sidewalk with the same sense of relief she felt each

time she completed a visit to her mother's hospital room. Inside, the building felt stifling, institutional. It resembled too many of the places where Cammy had spent long months of her childhood. On the best of days, it made her edgy.

Today, however, when she was already disconcerted from a mostly sleepless night, her mother's biting tongue had found its mark. The truth of her words, Cammy supposed, hurt more than the actual hearing of them. Laura had been right. Durstan Glynn couldn't tolerate imperfection.

Unbidden, and before she could stop it, a second memory assailed her. She was fifteen, and she'd failed to meet Durstan's expectations yet again.

"Why didn't you answer them, Cameo?" She read the cold accusation on Durstan Glynn's lips, felt the equally cold condemnation in his gaze.

She glanced at her mother. Laura was staring fixedly at the flower arrangement in the center of the table. "Durstan, did you give any more thought to attending that charity benefit next week?"

"Damn it, Laura—"

Cammy flinched. Though she couldn't hear the words, the vibration of her father's voice sent chills racing through her. She gathered a calm facade around her like a familiar blanket as she concentrated on her dinner.

Her mother swallowed the contents of her wine glass. "She didn't answer because she's deaf, Durstan. In case it escaped your notice."

Cammy didn't attempt to read her father's reply.

Her parents were shouting now. Soon, she knew, he'd leave. Her mother would rage at her for making him leave. Her fault for making him angry. Her fault for failing to impress his supporters. Her fault for his infidelity. Her fault for . . .

Forcibly, Cammy pushed the dark thought aside. She drew a long, tension-easing breath of the early spring air. Briefly, her eyes drifted shut as she mentally identified the sounds around her. A distant siren. A crumpled piece of paper tumbling down the sidewalk. The chatter from a nearby playground.

"Cammy?"

Her name. Her eyes popped open. Jackson stood beside her on the sidewalk, an intense expression on his angular face. He held a manila folder in one hand. "Hi."

"Hi."

"Are you all right?"

She frowned at him. "Are you?"

His expression gentled. "Yes. I was looking for you." His gaze narrowed. "You look like you're going to pass out."

"Do you think so?"

"Yes. You're pale."

"Really? It's probably not as bad as what I saw on your face last night."

He grimaced. "I can explain that. Sort of. That's what I wanted to talk to you about."

"How did you find me?"

"Costas."

She froze. "Mike? Mike told you I was here?"

"He said you were visiting a patient."

Relief washed over her. Mike would have known, she reassured herself, that she was far from ready to give Jackson Puller the complicated details of her personal life. She drew a calming breath. "I was."

"Is everything all right?"

"Fine, I—" She focused on his face. He looked exhausted. "I was worried about you."

"I know. What were you doing?"

"Doing?"

"Just now. Standing there with your eyes closed."

"Oh, that. It's just something I do."

His expression lightened for the first time. The customary teasing glint returned to his eyes. "You stand around in the middle of the city with your eyes closed? Are you trying to get mugged?"

"No. I'm listening."

Seconds passed before understanding dawned in his expression. On its heels came an aching tenderness that threatened to melt her into a puddle. "Oh. What do you hear?"

"Everything. Nothing." She drew a deep breath. "I hear the things that most people take for granted."

"You know what I did last night?"

Several seconds passed before she adjusted to the abrupt change of subject. She decided to risk a joke, hoping it would ease him into the topic. "Went home and called dial-a-shrink?"

He laughed, a genuine laugh that warmed her heart. "Not exactly." He looped his hand beneath her elbow and began walking down the street. "If I'd wanted to call a shrink, I'd have dialed your number."

"I was up."

He glanced at her. "Really?"

"You had me worried."

"Should I be flattered?"

"Strictly professional interest, I assure you."

"Damn. I was hoping Amy's roses would buy me twenty-four hours of hero worship."

"She's your friend for life."

"I wasn't talking about her."

"Oh. And here I thought your interest in me was all for the sake of a story."

Almost before she knew what was happening, he tugged her into a doorway out of the bustling traffic on the sidewalk. His hands settled on her upper arms, and his gaze landed squarely on her face. "You know, that's one thing I'd just like to go ahead and get straight. I'm writing a story, that's my job. But that doesn't even begin to cover what I want to know about you. Despite what you may think, I'm perfectly capable of keeping my professional life and my personal life separate. I know the difference, Cammy. I'm a big boy."

The vehemence of the statement surprised her. "I didn't mean to suggest—"

His hands tightened on her arms, guided her closer. "What I want from you professionally is a few answers to some general questions." His voice had lowered to a husky rasp. "I'm not even sure I can put into words what I want personally."

"Jackson—"

"Oh, to hell with it," he muttered as he lowered his mouth to hers.

The kiss was electrifyingly warm and very, very thorough. After her initial surprise, Cammy felt her hands gliding up the soft fabric of his well-worn shirt. Her fingers settled at his nape as he thoroughly explored her lips. She had the sensation of drifting in a warm sea where the sound of his heartbeat kept time with hers. His thumbs urged her mouth open so he could deepen the kiss. The warm sea became an ocean of sensation, where she felt drenched, enveloped. As his lips moved over hers, she felt her hands thread into the thick weight of his hair. Before she realized it, she was clutching him to her with something close to desperation.

Jackson shifted so she was pressed fully against him. He deepened the kiss, tugging at her mouth, exploring her with a frank sensuality that made her ears ring. When he lifted his head, she blinked three times and still couldn't quite bring him into focus. With a slight chuckle, he dropped her glasses back on her nose. She hadn't even realized he'd removed them.

"Are we clear on that?" he asked.

He didn't have to sound so damned calm, she thought irritably. Not when her own feet were having trouble making contact with the sidewalk. "I guess we are."

She would have moved away from him, but Jackson grabbed her hand and pressed it to his chest, where his heart pounded a steady rhythm. "Feel it?" He waited for her nod. "Sometimes, I'm not sure you really hear what I'm saying. I want to make sure you don't misunderstand me."

She stared at him several seconds, then released a long breath. "I understand."

"Good." He guided her back to the sidewalk. "Can I buy you a cup of coffee? Do you have somewhere you need to be?"

Somehow, she didn't think he should sound so calm, so normal, as if he hadn't just rearranged her mind and cemented himself in her thoughts. She forced herself to glance at her watch. "I have a little time."

"I'm glad. I wanted to explain what happened to me last night." He pulled open the door of the coffee shop.

"The kids affected you, didn't they?"

"You could say that." He fixed her with a direct look. "After I left, I went home and tried not to hear anything."

Warmth, and something dangerously close to the feeling she'd had when she'd watched him give Amy those roses, filled her. "You did?"

"You have things you do." A wry smile pulled at his lips. "I have things I do. Part of what makes me good at my job is that I try to relate to the people I write about."

"It also makes you a nice person."

"Don't let that get around. I have a reputation as an unscrupulous, power-hungry, filth monger to protect."

She had to laugh. The feeling surprised her. It generally took her several hours to shake the dark feelings she experienced after each visit with her mother. Today, Jackson had managed to send her through an entire cycle of emotions in the span of twenty minutes. "I'll keep it between us."

His gaze turned curious. "So can I safely assume that you've revised your opinion of me?"

She forced herself not to look away. "I told you not to take it personally."

"Force of habit."

"I never said 'filth monger.' "

"You thought it."

"Guilty."

He frowned. "I knew it." With a tilt of his head, he indicated the menu. "You want anything?"

"Black coffee."

His eyebrows lifted. The shop was notorious for its wide selection of specialty blends and flavored roasts. "What? No French vanilla, cinnamon bon-bon latte with heavy foam and a decaf chaser?"

"In case you hadn't noticed, I'm a plain-Jane kind of girl. Besides, I get confused when I try to read the menu."

He handed her the folder he still carried. "Why don't you grab us a seat? I'll get the coffee."

She settled herself in a booth by the window. To avoid the temptation of glancing through the folder, she studied Jackson's back while he ordered. He had such broad shoulders. But still not broad enough for the burden of Leo's death. She'd tried several times to get him to talk about it. He'd neatly avoided the conversation with a verbal two-step that would have shamed Gene Kelly. She resolved, again, to get inside him.

The thought sent a flutter along her nerve endings.

If that kiss he'd given her was any indication, she wasn't the only one having those kinds of thoughts.

He turned from the counter to catch her watching him. Deliberately, she held his gaze while he eased his way through the crowded shop. He set the coffee on the table, then slid into the booth. He took a long swallow of his coffee, then indicated the manila folder. "Do you know what that is?"

"I didn't look at it."

"You could have."

"You didn't give me permission. I make a habit of keeping my nose very firmly where it belongs."

He tilted his head to one side. "Unlike me who is constantly sticking mine right into other people's business."

"You said it."

He shook his head, then downed a sip of his coffee. He laid his bandaged palm on the folder. "I wrote this last night when I went home."

She stilled, inside and out. "Oh?"

"It's the first installment in the series about you and Wishing Star. I'm turning it in this afternoon. I wanted you to read it before you saw it in the paper."

"I see."

"Cam—" He paused. "I told you yesterday that I'd read your background file."

"And that you didn't necessarily approve of my father."

"He shouldn't have used you the way he did."

"What makes you say that?"

"Hell, all those pictures of you standing with him at press events while he pretended he wasn't using you for sympathy votes and good PR. I'm not a rookie, Cam. I know how it works.''

"It wasn't that bad.''

"Did he give you the time of day if there weren't reporters around?''

She hesitated. "Not generally.''

Jackson swore beneath his breath. "I didn't think so.''

"Maybe if they'd stopped taking pictures, he would have stopped inviting them to do it.''

His gaze narrowed. "You felt like a science experiment, didn't you?''

"It was scary and confusing. All those lights. I couldn't hear what was going on. They'd ask me questions, and I couldn't hear them. My father always seemed angry after it was over.''

"And you hated it.''

"I wouldn't say I *hated* it. It just didn't make me feel very good about myself.''

"You're afraid that's going to happen to your Wishing Star kids, aren't you?''

"Yes. When your story appears, it'll make waves. People will notice. The press is like that. They look for smoke, and if they don't find a fire, they start one.''

"Cammy—''

She held up a hand in surrender. "Okay, not all of you. Just some of you.''

"We're not a separate species, you know? We're just like anyone else. There are good reporters and bad reporters. Reporters with scruples and reporters without 'em.''

"But you have power. And a lot of you misuse it."

"Some do," he conceded. "I can't change that."

"But you wanted to."

The statement made his gaze narrow. "What do you mean?"

She shrugged. "It's just a feeling I have. Some things you've said—I take it you aren't always enchanted with the way the members of your profession behave."

"Journalism is like any other job in the world. We have our share of snakes."

"Still, Jackson. Why so wary? Level with me." She paused. "You owe me."

"How do you figure that?"

"That kiss you gave me. It says you want a little more from me than a good scoop."

He took a long sip of his coffee. "You could say that."

"So for that, don't I get to know a little more about you than the rest of the general public?"

"You think I'm hiding something?"

"I didn't say that. You're acting suspicious."

"I don't want you to analyze me."

"Fair enough. How about if I just take what you tell me at face value and leave the analysis to you?"

His full mouth twitched. "Are you kidding?"

"No."

"You can't do that, and you know it."

"Sure I can."

He snorted. "I'll bet. I can't walk away from a good tip, and I'll bet you can't walk away from the spilled guts of a bona fide nutcase."

"Are you?"

"A nut? I don't think so."

"Then you're safe with me."

Awareness glittered in his gaze. "You think so?"

She refused to take the bait. "You're safer with me than just about anyone else I know. I keep secrets."

"And you think I have some."

"I'm sure of it. I just want to know what makes you tick. How did you become the avenging angel of the downtrodden and helpless?"

His hands tightened on his coffee cup. He shifted his gaze to study the dark liquid. "I don't know. It wasn't a decision I made one day. And to be honest, I'm not sure I'm comfortable with the way people characterize what I do."

"You don't like the accusations, do you?"

"I don't like being told that I go into a story looking for some kid's life to exploit. No."

"I didn't think so."

"I became a journalist because it seemed like a noble thing to do. I could write a little. People seemed to respond to the way I told stories. I was attracted to the pace and the pressure of the business. Like most college journalism majors, I had dreams of being the next Bob Woodward."

"Someone ruined your dreams, didn't they?"

He shook his head. "It wasn't someone, it was a series of events. I got to Washington thinking I knew everything, that I could count on the world to judge me for my talent." His cynicism was unmistakable.

"It didn't work out that way."

He grunted. "I got a job. I was a copy editor at the

Post. I started watching the way things worked. I saw people get used, people's lives get ruined for the sake of a story.''

Several seconds of silence passed between them. Cammy slipped her hand across the table to squeeze his fist. "Young dreams are the hardest kind to let go."

He studied her for a minute. "How many of your dreams did you lose along the way, Cammy?"

She shrugged. His gaze narrowed. "More than I did, I bet," he said. "Why are you afraid to let me do this story? What don't you want me to find?"

His verbal arrow hit its mark, and he knew it. The regret in his gaze wouldn't allow her to resent him for it. "It's not that," she admitted. "I don't have anything to hide."

"But there are things you'd rather I didn't find out?"

"Maybe. The way things went in my life, well, it's not a very pretty story. It's not especially gruesome. I mean there's nothing really awful about it, but I don't really like to tell it unless I have to. It seems like a waste of energy to kick all those old ghosts around.

"Speaking of which . . ." she continued. Her hand still gripped his fist. Gently, she turned it over and spread the fingers so she could rub her finger on his bandage. "Are you ready to tell me about last night?"

He hesitated, then tapped the folder. "It's in there," he said. "What I was feeling is in there. I think you'll know when you read it."

"What about Leo?"

She waited, but the shutters she expected never fell. His expression remained open, almost vulnerable despite his strength. He absently touched the bandage. "Not today," he finally said.

"Soon?"

"Probably."

She released his hand. "I understand."

"You're not going to push?"

"I'm your friend, not your therapist. You want someone to push you, call Mike."

His face relaxed. "Do you think I should?"

"I would if I were you."

"But you aren't going to insist?"

"Not yet."

"What'll push your buttons?"

She waved the folder at him. "I haven't read this yet. If I think you're dancing on the dark side, I'll quit giving you free professional advice and insist you start paying for it. From him, not me."

"You wouldn't treat me."

She paused, considering carefully the risk in what she was about to reveal, then decided she owed him her honesty. "There's a rule in this business that says a good doctor never shrinks a head she's grown fond of."

He leaned across the table, his grin engaging. "Are you fond of my head?"

"Guilty."

"Fond of anything else?"

"You might be embarrassed."

"Try me."

"Well, your butt's not so bad, either."

A smile twitched at the corner of his mouth. "I kind of like yours too."

"And here I thought you were interested in my mind."

"It's wrapped awfully nice."

"I see. So it's purely a physical thing with you?"

"You have no idea."

"Is this a good time for me to ask you if you had an unusually strong relationship with your mother?"

He laughed. It felt good, she realized, to hear him laugh again. "Worried about my id, my ego, or my sexual problems?"

"Do you have sexual problems?"

"Want to find out?"

"Well, whatever's wrong with you, it's definitely not your ego. Besides, I'm a Jungian. You want Freud, you have to talk to Mike."

Jackson leaned back in his chair. "What if Costas says I have sexual hang-ups?"

"Knowing you, you'd probably take it as a compliment."

His low chuckle made her toes tingle. Cammy was struck by the warm feeling that had begun to work its way through her limbs as she studied him in the early morning light. There was something incredibly potent in that charisma of his. Being in his presence had the power to make her feel weightless and buoyant. He reached for her hand, then pulled it to his mouth to kiss the palm. "I'm glad I found you today. I feel much better now."

"Me too," she confessed.

"Better enough to agree to have dinner with me Friday after next?"

Her eyebrows lifted. "Is there a catch?"

"So suspicious."

"Only because Mike told me he'd talked to your boss and we're expected at the Harrises' on Friday. Were you going to tell me that ahead of time, or did you just want to spring it on me?"

"I was working my way around to it."

"Do you think you could have dreamed up a worse hell for me? I mean, I'll be trapped at the table with two journalists and my business partner."

"Hey," he squeezed her hand. "I'll be stuck with two shrinks and my *boss*. It's worse for me than it is for you."

She shook her head. "Shrinks don't bite."

He grinned. "You still haven't told me whether or not you'll go on Friday."

"I was under the impression it was required."

"We could play hooky."

"We'd start rumors."

"Would that be so bad?"

"I wouldn't want to explain it to Mike."

"If I were you, I'd worry more about Sheila Harris."

"Matchmaking?"

"Like a mother hen."

"Oh dear."

His eyes twinkled. She wasn't sure she'd actually seen anyone twinkle before. "Want to give them something to talk about?"

"Not especially."

"Damn."

"I'll think about it between now and then, and I'll let you know. If I were you, I wouldn't hold my breath."

He blinked. "I didn't mean I wanted to wait that long to see you again."

She indicated the folder. "I have to read this before I decide if I'm still speaking to you."

"Cam—"

"I'm kidding." Before she could think better of it, she pressed a quick kiss to his lips. "No matter how awful it is, I'll forgive you."

"It's not awful."

She rose from the table. "See? I told you that there was nothing wrong with your ego."

Jackson drummed his fingers on his desk as he continued to stare at his phone. "Ring, damn it." Somewhere in the back of his mind, he decided he was acting like a teenager waiting for a date. He'd been edgy since he'd handed Cammy his story that morning. Scratch that. He'd been edgy since the first time he'd walked into Mike Costas's office and found her looking him over like a lab specimen.

A sharp knock arrested his attention. He glanced up irritably to find Krista watching him with undisguised curiosity. "What do you need?" The sharp note in his voice made him wince.

Her eyebrows lifted. "You never told me which photos you want to run with the Glynn story. Layout is asking for negatives."

"Sorry." He began to forage through the contents on his desk. "I got distracted."

"I'll bet."

He ignored the remark as he rummaged through foam coffee cups and overstuffed envelopes. Finally, he found the pile he wanted, flipped quickly through the pictures, then handed Krista the one he'd checked. "That one. It's a great shot."

She took it but didn't budge. Seconds ticked by. She waited, looking expectant. He searched his brain but came up empty. "What?"

"The other shot," she prompted.

"What other shot?"

Krista rolled her eyes as she advanced toward his desk. "Geez, Jack. Sometimes, I don't know why I bother. I shot a roll of Dr. Glynn the day after we attended her session. You wanted some individual pictures. Remember?"

"Oh." He gave her a sheepish look. "And you took them, and very thoughtfully placed them somewhere on this hellhole I call a desk."

"Good guess." She rounded his desk to jerk open the second drawer. "I was afraid the floor would cave in if I added anything to the top. I put them in your drawer. I put the sticky note *telling* you they were in your drawer on top."

"Wonderful. You expected me to notice a sticky note?"

"I marked it Urgent." She located the folder and dropped it on his lap.

"You should have marked it Moron. I might have paid attention."

Krista laughed. "Next time, I'll remember. Pick one, Jack. Layout's driving me nuts."

He flipped open the folder and stifled a groan. Cammy Glynn had turned him into a first-class idiot, he concluded. He couldn't even remember the last time he'd mooned over a picture. Most likely some super-model in a bikini held the honor. All Cammy had to do was wear some loose-fitting dress and look into Krista's camera to make his head spin. "Nice stuff," he said as he flipped through the stack.

"I like the top one," she told him.

He returned to it. Cammy was standing near the window of her office, talking on the phone. Krista had caught her at an unguarded moment, with the phone propped on her shoulder and her hands thrown wide, as she communicated something that her expression told him she felt extremely passionate about. "I like it too," he said, then flipped back through the folder to a more formal shot of Cammy behind her desk. "But I think Dr. Glynn would prefer this one."

"Hmm. If you say so. The top one catches her personality more."

"I know." He offered her the picture he'd selected. "Some people don't like to see themselves in the newspaper."

She shrugged. "If that's what you want." She would have collected the folder, but his hands tightened on it. "No, leave it. We've got three more articles in the series. I might use some of them."

"You, uh, want anything enlarged?"

He glanced sharply at the innocent expression on her face. "Meaning?"

Krista tapped the two pictures she held against her jean-clad thigh. "I just shoot what I see, Jack. I don't make editorial comments. That's your job."

A reluctant smile tugged at the corner of his mouth. "Okay, so I'm a little enamored of my subject. You've seen it happen before."

"Your subjects are usually under the age of ten, and sure, you like them. But you *like* her."

"What's not to like?"

Krista nodded. "You got a point there. Not the usual type at all. She's very genuine. She even gave me an invitation to that fund-raiser she's having. Can you believe that? Said I could bring a date and everything, and that she'd be personally offended if I felt I had to take pictures while I was there."

Jackson's brows drew together. "Fund-raiser?"

"Yeah, you know. The Wishing Star reception."

"I don't think she mentioned it."

"She must have. It's in the press releases in her PR packets." She gave him a dry look. "You didn't read them, did you?"

"What makes you think that?"

"I know you. Geez, Jack. You could have at least read her press releases. You might have learned something."

"Every reporter knows that you never learn anything from a press release."

"Well, this time you would have. She's having a big to-do at the Wilson. Gordon Stratton is supposed to be there."

"*President* Gordon Stratton?"

"You know another one? His daughter is handling the publicity."

"Macon," he muttered.

"Who?"

"Never mind. When is this thing? Exactly."

"Thursday the fifteenth of June at eight o'clock." Krista tipped her head to one side. "I wonder if she'll invite you."

"Probably not."

"Maybe you could get a press pass."

He glared at her. "You're a laugh a minute, you know that?"

"So I've heard. Anyway, you'd better check with her. You could do her some serious good if you covered the fund-raiser in one of your installments."

"I could," he concurred. The intercom on his desk buzzed. He cursed, then reached for it. "Puller."

"Jackson, it's Edna. I need pictures. I needed them yesterday."

He glanced at the photographer. "She's on her way."

"Yesterday, Jackson. I needed them yesterday."

"Okay, okay. She's on her way *now.*" Krista started toward the door. "She's walking toward the door," he assured Edna.

Krista pulled open the door as he hung up. "I'll run these down," she told him over her shoulder. "Sure you don't want me to make that enlargement for you?"

Jackson hurled a wadded copy of yesterday's front page at her retreating back.

✨♡ five

Frustrated, Jackson pounded on her apartment door one last time. "Cammy, I know you're in there. I talked to your doorman." He paused. "If you're pissed at me over the column, can you at least tell me you're all right?"

Nothing. He leaned his head against the door in frustration. He'd been trying to reach her for the better part of the afternoon. Costas's assurances that she was tied up in therapy sessions had done little to calm his nerves. She'd left for the day without returning his phone calls. That had sent him over the edge.

Twice he'd tried to phone her at her apartment. When he didn't get an answer, he took the only option open for a reasonable man. He swiped her address from his file at work, took a cab to her apartment in Crystal City, grilled her doorman for information, then scammed his way past her building security to beat on her door.

That wasn't doing him any good either. "This isn't

like you," he announced to her gargoyle door knocker. "You're a fighter, not a coward."

The gargoyle glared at him. With a dark curse, Jackson flipped open the notepad on his clipboard. He scrawled a quick note demanding that she call him, then stuffed it under the door. On his way down the corridor, he contemplated just how he'd allowed this woman to make him so crazy so fast. He was reaching for the elevator button when he heard his name.

He jerked around to find Cammy, dressed in baggy pants and a monstrously oversized T-shirt, staring at him from her doorway. A kick of desire squeezed his gut. He was going to have to start getting used to that, he decided. Cammy clutched his note in her hand. "Come back," she urged him.

"Damn it, Cammy. It took you long enough." He stalked down the hall. Her hair, he noted, was damp. She'd pulled it into a loose ponytail that somehow begged for the attention of his fingers. He suddenly felt like a first-class fool for lurking around by her door. She did that to him. She had a way of turning him into mush. "Why didn't you answer your door?" He frowned at her. "Why didn't you return my phone calls? I got worried."

She held up a hand. "Stop. Stop."

He advanced the final few steps to glare down at her. "Hell, if you were mad, you could have just told me."

"Jackson, will you stop." She pointed to her ear. "No transmitter. I can't hear you."

He blinked. "What?"

She grabbed his hand to pull him through her door.

"I don't have my transmitter on. The implant doesn't work without the transmitter."

"You took—" he muttered a frustrated oath. "Oh, hell."

She gave him a sympathetic look. "No need to swear. I can read your lips, you know?"

He mouthed a succinct opinion. She laughed. That laugh, he thought, probably shouldn't feel like buttered rum on a winter night, but it glided over his frayed nerves and sent blood pouring through his veins again. Cammy shook her head. "Wait a minute. I'll put it on."

As he watched her retreat to her bedroom, he wondered just how an oversized shirt could look so alluring. From every angle. He tilted his head as she rounded the corner. Lord, she was making him nuts. She emerged, seconds later, with the tiny black box clipped to her waistband. "Hi."

He managed a weak smile. "Hi."

"How long did you knock on the door?"

"Ten minutes."

"Were you loud?"

"Maybe. Probably. You might want to apologize to your neighbors."

She smiled that secret smile that usually made him dizzy. "No need. Most of them are deaf."

He exhaled a long breath as he tipped his head back against the door. "I get it now."

"Get what?" She walked toward the kitchen. "This building. There's no noise. Where I live there's plenty of noise. Radios, TVs, telephones. There's no noise here."

"How did you get past security?"

He indicated the clipboard. "Old street reporter's trick. A confident wave and a clipboard will get you past any security guard in the world."

She gave him a bemused look. "You could have asked him to buzz me."

"Would you have heard it?"

"When someone buzzes in, the lights dim. The building is specially equipped for the needs of the deaf."

Which is why, he realized, she'd chosen to live here in this somewhat run-down building. Being willing to admit she had certain needs gave her a certain strength. Why hadn't he managed to learn that lesson about himself? "I thought you might not let me up," he confessed.

She plunked an ice cube in a glass before she looked at him with raised eyebrows. "Really?"

If she hadn't used that tone, the same one he was sure she reserved for patients on the brink of a monumental confession, he might not have reacted. He simply could not, however, resist the urge to clear that look of professional inquiry off her face and replace it with something, *anything*, more real. He crossed her kitchen in three quick strides. With a hand on either side of her waist, he pinned her to the counter. "Really," he muttered as he lowered his head.

He covered her mouth in a leisurely exploration that made up for the nagging regret that he hadn't been slower that morning. She was soft when he pressed her against the length of his body. So incredibly, gloriously soft. Even her worn T-shirt felt comforting to his quickly inflamed skin. He rubbed his mouth against hers in gentle persuasion. With a murmur of surrender, she leaned into him as she wrapped her arms around his waist.

Passion swept through him as his hands roamed her back. He wanted her, he realized, like a dying man wants time. With little encouragement, she could become an obsession. He could need her. Desperately and dangerously.

In the dark places, where Leo's memory haunted him, Cammy lit him up. She brought life where he'd begun to wonder if he'd ever feel again. He drank at that fountain like a man dying of thirst. His hands tightened on her upper arms. His mouth demanded. Blissfully, hers yielded. He pulled her closer, as close as he could get her. And still it wasn't enough. He was beginning to wonder if it would ever be enough. With a groan, he deepened the kiss. She responded with an abandon that had his body heat nearing overload.

Desperate for the feel of her, he slid his hands beneath the T-shirt to rest on the silkiness of her bare skin. Cammy breathed his name against his lips in a sigh of surrender. Her hands moved to his chest, over his shoulders and into his hair. "Jackson—" she muttered again, as she caressed him.

His body was surging, he pulled back from the brink with his last shred of restraint. With a ragged groan, he tore his mouth from hers to press his face against her neck. Her hands cradled him to her. His heart pounded an uneven rhythm that echoed the shredded cadence of his breath. "Cammy." He had nothing else to say.

Her fingers threaded through his hair as she softly stroked his head. Pressing a light kiss to his ear, she eased slightly away. "Feeling better?" she asked.

He shook his head. "Worse." His hands, still tucked beneath her T-shirt, moved over her spine.

A flicker of amusement played at the corner of her swollen lips. He found the sight almost unbearably tempting. He tilted his head again, but she stopped him with a firm hand on his chest. "Then you should stop this kind of activity. In therapy, we call it destructive behavior." She eased away from him, then pushed a glass of soda into his now empty hands. The flush in her cheeks told him she wasn't as collected as she'd have him believe. "I think I've had all I can take for one night."

He narrowed his gaze but didn't comment. Cammy studied him in the bright kitchen light. "Are you going to tell me what you're doing here, or are you going to stand there and watch me all night?"

"Don't tempt me."

"Jackson—" She stopped, fiddled for a few seconds with the earpiece of her transmitter, then met his gaze once more. "Something's *wrong*. I can tell. I'd like you to trust me enough to tell me what it is."

He fought for his equilibrium. "You're the professional. You tell me."

"You haven't even shaved. I mean, this morning, you looked like hell, but you told me you'd stayed up all night." Behind her glasses her eyes registered concern. "Did you go home at all today?"

"No."

"Why not? You met your deadline."

"I was waiting for you to call." He downed the soda in four swallows, uncomfortable with the admission. "I want to know what you thought."

Her eyes widened. He felt some of the tension leave him. "Of the column, Cammy," he clarified. "I know damn well what you thought of the kiss."

She visibly swallowed. "Oh."

When she didn't say anything else, he wiped a hand over his face in frustration. The woman made him nuts. "Damn it, Cammy—"

"I had no idea you'd be this concerned with my reaction."

He stared at her. "You had—" He swore again.

She tapped her earpiece. "It's working now. No need to shout."

"I'm not shouting."

"You're swearing."

"I'm frustrated as hell."

"Why is that?"

He could feel his teeth clenching. "If you don't stop trying to crawl inside my head—"

Cammy interrupted him by pressing a hand to his cheek. "Jackson, I'm concerned. I'm not analyzing."

He reached for her hand, held it. Tight. "And the temptation is almost impossible to resist, isn't it?"

That half-smile danced on her lips again. "A little."

"Do you think I'm crazy?"

"Do you want a personal opinion, or a professional one?"

"Can I have both?"

"It'll cost you."

"Name your price."

"I tell you what I think is going on in your head, and you tell me about Leo."

"I don't think—"

She held up a hand. "That's it. All or nothing."

He thought it over. "Nothing."

She surprised him with a brief nod. "I thought so." She pointed to his glass. "Do you want more soda, or not?"

"Have you eaten?"

"Yes. Have you?"

"Not since this morning. I was going to take you somewhere."

"I'm down for the night. I can make you a sandwich if you want."

"You don't have to."

She laughed. "I know that. I'm a professional woman with the highest educational credentials possible in my field. I've won multiple awards, I've published articles in half a dozen professional journals, and I'm in high demand as a speaker and lecturer. Believe me, if I didn't want to feed you, I'd make you do it yourself."

She absolutely delighted him. He even found himself looking forward to the roller coaster of emotions she sent him through. That had to be the secret. In a world overpopulated by artificial people, Cammy Glynn was the genuine article. "I'll make it myself," he offered.

"You'll probably mess up my kitchen." She

pointed to a counter stool. "Sit and entertain me. It'll do you good for a change."

He dutifully sat and watched, reveling in the feeling of contentment he felt with her. It was such a novelty, he realized, that he'd momentarily forgotten the purpose of his unorthodox visit. He drew a long breath as he prepared for verbal combat. Cammy had a gift for keeping a conversation exactly where she wanted it. "So, are you going to keep me in suspense for the rest of the evening, or are you going to tell me what you're thinking?"

She stared into the bottom of a glass jar. "I'm thinking I need to buy more mayonnaise. I didn't realize I was almost out." She gave him a benign look. "Do you want mustard on this, or not?"

"Cammy—"

"I have yellow, brown, and Dijon."

"I don't think—"

"Of course, for a man whose idea of refrigerator stock is a quart of milk and an apple," she shrugged, "you're probably not very particular, are you?"

The quip about his refrigerator made him feel like he'd just successfully stormed the Bastille. He'd written that line in his column. In the piece, it fell somewhere between his description of listening to his appliances for the first time and his recounting of the dance recital. "You read it, didn't you?"

"Of course I read it." She spread two pieces of lettuce on the sandwich. "That's why you gave it to me."

He waited. It almost killed him, but he waited. She spread mustard on the top slice of bread with culinary precision. She completed the sandwich, then sliced it diagonally. He wondered if she'd cut the crust off merely to stall for time. Finally, she pushed the plate toward him. When her gaze met his, he saw the glimmer of tears in her eyes.

"It hurt," she whispered.

That hit him like a blow to the head. Of all the things he'd guessed she'd say, that had never entered his mind. Frantically, he searched his brain for some reason, some word, some mishandled phrase that might have put that vulnerable look on her face. Alarmed, he left the stool. "Cammy—"

She shook her head. "No, no, you don't understand."

"I didn't mean to—"

"I know." She pushed him back on the stool with a gentle shove. Wiping beneath her glasses with the tip of her finger, she gave him a sheepish smile. "I didn't mean to imply you hurt *me*. Mike says I'm too economical with words sometimes."

"You didn't have any until you were eighteen. I guess that makes sense." He wished he could crawl inside her head. Never in his life, he realized, had he wanted that level of intimacy, but this woman had untold mysteries in there.

"When I did have them," she continued, "they weren't always easy to say." She straightened her glasses. "And there wasn't always someone who wanted to listen to them."

He heard the aching loneliness in the comment and carefully tucked it away in the place where he treasured the few insights she gave him. He'd spent his career learning how to read people, how to watch their expressions and guess what they were thinking. Cammy Glynn was harder to read than most, but he was learning. Each little glimpse she gave him tantalized him. Those treasures, he knew, would eventually help him decipher the rest of her. "I'm listening." He rubbed his hands on his jeans. "In fact, I can categorically say that I love listening to you."

"Even when I'm analyzing you?"

He chuckled. "Except then."

Her smile warmed him. "If you love listening to me so much, why do you complain that I'm always trying to divert your attention?"

"Because you are. You're doing it right now."

"I'm very good at it."

"I've noticed."

"What else have you noticed?"

He picked up his sandwich. "I've noticed that you're doing your damnedest to keep from talking to me about my column. If I had an artist's ego, I'd be crushed."

"I already told you what I think about your ego."

"Sure. You just won't tell me what you think about my writing." He took a bite.

She exhaled a long breath that seemed to come from her toes. "You know, I can see why you went into the newspaper business. You're relentless."

"Don't forget it, either." He gave her a meaningful look. "I'm like a dog with a bone."

"Do they *pay* you to come up with original material like that, or is it just a bonus?"

"Cammy—" His voice held a warning note.

Her eyebrows lifted.

He picked up the other half of his sandwich. "This isn't working."

"You don't like the mustard?"

"I'm not being deterred. If you think you're going to get away with telling me I hurt you, then duck the conversation, you can forget it."

"I didn't say you hurt me."

"I jumped to conclusions. Help me find my way back."

He watched her struggle for a minute, then sensed her surrender. The energy seemed to flow out of her like air from a balloon. She edged past him to sit on the other stool. "Sorry. I wasn't trying to irritate you."

"I'm not irritated. I'm just trying to learn the rules."

"Jackson—"

"Seriously. I realized it last night while I was writing that column. I have all the information I could possibly want on your charity, your kids, your vision, and your background. I know your dad was a senator with high-flying political aspirations who thought you and your mother were liabilities. I know your mother is in a mental hospital—" He paused. "That's where you were this morning, wasn't it? You were visiting her."

She hesitated, then nodded. "Yes."

"Hell." He shook his head. "That's exactly what I mean. I can't believe I didn't figure that out until now. I know everything there is to know about the public *you*—like the fact that you overcame terrific obstacles to make that little box you wear a workable option for you. But what I know about you personally wouldn't fill a single page of my notepad.''

"You know a lot about me—''

"I know who your friends are. I know how you spend your time. I know what your goals are for Wishing Star. I know you have a deep commitment to help make the world an easier place for deaf children, but I haven't got a clue as to what makes Cammy Glynn tick. I'm not used to that. I read people for a living. It generally comes easily to me.''

"Sorry I'm so frustrating.''

He ignored that. "Until I got here, I wasn't even sure you intended to read my column.''

"Why wouldn't I read it?''

"See? You're doing it again. Every time I think I have you pegged, you find a way to wiggle away from me.''

"I'm really not that complicated.''

"It was supposed to be a compliment.'' He rubbed a hand over his face. "Here's the rub, Cam. Somehow in the back of my mind I just can't get past resenting that you feel like it's perfectly acceptable for you and Costas to figure out what's going on inside my head, but I don't get to know what's in yours.'' He leveled a look at her. "Did you know that when Krista told me this afternoon that you were planning a Wishing Star fund-raiser, I actually spent a half hour wondering if you'd try to manipulate me into promoting it for you?''

She looked stung. "I wouldn't do that.''

"A lot of people in your position would.''

"I'm not a lot of people. I was the one who tried to talk you out of this story, remember?"

"Sure, but by this afternoon, I was past anxiety, turning the corner on resentment, and headed straight for desperation." He shoved his plate away from him. "Here it is in a nutshell. I like you." He gave her a narrow look. "I could like you a lot. I'm attracted to you. I haven't made a secret of that. Hell, I light up every time I touch you. And unless my instincts have gone completely haywire, you aren't exactly oblivious to me either."

"I'm not."

"See? That's part of it. You shoot straight. I haven't met many people lately who are quite that direct."

"It's that economy of words thing again."

"Yeah, well, there's a law about having good aim—when you have it, you have to exercise restraint. Because when you pull the trigger, you're bound to hit something."

"That's cryptic."

"So be direct with me. Tell me why you said that column hurt you." He reached for her hand. "Please, Cam. Help me understand." He searched her gaze. "You can't even begin to imagine how much I want to understand you."

Her fingers fluttered in his. "It was you," she said quietly. "There was so much of you in there. I could tell from the way you talked about trying to listen to the silence, and your descriptions of the kids and how hard they work. During the recital, I knew you were struggling." She clasped his hand in both of hers.

"Leo's memory is hurting you. I can see it. Every now and then, when you think no one's looking, there's this kind of naked pain in your eyes. It's eating you alive. Consequently, it's hurting me."

He blinked. The impact of her statement momentarily winded him. Whatever he'd been prepared to hear, it hadn't been this. Nothing could have readied him for the effect of her empathy. He had too much guilt, too much anger about what had happened to let himself accept it. His hands, he realized, were shaking. He drew a deep breath. "You think I'm cracking up, don't you?"

"No." She squeezed his hand. "I think you're in pain. I think you're up to your eyeballs in grief, and you're not exactly sure how to find your way out. And I think I'd like to help you deal with that."

His eyes narrowed. "I don't want you to be my therapist, Cam."

"What if I just tried to be your friend?"

"I'm not sure friendship is what I have in mind."

"It's a good jumping-off point."

"As long as we aren't jumping off a bridge."

"That's your department. You're the one who's depressed."

He gave her an incredulous look. With a soft laugh, Cammy released his hand. "Sorry. It's shrink humor. It isn't even good shrink humor."

"I am *not* depressed."

"I thought we agreed that I'd be the psychiatrist in this relationship."

His eyes drifted momentarily shut. "Lord. I thought I'd never get you to say that word."

"Psychiatrist?"

"Relationship."

"Oh. It's a very complicated word. All kinds of ramifications attached to it."

"Believe me, I know. I've been turning it over in my head for a week."

She paused. "Me too."

He traced a finger over the curve of her cheek. "Are you serious?"

"I'd never lie to you. Lying to the media is a prescription for doom."

"Damn it—"

"And," she continued, "I wouldn't lie just because I don't, and because you're you and I'm me. I could never lie to you, of all people. It wouldn't be right."

He wondered if these little victories would feel quite as good if he didn't have to fight so hard for them. "I know." He was having one hell of a time not pulling her back into his arms. He was still reeling from her earlier comments about Leo. The temptation to simply lose himself in her, put the bitter memories behind him for even a few minutes, nearly overwhelmed him. He concentrated on steadying his heartbeat. "It's part of your charm."

"Why do you think you have me so worried?" she asked him. "I could fall for you."

Something exploded in his heart. "That's quite possibly the best news I have had in years."

She frowned, but continued. "I could fall very hard, I think. I swore to myself I wouldn't get involved."

"Involved with me, or involved period?"

"Both. I'm not good at involvements."

Except that she practically threw herself into the lives of her kids. He decided not to mention that. "That's an interesting theory."

She ignored him. "Not only are you a dreaded reporter, of *all* things, but I'm concerned about your mental health on top of that. I mean, I'd have to be more than a little nuts myself to even think about getting seriously involved with you."

"Are you?" He wondered if she noticed the odd note in his voice. He sensed there was far more to this than she was telling, but he knew better than to press her. He'd gained enough ground for one night.

"Nuts," she asked, "or thinking about it?"

"Either."

"Both." She tilted her head to look at him. "See? I'm not even being evasive. It's a nice change, isn't it?"

He studied her, his gaze intent and seeking. "You're demolishing my equilibrium, you know."

"Fair's fair. Mine's been spinning out of control since the day I met you. I've been so preoccupied, I haven't even had time to worry about what you were going to put in your column. That's a big step for me. I generally regard media coverage on par with major surgery."

His fingers found her nape. He gave her neck a gentle squeeze. "Was it as bad as you thought?"

"Fishing for compliments?"

"Trying to survive."

Her smile tugged his heart. "Let's just say I never even feared it would be a hatchet job."

"I'm flattered."

"You should be."

He stared at her for a minute. "You liked it, didn't you?"

"Decided to risk it all?"

"I'm a gambling kind of man."

"I liked it," she admitted. "I liked it a lot." She slid off her stool and carried his plate to the kitchen sink.

He released the breath he hadn't realized he'd been holding. "You know, I've had an easier time getting an on-record quote from the CIA than I did getting that out of you."

She chuckled. "Was it worth it?"

"You bet." He didn't want to resist the urge to touch her any longer. Easing up behind her, he settled his hands on her shoulders to gently rub her flesh through the thin shirt. "That's why I want to ask you a favor."

Tension corded her neck muscles. "What could you possibly want from me?"

He rubbed at her nape with his thumbs. "You have no idea."

"I think I'm beginning to get one."

Tracing a finger on the curve of her jaw, he found her speculative gaze in the reflection of the window above the sink. Wary as hell. He'd give money to find out just who put that look in her eyes. Durstan Glynn had done his share of the damage, but someone else had finished the job. He squelched an irritated oath at the idea that he was competing with some faceless jerk who'd danced a demolition routine on her confidence. "I'm not talking about that. We'll get to that later."

"I don't suppose I could talk you out of it."

"Probably not."

Her shoulders relaxed beneath his hands. "I didn't think so."

Using the opportunity to pull her closer, he turned her to face him, glided his hands over her shoulder blades and down to the center of her back. When her body was fully aligned with his, he tipped his head to tease the corner of her mouth.

She raised a hand to his head. "Jackson—"

Soft. Her skin was so unspeakably soft. He guided her closer, aligning her against him, so he could nuzzle her neck. "That favor, Cam—"

A sharp gasp escaped her when he found the juncture of her collarbone and her shoulder. He raised his head, inexplicably pleased that he'd found one of her "spots." With a slight smile, he pressed his thumb to it, then waited for her to meet his gaze.

"What favor?" she whispered.

"I'd like to interview Amy for the next installment in the series."

She stiffened. "I'm not sure that's a good idea."

"Honey, I just want you to trust me. I swear I'm not going to drag her through the mud. That's one of the reasons I want you to be there. I'd like you to observe the interview. You can set whatever boundaries you want."

"She might be uncomfortable."

"She might. I think she'll feel less uncomfortable if you're there to interpret."

He sensed her indecision and pressed a kiss to her ear. "It's going to be okay," he urged. "I promise."

She released a reluctant sigh. "I'm powerless to resist you, you know?"

At her miserable tone, he laughed. "I'm banking on that."

✦☆ ♡ six

On Sunday morning, Cammy looked closely at Amy. She looked all right. Actually, she looked better than all right. She looked like she'd just been anointed queen of the universe. She was grinning at Jackson, and he was grinning back. The two had some kind of fast and firm bond Cammy couldn't begin to fathom. She remembered the look on Amy's face when Jackson had given her the flowers. She'd had the same look when Cammy had dropped by the children's home where Amy lived to tell her Jackson would like to interview her. On her way back from visiting her mother, Cammy had decided to swing by and visit with Amy. The prospect of seeing Jackson again had thrilled the child. Cammy knew the feeling.

She'd called him the evening of her visit with Amy to set the appointment for Sunday, and spent the rest of the hours in between trying to come to terms with why he affected her so deeply. Thus far, she had no answers, and a lot more questions than when she began. Resolutely, she pushed the thought from her mind and concentrated on the interchange between Amy and Jackson. She reminded herself that she planned to use the opportunity to observe how Amy responded to him—a virtual stranger—not obsess over why she'd been unable to stop thinking about him since his visit to her apartment.

Amy was signing slowly, waiting to be sure Jackson understood her. Amazingly, he seemed to grasp the gist of the report on the dance recital. He even signed back a time or two. Cammy conceded several thousand points in his favor for making such an obvious effort to master sign language.

He glanced at her with a frown. "She lost me."

Cammy pulled herself away from her observation and back to the task at hand. "What did you tell him?" she signed to Amy.

"He's slow," Amy signed back. "Can't keep up. I asked him how he liked the ballet part of the recital."

Cammy looked at Jackson. "What did you think of the ballet segment at the dance recital?"

"Is that what that is?" He copied the sign by wiggling his fingers. "Who knew?" Turning his attention back to Amy, he told her, "I thought it was boring."

She giggled and responded, "Me too."

Cammy looked at her in amazement. To her knowledge, she'd never heard the child giggle. Amy was bright and engaging, easy to love, but not lighthearted. Her too serious circumstances in life had drained away her childhood wonder. Until now.

Jackson concentrated briefly on what Amy was telling him, then pulled out his notebook. "I'd like to ask you a few questions,'' he told Amy. ''For a story in the newspaper. I thought it might be easier if Cammy interpreted.'' He flashed his engaging grin. ''Since I'm slow.''

Amy pursed her lips. ''Are you going to take my picture?''

Pulling a photo from a folder, he showed it to her. ''I have a picture. My friend Krista took it the day I met you.''

Amy studied it, then looked at Jackson. ''Will I be in the paper?''

''Yes.''

''I want to wear my green overalls in the paper.''

He glanced at Cammy, who quickly interpreted the statement. With a shake of his head, Jackson said, ''There speaks the eternal woman.'' He looked at Amy again. ''If Krista comes back on Tuesday, will you wear them?''

Amy nodded vigorously.

''If I promise to use a picture of you wearing green overalls in the newspaper, may I ask questions?''

She nodded again.

''Well, I'm glad that's settled,'' he quipped. He flipped open the notebook. ''Okay, it's a deal. Let's go.''

They settled into a comfortable rhythm. Jackson asked casual questions, Cammy interpreted, and Amy answered. For twenty minutes, Amy talked about school, her favorite subjects, dancing, the kids she liked and didn't like, in an open, carefree way. They didn't hit their first bump in the road until Jackson asked her how she had come to live at the children's home.

Her expression altered, turned guarded. She looked at Cammy for guidance. Cammy hastened to assure her. "You don't have to tell him if you don't want to."

Amy turned to Jackson. She searched his face for long moments, then replied, "My mother left me there."

Cammy saw the storm clouds beginning to gather in Jackson's gaze. "How long ago?" he asked.

Amy hesitated, then shrugged. Cammy waited. The child clearly didn't want to answer the question. The air grew still. Even the building air conditioner seemed to realize the gravity of the moment. It shuddered to a halt with the groaning of a mechanical monster. The steady tick of the clock on her desk punctuated the confines of the suddenly too-small room.

Jackson leaned closer to Amy, set his hand on her small knee, then tried a different approach. "Do you want her to come back?"

Amy shook her head and simply said, "She left me."

Jackson met Cammy's gaze. "I'm not going to print that," he said in a quiet voice. "I wouldn't exploit something like that."

She struggled with her mistrust. "Your call."

"I promised you I wouldn't."

"I know."

"And you don't believe me."

Amy laid a small hand on Cammy's arm. Cammy

realized she'd momentarily forgotten the child's presence. She smiled reassuringly. "It's okay, Amy. Jackson and I were talking about the story."

"I like him," Amy told her.

Cammy met Jackson's gaze again as she signed, "I like him too."

Amy refocused her attention on Jackson. In quick, abbreviated signs, she explained the few memories she had of her life before the children's home. Shelters, bus stations, and a succession of strange men and confusing circumstances figured prominently.

Cammy interpreted without inflection or comment. The expression on Jackson's face, she noted, turned increasingly grim. She felt the anger, the frustration brewing in him. They closely mirrored the feelings she had whenever she allowed herself to get too close to the stories of Wishing Star's children. Kids like Trevor Blackfort were the exception, not the rule. Too many children faced the same circumstances as Amy.

Amy's agitation was growing. Her signs became increasingly broader, more expressive. Jackson prompted her occasionally, with a question or an understanding nod. When Amy paused, suddenly, he gave Cammy an inquisitive look. "What?"

She continued to watch Amy. "Do you want to tell him?"

The child seemed to weigh the question. She looked from Jackson, to Cammy, and back again. Slowly, she shook her head, then pointed to Cammy. Cammy frowned. "You want me to tell him?"

Amy shrugged. Jackson shut the notebook with a soft slap and slid it back into his shirt pocket. "Tell her it's okay," he instructed. "Nobody needs to tell me anything she doesn't want me to know."

Cammy signed the message. Amy's expression softened as she looked at him. She slid from the sofa to wrap her thin arms around his neck. Cammy's insides began to tighten as she watched the unexpected gesture of trust. Jackson enfolded the child, his long arms engulfing her slender frame. When he set her away from him, she grinned and told him, "Thank you."

He signed his response, and Amy ran from the room.

Seconds ticked by while they simply sat in the lingering quiet. He exhaled a slow breath. "Damn it."

Cammy understood. He was angry at the world, at the circumstances that made a bright, exuberant child reticent and afraid. "I'm sorry I doubted you," she told him. "You were wonderful with her."

"How do you do it?"

"Listen to them?"

He nodded. "Doesn't it make you angry?"

"Unbelievably. Amy's story is one of the worst. I've only touched the surface of what her life was like when she lived with her mother. There are things—" she paused. "You wouldn't want to know."

"I'm sure I wouldn't." His expression remained dark. "At the end. What she didn't tell me. It would have rattled my nerves, wouldn't it?"

"Probably."

He nodded. "I thought so. I talk to enough kids to know that the world isn't very nice to a lot of them."

"You are," she said quietly.

He looked at her closely. "What?"

"You're nice to them, and you respect them. You obviously realize that children have things to say that are worth listening to."

He thought about it for a minute. "You're right. I guess I got tired of listening to adults. They lie a lot."

She heard the bitterness in his tone. "Especially to reporters?"

"In this town, a lot of people lie about a lot of things. I didn't come here expecting that. I was naive, a little idealistic maybe."

She wished she'd known him then. "You got burned."

"I took the word of a few unreliable sources when I shouldn't have. I believed some things I hadn't properly checked out, and some people got hurt in the process. I got stung. It was a learning experience, not the end of the world."

Cammy sensed there was more to the story, but decided to let it drop—for now. "I'm sorry."

"I'm not. It made me a better journalist. I learned to trust my intuition more and people less. The harder you look for a story, the better it is."

"Your instincts are excellent. You related to Amy right away."

"Unfortunately, I didn't have a very difficult time guessing what she had to tell me. The world can be a crummy place for little kids."

"Yes."

He met her gaze, his eyes intent. "I guess no one knows that better than you."

She sensed that he wasn't talking about the children she treated. "I guess not."

"If I ever get your story out of you, am I going to feel the same way I do now?"

"How do you feel?"

"Trying to divert my attention again?"

"Of course. Very much of course."

"I thought so."

"You haven't answered my question."

He frowned. "You haven't answered mine either."

"So we're at an impasse."

"Lord, you're stubborn."

"You're just figuring that out?"

"No, I'm just figuring out how to cope with it." He shook his head. "All right, I'll let you win this round."

"Thanks. How do you feel?"

"Frustrated. Angry. Helpless." He dragged a hand over his face. "Hell, I don't know. Like I wish I hadn't asked. Not because I don't want to know the truth, but because I don't want her to think about it. Does that make sense?"

"Yes."

"The place where Amy lives? What's it like?"

"Better than most, actually. It's very well run. Almost all of the children there have some type of special challenge, so the staff is trained and equipped to care for them."

"What percentage of the kids get adopted?"

"It's a small number." She kept her voice neutral. "People want perfect children."

He searched her face, probing. "What happens if no one takes them?"

"They go to school. They grow up. They learn some skills, how to cope. They turn eighteen, and they're on their own."

With a burst of energy, he surged from his chair to pace the confines of her office. "So if she doesn't get an implant, or the implant doesn't work, she'll probably live in places like that for the rest of her childhood and adolescence."

"Yes."

"How much is an implant operation?"

"Around fifty thousand dollars. But it's more complicated than that. She may not be a good candidate."

"They don't work on everyone, do they?"

Cammy shook her head. "It's not the cure for deafness. It enables some deaf people to hear most sounds. Whether or not they can interpret those sounds into meaningful communication is impossible to predict. Lucky recipients develop comprehensible language skills. Many don't ever have normal speech. It helps if they receive the implant when they're very young, or if they went deaf later in life. Children who are profoundly deaf from birth have the most difficulty learning auditory skills."

"But you were born deaf. You didn't get your implant until you were eighteen, and your speech is nearly perfect."

Her smile was sad. "Every rule has exceptions."

He looked at her with narrowed eyes. "How hard was it, Cam?"

"How hard was what?"

"After you received the implant, how hard did you have to work to learn to talk?"

She hesitated. "Hard."

"Durstan pushed you."

"If he hadn't, I might not have learned."

"It was never good enough for him, was it?"

Cringing inwardly, she forced herself to hold his gaze. "He was impatient with my progress."

"How many years did it take?"

"Several."

"And you still struggle, don't you?"

Surprised, she tipped her head to one side. "How do you know that?"

His broad shoulders rippled when he shrugged. "I watch you. Sometimes, when you think no one is looking, you practice saying words. When you're really tired, you drop a few Ls and Rs. It's barely noticeable."

"But *you* noticed."

"I'm observant."

She felt oddly flattered. "Thank you."

His tender smile made her heart turn over. "My pleasure."

"You're a very remarkable person."

"I've got nothing on you," he assured her. Exhaling a harsh breath, he tapped his notebook against his leg. "You know, there are kids like Amy all over the world. I see it everywhere. It never fails to affect me. I always want to fix it, and have to tell myself I can't."

"You're a better person because you allow it to frustrate you, to hurt you. Don't beat yourself up for it. It's a sad story. You'd be a jerk if you didn't respond to it."

He rubbed at the muscles of his neck and slanted her a sheepish look. "Sorry. Injustice has a way of riling my temper. I should warn you. I'm occasionally prone to spontaneous diatribes."

She laughed. "I understand. I started Wishing Star because of feelings like that. When I jump on a soapbox, I can do it behind the very respectable front of a charitable organization. No one has to know that I harbor secret urges to whack society over the head."

A smile tugged at the corner of his mouth. "May I print that?"

She checked her watch. "Depends."

"On what?"

"On whether or not you're willing to take me to lunch. I'm starved."

He laughed then. His dark mood scattered like leaves in the wind. "I'll make you a bargain."

"You want more for lunch than the right to print my quote?"

"I plan to take you somewhere expensive."

"I can't be bought, you know?"

"This place has a six-page dessert menu." He formed a C with his right hand, and rotated it counterclockwise on his left in the sign for *chocolate*. "Six-tier chocolate cake is their specialty."

"Okay, so let's say I'm more than a little susceptible to bribes of this particular nature—"

He slanted a look at the large candy jar on her desk. "A little?"

"That's for the children."

"You give your patients Godiva chocolate? Wouldn't they be satisfied with something a little less pricey?"

"I like to indulge them."

"If I looked in your trash can, how many gold wrappers would I find?"

"That would be snooping."

"No avoiding the question."

"A few," she admitted.

"A lot," he countered. "Is this a good time to tell you that Krista told me an order arrived special delivery while she was here taking your picture?"

"The fink. I'll bet you tortured it out of her."

He spread his hands in an innocent gesture. "I will have you know that I have never tortured anyone for information. They just tend to fork it over."

"Except for me?"

"You, I'd consider torturing."

"Which brings us back to this lunch issue. What exactly do I have to agree to if I want to know where this cake gets served?"

He turned suddenly serious. "I'm not really trying to bribe you, Cam. I just want to share something with you."

She tipped her head to the side. "You're serious."

"Yes."

"What do you want?"

"I want you to come home with me."

"Home?"

"To meet my parents. I'm going out to their place in the Shenandoah Valley next weekend, and I'd like you to come."

"Meet your parents? Are you crazy?"

"I don't know." He flashed her a half smile. "You're the expert. You tell me."

She stared at him. "Are you in the habit of bringing women home to meet your parents?"

"No. You're the first."

"Do you have any idea what kind of conclusions they'll draw from that?"

"The right ones, I hope."

Cammy felt herself redden. "How could you possibly want to open yourself up to that kind of scrutiny?"

"I don't mind scrutiny the same way you do, and besides, they're very reasonable people. I promise they won't grill you for answers. At least, not until they've fed you. After that, you're on your own."

"I don't know, Jackson. It doesn't seem like a good idea. I'm not sure I'd feel right about—"

He held up a hand. "Cammy, all kidding aside, it's not what you think. I just have this . . . need . . . to go home. It's peaceful there. I need some time to think. About Leo," he added, knowing it would give him an edge. "That's a great place to do it. It's a part of me, and I'd like you to share it. That's it. No strings." He paused. When she lifted her eyebrows he said, "I swear."

She pursed her lips as she thought about it. The opportunity to observe him interacting with his family was almost irresistible. He was almost irresistible. "I will. On one condition. I want you to come with me tomorrow night to one of Lynette's rehearsals. I think it will help you write that story if you can experience a little of what it's like to be a deaf child in a hearing world. So far, you've seen the children together, and you've seen them with adults who speak their language. To watch them function in an environment where all the odds are stacked against them would be important.''

He nodded. ''I'd like that.''

''You would?''

''Yes.'' He gave her a meaningful look. ''I would.''

She watched him from the corner of her eye. His gaze was fixed on the small stage in Lynette's rehearsal hall, where she carefully demonstrated the count for a complicated sequence of choreography.

''You kick,'' Lynette said, demonstrating, ''then Lindy to the left, scissor right, Lindy left, Lindy right, stomp.'' She turned to face her young pupils. ''Who's got it?''

Trevor Blackfort's hand shot up. Lynette smiled at him. ''Why am I not surprised? All right.'' She looked at the group of children. ''Kathleen, do you want to help Trevor with the count?''

Kathleen nodded, and she and Trevor walked to the front of the group.

When Lynette crossed to the CD player, Jackson glanced at Cammy. ''What are they doing?''

''Kathleen can hear,'' Cammy explained. ''She's going to help Trevor find the beat. The deaf kids can count, and they can watch the other dancers for their cues, but unless a hearing child helps them, they could never match the rhythm.'' She leaned forward in her chair as the music began to play. "Watch."

Kathleen let two measures of the music pass, then began steadily moving her feet. Trevor watched her intently. After a few more measures, he mimicked her foot motions. When Kathleen nodded, he repeated the sequence of steps Lynette had demonstrated. The group applauded, and Jackson shook his head in amazement. "I had no idea," he told Cammy.

She nodded. "You can't imagine what it's like to grasp something as basic as rhythm with no sense of hearing. They feel the vibrations, so they know when the music stops and starts, but beat is an entirely alien concept to them. That's what makes Lynette's work here so amazing. The hearing children and the deaf children learn from each other."

Lynette encouraged all the children to rise and attempt the steps. They paired off, and the procedure began again. Cammy pointed out nuances of Lynette's technique throughout the rehearsal. Jackson took a few notes, but basically just watched as the children conquered the difficult process of counting and watching without the benefit of sound.

When Lynette dismissed the children, Jackson gave Cammy a warm look. "Thank you for bringing me."

"Thank you for coming," she told him.

"I'd like to talk to Lynette awhile." He rested his hand on Cammy's waist in an unconscious gesture of affection. "Do you think the three of us could go somewhere and chat?"

Cammy hesitated. Jackson's hand was sending currents through her bloodstream. She wasn't prepared, she knew, for the inevitable questions that would arise from their togetherness. And he certainly gave the impression that they were very much together. "It's late," she said.

"Only eight," he countered. "I don't think it'll take long. I just want to clarify some things."

Lynette was bearing down on them. Cammy fought the urge to turn away from his half-embrace. The curious look in her friend's eyes warned her it was too late, anyway. Lynette had seen, and she had questions. "All right. Why don't you ask her? I want to say good-night to the kids."

Jackson listened intently while Lynette, who had rapidly warmed to her subject, discussed the combination of methods she used to conduct her dance classes. She was a warm, vibrant person whose passion for deaf children began in her own home. Her nine-year-old brother was deaf, and one of her star pupils.

"They benefit so much," she explained, "from their interaction with each other. As dancers, the hearing children learn to concentrate harder. They know the deaf children watch them for rhythm cues and timing. They can't afford to miss a step. Even more, they develop a special sensitivity to the challenges of life."

"And the deaf children," he prompted, risking a glance at Cammy. She'd been quiet since they'd left the dance studio. He was beginning to recognize that stillness as her mask for nerves. He should have seen it the day he'd met her. Then, she'd ignored her hair.

"The deaf children," Lynette said, "have the chance to try something they've never known. They can 'listen' to music in a special way. Their confidence grows as they master the steps, and they learn to appreciate their own abilities when they're able to help the hearing children focus. I try to intermingle sequences I know will benefit each group. They teach each other as much as I teach them.''

No woman, he noted as Cammy ran a finger absently on the rim of her water glass, ignored her hair for nothing. ''Cammy?''

At his prompt, she visibly started. ''Sorry. I was thinking.''

Lynette gave her a knowing look. ''I can tell.''

''Did you want something?'' she asked Jackson, her smile overly bright.

She had no idea what he wanted, he decided. At that particular moment, he was struggling with the fact that he wanted to haul her off somewhere very private and explore every one of the secrets that were starting to haunt him. He cleared his throat. ''I was curious why you felt Lynette's classes were such a good investment for Wishing Star.''

She drew a deep breath. He'd have sworn she was relieved. ''The goal of the foundation is to help mainstream deaf children. Some advocates think the best way to mainstream them is to give every deaf child a cochlear implant.''

''You don't?''

''It's not a lucky charm.'' Her forehead puckered in a look he was coming to recognize as intense concentration. She was filtering—noise, distractions— until she could hone carefully in on what she wished to say. He found the effect simultaneously disconcerting and intriguing. The idea that he might one day get her to turn the full force of that concentration on him sent heat skittering along his nerve endings.

Cammy tapped her finger absently on the table. "I've told you before, not every child is a candidate for a cochlear. The implants don't always succeed, and sometimes, if a child has more difficulty than usual learning to speak, it can do more harm than good."

He resisted the urge, barely, to cover her hand with his own. Instead, he prodded her to continue. "So if a cochlear is not in their future, then what?"

"I believe deaf children should learn to function in a hearing world, just as children with other challenges have to function in a world that's not really designed for them."

Lynette interjected, "I think she's right, but not everyone agrees with Cammy's methods."

His gaze narrowed. "Why not?"

"There are people," Lynette said quietly, "like Jeffrey Herrington—"

At Jackson's raised eyebrows, Cammy gave him a quelling look. "You didn't read the press releases, did you?" she said in a pained voice.

"Okay. Okay." He looked at Lynette. "You want to bail me out, here?"

Lynette laughed. "Herrington calls himself an 'activist for the rights of differently-abled Americans.' "

"Calls himself?"

"As far as I can tell, he's very active at taking people's money, and not so active at doing a lot with it. Anyway, he's deaf, and he's one of a substantial portion of the deaf community who believe that deafness is simply a matter of speaking a different language. He doesn't acknowledge that deaf children, and deaf adults, for that matter, face challenges in a hearing world. According to Herrington and his supporters, deafness isn't a disability, but they want it covered under the Americans with Disabilities Act.''

''And they support separation?''

Cammy nodded. ''Yes. Herrington has been at odds with me for years. He believes that Wishing Star raises the expectations of deaf children to unreasonable heights—that it gives them the idea they'll be able to successfully integrate with a hearing public.''

He blinked. ''Can't they?''

Lynette laughed. ''That's the point, I guess. Cammy believes a deaf person is just like anyone else, they just have to learn to deal with certain obstacles. A lot of people believe that.''

''But not Herrington.''

Cammy waved a hand in his direction. ''Jeffrey is very driven. He's passionate about what he believes. Being deaf, he knows how hard it can be. He feels just as strongly as I do, we just haven't reached the same conclusions.''

Jackson looked at the two women, he could feel Cammy's intent gaze. He gave her an unabashed grin. ''Then, I guess he hasn't been to a dance recital lately.''

✧✧♡ seven

"*I'm a grown woman,*" Cammy mumbled. "How did I get talked into this?" She sat on the bed next to her half-packed suitcase and stared at her reflection in the mirror. "Cammy, you fool."

She knew exactly when it had happened. After his startling request to accompany him on a visit to his parents, she'd spent the rest of the week offering him excuses why she couldn't go.

But she'd read the article, and that, coupled with the indelible memory of his expression when Amy had told him her story, had made her head spin and made her decision for her.

Like a vision in a dream, she could recall almost every word of his haunting column.

The world is an incredibly noisy place. If you sit for a while, and try to filter the sounds that clutter up your ears, you find that everything makes noise. First, I shut off the obvious things. I isolated myself from the sound of traffic and crowds. Then the telephone, the TV, the radio. The thrum of activity persisted. I switched off my appliances, at the risk of losing the one bottle of milk and the apple I keep in my refrigerator. Light bulbs, I learned, make a buzzing kind of sound that's excruciatingly loud when you listen to it. I threw the master breaker in my townhouse, retreated to my most interior room to sit in the dark and listen to silence.

Noise continued to interrupt. The distant sound of a siren. The vibrations of street traffic. The ring of a neighbor's telephone. In desperation, I filled my bathtub with water, held my breath and submerged my head. I could still hear my heart beat.

Tonight, I witnessed a remarkable, even astounding, artistic performance. In my life, I've seen the greatest artists in the world perform on the most prestigious stages for audiences equally sophisticated. I've watched the premier performances of works which are now classics. What I saw tonight, and the impact it had on me, eclipsed them all. At seven fifteen this evening, I watched thirteen kids dance to the sound of silence. There was music, of course. I heard it. Most of the audience heard it. The dancers, however, did not.

At the corner of Fifteenth and P Streets, in a nondescript looking building, a miracle took place.

With a shake of her head, Cammy forced herself from her reverie. With his characteristically lyrical flow, the column read like a letter from Jackson to an individual reader.

Filtered through her own experience with him, through the lens of his behavior during the recital and later, she sensed again the almost overwhelming cloud of sorrow that he wore like a mantle. Haunted by his memories of Leo, Jackson needed her.

That had clinched it. She'd told herself a hundred times that he didn't need *her* specifically. She merely stood in the spot where his need happened to focus. Anyone else might have tumbled into the role. But as the week progressed, the argument weakened, until she found herself on the precipice of a very dangerous ledge. If she allowed herself to fall for him, he'd break her heart. There couldn't be anything between them. She knew that. A man like Jackson Puller needed a stable family life, half a dozen kids, and a woman who could love him without reservation.

She made an effort to remind herself sternly that she wasn't that woman. Not only couldn't she give him children but she'd also concluded long ago that she couldn't make herself love without strings attached. She had all kinds of excellent psychological reasons for the affliction. It wouldn't be fair to him, or to her, if they went down that road. Eventually, he'd resent her, she'd resent him, and she would have made them both miserable.

It was the most logical, educated, professional analysis in the world. During graduate school, she'd diagnosed it as ''chronic disassociation.'' She cared for people—deeply. But she was incapable of letting their existence in her life matter beyond their immediate circumstances. In the end, she always managed to hurt them.

The hold that argument had on her, however, had flown right out the window. Between his behavior at the dance class on Monday night; the interview with

Lynette; and the fact that he'd couriered the next installment of his series to her that afternoon, all he'd had to say was "Please," and she'd wilted like a flower. The effect of this latest column on her was no less devastating than the last one. He'd told Amy's story with a minimum of frills, drawing sharp contrasts between the realities of the child's life and the size of her dreams and aspirations. The terribly poignant image of Amy clutching his roses to her chest had lingered in Cammy's heart to melt whatever resistance she had left.

How had she ever thought she'd have the will to tell him no?

Again she met her gaze in the mirror. "This is a fine mess you've gotten us into," she muttered.

She was telling herself the same thing two hours later as his car ate up the miles between Washington and his family home in the Shenandoah Valley. When he'd picked her up, he'd rushed her to the car with some mumbled explanation about missing the bulk of rush hour traffic. She didn't buy it. He'd been wisely aware that if he gave her enough time to formulate a plan, she'd back out. Before she could protest, almost before she could think about protesting, he was on the highway.

They'd spoken little, and when they had, they'd discussed their respective weeks in the vaguest of terms. But now, with the traffic beginning to thin and the road laid before them like a black ribbon winding its way across the verdant landscape, she said, "I can't believe I let you talk me into this."

He slanted her that devilish little-boy grin of his as he reached for her hand. "I can't believe you did either."

"Have you decided just how you're going to handle it when your family jumps to the conclusion that you and I are seriously enough involved that you're dragging me home to meet them?" She pushed a strand of hair off her forehead. The cool breeze that wafted through the sunroof of his car did little to calm her nerves. Even the weather had cooperated with him. "I warned you."

"They won't be totally wrong." He pressed a kiss to the back of her hand, then settled it on his thigh. "You may not be involved with me," his wide shoulders lifted in a shrug, "but that doesn't mean I'm not involved with you."

She glared at him. "You aren't taking me seriously at all, are you?"

He laughed. "Are you kidding? I'm taking you as seriously as I take earthquakes and hurricanes."

Her ears were beginning to ring. She wished she could blame it on the batteries in her transmitter, but she knew better. The pressure of his fingers on her hand, the feel of his muscled thigh was making her blood pressure soar. "Jackson—"

He glanced at her. "Okay. Okay. I'll back off."

"Since when did you master the art of backing off?"

"Since about noon yesterday when you told me you'd cancel if I made one more comment like that." He pulled his gaze from the highway to glance at her.

"I can't explain it, Cam. I needed to go home this weekend. I needed the peace of this place, and I needed to share it with you. I haven't been home since Leo," he said quietly.

Her heart fluttered. "Really?"

"Yes. I just feel like I'll find some answers there." He shrugged. "I don't know. It's complicated. Believe me, if you manage to figure out why all that's jumbled around in my head, then let me know. I've been going crazy trying to sort through it."

She exhaled a slow breath. Her fingers relaxed in his grip. "Sorry," she mumbled. "I'm letting my neurosis dictate my moods again. I hate that."

Without warning, he pulled his car onto the shoulder, then killed the engine. In the subsequent silence, he cradled her face in his large hands as he tipped his head to kiss her. Long and thorough, the kiss sent little licks of flame skittering along her flesh. The feel of his hands on her face sent her pulse into overdrive. In seconds, he had her clinging to him. Her fingers curled around his wrists to hold him in place while she returned the kiss.

With a slight groan, Jackson shifted so their bodies were closer. He played with her lips, brushing his mouth over hers in the most tantalizing of rhythms. When he finally lifted his mouth from hers, his fingers continued to rub mesmerizing little circles beneath her ears. Several seconds passed before he opened his eyes. "There," he said, his voice a low rumble. "That'll hold me."

She shook her head slightly to clear it. "What was that for?"

"You do that to me. One simple diagnosis falls from your lips, and I'm hooked."

"Not funny."

"You don't believe shrink talk turns me on?"

"Sure, that's why you've been to so many."

He laughed. "Okay. How about this?" The callused pad of his thumb rubbed her tingling lips. "I've been thinking about kissing you for a week. I've barely seen you since Monday. We've both been so busy."

"Your column made my phones go haywire. I spent so much time answering inquiries, I hardly got any work done."

He watched her intently. "I've been up to my eyeballs in paperwork and meetings. The damned Slavs had to go and have free elections, and the news business just went sort of nuts."

Why, she wondered, did he have to look so attractive when his eyes sparkled like that? As quickly as her world had tilted, he'd helped right it again. "It would have been nice if they'd called you first."

"Uh-huh. Or if the president had consulted with us before he authorized an air strike in the Mideast." He swept his thumb over her lower lip.

She ignored the leap in her pulse rate. "Poor guy. You must have worked yourself to death. I thought your consequence had earned you all the plum assignments."

"Plum assignments like digging through ten-year-old archives for the complete history of the Bezin Peninsula?"

"No. Assignments like hanging out with some

crazy female shrink and her fly-by-night charity.''

Above the rim of her glasses, he traced his fingertip along her eyebrow. ''Would it surprise you to learn that my consequence isn't worth squat around there?''

''My kids are pretty impressed with it.''

''How about you?'' He bent his head to nuzzle her neck.

Beyond his shoulder, she could see the weekend traffic racing by, but somehow, within the confines of his car, she felt cocooned. She lifted a hand to the back of his head. Her fingers wove into the crisp silk of his hair. ''I'm pretty impressed with it, too,'' she admitted.

He kissed her again. This time, he gently, slowly explored her, as if they weren't parked on the side of a highway, or as if things between them could ever be normal.

The thought brought her firmly back to reality. Threading her fingers in his hair, she tugged until he lifted his mouth. His eyes clouded as he watched her. ''Cam?''

She shook her head. ''I don't think this is a good idea. I want to be your friend. Your *good* friend,'' she clarified at his scowl, ''but I don't think it's particularly wise for us to get emotionally involved.'' She gave him a narrow look. ''It's not the best choice for you.''

''Where did you get the idea you can control something like that?''

''I paid one hundred and sixty-five thousand dollars on education to learn the secret.''

''Then you got ripped off. It's not going to work.''

"I keep trying to tell you that."

"Cute."

She shook her head. "Sorry. I'm really not trying to pick a fight with you."

"You're sure?"

"I'm sure. I just think we could both benefit from exercising a little discretion. I feel like we're playing with fire." She paused. "I'd rather not be the one who gets burned."

She saw his desire to argue clearly reflected in his gaze, but he pushed it aside. Gently, he set her back in her seat, checked her seat belt, then guided his car back onto the highway. Several minutes passed before he spoke again. "You know what I think?"

"Would it surprise you to find out that I have no idea what you think?"

He slanted her a grin. "The feeling is mutual."

"That's comforting."

"I think," he continued, "that you can argue all you want, but one day, you're going to wake up and find out you're hooked."

"Jackson—"

He reached for her hand. "It's okay, Cam. I'll wait." He squeezed her fingers. "Now, why don't you fill me in on this fund-raiser you're planning. I'd rather hear it from you than trying to muddle through your press releases."

She hesitated, but allowed him to change the subject. They spent the next couple of hours talking about her plans. He listened, made suggestions, asked questions, and kept her hand cradled in his warm palm. The bandage, she realized, was gone. In its place was a jagged scar that pressed against her tender skin as a constant reminder that he had his share of demons, too.

Almost before she realized it, he was turning down a tree-lined road, where a sprawling white farmhouse sat amid rolling hills and towering oaks. She sensed his inward stillness.

"Home?" she prompted.

His gaze remained fixed on the house. "Home."

eight

Cammy looked around the comfortable room with a twinge of envy. She'd never met a family like Jackson's.

She caught her reflection in the mirror and frowned at it. She'd once *dreamed* of a family like Jackson's. They'd barely turned into the drive when his mother bustled from the house, flanked by a handful of Jackson's nieces and nephews, an aging golden retriever, and the scents and sounds of his home.

Jackson was engulfed in the warm circle of love. His sisters and brothers-in-law soon joined the fray. Amid the laughter and delighted squeals of his young nieces and nephews, introductions were made, plans were established, and his father rounded the back of the house with a welcoming smile on his sun-weathered face.

Cammy had been ushered into the house in grand ceremony. One of Jackson's brothers-in-law had seized her bag from the trunk. His oldest nephew had taken her hand to guide her to the spacious room on the upper floor of the house. His nieces had bounced merrily on her bed, while their mothers attempted, in vain, to regain control. The dog barked. The children shouted. Jackson's mother stood to one side, delicately wiping her teary eyes with the corner of her apron.

At a softly spoken command from Jackson's father, the boisterous crew swept out of the room in a whirlwind of sound. Even Jackson, Cammy realized, had gone out with the tide. Alone, she sat on the edge of the bed in the aftermath of the storm. The one time she remembered bringing a roommate home from college, her parents' maid had shown the girl to her room. Cammy had learned that evening that her father had planned an impromptu campaign trip and that she and her friend would spend the holiday alone.

At the sharp knock on her door, she raised her head to meet Jackson's gaze. His expression sheepish, he strolled into her room. " 'Fess up," he urged. "Did it feel like one of your father's press conferences?"

She managed a slight laugh. "They're a bit overwhelming."

"Sorry." He sat on the edge of the bed. "Everyone lives nearby, so I knew we'd see them. I just didn't think it would be all at once."

"Is there going to be a quiz on all the names?"

"How would you do?"

"Your parents are Mr. and Mrs. Puller. That's the easy one."

"They'd rather you called them George and Marie."

"They'll have to adjust." She pursed her lips as

she scrolled through her memory. "Your sisters are Karen, Mary Beth, and Jordan?"

"Right. And they're married to Bud, William, and Anthony. Wanna try the nieces and nephews for the bonus round?"

"Jaime and Andy belong to Karen and Bud. Tommy, Philip, and Leah go with Mary Beth and William. And Jordan and Anthony get Fiona."

"I'm impressed."

"I've had practice. Between politics and group therapy, I've learned all the tricks for name recognition." She met his gaze. "When was the last time you were home?"

He thought it over. "Christmas three years ago." At her surprised look, he held up a hand. "I've seen them all individually several times since. Mom and Dad came into Washington last summer. I've played tour guide for all my sisters' families. Heck, I was Andy's show-and-tell exhibit at her preschool's career day."

"They adore you."

He studied her carefully. "They're my family."

"You got a good one." She pushed aside her lingering grim mood as she eased herself from the bed. Busying herself with hanging the clothes from her suitcase, she tried to ignore the nervous feelings tumbling through her. "Are you going to tell me what they said about me, or are you going to make me sweat?"

"I should, you know. It'd be payback for what you did to me over that column."

She shook the wrinkles from a green sundress, then

concentrated on adjusting it on the hanger. She fiddled with the straps, as if arranging them just so had become the most crucial task in the world. She focused so intently on the small job that she didn't realize he'd come up behind her until his hand settled on her shoulder.

He eased the hanger from her stiff fingers to place the dress in the closet. Carefully, he turned her to face him. "Cam," he whispered as he traced a finger along the curve of her collarbone, "they said they were very glad you were here. They can't wait to get to know you. Andy wanted to know what this black box is you have clipped to your belt." He rubbed the stem of her glasses where the implant earpiece rested. "I told her to ask you yourself." He pressed a kiss to her forehead. "And they said they were glad to know I had the good sense to recognize what a great person you are."

She met his gaze. "Oh."

A smile played at the corner of his mouth. "Do you know that I think you're adorable?"

"Even when you wish you were wringing my neck?"

With a soft laugh, he mumbled something that sounded like "even then," an instant before he claimed her mouth with the same hungry ardor she'd learned to recognize. And as it always did, it melted her resistance. She flowed against him, wrapping her arms around his waist, tilting her head to give him better access. He cradled her head in one large hand, while pressing her closer with the other. His tongue slid between her lips, and she melted. His mouth glided over hers, tantalizingly soft, temptingly demanding. A flutter of excitement tripped along her nerve endings. She was trembling when she heard the giggle from the doorway.

With a muttered oath, he lifted his head. Cammy stifled a groan when she saw the child watching them with avid interest. Jackson, apparently, had no such qualms. "Andy, what are you doing?"

The genuine affection in his voice and the smile he gave the girl eased some of Cammy's discomfort. Andy beamed at him. "You're kissing." Her tone left no question that she found that truth absolutely hysterical.

"Uh-huh." He ran a hand down Cammy's back. "Why are you watching?"

She shrugged. " 'Cause."

"It's not polite."

"The door wasn't shut," she argued. "If I wasn't s'posed to look, how come you didn't shut the door?"

He laughed. "Do you still want to be a reporter when you grow up?"

"Just like you."

"You're going to be great at it. I can tell."

Andy looked at him in puzzlement. "Why?"

"I'm smart that way. You didn't tell me why you came up here."

"Grammy said if you didn't eat dinner, she has some ready."

He gave Cammy an apologetic look. "My mother believes that the answer to society's ills is home-cooked food. We'll probably both gain ten pounds before we leave."

She had eased away from him when he'd begun

talking to his niece. She finished the task of hanging her clothes, then met his gaze. "I think the last time I ate a home-cooked meal that didn't come in a microwaveable container was my senior year in high school."

"Brace yourself," he warned. "My mother takes the biblical directive to eat of the fat of the land in dead earnest."

"I doubt my arteries are going to clog in one weekend."

"You ever tried buttermilk biscuits with sausage gravy?"

"Are you kidding? My father was from Syracuse. Our idea of a gourmet breakfast was half a grapefruit and a bagel."

Jackson's laugh eased what was left of her tension. He looked more relaxed, more content than she'd ever seen him. In that instant, she made a conscious decision to simply enjoy the warmth of his family and deliberately push from her mind the idea that this hazy utopia he'd shown her couldn't possibly last. She simply refused to allow her misgivings to knock the shine from his eyes.

"Uncle Jackson." Andy was pulling on his blue jean pocket. Belatedly, Cammy realized that Jackson had been holding her gaze, while she had been holding her breath.

He glanced at Andy. "What, baby doll?"

"Can I ask her about the box now?" Andy pressed.

He squatted down so his face was eye level with hers. Gently, he smoothed a reddish curl off the girl's forehead. "Maybe she'd like to eat first."

Andy looked crestfallen. "But you said—"

Jackson pressed a finger to her lips. "Be polite, and I'll tell you an extra bedtime story tonight."

"The scary kind?"

"If you want."

The child seemed to think it over. She glanced at Cammy's transmitter, visibly weighing the temptation. Cammy was about to tell Jackson she didn't mind when Andy placed her small hands on either side of his face and said, "Uncle Jackson?"

"What?"

"Is she your girlfriend?"

A cough squeezed from Cammy's chest. Jackson gave her an amused look. "I'm working on it," he told Andy.

"But she's not?"

"Not yet."

Andy looked at Cammy. "Why not?" The earnest question told her that Andy knew any woman would be lucky to snag a man like her uncle.

Jackson looked like he wanted to laugh. Cammy thought about kicking him in the shin. Instead, she offered the child a smile. "He's not always easy to get along with."

"Uncle Jackson," Andy looked at him solemnly, "you have to be nice if you want her to like you."

His eyes were shining with mirth. "You think so?"

Andy nodded. "It's a rule. Like sharing. And flushing."

He couldn't seem to contain himself any longer. He laughed, a genuine, throaty laugh, as he swept Andy into his arms. Standing, he swung her around twice before he hugged her to his chest. "I love you."

She giggled. "I love you, too."

"Thanks for the advice."

She leaned back so she could press a quick kiss to his cheek. "Is it okay if I ask her now?"

Jackson looked at Cammy. His shoulders were shaking. "At what age do they start teaching girls to manipulate men with open displays of affection?"

"Preschool, I think. Around the time they hand out the rules about sharing and flushing. They take us aside and fill us in on the effective use of feminine wiles."

"Just for the record," he said, "it's going to work on me just about every time."

"I'll remember that."

"I'll look forward to it."

"Uncle Jackson—" Andy's voice had grown impatient.

"Okay, okay." He stood her on a chair so she could face Cammy. "I'll test the waters for you." He looked at Cammy. "Do you mind?"

"Not at all."

He chucked Andy under the chin. "I'll go see what Grammy has for dinner while you talk to Cammy. Be polite."

"I will."

"Don't ask too many questions."

"I won't."

To Cammy, he said, "Don't let her railroad you."

"I'm an expert at this type of thing."

"If you're not downstairs in ten minutes, I'll come rescue you."

He walked from the room with long, graceful strides. Cammy allowed her gaze to rest on the breadth of his shoulders where they rolled beneath the soft chambray of his shirt. Being rescued by Jackson Puller, she mused, could become an extremely dangerous temptation.

Jackson found his mother in the kitchen, standing at the sink peeling apples. Casey, the golden retriever he'd known since adolescence, thumped a tail on her braided rug at Jackson's entrance. He stopped to rub the dog's silky head, then walked up behind his mother to wrap his arms around her ample girth. "Hi, Mama." He dropped a kiss on her cheek.

She jabbed his ribs with her elbow when he reached for an apple wedge. "Ah. They're for the pie."

He snatched the wedge anyway. "And you have too many apples. You always do." He chewed the tart fruit. "Where's everyone?"

"On the porch. It's a nice night. We thought we'd sit outside and enjoy it."

"And they left you here alone in the kitchen," he teased. He knew from experience that his mother had finally had all the activity she could stand and sent a silent command to her father to usher the large group out of her territory.

"I wanted to finish the apples." She glanced at him. "Is Cammy coming down to eat?"

"She'll be here in a minute. She's explaining her cochlear implant to Andy."

His mother nodded. "We read your column. She seems like a remarkable woman."

"And your curiosity is killing you?"

"It's not killing me exactly." She set the apple down, then wiped her hands on her apron. "I'm just very glad you decided to come, and that you brought her with you."

"You'll be happy to know that she has the very good sense to resist every advance I've made."

"Knowing you, you've been making plenty."

He grinned at her. "Every chance I get."

She patted his cheek. "She couldn't have been resisting that much. She's here, isn't she?"

"I badgered her to death. She finally had to agree just to get me out of her hair."

She snorted. "That's a switch. Since when do the girls want you out of their hair?"

It felt good, he realized, to share this banter again. He hadn't realized how hungry he'd been for it until he'd gotten here. "I hate to break this to you, Mom, but just because you find me irresistible doesn't mean the rest of the world does."

She ignored that. "Still, from what I read in your column, Dr. Glynn isn't the kind of woman who's easily manipulated into doing anything she doesn't want to do."

"No. You're right."

His mother pointed at the cabinet behind him. "Get two plates and silverware. I'll pour you some tea."

He felt rather than saw his mother's gaze fixed on the wide scar that marred his palm. "It's okay," he assured her as he reached for the plates.

She plunked a glass down on the counter, then reached for his hand. Pressing her lips into the center of his palm, she raised tear-filled eyes to his. "I've been very worried."

"I know. I'm sorry." He cradled her face. "I'm getting better."

She tapped his chest with her index finger. "Here, too?"

Over her shoulder, he saw Cammy enter the room. Andy held her hand and chattered aimlessly as they crossed the wide kitchen. He met Cammy's gaze, held it, then wrapped his mother in his arms. "There, too," he assured her.

"It's better this way," Durstan assured her. "You couldn't have given him what he wanted."

The accusation found its mark. Cammy gasped as the wound in her heart stretched wider. Wiping her tears with the back of her hand, she glared at her father. "You don't know that."

"Well, he's gone, isn't he?"

"Because of you."

"Because I told him the truth." Durstan's expression turned harsh. "You didn't really think Leslie wanted to marry you?"

She refused to answer. Her mind traveled to the picture of the wedding dress she kept tucked in her desk drawer. Durstan studied her face with disbelief. "You did. You thought he was serious."

"You shouldn't have interfered."

"For the love of—" Her father swore. "It's time you learned something about life, Cameo. Leslie is a political animal with high aspirations. Boys like him want two things from the girls they date. Sex and po-

litical connections. God knows you weren't giving him the first—at least not very satisfactorily.''

She gasped aloud. Her father's gaze narrowed. ''Were you?''

''I don't have to answer that.''

''You don't have to. He wouldn't have come sniveling to me if you had been.''

''Father—''

He held up his hand. ''What he wanted from you was my blessing on his political aspirations. I told him if he wanted to succeed in this business, then he'd better find a wife who could help him campaign, support him once he got elected, and give him lots of healthy children. Just marrying into a political family wasn't going to be enough.''

Cammy's tears were scalding her eyes now. She stared at him in horror. ''I can't believe you—''

He interrupted her. ''It's all true. No one knows that better than me. I married your mother for access to her family name. What I ended up with was a crazy wife and a handicapped child. I did Leslie a favor.'' He pinned her with a pointed look. ''One day, you'll see that I did you a favor, too. You couldn't have made him happy, Cameo. You weren't what he wanted.''

Cammy forcibly pushed the painful memory aside as she gazed into the clear night sky. Standing on Jackson's porch, she studied the twinkle of starlight in the black velvet canopy. Here the sky seemed larger, darker, than it did in the city. The rustling of leaves, spurred by a warm breeze, provided the only interruption to the stillness. Cammy concentrated for a few minutes on the sound, savoring its lulling rhythm.

She'd lain in bed for nearly an hour before she admitted she wouldn't be able to sleep. Pulling on a robe, she'd slipped quietly downstairs to the porch. The bitter memory, she now realized, had been lurking at the edges of her consciousness, waiting for her to let her guard down. The vastness of the night had freed it to taunt her. Often, she'd escaped those angry confrontations by seeking solace on the roof of her parents' Washington town house. Then, she'd believed in the power of wishes and stars. Years of disappointment had taught her the folly of believing in miracles.

She pulled the belt of her robe a little tighter. She'd almost forgotten that lesson today. The warmth of Jackson's family, the way he made her feel, the inescapable truth of the way he pulled at her heart, tempted her to ignore the consequences. She was nine years old when she first confided to her mother that she escaped to the roof to wish on the stars. Her mother had informed her that evidently she'd been wishing on the wrong ones.

The memory of Jackson lying in the front yard, swamped by his giggling nieces and nephews, looking younger and less strained than she'd ever seen him, reminded her that some stars, and the wishes that went with them, belonged to someone else.

The obvious warmth of his family shed some light on her observations of him. He'd grown up in a world where children were accepted and loved and wanted.

He'd enjoyed a close family full of warmth and compassion. Understandably, he'd expected the world to be the same way. The cold reality he'd experienced in his job had sent him scrambling to reevaluate. She'd stake her professional reputation on the fact that every disappointment in Jackson's adult life had helped him reach the same conclusion. Someone had looked out for him as a child. Someone had stuck up for him when he'd gotten bullied. There had always been someone to share his triumphs and his sorrows, his successes and his failures. And somewhere, in the center of his soul, where the forces lay that made him the incredible man that he was, he fervently believed that *everyone* deserved a crusader. When he found people without one, he made up his mind to fill the role.

The thought saddened her almost beyond belief. When she thought of him fighting the world's battles, taking on every lost cause and hopeless case in his path, she saw his passion and his deep, vibrant love for life. She could never, she knew, give him what he wanted, what he needed. Jackson deserved a life full of children to love who loved him back. He deserved an uncomplicated relationship with a woman who still had all her pieces. He'd have to find that in someone else. When he realized that, she could easily end up with a heart so broken that it might not be fixable.

But then, a niggling voice reminded, she didn't have any future plans for it.

He had so much to give, so many things to offer the world, and for reasons she didn't begin to understand, God seemed to have plunked him down in her path so she could help him find them again. The trick was to make sure Jackson didn't get hurt in the process. She could give him so much, as long as she made him understand why he couldn't fall in love with her. He needed to keep that for a woman who could make him happy.

Achingly familiar, a set of strong arms slipped around her waist. She leaned back against his chest. "Hi."

She felt his hand slide to her waist, check for her transmitter. "Hi." His breath tickled her ear. "Couldn't sleep?"

"No."

He pressed a kiss to her neck. "Did they overwhelm you tonight with all those questions?"

"I like them."

"They like you."

A smile played at the corner of her mouth. "How do you know? They all talk at once."

With a slight laugh, he turned her to face him. Clad in jeans and no shirt, the expanse of his chest assailed all of her senses. Some women, she'd heard, were leg women, or butt women, or even brain women. From now on, she decided while studying the smooth sculpted lines, she could definitely be known as a chest woman. She didn't even resist the urge to trace a finger over the ridge of his collarbone.

Jackson pressed a hand to the small of her back and said, "I just know. Besides, *I* like you." He shrugged. "What choice do they have?"

"Do they always give you everything you want?"

"Hell no. They just know I'm extremely difficult

to talk out of something I want once I've made my mind up.''

Her finger trailed to the other side. ''Is your mind made up?''

''About wanting you? Sure. I know exactly what I want. You're the one who needs convincing.''

''You're very good at it.''

She felt him still. ''Cam?''

''Convincing me, I mean.''

''Honey, you're sending me some mixed signals here.''

She met his gaze. ''Really?''

''You were pretty clear this afternoon that you weren't ready to go here, yet.''

Her fingers threaded through the dusting of dark hair on his chest. ''I was?''

''I remember it vividly.''

''Girls change their minds, sometimes. Didn't anyone ever tell you that?''

''Are you saying what I think you're saying?''

She pressed a kiss to his oh-so-tempting pectoral muscle. ''Is that any clearer?''

''Hell.'' His breath left his body in a *whoosh*. ''Why in damnation would you say something like that to me when we're trapped in a house full of my family?''

She rubbed the frown from between his eyebrows. ''Mike would say I have a passive aggressive need to control my environment by manipulating my external circumstances to suit my personal gratification.''

He grunted. ''I can see I have a lot to explain to you about gratification.''

A giggle escaped her. "Please do."

Without warning, he cupped the back of her head in his large palm, aligned her body closely with his, and captured her mouth in an aching kiss of mindless need and barely-banked fire. She pressed her hands to his shoulders, holding him to her like a treasure finally found. His mouth molded hers to fit the shape and feel of his. His whispered endearments tripped the hidden triggers in her spirit.

He cradled her, she realized. When Jackson kissed her, his hands cradled her with a fierce tenderness. Even the hunger she felt in him, sensed in him as he deepened the kiss, told her that he cherished her. The feeling was singularly devastating.

She pressed herself to him, moved her hands over his bare back, threaded them into the crisp silk of his hair. "Jackson," she breathed.

"I love the way you say my name," he told her. His lips moved to her cheek, glided along her jaw-bone, then found the spot at her shoulder.

Cammy gasped. "Have I ever told you that I love the way you touch me," she confessed.

He kissed her again, a kiss rife with tenderness and longing. Tendrils of need licked through her. His hands were warm and reassuring through her cotton robe as they roamed her body. When he slid one large hand inside to stroke the sensitive flesh of her belly, she felt the caress to the very core of her body. She gasped. He swept his hand upward in a searing exploration.

Cammy breathed his name and pressed herself into his palm. When he raised his head, she was sure the stars she'd seen in the sky now shone in her eyes. Overwhelmed by the depth of her feeling, she pressed her head to his chest.

She felt his hand tremble as it slowly eased from her robe. "If you even mention," he said, his voice a husky rasp, "the words 'delayed gratification' to me in the next two days, I'm going to strangle you."

Cammy laughed as she raised her flushed face to his. "No you won't. I'm too useful."

"And you're trying to torture me with that fact, aren't you?"

"It builds character."

"That's not all it builds," he grumbled. With a hand between her shoulder blades, he guided her to the porch swing. "And if I don't come up for air very soon, you're going to have to commit me."

"I'm not trying to be hard on you."

"For the record," he told her, his eyebrows raised, "you have an absolutely devastating effect on me. I'd advise you not to misuse it."

"I wasn't—"

He interrupted her with a quick kiss. "I'm not finding fault, just laying down ground rules. For the most part, whatever you're asking for with that look in your eyes, the answer is an unqualified yes."

She smiled. "Really?"

"Really."

"That's probably the most intriguing offer I've ever had."

"And I aim to keep it that way." He indicated the porch swing with a tilt of his head. "Since this obviously isn't going anywhere tonight, what do you say we swing for a while? Unless you're sleepy."

"I'm not." She studied the swing. "I've never been on one of these."

A rough chuckle pulled from his chest as he seated himself. "It's a Southern courtship ritual."

"Swinging?"

"Uh-huh." He nodded his head toward the living room window. "Couples can sit on the swing while nosy parents watch Lawrence Welk and chaperone."

"Is that what your parents did?"

"That's what they did to my sisters. I was smart enough not to sit on the swing in the first place." He held out a hand to her. "It's restrictive."

She glanced at him in surprise. "What do you mean?"

With a slight smile, he shifted so his back rested against the corner. He extended one jean-clad leg, then guided Cammy so her back rested against his chest, and she sat securely in the V of his legs. His hand tickled the hairs at the nape of her neck. "I mean, that there's not a whole lot of trouble you can get into on one of these. Some Southern father designed them to guarantee minimal hanky-panky."

She settled against him, savoring the feeling. "Come on, adolescent males are the most ingenious creatures alive when it comes to making time with adolescent girls."

With a shove of his foot, he set the swing in motion. "Honey, believe me. If there was a way to fool around on this thing, I'd have figured it out years ago." He trailed a finger along her arm as they lapsed into a comfortable silence. Several long minutes passed before he spoke again. "Cam?"

She was feeling lulled by the warmth of his embrace, the solid feel of his body behind her. "Um hmm?"

"So, you want to tell me why you looked so sad when I came out here, or do I have to drag it out of you?"

She thought it over and realized, with some surprise, that she found the idea of talking things over with him oddly comforting. She'd talked about her childhood before, often with her colleagues and even, on occasion, with patients who needed to feel they could trust her to relate to them. But she'd never wanted to. She turned the thought over in her head for several seconds. Jackson waited in silence, his touch reassuring but patient. "I was thinking about my parents."

His hand momentarily stilled, then continued its gentle stroking of her forearm. He waited in silence. The caress of his hand mesmerized her into a comfortable lassitude. "The only time I ever brought someone home with me, my parents went out of town." A sad smile tugged at the corner of her mouth. "I was secretly relieved."

"What did he think?"

"He who?"

"Your boyfriend."

"Oh. It wasn't a boyfriend. I never brought a boyfriend home. It was my college roommate. She didn't have anywhere to go for Thanksgiving. I knew if my parents had been there, we would have ended up fighting in front of her.''

"It was lonely, wasn't it?"

She didn't pretend to misunderstand. He wasn't talking about a single holiday, he was talking about the tone of her life. "Sometimes. My mother wasn't well. *Isn't* well. My father didn't know how to handle a sick child and a sick wife.''

"You weren't sick, Cam.''

"Haven't you ever noticed that when people put you down long enough, you start to believe them?''

He snorted. "You're smart enough to know better. You're an extraordinary woman. In case I haven't told you lately, I'm phenomenally impressed with you. Truth is, I'm almost beside myself with awe that you even have anything to do with me.''

She pinched his arm. "Liar. You are not going to trap me into believing that your self-esteem isn't perfectly whole.''

"Can I at least get you to realize you're an amazingly gifted woman?''

She hesitated. "The bad stuff is easier to believe.''

"I hate it that you think that.''

"It's okay, Jackson. I'm old enough now to understand that my father had some very serious problems. Whether he found my deafness unendurable or not doesn't change what it was. The world's more tolerant today, and it's easy for people to condemn him for his attitude.''

"He was a bastard.''

"Thanks for your loyalty.''

"I'm serious.''

"I know." She squeezed his hand. "Durstan was . . . ill-suited to the demands of a challenging relationship. He married my mother because she came from a well-respected, wealthy family. She was supposed to be a political asset. He didn't count on mental illness."

"What happened to 'in sickness and in health'?"

"Don't be so hard on him," she warned. "My mother didn't exactly think he was the love of her life, either. They had what I consider to be a fairly typical political marriage. It was a partnership, not a commitment. You know the type."

"Unfortunately."

"It works very well for some people."

"Maybe it does. They should know better than to have children, though."

"My parents didn't plan to. Accidents happen."

"And, naturally, they felt obligated to inform you of this fact so you could walk around with the knowledge that you were an accident. I just like them more and more."

She heard the scorn in his voice. With a smile of amusement, she stroked the back of his hand. "Even before she grew chronically psychologically ill, my mother was prone to lapses in her mental stability. She'd rant. Sometimes she said things she shouldn't. I can't really hold that against her, and I stopped letting it hurt me."

His arms tightened. "It makes me mad."

"That doesn't surprise me. You have a very strong sense of justice and responsibility and compassion.

It's a powerful combination. It's bound to evoke powerful emotions.''

"And you don't like it.''

She looked at him in surprise. "I didn't say that.''

"You think I'm too passionate.''

"I think you're impulsive. That makes you different from me. Not wrong different, just different.''

He looked at her for a long moment, his gaze probing for secrets. "Do I scare you, Cammy?''

She swallowed. She didn't know how to answer that. She felt fear when she was with him. She knew that much, but she'd be lying if she pinned the source of that fear on him. The expression in his eyes told her he knew that. And he'd wisely refused to give her the out. "No.'' She stroked the back of his hand. "Sometimes, I fear the person I am when I'm with you.''

He stopped breathing. "Why?''

"I haven't figured it out yet.''

The swing rocked back and forth as they sat several moments in silence. "Did you ever wonder,'' he finally said, picking up the thread of their earlier conversation, "why your parents were so self-indulgent?''

"Some people are. They come by it naturally.''

"I used to think that the material wealth of this country contributed to self-indulgent adults like your parents.''

"I'm sure it does.''

"You'd be surprised. The first time I did a feature story on children was about seven years ago. I was covering a summit meeting in the Baltics when I met this kid outside the U.S. Embassy. His father was an attaché. He'd had to move in the middle of the school year, so he'd left all his friends behind.'' She felt him smile. "His name was Rodney, and he loved to play soccer. He was standing by the gate bouncing a soccer ball on his knee. It was midafternoon. I struck up a conversation with him, asked him what he was doing. He told me he'd observed that the local kids got out of school about that time. He figured if he waited until they walked past, he'd draw enough of a crowd with that soccer ball that he could pull a game together. I asked him if he spoke their language, and he just looked at me with the most serious expression and said, 'Sure. I speak soccer.' ''

Cammy laughed. "Smart kid."

"They usually are. It was just so refreshing. I'd been following these politicians around for months, watching them operate, watching them use people, then here was this kid with all the confidence in the world that a soccer ball and a grin could get him to the people that mattered."

"And you wrote about him."

"I used the idea that while the politicians were holed up fighting over territorial water rights and ethnic divisions, the kids were down in the street playing soccer."

"Not everyone would have seen the poetry in that."

"Maybe not, but a lot of people did. That story struck a chord. People liked it."

"I remember it. People talked about it for weeks."

He paused. "I suppose even more important to me

than the way people reacted to it was the way I reacted to it. *I* liked it. I liked what it said and what it
accomplished.''

''I can see why.''

''I was recovering from a pretty healthy dose of
disillusionment when I wrote that story. I had just
gotten burned by a senator's aide who'd deliberately
fed me misinformation about her boss's opponent.''

''Were you involved with her?''

''Yes.''

She nodded. ''That's the worst kind of betrayal.
When it comes from someone you trust.''

''I should have seen it coming.''

''How old were you?''

''Twenty-two.''

''Then maybe you should cut yourself some slack.
You were inexperienced. Did you write the story
yourself?''

''No. I was still a copy editor in those days. I gave
it to an older journalist, a man I had a lot of respect
for.''

''And he ran with it?''

''He didn't double-check it like he should have.
When the fallout came, he let me take the blame.''

''It was his byline?''

''Yes.''

''Then it was his fault.''

He shrugged. ''I'm no saint, Cammy, but I'm pretty
sure I wouldn't let some copy editor take a hit for my
own incompetence.''

''It hurt you, didn't it?''

''He was one of my heroes.''

Jackson visibly wrestled with the memory, then pressed ahead. "That's actually how I met Chris Harris. I got fired from that job and threw myself on Chris's mercy. AW was a new enterprise then, and they'd take just about anyone. Chris hired me and sent me to help another journalist cover the Baltics event."

"He ran your story on Rodney?"

"He did. I was surprised when it got picked up by papers across the country. I felt vindicated, and cleansed, somehow, like I'd finally found something worth doing. I started looking, then, for those kind of ironies in the world. And I found out that most of the time, children are just honest—with themselves and the people around them. When you talk to kids, you find out what counts and what doesn't, who matters and who doesn't. The older I get, and the more I see of it, I find I'm less and less tolerant of scheming adults."

"I saw the special you did last year with those children during the war in the Middle East. I'm not surprised you got an award for that."

"They had questions. I thought someone should answer them. Andy gave me the idea. She called me to ask me why President Stratton was so angry all the time. I started talking to her, and found out she'd heard enough information to be scared, but not enough to feel secure." He shrugged. "For some reason, she felt like she could ask me."

"She knew you'd tell her the truth. There aren't many people children trust like that. I see that with my therapy kids all the time. They know adults patronize them. You have a way of talking to them—I saw it that day you sat in on one of my sessions. You show them that you respect them. They sense it.''

''You never got that from your parents, did you?'' he asked, his voice quietly intent.

''No. My mother wasn't psychologically capable. My father wasn't emotionally capable. It wasn't idyllic, but it wasn't awful either. It wasn't like I was abused.''

''Why didn't you ever bring a boyfriend home?''

''What?''

''You said you never brought a boyfriend home. Why not?''

''Oh, that. I don't know. I never had many, that was part of it. There aren't very many teenage boys who want to date deaf girls.''

''What about later?''

''After the implant?''

He made a sound of impatience. ''No, later in life. College, adulthood.''

''I don't know. I attended Gallaudet, the deaf university. I had my implant then. It made me something of a pariah. I've told you that it's not widely accepted in the deaf community. It doesn't work for everyone, and there are a lot of deaf people who firmly believe it represents a concession to the rest of the world. People like Jeffrey Herrington, the activist Lynette told you about, are actively opposed to the technology. When I was eighteen and in college, I was learning to use it, learning to speak. I was serious and extraordinarily focused, and I didn't really have a lot of time for a social life.''

"Come on, Cam, you had to fall for somebody, sometime."

"I never really felt serious enough about the few guys I dated to expose them to my family. But there was one I fell pretty hard for." The admission slipped out with an ease that amazed her. The memory had seemed so vile, but wrapped in the warm circle of Jackson's arms, with the gentle creak of the swing and the sounds of the night filling the air, the edge was gone.

"Tell me," he urged, as his hands slid up her forearms. He pressed a kiss to her nape. "I want to know."

She shivered from the warm contact. "He worked on my father's staff. It was the last year my father ran for the Senate. Leslie was assigned to do my scheduling for the campaign."

Jackson snorted, then glided his mouth along her shoulder. "His name was Leslie? That should have been your first clue."

She jabbed him in the ribs. "He took care of my advance work for any public appearances, made sure I got where I needed to be. We were together a lot. My implant was new to me then, and the press conferences were still confusing. I had a lot of trouble sorting out all the sound. Leslie handled things. He fielded questions, and just sort of took care of me."

"What happened?" He had found the verge of her collarbone. He seemed fascinated by the tiny strip of flesh.

"He paid a lot of attention to me. He treated me like a queen, and I reveled in it." She moaned softly when he licked an especially sensitive spot. "Oh."

He raised his head. "Sorry. I wasn't trying to distract you."

"Liar."

His boyish grin made her heart tumble. "I wasn't. I'm interested." At her dubious look, he tightened his arms at her waist. "I am."

She searched his gaze for several seconds, then tipped her head back against his shoulder. "My father seemed to like him," she continued, "which helped. I spun all kinds of fantasies in my head, and started reading *Bride* magazine. I wanted a spring wedding. Sometime after the Inauguration."

"Did Leslie have other ideas?" He rested his chin on top of her head.

For once, her father had been right. Leslie had wanted an advantageous political marriage that would bolster his political career. For a while, he'd believed that Durstan Glynn's daughter could give him that. Then Durstan had taken him aside to explain the harsh facts. She could never have children; she'd never be able to pose with him in perfect campaign photos with fair-headed sons and a golden retriever; her mother was insane; and, given Cammy's other birth defects, chances were she might end up that way, too. The price had seemed too high for Leslie. She drew a shaky breath. "He just decided he wasn't ready for that much responsibility."

"Where is he now?" Jackson asked.

"I don't know. He ran for Congress several years ago, but he lost. I suppose he's planning his next move."

Jackson muttered a dark curse. She glanced at him in surprise. "I recovered, Jackson. No need for full-blown outrage on my behalf."

"I've been suspecting for days that some faceless jerk was causing the bulk of my problems with you."

"You don't have any problems with me."

"Shall I list them?"

"Better not. We'll be awake half the night."

"I just knew there was some creep who'd done a number on you. I was sort of looking forward to stalking him down and terrorizing him a little."

She laughed. "That's hardly your style."

"I'm a real SOB when I get provoked."

"I assure you, there's no need to even give it a passing thought. I'm much better off without him. Can you really imagine me married to a congressman?"

"He was a jerk."

"Probably, but I'd have been a jerk's wife if I'd married him, so he did me a favor."

Jackson didn't comment. Cammy waited a few seconds, then prompted. "Jackson?"

"Hmm?"

"Are you going to tell me about Leo while we're here?"

His arms tightened. "Tomorrow," he promised. "When I'm stronger."

nine

The conversation still ringing in his ears, Jackson led the way up a long hill to his favorite place on his parents' farm. Breakfast had been an especially boisterous affair, with questions and laughter filling the confines of his mother's kitchen. Twice he'd glanced at Cammy to see if she looked uncomfortable. She'd met his gaze with a slight smile and a reassuring nod. She was coping. As she always had.

Long after he'd kissed her good night at the door of her room, he'd lain in bed replaying the scene on the porch. She'd looked close to tears when he'd found her staring out into the night. He had a suspicion that the matter-of-fact account she'd given of her family life had barely touched the surface of long years of disappointment and sorrow.

Then she'd knocked him flat on his butt. It had taken more self-control than she'd ever realize for him not to simply carry her off to bed before she had time to change her mind. But there was a hell of a lot more about Cammy he wanted to know than he'd learn if he rushed her into a serious physical relationship. He was fairly impressed that he'd managed to figure that out while his hormones were moving from overdrive to light speed.

He glanced at her now. She showed no ill effects of their late night or any sign that she remembered what she'd told him. He stifled a frustrated sigh. "We're almost there," he told her.

She smiled at him. "You were right. It's beautiful up here."

He noted the slight flush on her cheeks and the way the sun glinted in her blonder than red hair, and he found himself in wholehearted agreement. "This was my favorite place when I was a kid. It's a bit of a climb, but the view is worth the bother."

They crested the hill. Jackson extended a hand to Cammy to assist her up the final few steps. When she reached the apex, he took a few seconds to savor the view, savor the sensation of sharing it with her.

"Oh, Jackson." She gazed across the vista of the Shenandoah Valley. "It's breathtaking."

The light in her eyes made his mind go blank. He didn't even resist the urge to kiss her. He drowned his senses in the exquisite sensation, relished the feel of her pressed close to him. Drank deeply from her fresh, sweet taste. When he finally raised his head, he released a long breath. "I've been waiting to do that all morning."

Her laugh filled him with joy. "If the looks your father was giving me meant anything, I think he was waiting for you to do it all morning, too."

"He's a wise old guy."

"He knows you very well."

"I ran into him in the hall on my way to the shower. He told me he'd left me all the cold water."

She tucked her face against his chest. "I'm glad you have them."

As usual, her honesty had him reeling. He rubbed his hands up and down her back, smoothing the nubby cotton of her light sweater. "Me too."

They studied the view for long minutes while Jackson contemplated his sudden lightheartedness. It had been months, maybe even years, since he'd felt this peaceful. When he'd finally drifted to sleep last night, he'd slept better than he had in all the months since Leo's death. Cammy was good for him. He'd known that since almost the moment he'd met her. All he needed to do was find a way to show her how good they'd be together.

No matter what she'd said last night, he still felt her reticence. Each time he thought about how easily she could slip away, he had to fight down a wave of panic. He was a smart man, with an excellent talent for persuading people to trust him. The skill had worked for him all over the world. He had to make it work for her.

Drawing a deep breath, he tipped her away so he could look at her. "Wanna sit?"

She didn't pretend not to know where he was headed. "If you'd told me, I'd have brought my roll-out couch."

"We won't need it." He guided her toward a large elm. "When I was a kid growing up here, we mostly just used this tree." They reached the base, and he pointed to the branches. "Welcome to my sanctum."

Fascinated, Cammy looked at the tree house, well-maintained despite its obvious age, then at Jackson. "Yours?"

"My nephews' now, but yeah. Dad and I built it one summer." He laughed. "Actually, he built it, and graciously pretended that I was helping. I think I bent most of the nails and cut at least half the boards too short." He tilted his head to one side as he studied her. "Did you have a sanctum when you were growing up?"

"I didn't have to go anywhere to find peace and quiet," she quipped.

His expression remained intent. "Cammy—"

"Sorry. I'm doing it again. Old habits die hard."

"You're the most confusing woman I have ever known."

He looked so baffled that she had to laugh. "At least I'm not boring."

"Not even close."

She nodded toward the tree house. "So, you wanna take the lead, or shall I?"

"Are you kidding? I haven't gotten to lead since I met you. I'm not turning that kind of offer down." He reached for the bottom rung of the ladder.

Cammy tapped a finger on the hand-painted wooden sign that read ABSOLUTELY NO GIRLS. "Should I be insulted or gratified?"

"My nephews added that. Believe me, I would never have come up with a rule like that."

"I can imagine you always had a fairly healthy appreciation for the opposite sex."

His expression turned devilish. "That. And I had three sisters who would have knocked me flat."

Cammy laughed even as she realized she was losing a piece of her heart to the picture he was painting of his childhood. Jackson climbed several steps, then glanced at her. "Watch your step. The rungs are a little slippery."

She waited until he had hoisted himself onto the platform before she began the climb. The tree house was well designed to provide maximum space among the large limbs. A few rungs of the ladder had her easing onto the first platform. Only then did she realize the complexity of the structure. Three levels, it resembled a pirate ship wedged into the thick branches of the elm. Jackson had advanced to the bow, which jutted out toward the sweeping vista of the valley. He held out a hand to her. Charmed by this scene from his childhood, by the morning, and mostly by him, she accepted it as she seated herself beside him.

For long moments, he held her hand in companionable silence. "I loved this place," he finally said. "I used to dream here."

"My dreams were about having a pony. What were yours?"

"They weren't about watching an eight-year-old kid get killed and knowing I should have stopped it."

Cammy slipped her arm around his waist and waited, sensing his internal struggle. Long seconds passed before he said, "Thank you."

"For what?"

"For not telling me that it wasn't my fault."

"Would you have believed me?"

"No."

"I don't like to waste words, even if they're true words."

His hand stroked her hair. He lingered at the curve of her ear, then trailed his fingers downward to gently caress her cheek. When he spoke again, his voice sounded raw. "Did I tell you how I met Leo?"

"No."

"He stole my cassette recorder." He made a slight sound that might have been a laugh. "The kid was probably the best pickpocket in the city. He bumped into me, literally, outside this small grocery store, and before I knew it, he'd lifted my microrecorder and taken off."

"Take anything else?"

"If I'd been carrying a wallet, I'm sure he'd have lifted it."

"How did you catch him?"

"He caught me." He looked at her then, and the shadows, she noted, had begun to cluster in his eyes, turning their color to the shade of a stormy sky. "The press corps had a regular hotel where we stayed. The locals knew it. Leo hunted me down that night and hurled the thing at me." Jackson shook his head. "When he stole it, he thought it was a radio. It pissed him off when he found out that it didn't play music. All it played was the sound of my voice."

Cammy laughed softly. "My kind of kid."

He nodded. "You'd have liked him a lot. He was sharp. He was also distrustful. He didn't want to talk to me. None of the usual stuff worked."

"You couldn't bribe him with bubble gum and a snapshot?"

"Not Leo. He wasn't the kind of kid who'd fall for a simple trick. He was the oldest of five children. His father had been killed in the war. Leo took on a lot of responsibilities—the kind kids his age aren't even supposed to know about. His mother worked several jobs, and he learned how to pick pockets so nobody in his family had to starve."

"Hmm." She waited again. She doubted he realized he'd put his arm around her shoulders and was nearly squeezing the breath out of her.

"He had a girlfriend. Bianca. She was sixteen."

"I've always admired men who felt secure enough to date older women."

She thought she felt some of his tension ebb. "I think that Leo's life didn't lend itself to insecurity. Surviving took courage and sharp wits. The more his family counted on him, the more he learned to depend on himself, and no one else." He frowned. "He had magnetism. There was something about Leo that made people trust him."

"Like you?"

"No. Leo made me curious. Emotionally, he was a grown man. He had a whole gang of boys who followed his lead. Everyone depended on him, and he always delivered. He never seemed to feel the pressure of meeting their expectations. Even Bianca—" Jackson shook his head. "He'd give her a few coins and send her off to buy something for herself while we talked 'business.' "

Cammy laughed. "No wonder you were charmed."

"I was. I couldn't shake the feeling that a child was lost inside that confident facade. Something about that made me inexpressibly sad. It didn't seem right that this kid's life should have gotten preempted by things he barely understood. I kept digging, probing. I wanted him to trust me enough to show me who he was when no one else was looking."

"Did he?"

"He resisted me for a while, but I wasn't ready to let it go. He turned up too often not to make me think he wanted something. I was watching him scam an American Marine out of his watch when I realized my mistake." He sat, silent for a moment. "Leo was used to people wanting things from him. He wasn't used to having people respect him."

Cammy's hand glided over the scar on his palm. "But you did?" she prompted.

"I told him I needed to work a deal with him. He liked that. It felt like business. He sent Bianca to get us some coffee. He wanted to know if I wanted liquor in mine."

"Did he take liquor in his?"

"Nope. He told me he never drank. Didn't like the way it dulled his wits."

"Smart kid."

"Definitely. Once he realized I was serious about treating him like an adult—one who had something I wanted—he was willing to talk to me. I told him I needed a guide to show me around the city, help me find out what was really going on. I figured that nobody knew that city better than he did."

"What did he want in return?"

Jackson gave her a slight smile. "It took me almost an hour to get it out of him. He resisted for a while. I could tell he didn't want to tell me."

"But he cracked."

"Sort of. Actually, I cracked. I offered him a cigarette. He pointed out that I didn't have any, and that he knew that because he'd picked my pocket before we sat down to talk."

Cammy laughed. "No wonder you liked him so much."

Jackson shrugged. "I think he decided he could trust me because I congratulated him on the excellent job he'd done in robbing me blind."

"I can imagine." She rubbed her cheek on his shoulder. "Did he agree to help you?"

"If I got him a transistor radio, he said he'd show me around."

"How hard is it to get a transistor radio in Bosnia?"

"You have no idea." He laughed, as if the warmth of the memory had eased some of the hurt. "Chris Harris almost killed me. I had him calling every delivery company in town trying to figure out how to ship one to me."

She plied him with another question to keep him talking. "How did you get it?"

"American Marine on his way home. He sold it to me for twenty bucks."

"And Leo became your tour guide."

"Yeah. He hadn't expected me to come through. In his experience, adults didn't come through very often. When I produced the radio, it was like something incredible happened. It was one of the few times I ever saw him act like a kid. We must have sat on the curb for half an hour while he tuned in all the stations.''

''What kind of music did he like?''

''The Beatles.''

''They get the Beatles in Bosnia?''

''Honey, they get the Beatles everywhere. 'I Wanna Hold Your Hand' was his favorite song. He wanted to grow up and be a Beatle.'' Jackson shook his head. ''It was such a simple dream, the kind every kid should have. Leo's life didn't allow for a lot of dreaming. I didn't have the heart to tell him there weren't any Beatles anymore.''

''Things were bad.'' She'd stopped asking questions and begun offering prompts. Professionally, she felt him sinking into the pseudo-trance her colleagues referred to as ''disassociated recollection.'' Personally, she felt him ripping her heart out.

''Things were bad,'' he concurred. ''His family lived in a one-room apartment in a building with more bomb holes than walls. The place was clean, relatively speaking, but everyone shared one bed. His mother insisted on feeding me each time I went there. I started dropping off bags of groceries to cover the expense. Leo didn't like it. Charity bugged him. But he didn't complain either.''

''I read your series. It was obvious that you cared for him very much. He was very engaging.''

He gave her a wry look. ''*You* read my series?''

''I read the newspaper. I just don't believe most of it.''

Gently, he pushed a lock of her hair off her cheek. "You're right. He was engaging. An amazing kid with an incredible wit. Sharp, talented, bright. I loved to talk to him. I always learned something from Leo." His expression turned rueful. "I'm even pretty good at picking pockets now."

Cammy stroked his arm softly. His expression was beginning to darken. "Did you ever feel that strongly about another one of the kids you wrote about?"

He didn't hesitate before he shook his head. "Never. Leo was unique. If he'd been raised in this country, he could have had every opportunity he deserved. Every door in the world would have been open to him."

"But there aren't many doors there, are there?"

"About the only hope he really had of getting out of that place was joining the army. There weren't a lot of choices, and his family needed him. Hell, they couldn't have survived without him."

"You wanted to help him."

His eyes drifted shut. "Desperately."

She smoothed the frown from his forehead with her thumb. "It hurts when you can't. It's frustrating, and sometimes, it's terrifying. I know how it feels."

He met her gaze again. "I guess you do."

"The kids who come to my sessions—I want to do so much for them."

"Wishing Star helps."

"Sometimes. Not as much as I'd like. You saw it. You wrote about it. Look at Trevor. He has every advantage he can have. He's got great parents. They love him. They have money. He'll flourish. Then look at Amy. What's waiting for her?''

''She told me she wants an implant so she can dance.'' He tapped the box at her waist. ''Like yours.''

Cammy's eyes widened. ''She told you? When?''

''At the session I attended. One of the volunteers interpreted for us. You were working with some other kids at the time.''

''I didn't know. She's never talked about it with me.''

''Big dreams are like that. The less you talk about them, the less scary they are.''

Cammy felt herself move dangerously close to that emotional cliff. ''No wonder.''

''What?''

''No wonder kids trust you. There aren't many people who understand them like you do.''

With a shrug of his broad shoulders, he turned his gaze back to the valley. ''All you have to do is listen.''

''I know. I listen for a living. But you have a gift. They warm up to you so fast.''

''Some people would tell you it's because I'm the same age. It takes one to know one.''

She laughed. ''I guess some would.''

Jackson inhaled a deep breath of the crisp air. ''Unfortunately, I've seen too much to ever pretend I'm a kid again.''

''But you haven't lost your wonder.'' She tapped a finger on his chest. ''That's where it counts.''

Fixing her with an intent look, he captured her

hand. "Dr. Glynn, that's almost a compliment."

"I'm feeling a little loose tongued at the moment."

His eyebrows lifted. "Really?"

"Don't get any ideas. You're not going to divert my attention that easily."

"I could try."

"You'd fail."

"Wanna bet?"

"No. I'd rather hear the rest of the story."

The corner of his mouth twitched. "Sorry, babe, that's some other reporter's scoop."

"Is this your way of telling me we're not going any farther with this today?"

He thought about it, then nodded. "Do you mind?"

She shook her head. "No. You'll tell me when you're ready."

His expression altered so swiftly that it stole her breath. One moment, he was watching her with wry amusement, the next, his gaze turned stark. "Lord, Cammy," he whispered, his large hands coming up to cradle her face. "Where the hell have you been all my life?"

The rest of the day passed quietly. Jackson talked at length with his sisters, while Cammy endured, with her usual grace, the good-natured teasing of his family. Twice, he caught her watching him as he played games with his nieces and nephews. He was almost certain he read a lingering sadness in her gaze, the same sadness he'd seen the night before when he'd joined her on the porch. But she masked it so quickly that he couldn't be sure.

He found himself admitting that he was falling. Hard. Demolition hard.

To describe what he was feeling as just physical attraction or chemistry made it seem unbearably tawdry. Even if he'd wanted to deny it, his conversation with her that morning had cinched it. Thoughts of Leo had come amazingly easy with Cammy. She listened intently, he realized. Perhaps because she'd spent so many years unable to, she'd learned to listen with a deep stillness that drew him. She had none of the nervous gestures or fidgets of average people. Instead, he'd noticed after the first day he'd met her, she could sit, perfectly still, waiting, listening.

There was a calmness about her that offered his too-weary soul a solace it urgently needed. He wanted her, in so many ways. As the sun set, and his family enjoyed the noisy exuberance of the dinner table, he used the chaos to disguise his continued study of her. He saw that she'd noticed that Andy and Tommy, who sat directly across from each other at the large table, continued to pass serving dishes through the hands of adults distracted by the dinner conversation. When Cammy handed over the mashed potato bowl for the third time, she gave Andy a knowing look. The little girl giggled.

Cammy seemed to sense his gaze. She met it across the table. He looked, hard, for that hint of sadness, but it remained firmly hidden behind her glasses and her clear, gray eyes. In the distance, he heard the phone ring and realized that his sister had risen from the table to answer it. Still, he held Cammy's gaze.

She seemed momentarily frozen by his probing glance.

He'd never realized the power of nonverbal communication until he'd met her. He could virtually feel her begging him not to look so closely—to take what she'd offered and leave the rest alone. He was fairly certain he'd have to disappoint her on that count.

"Cammy?" Jackson's sister stuck her head into the dining room. "The phone's for you."

Jackson sent her a sharp look. "Were you expecting a call?"

She looked anxious as she pushed her chair back from the table. "Mike knows I'm here. In case of an emergency." The room quieted as she headed for the kitchen. "I'm sure it's nothing. Probably a patient."

Jackson watched her disappear through the door, hesitated half a second, then rose to follow her. He considered himself fairly expert at studying human behavior. It was what had made him so good at his job. With Cammy, he was beginning to get used to her economy of words. The more agitated she grew, the fewer words she tended to use. The unguarded time she'd spent with him last night, and again this morning, had given him some fresh insights into her complexity. Most people, he'd learned, tossed words around, never thinking further about their import. Cammy picked and chose each one as if it were an expensive purchase. Often, what she didn't say had even more impact than what she did.

That's why he knew for a fact that, despite her outward calm, she was damned nervous about whoever was on that phone. She had a white knuckled grip on the receiver. "When?" Her voice sounded rough.

He heard the deep sounds of a man's voice on the other end. Jackson placed his hands on her shoulders. She frowned at his shirt front. "Are they sure? Did you talk to Brian yourself?"

Costas answered her. Jackson kneaded the tense muscles in her shoulders. "Yes," she said. "Yes, all right." She met Jackson's gaze with stricken eyes. "Thanks for calling."

He pried the phone from her hand. "What's wrong?"

"It's my mother. She's—having a rough night."

"We can be on the road in an hour."

"You don't understand." Her face was a mask of anxiety. "I'm not sure I need to go back. Her doctor called Mike to tell him she's more agitated than usual. They're going to sedate her, see if they can calm her down. He wanted me to know, but I'm not sure it would do any good if I were there."

He frowned. "Why risk it?"

"It could make things worse if I go. I told her I wouldn't be by to see her this weekend. I generally go on Saturdays. This could be—" she exhaled a long breath "—this could be a reaction to the change. If it is, seeing me is going to make her angrier, not better."

His father stuck his head in the door. "Is everything all right?"

"No," Jackson said.

"Yes," Cammy muttered at the same time.

He gave her shoulders a squeeze. "Cammy's mother isn't well. We need to go back tonight."

His father looked at her with a tender sympathy that reminded her of his son. "I'm so sorry, Cammy."

"I—I'm sure she's fine. She's been unwell for some time. The doctors don't think this is really serious."

"Still," Jackson said, "we're going back to Washington."

She shook her head. "I don't want to ruin the rest of your visit."

His father advanced into the room, where he scooped Jackson's car keys off the counter. "Tell you what. I'll go gas up your car while you pack."

"Good idea, Dad. Thanks."

"I'll tell your mother, too," he said as he headed for the door. He shot Jackson a dry look. "She'll want to send food along. She hasn't figured out that there's a fast-food restaurant at every exit."

When he left, Cammy's fingers tightened in the folds of his shirt. "You don't have to go to this much trouble."

"Honey," he tipped her head back so he could look at her. "What's going on here?"

"Mike assured me that her doctor just wanted to keep me informed. There's no cause for alarm."

He thought he detected a note of bitterness in her voice. "If there isn't, there isn't." He tucked a tendril of hair behind her ear. "If we end up with tomorrow free, I'll meet you at your place with a video. You bring the popcorn."

"You could be here with your family."

"Or I could be alone with you. Hell of a sacrifice, I admit, but I think I'll survive it." His gaze narrowed. "Especially after last night. I've been pretty much dying to get you alone."

"This has happened before," Cammy whispered. "I really don't want it to spoil your weekend."

He could see the strain of this new burden weighing her down. He wanted, desperately, to ease it. "We'll have time to talk about it on the way home."

Her stricken gaze met his. "It's not that I don't care."

"I know."

"I'm not even angry with her."

"I know."

"It's so complicated. I just didn't want to drag you into this. It's not fair to you."

He considered her for a moment, then pressed a quick kiss to her forehead. "I'm in, Cam. I think you'd better start adjusting."

By the time they reached the highway, her withdrawal was complete. He felt it. He hated it.

Her cold hand lay passively in his. Her gaze remained trained on the road.

"Do you want to talk about it?" he prompted.

"No."

He waited. She didn't elaborate. "I do," he told her.

That pulled her gaze from the double yellow line to his profile. "You do?"

"Yes."

"All right. What would you like to know?"

He sighed an exasperated sigh. "I don't want a

clinical lecture, Cam. I want you to tell me what's going on inside your head.''

Her fingers trembled. ''Sorry.''

Pressing the back of her hand to his lips, he muttered. ''Me too. I know you're hurting right now. I didn't mean to sound impatient.''

''I have a certain knack for sparking people's tempers.''

''I hadn't noticed.''

''Liar.''

The banter eased his fear. She wasn't lost to him, just distanced. For now. ''You don't have to tell me if you don't want to,'' he assured her. ''I just want you to know that you can.''

''You know, with a philosophy like that, I'm surprised you ever got very far in journalism. What happened to rooting out the truth and uncovering the muck?''

''Why do you think I became a columnist instead of an investigative reporter?''

''You get to work your own hours?''

He laughed. ''Are you kidding? I work everyone's hours but my own.'' He briefly met her gaze. ''I became a columnist because I'm a lousy investigator.''

She shook her head. ''You care too much to stick to hard facts. You like to tell your own story. You don't get hung up on black and white. You're too interested in the things that make the world gray.''

''I think that's the nicest thing you've ever said to me.''

''Don't get used to it. I'm sure I'll find a way to insult you again soon.''

"I'd miss it if you didn't."

"If I run out of material, I'll just borrow some from my mother. She's got a complete arsenal."

He heard the pain behind the quip, and decided to wait. Cammy, he knew, was picking and choosing words again. He was a very patient man.

"She's been in St. Elizabeth's off and on for the past twelve years."

He knew from Cammy's background file that her mother's long history of mental illness had finally resulted in her permanent admittance to the mental hospital. Rubbing a thumb along the back of her hand, he said, "I know. I read that in your file."

"It started a long time ago. She was never chemically or emotionally balanced. She has delusional tendencies, repressed anxiety, and severe manic depression." Her voice had taken on a clinical edge. She could have been giving a briefing to a group of medical colleagues. He recognized it as an evasion tactic, but he forced himself to wait through another extended silence.

When Cammy spoke again, her fingers had tightened on his hand. "She's generally cognizant enough to know where she is. She hates me for putting her there."

He resisted the urge to argue with her, resisted the urge to offer some comforting platitude. Guilt, he knew, could eat a hole in a person's gut quicker than acid. "I'm sorry." He could give her that, at least.

"I really think," she said, her voice painfully calm, "that she actually started hating me long before I admitted her to St. Elizabeth's."

"Cam—"

"No, it's true. My mother always believed that my father resented her for my deafness, and . . ." She trailed off.

"And?"

"Other things."

He wasn't buying it, but he chose not to press. Not yet. "She hurt you." It wasn't a question.

"Yes."

"She still hurts you."

"She's my mother. She'll probably always have the power to hurt me. If I refused to let her inside me like that what kind of person would I be?"

She'd done it again. With a few choice words, she'd blown him away. Cammy had a way of shining a light into his soul that made him see things he hadn't even known existed. Until that morning, when she'd sat in his tree house and calmly told him she didn't expect anything from him that he wasn't ready to give, he'd seriously considered that a part of him had died with Leo. For as long as he could remember, people had demanded that he feel things, say things, write things that would move them.

For years, he'd relished the role.

He enjoyed helping people see things from a new perspective. But in the long days following Leo's death, he'd begun to question everything, from his integrity to his own sanity. Ever-present in his mind was the nagging doubt that he'd pushed too hard, asked too much. If he'd backed off in his pursuit of Leo's story, things might have been different. In the stillness of night, when he had nothing but his conscience and his memories for company, the insidious memory of knowing Leo's life represented award-winning material would creep into his soul and leave a mile-wide path of guilt and destruction in its wake. Somewhere deep inside him, a voice whispered that Leo was dead because of him. And that was the same as murdering the kid himself.

While he'd been writing the series, he'd justified his actions to himself with the idea that Leo's story hadn't changed simply because Jackson had been present to tell it. The world had met Leo through his columns, but the tragic circumstances of the child's life had existed long before Jackson put them in print.

During the weeks he'd spent with Leo and his family, the argument had worked. Jackson had made himself believe it. The sight and feel of Leo dying in his arms, however, had ripped bare the awful truth: he'd become what he despised. Somewhere along the way, with the clamoring of the public and his colleagues in his ears, he'd lost his eye for truth. The stories had become more important than the people. One step at a time, he'd moved so far away from who he was that after he'd taken a hard look at himself he realized he'd lost his way.

And until that morning, he'd more or less convinced himself that he'd never find it again. Then Cammy, who had endured so much more than he ever had, had shown him a picture of grace. He'd almost forgotten, he realized, just what grace looked like.

He clung to her hand, wishing he could absorb some of the turmoil she felt. She'd given him an un-believable gift that day. He wished he could give it back to her. "Cammy." His voice seemed to edge past the tightness in his throat. "Did you know that you are probably the most remarkable person I know?"

In the semidarkness he felt, rather than saw, her surprised look. "Why would you say that?"

"Because it's true. And don't let anyone, especially not your mother, convince you otherwise."

"Jackson—"

"I mean it. You're one of a kind, and I don't think I've ever respected anyone more than I respect you. I've seen a lot of the world. Heck, I've *interviewed* most of it. You have more character and grace than all of them combined. If you find yourself doubting that, I'll be at your elbow reminding you."

"Okay." He almost couldn't hear her whispered response.

He met her gaze again. "And promise you'll trust me."

"I do."

"Promise you'll trust me with the whole story."

She hesitated. "It's not a very nice story."

"But it's your story." He settled their joined hands on his thigh. "That's why I want it."

✧✧
✧ ♡ *ten*

"How is she?" Mike pushed a cup of coffee into her hand.

"About the same." Cammy shook her head. "She's not speaking to me."

"Have you talked to Bruce?"

Bruce Philpott, her mother's psychiatrist, had just left. "You just missed him. He changed her meds."

Mike dropped into the vinyl chair next to her. "How are you doing?" he asked.

She took a sip of her coffee. "Don't you want to know what Bruce prescribed?"

"Not particularly. I'd rather know how my friend is holding up under this kind of pressure."

"I'm surviving."

"Cam—"

She laid her hand on his sleeve. "It's okay, Mike. I'm fine."

"I'm worried about you."

"Think I'm as crazy as she is?"

"I think you've got a right to be mad as hell, and

you're starting to scare me with how rational you are.''

"Nothing's going to change if I get angry, Mike."

"You want my professional opinion?"

"Not really."

"Tough. You're getting it. I don't think it's a question of getting mad. I think you are furious. And the longer you deny it, the worse it's going to get."

"I know the drill, you know. I took Denial 101 as an undergrad."

"Yeah? Then you also know that you can't possibly be objective about what you're feeling." He captured her gaze and held it. "You've got to trust somebody, Cameo. Sooner or later, you've got to unload this."

"It's not a trust issue." His eyebrows arched. "It's not," she insisted. "I just decided years ago that there was nothing healthy about brooding over the hand I got dealt. She's my mother. She didn't always treat me very well, but then, she wasn't exactly mentally responsible, either. So what's the point in taking offense?" At his frustrated oath, she laid a hand on his. "It's okay, Mike. I promise."

"Hell. You make me crazy, do you know that?"

"Yes. Thank you for putting up with me."

"I'm sorry I had to call you at Puller's about this. Bruce seemed to think you should know."

"I'm glad you did."

"Does he think there are any physical symptoms this time?"

"Her heartbeat is irregular, but that's happened before. Bruce told me he'd been experimenting with B_{12}

shots to try and treat her lethargy. It probably reacted, finally, with some of her other medication. She was a little odd when I saw her last week.''

''Odd how?''

Cammy shrugged. ''She mentioned something about expecting my father to take her to an embassy ball. It's been a while since she's lapsed like that. Generally, she's aware that he's gone, just not that he's dead. It's been months since she's referred to him as if they were still married.''

''Hmm.''

She frowned. ''What?''

''I don't know. I'm just wondering if Bruce should have a geriatric specialist check her. I've been reading some things in the journals lately that make me wonder if her physical health isn't more of a problem than we realize.''

''There aren't any indications of that.''

''Still, it wouldn't hurt.''

''No.'' She exhaled a long breath as she leaned back in her chair. ''I guess not.''

''You want me to handle it?''

''Would you mind?''

''No.'' He stood. ''Can I drive you home?''

''I'm going to stay here for several more hours tonight. It generally helps if I'm around.''

''Don't wear yourself out.''

''I won't.''

He frowned at her. ''Promise you'll call if you need anything.''

''Yes.''

''Promise,'' he pressed.

She offered him a weary smile. "I do. I will. Go find your wife."

"All right. I'll talk to Bruce on the way out."

"Thanks, Mike."

He turned to leave, then paused. "Does Puller know what's going on?"

"Mostly."

"Does he know you're spending the night here?"

"I don't know. I had him drop me off."

"Did you ask him to stay with you?"

"He wanted to."

"And?"

She hesitated. "I told him he couldn't."

"You could have signed him in."

"This is a secure floor, Mike."

"You could have signed him in," he said again.

"I know."

"Why didn't you?"

She didn't want to think about it. "I don't know."

"I'll call him."

"Mike—"

He held up his hand. "Don't try to talk me out of it. You could stand to have a little moral indignation in your corner right now, Cam. If you're not going to get mad on your own behalf, somebody should do it for you. Puller's just the guy. This is his thing."

"Mike, really."

"Really." He bent to drop a quick kiss on her forehead. "Trust me. I'm a pro."

Cammy hesitated, then nodded. "All right. Call him. But don't be surprised if this blows up in your face."

He squeezed her shoulder. "It won't. I've got good instincts."

With a sense of resignation, she watched him stride down the corridor. She should have listened, she told herself, to all those warning bells that kept clanging in her head. Sooner or later, Jackson Puller would have to know just why she couldn't let him too close to her. For a few brief days, she'd convinced herself she could forestall the inevitable.

The respite was over. If she'd doubted it before, the hollow wailing that now sounded from her mother's room convinced her.

Jackson paced the confines of his apartment with increased agitation as he lectured himself on the vastness of his own stupidity. "You shouldn't have left her, you moron," he muttered as the pounding condemnation in his head threatened to overwhelm him. He'd been berating himself for the last three hours— since the moment he'd let Cammy flee his car and hurry through the entrance of the hospital. She'd assured him he couldn't go in with her. She'd promised him she was all right. She'd patted his hand and told him to go home and get some rest, that she'd call him in the morning.

She'd looked him right in the eye and lied through her teeth. And he'd let her. "Asshole," he mumbled.

When the phone rang, he dove for it, like a shortstop for a game-winning ground ball. "Cam?"

"No, it's Mike Costas." He sounded grave.

"How is she?"

"I'm not sure."

Jackson's heartbeat kicked into overdrive. "What the hell do you mean, you're not sure? Where is she?"

"She's still at the hospital. She's going to stay most of the night."

Jackson swore. "Is her mother's condition that serious?"

"I'm not sure," Mike repeated.

"Then what the hell do you know?" His frustration seemed to amuse the other man.

Mike's chuckles grated across Jackson's already too tight nerves. "I know that she won't talk to me, and that she needs someone to be at her side tonight."

Jackson didn't hesitate. "I'm on my way."

"They won't let you in the front door. You'll—"

Jackson swore again. "I'm not leaving her in there by herself."

"Ease up, Puller. I was just about to tell you that if you'll meet me at the parking entrance, I'll sign you in."

Jackson dragged a hand through his rumpled hair. "Thanks. Sorry. She scared me."

"Me too."

He didn't like the sound of that. "I can be there in fifteen minutes."

"Bring some coffee. The stuff in the lounge sucks."

"Right." Balancing the cordless phone on his shoulder, he was already scooping grounds into a clean filter. "Anything else I should know?"

"It's not pretty. She isn't going to want you there."

"I know that."

"Cammy's more fragile on this count than she lets on. This isn't something she shares with people."

"Got it."

"She's under a lot of emotional pressure." Mike paused. "Add a healthy measure of guilt to that, and it's a pretty volatile situation."

"Volatile. Right." He switched the coffeepot on, then headed for his bedroom to change clothes.

"I called you because I care about her, Puller. I'm personally and professionally worried."

"I understand. Anything else?"

Mike exhaled harshly. "Yeah. Don't screw up, or I'll kick your ass."

Jackson strode down the sterile hall, his gaze trained on Cammy. She sat hunched in a chair, staring fixedly at a poor copy of Van Gogh's *Starry Night*. She looked like hell. His guts twisted into another complicated knot—their countless turn of the evening. His stomach felt sore from the turmoil. She didn't look up when he reached her. He set the thermos of coffee on the plastic table, then eased into the chair beside her. "Hi."

She met his gaze. Sort of. There was a hollowness in her expression he didn't like. "How did you get in here?"

"Mike." He studied her carefully. "You okay?"

"He shouldn't have called you."

"I shouldn't have left you."

"I told you to."

He shrugged. "Doesn't matter. I shouldn't have left."

"I never would have signed you in."

He reached for her hand. It felt cold. He rubbed it between both of his. "I won't make this mistake again."

"Jackson—"

He shook his head to interrupt her. "It doesn't matter now. I'm here. How is she?"

As if on cue, an angry scream sounded from the room across the hall. Cammy's mouth twitched into a sad smile. "Crazy as a loon."

"Physically?" he prompted.

"Who knows? Her heartbeat's irregular. And she's lapsed into unconsciousness a couple of times. She's not speaking to me." The screaming turned to a howling wail that brought an orderly down the hall. The young man gave Cammy an apologetic look as he hurried into the room.

"Do you want to go in?" Jackson asked.

She shook her head. "It won't help right now—not until she's calmer. She'll get angry if she sees me."

He waited. The pain in Cammy's eyes threatened to undo him. Nothing in his entire worldly existence, he realized, had prepared him for this moment. There was a cauldron of emotion in her that both confused and frustrated him.

And it hurt him, he realized.

At the lacerated look in her eyes, the feelings he had locked away were ruthlessly pushing themselves through the frozen barricades in his heart.

Wanting to offer her something, *anything* that might ease that rawness, he pressed her hand to his lips. "Please, tell me," he said, his voice a low whisper. "Just tell me."

For a moment, he thought she'd refuse. Then he felt the reserve flow out of her as she leaned against his shoulder. He almost drowned in relief. He pressed a kiss to the top of her head as he drew her into his embrace. "There's nothing you can tell me," he assured her, "that I don't want to listen to."

"You're the first guy I ever met who wanted to talk about his feelings."

He managed to choke a laugh past the knot in his throat. "Don't give me too much credit. I want to talk about *your* feelings. Not mine."

She exhaled a slow breath. "Still, I—" she seemed to catch herself. With a brief shake of her head, she gave him an apologetic look. "Sorry. Old habits die hard."

"You're going to have to learn that I'm not easily distracted."

"I'm beginning to get the picture that I may have finally met my verbal match."

He offered her a lopsided grin. "I've been in training my entire life just for you."

"It obviously worked."

"Does this mean you're going to talk to me now?"

Another wail carried through the door. She flinched, but didn't take her gaze from his. "You're sure?"

"Positive."

"You can't say later that I didn't warn you."

"I won't."

He watched her waver in indecision while he silently willed her to trust him. He'd almost given up hope when she finally said, "I've always wondered why our society thinks insanity is funny." She removed her glasses so she could press her face to his chest. "Have you noticed that?"

"Tell me." He threaded a hand through her hair.

"Movies and books, television, it's everywhere. People think insanity is some kind of naive state of bliss where the mind allows its owner to take time off from the pressures of life." The breath she exhaled sounded bone-weary. "I didn't want you to see this."

"It's all right."

She shook her head. "You don't understand. I feel—ashamed."

"Honey—"

"No." She placed a hand on his chest. "Not about this, not about what it's like. I feel ashamed that I didn't want you to know. It makes me feel small. It's not her fault."

He studied her for a moment. "It isn't your fault, either."

Surprise registered in her gaze. He captured the expression and clung to it. "What?"

"It's not your fault."

"I know that. I have a fistful of degrees that say—"

Jackson pressed his hand to her mouth. "You don't have to convince me. I wouldn't have believed you if you told me that about Leo, either. Remember?"

"But, Jackson—"

"I just wanted to make sure you know that I know.

It's not your fault, Cam. I'd never think it was your fault."

She blinked several times and simply stared at him. "No one ever said that to me before."

"I know."

"I didn't think . . . it shouldn't make that much of a difference."

He felt pleased. His anxiety began to fade as he watched her wrestle with the admission. She was coming back to him. "I'm glad I was here to say it."

"I am, too." She sounded shocked.

He found his first smile of the evening. "Do you have to sound so surprised?"

"This is a little new to me."

"You've never been through this with anyone else, have you?"

"Only my father."

"Who wasn't exactly the Rock of Gibraltar."

"He couldn't handle it."

"How old were you? The first time?"

"Thirteen."

He swore. "Lord, Cam."

She laid her hand on his face. "It's part of what makes me who I am. I wouldn't be me without this." With a wave of her hand, she indicated her mother's room. "She has these lapses where she's just completely unreachable. Clinically, we call it severe delusional schizophrenia. It's like a demon overtakes her, and she just can't control herself."

"Does she get violent?"

"Not really."

"Never?"

"She breaks things sometimes."

He released the breath he'd been holding. He wasn't ready for the mental image of Cammy suffering physical abuse. "Has she ever hurt herself?"

"Yes. She attempted suicide twice before I finally agreed to admit her here. She needs constant supervision."

"What did you have to go through to admit her?"

"Hearings. Competency exams. It's not easy. Too many people try to take advantage of the system. There are several safeguards built in."

"It was hard on you." He didn't have to ask.

"I didn't want to do it. No one wants to lock up their parents, even for the best reasons. The fact that she wasn't consistently mentally incompetent made it worse. She'd have long periods of sanity where the bitterness between us escalated. She knew what I was doing, and she hated it."

"There were no other choices, were there?"

"I tried everything. I hired nurses. I worked more and more hours at home. I enrolled her in adult day care programs. But her mind continued to deteriorate until she reached the point where I couldn't leave her alone anymore." She rubbed her eyes with her thumb and forefinger. "Generally, she seems fairly content here. She's bitter, but she always has been. Depression tends to exaggerate destructive personality traits and eliminate positive ones."

He tilted his head toward the door. "How often does this happen?"

"It's happening more frequently." Her eyes drifted shut for long seconds. "Unfortunately, psychiatric research hasn't made many strides in the past several years. We still don't know much about the links between physiological disorders and mental disorders. Several studies have dealt extensively with depression in the elderly, but the subjects are generally well into their eighties or nineties. We don't know much about the disease in younger patients.''

''How old is your mother?''

''She'll be sixty-two in October. Physiologically, her body has the symptoms of a ninety-year-old.''

He absorbed that. ''You don't expect her to live long.'' His voice was just above a whisper.

''The life expectancy for the chronically mentally ill is very low. A lot of doctors believe that as their mind decays, they lose their will to live. Something in their subconscious seems to give up. From the point of diagnosis, they generally don't live more than three or four years. Many die within the first eighteen months.'' She paused. ''My mother has been here permanently for seven years.''

He waited. Long seconds ticked by. Her fingers fluttered over his shirtsleeve in an erratic rhythm. ''Cammy?'' he finally prompted.

She met his gaze. ''There are times when I wish it was over. For her, and for me.''

He sensed exactly how much she'd had to trust him to admit that. From what she'd told him about her childhood, he knew she'd spent a lifetime fearing the unreasonable expectations of a demanding father and irrational mother. She didn't like to disappoint people, but she'd trusted him enough to believe her admission wouldn't shock him. His hand visibly trembled when he lifted it to her face. Tracing the curve of her cheek with the pads of his fingers, he gently smoothed the lines of worry near her eyes. "Thank you," he whispered.

She didn't pretend not to understand. "I'm sorry it's all so complicated."

"No apology necessary." He felt the moment slide away as her expression changed to resignation.

"You're probably wishing by now that you'd picked someone normal to get involved with."

"Honey—" He nudged her chin up with his thumb. "I'm so damned pleased that I finally got you to say that that I'm thinking of sending Chris Harris and Mike Costas each a case of bourbon for their trouble."

"It doesn't count. I'm under duress."

"It counts. I've learned that about you. Every word counts."

Before she could respond, the orderly emerged from her mother's room to give Cammy a grim look. "She's sedated," he announced. "She should sleep through the night, now."

"Thanks," Cammy told him.

"Dr. Glynn, you really don't need to stay. There's nothing you'll be able to do until morning."

"I know."

The young man watched her for several seconds, then shrugged. "Dr. Philpott said to assure you that it's all right if you leave."

"He told me."

His gaze flicked to Jackson. "I'm supposed to make sure all unauthorized personnel are off the floor by midnight.'' He paused. ''It's after one-thirty.''

Jackson tightened his arm around Cammy's shoulders. ''I'm here as long as Dr. Glynn wants to stay.''

''I don't think—''

Cammy interrupted him. ''It's all right, Rocko. We're leaving soon.''

Jackson raised his eyebrows. ''Cammy—''

Rocko looked relieved. ''Thanks, Dr. Glynn.''

''You have my pager number?''

''On record. You know we'll call you if there's any change.''

She nodded. ''All right. We'll go.''

''We don't have to,'' Jackson assured her.

She slipped her glasses back on. ''I want to.'' She glanced at the door. ''I've done everything I can.''

He felt *her* emotional fatigue as she walked with him to his car. She didn't even balk when he informed her that he'd be taking her home. That was his first clue. Whatever was going on in her head, he sensed that there was far more to this incident than met the eye. Cammy was drifting, somewhere on some foreign sea of turmoil where he couldn't reach her. Unsettled and anxious, he drove through the city in silence.

By the time they reached her apartment, she'd grown so still that he thought she might be sleeping. She stirred, though, when he turned into a parking spot. ''Thank you for bringing me home.'' She dug into her purse for her keys. ''I could have taken a cab.''

With an exasperated sigh, he pulled the keys from her still-cold fingers. ''Who ever convinced you that all of life's battles have to be fought in solitude?''

''What?''

''Never mind.'' He reached across her to push open her door. ''I'll walk you upstairs.''

''You don't—''

He kissed her, quickly, to stop the protest. ''I will walk you upstairs.'' He pronounced each word deliberately. ''Stop arguing with me.''

''It's a habit.''

''Just for tonight, what do you say we break it?''

She held his gaze for brief seconds more, then slipped from the car without comment. When he opened the door to her apartment, she seemed to float across the threshold on a wave of fatigue. He took one look at her weary face, then made a decision. He threw the dead bolt home and dropped her keys on the foyer table. No way was he leaving her again. ''Why don't you sit down?'' He indicated the sofa with a wave of his hand. ''I'll get you something to drink.''

She stared at him. ''You don't have to stay with me. I'm going to be all right.''

''I know.'' He walked toward the kitchen. ''Do you want tea, or something else?''

''I'm really fine, Jackson. I've been through this before. I can take care of myself.''

He decided to ignore that. ''Do you have tea in here?''

She'd followed him into the kitchen. ''I don't need you to do this.''

He flashed her a brief smile. ''Humor me.'' Turning his attention back to the open cabinet, he produced a bottle of brandy. "All you offered me was soda."

"That's new. I bought it the morning after you were here."

"So I've driven you to drink," he quipped.

"You have no idea."

He gave her a sympathetic look. "Believe me, I know the feeling. Would you rather have tea or this?"

"I'd rather you left."

"Not going to happen, babe. Sorry." He decided on the brandy. Lord, she looked tired. If he didn't think her nerves were already stripped raw, he'd tell her that she looked like she was going to fall on the floor. "Have a seat. I'll heat this up."

"I don't want you here." Her voice had taken on an edge he'd never heard before.

Instinct told him they were reaching a turning point. She'd trusted him with so much at the hospital. He was willing to bet that she was still reeling from it, and she desperately wanted time to regain her equilibrium. Inclined as he was to give it to her, his gut told him to stay put. Too many people had left Cammy alone too many times. He wasn't about to add his name to the list of deserters. "I'm not leaving, Cam. You're stuck with me."

"You don't understand." Her eyes had begun to glitter. He sensed the emotional storm cresting the horizon and schooled his expression to remain passive. "There are things that I do—ways I have of handling this. They don't include you."

If he had a brain in his head, he supposed, he'd run like hell. She'd given him the perfect excuse. She said she didn't want him. But as he studied her drawn features, the slightly panicked look in her eyes, his heart got in the way. "They do now," he said quietly.

He watched her hands fist at her side. "You can't have this from me. I gave you the rest. You can't have this."

Drawing a deep breath, he plunged ahead. "You aren't going to turn into her, Cammy. It's not going to happen."

"You don't know what you're talking about."

"I know that you're not the same person she is. You're an incredibly passionate, caring, brilliant woman. I wish you could see what I see."

The first tear scalded a path down her cheek. "Damn you," she whispered.

"I don't want you to be afraid of this, of who you are, Cammy. And if you are, I don't want you to face that fear by yourself. Let me go there with you."

"Damn you," she said again, and this time, the storm overtook her. Her shoulders hunched as a soul-deep sob dragged from her body.

Jackson didn't hesitate. He plunked the bottle down on the counter and crossed the room in three long strides. Scooping her into his arms, he carried her into the living room. He settled his large frame on the sofa as he cradled her against his chest. Carefully, he lifted her glasses from her nose, then disconnected her ear piece. Setting both aside, he eased her across his lap so she lay sobbing against him. His heart broke with each jerk of her shoulders. As her tears soaked his shirt, he smoothed a hand through her hair, feeling helpless and irrationally angry at her pain and its causes.

Without the benefit of her earpiece, she couldn't hear him, he knew. He was spared the awkward task of offering meaningless words of comfort. Instead, he gently tendered the only things he knew to give: his presence and his companionship. Too many times, she'd faced this demon alone. She'd told him of escaping to the roof of her parents' home where she'd wished on stars, like thousands of children before her. He had a mental picture of a lonely child, staring into the heavens, confused and hurting. The image struck deep, made his insides ache with the rhythm of her sobbing.

His arms tightened. He buried his lips in her hair. And for the first time in his adult life, he sent a silent plea of his own to the heavens. *Please,* his heart begged, *please help me. I can't lose her.*

✲✧♡ *eleven*

"I can't believe you're canceling." Mike stood at her desk, five days later, glaring at her. "What am I supposed to tell Chris Harris?"

She shrugged. Jackson had called that afternoon to ask her how much she would mind skipping their command performance dinner at the Harris home that evening. She'd assured him she could be talked into staying home for something as uncomplicated as nursing a hangnail. "I didn't cancel. Jackson did."

"What am I supposed to tell Chris?"

"He's Jackson's boss. Let him worry about it."

"You know that the whole point of this thing was so Chris's wife could get the two of you together."

There was that word again: together. When had that become such a complicated concept? Sometime, she imagined, between her trip to his parents' home and waking up on her sofa with him. "Then she should be pleased. I'm seeing him tonight. We're just not going to dinner at the Harrises'."

"Why not?"

"I don't know. He didn't tell me."

Mike's eyes narrowed. "*You're* doing something spontaneous?"

"Don't look so shocked. I am capable, you know."

"Just not prone." He pursed his lips for a moment. "Maybe this guy is better for you than I thought."

She winced. For a week, she'd buried herself in enough work to keep her mind off Jackson Puller. At least, she'd tried. The fact that he'd called three or four times a day, attended both of her sessions with the children, turned up at lunch one day with Chinese takeout, and generally managed to edge his way into her thoughts whenever she lowered her guard had wreaked havoc with her well-planned strategy. As much as she wanted to deny it, he'd knocked her for a loop.

When he'd arrived at the hospital, she hadn't been sure what to expect. Nothing could have prepared her for waking up, still wrapped in his embrace, stretched out on her couch. He hadn't fled, or tried to extricate himself from the messier details of her life. He'd cushioned her head on his chest and stayed the night. When she thought about it, it made her head spin.

She'd hurried him out of her house, using some hastily concocted excuse about meeting with doctors and discussing her mother's case. He'd looked doubtful, but he'd succumbed.

The respite from his probing gaze appeared to be short-lived.

By Tuesday morning, a knot of queasy anxiety had begun to form in the pit of her stomach. She'd entered her office to find him waiting with a bag of pastries and two cups of coffee. He didn't give any indication that he'd given any deep thought to the other night. Instead, he'd inquired about her mother, then gracefully accepted her unsubtle change of subject. They'd discussed her morning session, talked about Jackson's interview with Amy, and the progress he was making on his second column.

He told her his parents had sent their regards and expressed their concern for her mother. She searched, hard, but found no signs of reticence or withdrawal in his expression or manner. She'd been sure she could show him the insurmountable odds they faced. He, however, refused to fall in line with her very sensible plan to convince him why he couldn't afford to get involved with her. Instead, he'd brought her Szechwan Chicken for lunch the next day.

And she felt herself slipping into a warm, blanketing haze that the warning bells couldn't penetrate.

"Cammy?" Mike's voice pulled her from her reverie.

She gave him a sheepish look. "Sorry. I was lost in thought."

"You were mooning." He sounded amazed.

"I was *not* mooning. I never moon."

"I know."

"Don't get carried away, Mike. Jackson and I are friends." His eyebrows lifted. "Good friends," she clarified.

"Are you going to tell me what's in that shopping bag you have under your desk?"

"How do you know about that?"

"While you were out, I came in to steal chocolate. I saw the bag. Very swank place. Not your usual style."

She folded her hands on top of her desk and tried not to think of the small fortune she'd spent on the black dress. "I needed something for the Wishing Star fund-raiser."

"Which is two months away."

"They were having a sale."

"And it wouldn't have anything to do with the fact that Puller called and asked you to wear black tonight?"

"How do you know *that*?"

"Stripped the message off the answering service. If you don't want me to know stuff, we should get separate numbers."

"Or you could have punched the button to skip it when you knew it was for me."

"I'm getting old. My reflexes are slow."

She rolled her eyes. "And I'm Marilyn Monroe."

"You might be in that dress."

"Did you look at it?"

He didn't even have the grace to look repentant. "Absolutely. Bess is going to want a full report."

Cammy laughed. "Mike, you're hopeless. If your wife knew how much stuff you blame on her, she'd kill you."

"I never pretended not to be curious."

"Nosy."

"Or nosy," he agreed. "Besides, it's a killer dress. Do I get to see what it looks like on?"

"No."

"What if I tell you that you can have the rest of the afternoon off to go buy slinky lingerie?"

"I don't need slinky lingerie. You don't control my hours, and if you weren't my very good friend, I'd warn you that you're dancing very close to sexual harassment."

"Hah. If anyone's harassed in this office it's me. My partner is snuggling with Super-Scoop and I have to cull the details from phone messages and credit card receipts."

"Don't feel left out. I think I'm in the dark as much as you are. He's something of an enigma."

"The two of you should be well-suited, then."

"I guess."

Mike's expression turned suddenly serious. "Kidding aside, Cam, I know this has been a rough week for you. Try not to let fear get in the way of following your heart."

"Sometimes my heart wants to go where it shouldn't. That's a lesson I've learned in life. It's not always a bad idea to burn a bridge *without* crossing it first."

"Your head doesn't always know best, either," he grumbled. "I'd give you a lecture about not allowing past experiences to dictate current responses, but you wouldn't listen."

"Probably not."

"So will you at least promise me that you'll try to enjoy the moment?"

The moment, she decided three hours later, would be easier to enjoy if she didn't feel like she was about to fall off a cliff. She squinted at her reflection in the mirror in her office. Without the benefit of her glasses, her image was a bit blurry. Not blurry enough, however, to make her secure with the picture she presented. What in the world, she wondered, had possessed her to buy this dress? Tugging at the hem, which seemed a full three inches shorter than it had in the store dressing room, she turned to look at the back. Had she simply failed to notice the way the oval cutout in the back revealed such a generous expanse of skin, or had that been a trick of the light?

She'd fallen for it, she supposed, because the cowl neckline gave her a place to hide her cochlear transmitter. She'd been able to disguise it in the folds of the dress rather than clipping it to her waist. Consequently, the black crepe skimmed her figure in uninterrupted lines that displayed every curve to advantage.

As if the dress, which dipped too low in the back, showed too much of her legs, and fitted too closely in the front, wasn't bad enough, she'd allowed Macon to talk her into a trip to the salon. While Macon's hairdresser had used scissors and a comb to attack her very sensible haircut, Macon had distracted her by talking about her publicity plans for the Wishing Star fund-raiser. By the time Cammy knew what was happening, René was blowing her hair dry.

When he finished, he spun the chair with a flourish. Cammy had stared at the mirror with the same sense of unreality she felt now. She hardly recognized herself. René and Macon called the scrunched, windswept look "sexy modern chic." As far as Cammy could tell, she looked like she'd spent four hours in a convertible. For the hundredth time that day, she resisted the compelling urge to take a brush to her hair. Besides, the dress seemed a more pressing problem.

The low whistle from the doorway clinched it. She was *not* going out like this. Gathering what she personally thought was admirable poise, she turned to face Jackson. He leaned against the door frame, looking positively devastating in a black suit and pristine white shirt. She was almost glad he was far enough away to look a little fuzzy. If he looked any better in focus, she might melt.

Jackson strode across the room in his characteristically long-limbed stride. The closer he got, the faster her pulse beat. By the time he stood a foot away, she was foundering about for something, *anything*, that might help her remember all the rules she kept firmly in place to keep her out of precisely this kind of trouble.

He didn't give her a chance to find one. He cradled her face in his hands and bent his head for a long, thorough kiss. As his lips glided over hers, and his fingertips caressed her sensitive skin, she curled her hands around his wrists. She seriously feared her knees might buckle beneath the sensual onslaught. When his tongue darted out to trace the curve of her lips, she sighed softly. He muttered a soft oath that sounded an awful lot like a compliment, then tore his lips from hers to trail a delicate path along her jaw. When he finally reached the juncture of nerves at her collarbone, she was clinging to him. A soft moan escaped her. At the sound, Jackson lifted his head.

The gleam in his eyes sent a shiver down her nearly bare spine. Her gaze remained riveted to his warm, firmly chiseled mouth. "Hello."

She wasn't sure if he'd said the word, or if he'd simply mouthed it. The blood roared so loudly in her ears that she couldn't hear. "Hi."

His hand skimmed her arm, her rib cage, the underside of her breast, then settled firmly at her waist. "Can you hear me?" he asked.

She blinked. How had he known? "What?"

"Your transmitter," he clarified. He touched the ear piece in her right ear. "You're not wearing the receiving box."

The fog finally lifted. "Oh." She forced her fingers from his wrist to touch her neckline. "It's in here."

Something flared in his eyes. Even his temperature seemed to raise a notch. She had a sudden heightened awareness of his scent. Soap and cologne and printer's ink mingled to intoxicate her. "Are you trying to kill me?" he rasped.

Her eyebrows lowered in confusion. "What?"

His gaze went meaningfully to her neckline. "First, there's this dress." His hand brushed her side as he moved it to the bare flesh of her back. "Which would have been a pretty solid line-drive double all on its own." His other hand twined a tendril of hair on his index finger. "Then there's your hair." He shook his head slightly, "which could more or less guarantee the outfielder is going to juggle the catch, and you can make it to third without even sliding."

Her lips twitched. "You really know how to charm

a girl, don't you? Sports talk always makes me swoon.''

He shifted his hips against hers, pressed her a little closer so his loose embrace turned intimate. ''And then, just to make sure there's no contest here, you tell me that little black box is buried somewhere,'' his gaze shifted meaningfully, ''down there. Which just about ensures that I'll spend a good portion of the evening wondering what would happen if I went looking for it.''

A surge of pure feminine power raced through her. And she liked it, she realized. ''Do I get a home run for that?''

''Honey,'' his gaze lifted to hers, ''you get me as your personal slave for the night for that.''

Despite his jesting tone, the remark sent sparks skittering through her blood. ''Oh.''

Jackson laughed. ''Never had one before, have you?''

''A what?''

''A slave?''

''Um, no. I had a dog once. And Charley Patterson had a crush on me in the third grade, which was somewhat slavish in nature, but this is a first.''

He ran one hand down her arm to lace her fingers with his. ''Want an etiquette lesson?''

Her eyebrows lifted. ''Exactly what do you know about having a slave?''

''I did a story, once, in Burma, where I enjoyed the attentions of a devoted personal servant.''

''Female, I presume?''

''Naturally.''

"That's barbaric."

"She didn't think so."

"I'll bet."

His lips twitched. She wished he'd stop doing that. Every time his mouth moved in that half-smile, her insides quaked. "Anyway, she taught me a few things."

"Oh, I can imagine."

"Can you really?"

She fought a blush. "Um-hmm."

"I had no idea."

"I have an excellent imagination."

"I used to think I did, too," he assured her.

"What changed your mind?"

"I saw you in this dress and found out I hadn't even come close."

Absurdly pleased, she drummed her fingers on his shoulder. "Confession time?"

"If you want."

"I wasn't exactly prepared for the way you'd look in this suit, either."

"And here I thought you were only interested in my, uh, rear attributes."

Cammy remembered their conversation from the coffee shop with a slight laugh. "I didn't say that was the only thing that I found interesting."

"You know, this conversation gets better and better."

"Actually, I'm much more interested in your mind than your visual layout."

"Like gentlemen who read men's magazines for the content?"

"Uh-huh. Like that."

"Is this a good time to tell you that I've never met a man who has actually even looked at one of the articles?"

She schooled her expression into shocked inquiry. "No?"

"Not a single one."

"So you're not buying it?"

"Not for a second. Guys make that up to snow women."

"It doesn't work."

"Really?"

"Nope. I've never actually met a woman who believed it." She met his gaze then, and allowed herself to drown for a moment in the sea of sensual promise she saw in his eyes. "Want to know another secret?"

"I'm on pins and needles."

"Your visual layout just about knocks my socks off."

He blinked, then lifted her hand to his mouth to press a soft kiss to her palm. "Ditto, kiddo."

Cammy exhaled a slow breath. "So, now that we have that settled, are you still willing to be seen in public with me?" She glanced over her shoulder at the mirror. "I hadn't realized this dress was quite so—"

"Devastating?"

"Revealing," she corrected. She touched the soft cowl of the bodice. "I bought it because of the neckline."

"Nice choice." His gaze rested there.

She thumped his shoulder with her forefinger.

"Lech. I meant I liked the fact that I could hide my transmitter in there."

"It doesn't hide much else."

"I know. Maybe I should change."

"Don't even think about it."

"I have a reputation to protect."

He laughed. "Trust me, honey. This dress, the whole package, as a matter of fact, is a complete knockout, but it's not going to get you arrested."

"I feel like it is."

"I like it."

"You're kidding." Her voice oozed sarcasm.

He pressed his hips closer, just enough to let her feel how much he liked it. "It's perfect."

She raised a hand to straighten the knot of his tie. "Macon picked it out."

"Then we're even. My mother picked my suit."

"Excuse me?"

"No kidding. My mother dressed me."

"She has very good taste."

"I wore this to my sister's wedding. Mom was afraid I'd show up in jeans, so she bought the suit for me."

"Does she know it makes you look lethal?"

"I don't think so. I guess she figured I wouldn't get a lot of wear out of it, so black was a safe bet. My mother's very frugal. She probably plans to bury me in this."

Cammy slipped her hand into his breast pocket, where she felt the steady thrum of his heartbeat. "Nope." His eyebrows lifted. "It's not a funeral suit," she explained. "It has pockets. Funeral suits don't have pockets."

"That's a charming thought."

"I have a fifth cousin who's a mortician."

"So you don't think she picked black to make it all-occasion?"

"I think she picked black because she knew you'd look delectable in it."

"Delectable?" An amused glint filled his gaze. "You know, I think I might reconsider my sense of fashion. I'm not normally the suit type."

"I hadn't noticed."

He ignored her quip. "I haven't worn it since the wedding."

"And you put it on for me? I'm impressed."

"You haven't begun to be impressed tonight."

"Has anyone ever told you that you have something of a humility problem?"

"Do you think so?"

"I told you before, I don't think there's a thing in the world wrong with your ego."

"I should probably warn you. It's going to get hugely inflated after I introduce you as my date."

She was starting to feel warm, inside and out. "It is?"

"Sure. First thing people will want to know is how a guy like me snagged a hot-looking dame like you."

She almost laughed out loud. Jackson Puller's face had been making female hearts quicken for years. "Must have been the suit."

"That's what I'm thinking. I'll have to remember to tell my mother."

"Do me one favor?"

"Anything."

"Don't tell her it made my knees weak."

"Gentlemen never kiss and tell."

"I wasn't aware you put yourself in that category."

His laugh rumbled along her nerve endings. "Rarely."

"What's different about tonight?"

So quickly it stole her breath, his expression turned serious. "A lot, Cammy. There's a lot different."

"I didn't mean—"

He pressed a long finger to her lips. "Shh. I know. I just wanted to say that I understand this week has been rough on you. Just for tonight, I wanted you to have permission to run away for a little while."

"Run away?"

"Retreat. I want us to go somewhere quiet and safe and peaceful where you can just relax."

"You should have told me to wear sweats."

Instead of taking the bait, he shook his head. "I wanted magic, Cam. For both of us. I wanted this to be like magic."

Fear goaded her to make another quip, but the intent look in his eyes stopped her. "It's always magic with you," she blurted.

His eyes widened for a moment, then turned indescribably tender. "You say the most amazing things."

"You make me feel them."

He kissed her again, a soft kiss, rife with promise and latent hunger. When he finally raised his head, her breathing had turned feathery. "If you're ready," he said, his voice a rough whisper, "we should go."

"Are we on a timetable?" Her voice sounded as gravelly as his own.

Briefly, he cupped her face in his hand. "No, honey. We've got all night."

With the promise hanging in the air, he tucked her hand in his and led her to the door.

Jackson leaned back against the wall of the U.S. Naval Observatory and breathed a deep sigh of contentment. Until that instant, he wasn't sure he'd made the right choice about the evening. Her week, he knew, had been hell. Her mother had made little progress. His second column had set off a firestorm of phone calls and information requests that had had her doing paperwork into the small hours of the morning. He knew her well enough to know that she'd used the deluge of mundane details to divert her attention from the more pressing problem of her mother's health, and, unless he missed his guess, from him. She'd made herself vulnerable to him. It scared her. He fully understood that, and also understood that she needed some leverage back to feel secure again.

So he'd picked tonight, and this place, to tell her the whole story about Leo.

As if she sensed his contemplative thoughts, she flashed him a gentle smile. "How did you do this?" she asked as she gazed in wonder at the large telescope. They were alone, with a broad canopy of stars overhead, a picnic dinner spread on a blanket, and the quiet thrum of the telescope for companionship. In one corner, a portable CD player pumped seductive music into the still atmosphere. The evening's arrangements, he'd found, had been as complicated as planning an inaugural gala. He'd pulled so many strings that week that his fingers should have blisters. And it had all been worth it for the look of tender wonder in her eyes.

He eased away from the wall. "I know a guy. He owed me a favor. I cashed it in."

Her eyes widened. "*You* pulled strings?"

"You'd be amazed at what I'd go through for you."

"I am," she assured him.

He studied her for long seconds, wondering why he always felt this nagging fear that somehow, she'd slip away from him. "You are?"

"You doubted it?" Her gaze narrowed.

"I'm never quite sure with you."

She blinked. "You're kidding."

"No. You're complicated. You know that."

"I never really thought so. I always seemed pretty simple to me."

He shook his head. "No way. There are more layers to you than baklava."

"Thanks. I think."

He managed a slight smile. "I meant it as a compliment."

"Then I'll take it as one." She narrowed her gaze. "Is something wrong, Jackson? You seem . . . distracted."

Ruthlessly, he pushed aside the lingering sense of fear that she was dancing just beyond his reach. "I'm fine. Just a little dazed from your compliment."

Her quiet laugh chased away his lingering doubts.

"Very smooth." She turned back to the telescope. "Can we use this?"

"Yes. Burt focused it for us. Just look through here." He came up behind her, then indicated the view glass with a tap of his fingers. "The heavens are yours."

Her hands cradled either side of the view glass. "No one ever offered me the heavens before."

"I'm glad I could be the first." He wondered if she could hear his voice catch.

She gazed through the glass with an exclamation of wonder. "You should look at this. It's beautiful."

"It pales next to you," he said quietly.

She shot him a teasing look over her shoulder. "Exactly what are you trying to accomplish tonight, Mr. Puller?"

His hands settled at her waist. "The impossible," he muttered.

"What?"

With a slight shake of his head, he guided her away from the telescope. "Never mind. Are you enjoying yourself?"

"It's magic," she assured him. "I never met a man who could work magic before." She returned her attention to the telescope while he fought for emotional balance.

Being told in the span of ten minutes that he was the first guy to give her the heavens *and* that she found him magical was enough to make his head spin. Cammy was not a woman who used words lightly. She meant what she said. Always. It was one of the many things he found so disarmingly attractive about her.

As he studied the tilt of her head, the slight wonder in her expression, he decided in that instant that, no matter what it took, he'd make everything all right. Together, they'd be incredible. He was sure of it. He needed her in so many ways.

The hunger to assuage those needs had begun spreading like an ache through him for weeks. It had come as something of a shock when he'd realized that the insatiable longing he felt involved her needs as well as his own. He needed to ease the worry from her eyes. He needed to hear her laugh without reservation, knowing he'd played a role in helping her get there. And he needed her to see herself as he saw her. She did something for him no other woman, no other *person*, ever had. He felt stronger with her than he did by himself. She reminded him, somehow, of the life-giving roots of a tree.

The thought made his lips twitch. He'd used a lot of lines on women. Some had been glamorous, others poetic, some even hokey. But even he had never stooped to telling a woman she reminded him of a root. She'd probably deck him.

With a soft laugh, he pressed his lips to her shoulder. Cammy gasped and turned from the telescope. "You're distracting me."

"That's the general idea."

"You went to all the trouble to arrange this, and now you don't want me to look?"

"Would it help if I told you that I'm famished, and

I'm hoping we can get to that meal over there before I get weak in the knees?''

With visible reluctance, she dropped her hands from the view glass. ''I suppose after you did all this''—she indicated the room with a sweep of her hand—''the least I can do is let you eat.''

He didn't give her a chance to change her mind. With a hand at the small of her back, he guided her to the blanket. ''Thanks. I'm getting light-headed.''

''I'd like to see that.''

''It's ugly. Trust me.'' He helped her settle amid the overstuffed pillows before he levered himself down near the basket. ''I hope this is good.''

''What is it?''

''I haven't got a clue. I have a friend who's a caterer. I pulled in a favor with him, too, and he sent the meal and decor over this afternoon.''

''*Another* favor? I had no idea.''

She really didn't, he thought wryly as he considered the numerous phone calls he'd made to secure access to a government facility after hours—a government facility that normally gave public tours at this time of night. It had taken a laundry list of promises and some pretty serious maneuvering, but the look on her face had been worth it. He plucked the top off the picnic basket then reached inside with a slight smile. Pulling out an elaborate-looking confection made with slices of star fruit, he showed it to her. ''Look. Theme food.''

''Very impressive. Are there Milky Ways in there?''

"You'd eat cheap chocolate?" he quipped. "I'm shocked."

"I'll take it almost any way I can get it. Now you know. I'm easily seduced."

A jolt of electricity shot through him. He was fairly certain his hand shook. He didn't trust himself to respond to that. Instead, he finished emptying the basket. He left only the last dish in the bottom. "Well, we won't go hungry anyway."

She looked dazed. "A small army wouldn't go hungry."

"I told my friend you were a big eater."

She hurled a strawberry at him. "Who are you kidding? I watched you down three pounds of bacon and a half-dozen biscuits at your mother's house."

"I was trying to be polite."

Her eyes twinkled, and he found it absolutely enchanting. "You're a glutton."

"Maybe." He removed the last dish. It held something dark and rich and undeniably chocolate. Tilting it so she could see it, he added, "But if you're not nice to me, I won't let you have any of this."

"You would, too."

"In a heartbeat, babe."

Cammy laughed, a fresh laugh that held none of the stress of the previous week. At the sound, warmth flooded him. "You're impossible."

"And you're adorable." He leaned closer to her so he could catch the scent of her perfume. It was subdued, but a little spicy. Like her. His head started to swim. "Do you know that?"

She tilted her head to one side. "You're on especially good behavior tonight."

"I talked to my niece this week. She gave me a few pointers."

"They're working."

"Are they really?"

Cammy reached for a plate. "Absolutely. You may tell her that I'm very impressed."

"I hope so," he said as he spooned various dishes onto her plate. "I've got big plans for the evening."

✨💗 *twelve*

Cammy allowed her eyes to drift shut as she listened to the steady rhythm of his heartbeat. They'd talked of nothing, and of everything, while they'd explored the various offerings in the picnic basket. Jackson had a way of listening to her that quickened her heartbeat and, she was sure, made at least some of those stars above their head lodge right in her eyes. Half-reclined as she was, with her head pillowed on his chest and his arms wrapped comfortably around her, she tried to remember a time in her life when she'd felt more at peace—more right.

And she came up short.

The idea made her smile. Here she'd gone and fallen—hard, fast, and irrevocably—for a *reporter*. Her father was spinning in his grave. And in the back of her mind lurked the terrible knowledge that her happiness couldn't last. Jackson needed more than she could ever give. But for tonight, in this place, with the stars as a ceiling and the gentle caress of his hands on hers, she shoved aside the doubts and the fears that had driven her for so long. If she lost him—when she lost him—she'd have memories like this to hold on to.

"What are you thinking?" His voice was a low rumble.

She drew a deep breath. If she told him she was thinking about the inadequacies of every idea she'd ever had of love, it would probably scare him to death. "I'm thinking," she shifted in his arms, "about what in the world I could have done to deserve this." She indicated the room with a sweep of her hand. "I'm smart enough to know you had to pull a lot more than a couple of strings to make this happen."

"It wasn't that bad." She looked at him with raised eyebrows. "It wasn't."

"How much positive press coverage did you promise away this week?"

The laughter in his eyes made her heart race. "Some."

"How much?"

"Fishing for compliments?"

"Trying to assuage my guilt."

"A lot."

"In laymen's terms."

His arms tightened. "Enough ink to fill a vat."

"I thought so."

He ran a hand up her arm. "I know what kind of week you've had. I'm pretty well known in this town, and you are too. I was afraid if I took you somewhere public, we'd have to answer questions. I wanted you all to myself." His eyebrows lifted in amusement. "Of course, if you'd warned me ahead of time about this dress, I might have made other plans. A guy's ego could really benefit from being seen with a woman like you.''

She laughed. "You're right about one thing. If we'd gone to a restaurant, you'd have been mobbed. And it has little or nothing to do with me. Your presence seems to have an astounding effect on people. I noticed it at the dance recital.''

"People in Washington are easily impressed by anyone they feel is in a position to do them a favor.''

"Just tell me you don't have to write restaurant critiques for your friend the caterer, and I won't feel so bad.''

He laughed. "I promise. Although I could probably do a fairly impressive job of summing up the decadence of that dessert.''

"I don't doubt it.''

"And''—he stretched out an arm to scoop up a folder he'd placed on the blanket—"speaking of articles, here's Monday's installment.''

"Is this the last one?''

His lips twitched. "I decided to do four. I'm a little enamored of my subject.''

She set the folder aside with a slight smile. "You're not much for subtlety, are you?''

"Never gets you anywhere.''

Turning slightly so she could lie on her side and closely observe his face, she traced a finger along a wrinkle in his shirt. "Actually, your blunt approach seems to be having something of an effect.''

"You don't say?''

A smile played at the corner of her mouth. "And

not just on me, either. I didn't have a chance to call you this afternoon and tell you what happened today." She'd been getting the haircut he couldn't seem to stop touching.

"Good news?" He twined a tendril around his finger.

"Extremely. Doctor Cornelius Van Root from the Sillred Institute read your last article."

"I'm very impressed."

She pinched him lightly. "You don't have a clue who he is, do you?"

His eyes twinkled. "Guilty."

"You know, you really should read my press releases."

"I'd rather hear it straight from you. It turns me on to watch your lips."

She deliberately ignored him. "Dr. Van Root is the world's expert on cochlear implants. He's the foremost surgeon in the field, and he specializes in difficult cases."

His expression turned serious. "He's interested in Amy?"

"Yes. He's flying through Washington this weekend on his way to an international medical conference, and he's agreed to examine her tomorrow afternoon."

"No kidding?"

"Nope. If Dr. Van Root believes she's a good candidate for an implant, he said he'd donate his surgical time. Wishing Star would finance the hospital costs and the implant and Amy's transportation to California."

"That's great."

"Incredibly great. I never dreamed I could get someone of Van Root's caliber on board. Not only can he help Amy but his support of Wishing Star will go a long way toward helping hundreds of other children, too."

"I'm glad."

"It's because of you."

"It is not," he insisted. "You're the one doing all the work. I just write it down."

She smiled at him. "Don't be modest. It doesn't suit you."

"It's true. I just tell stories, Cam. That's it. The story is only as good as the person it's about."

"You're a very nice man, you know."

His hands tightened at her waist. "I'm awfully glad you think so."

She laid her head against his chest again. "Anyway, the piece you did on Amy was more than I could ever have hoped. I'm very sorry I doubted you."

"You're forgiven."

Several heartbeats passed while she gathered her courage. "Jackson?"

"Hmm?" He sounded sleepy.

"I—I don't think I ever thanked you for what you did the other night."

"You didn't have to."

"Neither did you." She held his gaze. "I know it wasn't exactly a walk in the park for you."

"You were hurting, Cammy. I wanted to be there for you."

"I don't think you can possibly understand what that means to me."

"You don't?"

"No."

"I do."

She lifted her eyebrows. "What do you mean?"

"Honey, you sat in a tree house with me and listened." He brushed a tendril of hair off her forehead. "You didn't push me. You didn't lecture me. You even resisted the urge to share your analysis." He managed a slight smile. "You just listened to me. No one's ever done that before."

Her eyebrows knit together. "No one?"

"Not that I remember. My job, hell, my life, is made up of people who want something from me. You're the first person I've known in a long time who just takes me as I am."

"That's what friends are for, Jackson."

"How do you know?"

She smoothed the frown from between his forehead. "I have friends, you know?"

"I know. I just don't like to think of how much crap you carry alone. It shouldn't be like that."

Long seconds passed while she studied his face. "No one should grieve alone," she finally said. "Not even you."

A long breath left his body. "You know, don't you?" he asked.

"That you want to talk about Leo?"

He nodded.

"Yes. I know."

"*How* do you know?"

"You read faces for a living, and follow your instincts. I read faces, too. I just have different reasons.

I've known since you walked into my office tonight.''

"Do you mind?"

"Of course I don't mind. I think you need to talk about it, and I'm very glad you're willing to share it with me."

"I thought you wanted me to call Costas."

"I think Mike could help you professionally." She laid her hand against the column of his neck. "But I'm not going to listen to you as your doctor, I'm going to listen as your friend." Her thumb skimmed his jaw. "I'll take whatever you want to give me."

He swallowed. Hard. Then he pressed her head against his chest again. "I know how hard it was for you to trust me about your mom. I want you to know that."

"Yes. It was."

"At first I thought I could give you this so you'd feel like we were even."

"Psychological tit for tat?"

"Something like that."

"But now?"

"I don't want to carry it around anymore."

She nodded. "I understand. Make the pass, Jackson. It won't be nearly as hard as you think."

Almost a full minute passed while he wrestled with demons and she waited, still and silent.

"He had so much life," he said at last. "There was an energy in Leo that just sparkled. The entire time I was with his family, I kept trying to figure out how to get them out of there."

"How long have you had this addiction to saving the world?"

"Years. I guess. I think it started when Billy Phillips tried to beat up my sister in fifth grade."

"Only jerks beat up girls."

"Jordan wasn't exactly a typical girl. I think she took the first swing."

"And Billy swung back?"

"Yeah. He was twice my size, but I couldn't stand it. I dove on him and started beating the snot out of him."

"Did you get hurt?"

"Split lip."

"What about Billy?"

"Broken nose and a black eye." She heard the slight smile in his voice. It felt like a positive sign.

"And you saved Jordan?"

"I thought so, anyway. It felt good."

"So you kept on doing it."

"When the opportunity presented itself. I told you the other day that I've seen a lot of kids get stepped on. It bugs me."

"That's what makes you a good person."

"With Leo's family, though," he shrugged, "it was different." The tip of his forefinger traced a lazy path over her hand. "I *needed* to save them. For Leo's sake, I needed it."

"Did they want saving?"

"I don't know. They'd never known another life. Especially not Leo and his brothers and sisters. Even before his father's death, they were used to dodging sniper fire on their way to the market."

"What was a day in the life of Leo like?"

His chest ached with the force of emotion. "Explosions and gunfire echoed through the streets.

Everything was dirty, half-burned or destroyed. Leo thought nothing of finding a corpse in the street. He usually checked the body for valuables without even breaking his conversation with me. It's how they survived. He stole almost everything for them. His sister's prized possession was a plastic necklace he'd swiped from a dead tourist.''

"And you hated it."

"What I hated was the fact that adult problems had stolen his childhood." He paused. "I loved that kid. In many ways, he reminded me of myself. He had big dreams. Somehow, in the middle of all that, he'd managed to hold on to his wonder."

She smoothed her hand across his shoulder in a gentling caress. "What happened the day he died?" she finally asked.

A silent war raged in him. The tension in his muscles, the shallow rhythm of his breathing, the tightening of his hands on her shoulders all told her he was struggling. "I wanted an ending for the series," he said. "I wanted something that would show the stark contrast between Leo's life and the war on the streets. Somehow, I felt like I could capture that juxtaposition and make the war stop. If the war stopped, Leo's life would become normal. It sounds crazy."

"No, it doesn't."

He uttered a harsh curse. "I don't know what I was thinking. I was so captured by the entire thing—more involved than I should have been. It wasn't just a story. It's always supposed to be about the story. But it wasn't. I was seriously involved this time."

''That doesn't make you a bad person, Jackson. You know that.''

He ignored her. ''I took risks. I let Leo take risks.''

''Jackson—''

''No.'' His voice sounded raw. ''You don't understand. For days, Leo had been offering to take me into the west quarter of the city. The fighting is the worst there. It's dangerous, and I knew it. I wouldn't let him go.''

''But on that day, you did?''

''Yes.'' He fell silent. ''Aren't you going to ask me why?''

''Do you know why?''

''Because I'm a selfish bastard.''

She shook her head. ''No. You couldn't have known what would happen.''

''Would you let a kid guide you into the southeast section of this city?''

She leaned back to meet his gaze. The ravaged look in his eyes hurt her. She had to carefully school her expression. ''That's a ridiculous question. Did you consider, even once, that you might be putting Leo in danger?''

He hesitated. ''He made it easy to forget how young he was.''

''He knew the streets, Jackson. He knew how to survive.''

''I shouldn't have let him go.''

''How exactly did he get caught in that explosion?''

His eyes drifted shut. ''The guy driving the car stopped it in the middle of the street and fled. He left the driver door open. Leo wanted the radio. He took off for the car before I could stop him.''

''You suspected the bomb?''

''Something made the driver abandon the vehicle.''

''And before you realized it, Leo was in the car?''

''I was instructing my photographer. I turned around in time to see him climbing in. I shouted. He waved to me. And it blew up.''

''Oh, Jackson.'' She pressed herself tight against him. ''I'm so sorry.''

''The force of the blast ripped through a building. Everyone was screaming. I ran for the car. I pulled what was left of him out of the wreckage.''

''I saw the picture.'' The photo of Jackson, surrounded by a ball of fire, carrying a badly burned child, had run in every newspaper in the country.

''My photographer took it.''

Long moments passed. She wrapped her arms tightly around him, trying to absorb some of his grief. ''Was Leo dead when you reached him?'' she asked quietly.

''No.'' His body shuddered. ''I got him away from the car. He was still breathing. Most of his body was burned. He was in horrible pain. I kept talking to him, telling him I'd get help, threatening him. I did everything I could think of.'' His expression was ravaged. ''The last thing he did was ask for his mother.'' Wetness made his eyes gleam.

An answering tear slid down her cheek. ''Have you told anyone else this story?''

He shook his head. ''I finished my last article for AW, then I helped Leo's mother take care of the funeral arrangements. I dug his grave myself. I begged her to let me relocate her, but she wouldn't budge. Her entire life was there. I left her some money.'' He threw his head back with a harsh groan. ''God. I took her kid, and I left her a thousand dollars in cash. What the hell does that say about me?''

''What do you think it says?'' Her heart was breaking, but she carefully prodded him for the whole truth.

He wiped his eyes with the back of his hand. ''It says I'm a self-interested asshole who cared more about a damned story than I did about a kid's life. And now,'' he went on ruthlessly, ''they want to give me an award for it—a bunch of 'em, in fact. In the eyes of my media colleagues, I'm a hero because I didn't let my personal feelings get in the way of the story. I let a kid get blown up so the world could know what a rotten life he had. Can you believe that?''

She gripped his upper arms. ''Do you believe it?''

''Of course I believe it, Cam. Leo's dead, it's my fault, and I walk away from the whole thing with awards and honors for my trouble.''

Long seconds passed. His heart beat a pounding rhythm against her ear. ''Is it true?'' she finally asked.

''Is what true?''

''Is it true that you cared more about the story than you did about Leo?''

She felt him stop breathing, felt the stillness settle on his large frame. His mind virtually hummed while he probed the darkness within, looking for answers.

Cammy laid her hand against his face. ''Find anything?''

He shook his head. "No."

"Want some help?"

"Desperately."

"If you'd known that car was going to explode, would you have taken Leo into that part of the city?"

"No."

"If someone had told you that helping you would get him injured, much less killed, would you have allowed him to tag along?"

"No. Absolutely no."

"But you've convicted yourself anyway?"

He looked at her with a blank expression. "What?"

"If you believe it's your fault, despite the evidence to the contrary, then I can't talk you out of it. Do you want me to try?" He probed her with his gaze. She shrugged. "Ask yourself this question: what could I say to change your mind?"

He stared at her for long seconds. "Nothing," he answered.

"Exactly. No matter what I say, you're going to believe that Leo died because of you until you're ready to believe otherwise." She laid a hand against his cheek. "It doesn't matter that the man I know would have given his life for that child. Or that I believe Jackson Puller is an honorable, decent, caring human being who would never put his aspirations above the welfare of another person. Or that you would have done anything in your power to prevent Leo's death."

"Cammy—"

"It was awful, Jackson. I know that. I can't even imagine what the experience was like for you. Life hurts. Sometimes, it downright devastates. What happened wasn't fair or right or good, but because of you—because of your memories, and your stories, and your strength—a part of Leo is still alive. Sooner or later, that part will be the thing that heals you.''

"Sometimes I think it's going to kill me.''

"I know. It sneaks up on you, doesn't it?''

"Yes.''

"And there are times when you think you can't take another breath because the pain is so bad?''

"Yes.''

"But then you do, and the world keeps moving, and you keep moving, and the next thing you know, you have it almost under control again.''

"Something like that.''

"Grief takes time, Jackson. It hurts, but it finally passes. It is the guilt that will destroy you. You've got to find a way to let it go.''

"How am I supposed to do that?''

She smoothed the lines from around his eye with her fingertip. "All right. Let's say it was your fault.'' His eyes widened, but she continued. "Let's say you were reckless and you subjected yourself, your photographer, and Leo to unnecessary danger. If that's true, it was a dreadful mistake. You showed a serious lapse in judgment, and as a result, someone else got hurt. Did you mean for it to happen?''

"No.''

"Did you know there would be a bombing that day?''

"Of course not. Cam, I—''

"Wasn't sniper fire the most serious danger in the area?"

"Probably."

"And did you already consider that a young native child wasn't at any real risk from the snipers? Didn't an American journalist and photographer provide larger, more likely targets?"

He paused. "Yes."

"Did your photographer feel that the danger was too great a risk? Did he try to talk you out of going to that sector that day?"

"No."

"So ask yourself," she said quietly. "Did you really contribute to Leo's death, or was it an unbelievably tragic set of circumstances that happened to catch you in the middle?"

"I don't know."

"And you don't have to know," she assured him. "Not now. But even if you made a terrible mistake, a mistake with horrible consequences, it doesn't have to destroy you." She paused as she studied the intense look in his eyes. The subtle shift in his expression told her he was starting to come back to her. "I can forgive you," she whispered as she trailed her fingers over his eyebrow, "because there's nothing to forgive. But you can't forgive yourself right now. If I could, I'd absorb all this pain for you."

"I don't—"

She pressed a finger to his lips with a sad smile. "But I can't. So will you at least let me bandage a few wounds and clean your stitches?"

The ravaged lines on his face had begun to ease.

"Why are you so good to me?" he asked.

"Because you're good to me." She studied him for a moment. "I've never felt closer to a person than I feel to you."

His eyes drifted shut. "Have I ever told you how much the stuff you say affects me?"

"No." Her breath caught.

"Sometimes, we're cruising along having a perfectly normal conversation, and then, *wham*, one sentence will hit me out of the blue."

Cammy swallowed the sudden dryness in her throat. "I think that's the nicest thing you've ever said to me."

His eyebrows lifted. "You're kidding. It's not exactly poetic."

"Yes, it is. You have no idea how much I love the way you listen to me. Or what it does to me."

"We're evenly matched, then. You talk. I listen. And the next thing you know—it's fireworks."

Lord, he made her feel good. Smoothing a dark wave of hair off his forehead, she pressed a kiss to his chin. "Fireworks. Really?"

"Absolutely." His voice was still a little hoarse, but the turmoil seemed to have quieted.

"Hmm." She nuzzled his throat.

"Cam?" He tipped her head away, his warm palm cradling her face. "What are you up to?"

She studied his eyes. Grief still lingered there, but she sensed the peace in him. Telling the story had freed him of its grip. "I'm wondering just how much it would affect you if I reminded you of the conversation we had on your parents' porch."

He went as still as a breezeless day. "What?"

She ignored his strangled tone as she turned her face to kiss his palm. Spending time with Jackson had shown her an entirely new side of herself. Not in a million years would she have pictured herself telling him that night that she'd been ready to escalate their physical and emotional relationship. And here she was, ready to do it again. A part of her recognized that she wanted to give him this, this affirmation of life, to help ease his pain, but another part, the braver part, told her the truth: the man absolutely amazed her. "I've been thinking about that," she whispered.

"So have I. Night and day."

"In psychology, we call that an abnormal preoccupation."

"Obsession is more like it."

"You're sure?"

His eyes sparkled. "Honey, believe me. It's my body and my psyche. I'm sure." He eased his arm from around her shoulders and reached into the picnic basket. "Before we go any farther with this conversation, which I can pretty much guarantee is going to make me crazed, I have something for you."

"I can't eat another thing."

He playfully tugged a lock of her hair. "It's not food. It's a present."

She looked at him curiously. "Really?"

"Really." He handed her a rolled parchment. Cammy gave him a curious look, but accepted the paper. She untied the blue ribbon so she could open it. The certificate had been issued by the International

Star Registry. It pinpointed a specific star and named it: STARLIGHT, STAR BRIGHT. An astrological chart showed the location of the star, and assigned ownership to Dr. Cameo Glynn.

"I never had my own star before."

"All those wishes," he murmured. "I thought I'd give you a place to direct them."

Her heart swelled. She pressed a soft kiss to his mouth. "You are the most remarkable man I have ever known."

"I'm awfully glad you think so. I also think that if you don't let me off the hook soon, you might have a certifiable nutcase on your hands. You're destroying my brain."

"How could I possibly resist a man who gave me the stars?"

He clasped her hand in his and pressed it to his chest. The steady thump of his heart echoed her own. In a voice so raw that she recognized the urgent need in it, he whispered, "I need you, Cammy."

The simple admission captivated her. To the best of her knowledge, she'd never been needed before. The rawness she saw in his gaze revealed both his hunger and his hurt, and she was powerless to resist it. Like a flame, it beckoned her. Even if it burned her alive, she realized, she longed to feel the heat of it. He had given her an indescribable gift tonight, and no amount of fear, or doubt, or hesitation would stop her from returning it to him. She drew a deep breath. "I know the feeling."

His gaze darkened. "I can wait," he assured her, "I'm just not sure how long."

Resolute, and slightly giddy from a surge of adrenaline, she pressed a soft kiss to his lips, then met his gaze. "What's wrong with right now?"

✶✮♡ *thirteen*

Jackson pushed his way through layers of sleep, dimly aware that the blissful lassitude couldn't possibly last. His limbs seemed sensitized, his nerve endings thrummed with subtle energy. He hadn't felt this rested, or refreshed, or at peace since the day Leo had died.

The realization opened the floodgate of his memory. His eyes popped open, and he took a quick assessment of Cammy's bedroom. In the adjacent bathroom, the shower was running. His suit jacket hugged the ladder back of a chair. The black dress hung in the closet. His shirt lay across the end of the bed.

And contentment filled every muscle in his body. He spent one long minute savoring the absolutely mind-shattering feeling that coursed through him. There was every possibility that he'd never felt this good. She had responded to him with a deeply sensual abandon that had aroused him like nothing before. He'd realized one of the most profound moments of his life the instant she'd clung to his shoulders and found fulfillment in his arms.

The second and third times, inconceivably, were even better. With a deep growl of satisfaction, he tossed the sheets aside and strode to the bathroom. If he knew her as well as he thought, he'd bet real money she was in there trying to pretend that the events of the previous night hadn't irrevocably altered the course of their relationship. And he wasn't about to let her get away with it.

He pushed aside the shower curtain with a broad sweep of his hand. Cammy faced him, looking terrified. Too late, he realized she could never have heard his approach. Her cochlear transmitter and earpiece sat on the vanity. With a repentant smile, he stepped into the tub, then pried the soap from her white-knuckled grip. "Sorry," he signed. "Didn't mean to scare you."

She watched him, wariness and uncertainty filling her gaze. He found the idea of chasing away that look so fulfilling that he almost didn't recognize the slight feeling of unease that threatened to dissolve the rosy haze of serenity.

It niggled at him for a full half hour before he put a name to it. They were dressed, and she was toasting a bagel, and he was toweling the remaining dampness from his hair when he realized, with a sense of shock, precisely what was making his stomach clench with anxiety.

He loved her. And it scared him to death.

He drew in a shaky breath as he carefully placed the towel on the counter. She wasn't going to like this. He had a very distinct, very certain feeling that Cammy wouldn't like knowing he'd placed a name on his feelings. Especially not *that* name.

How many times had she told him she wouldn't get involved with him? A less intuitive man, he supposed, might assume that, after last night, they were as involved as two people could get.

He knew her well enough to know there was nothing uncomplicated about what had happened between them last night. He'd stake his life on the fact that she didn't have much experience, an insight which had made her sweetness and her passion all the more electrifying. She hadn't rushed into bed with him for some emotionally detached one-night stand. It had meant more than that to her. He'd also bet that she'd known it would happen from the minute she'd put on that black dress. She had planned his seduction. And it had been absolute.

He'd spent the entire night completely under her spell. She'd been in control, just as she'd planned. He studied her now, with her hair pulled into a loose ponytail, her oversized sweatshirt masking all the curves he'd adored during the night. On the surface, she showed none of the emotional turmoil he felt, but he sensed it. The physical link between them only served to deepen his developing understanding of her. At times, he almost felt like he read her mind. With his own feelings held so deeply, he was especially attuned, he found, to hers.

And unless he missed his guess, she was struggling to maintain distance, regain the upper hand she'd previously held. Her body was calm, but her mind was in overdrive. Somehow, she was trying to find a way to hold him at an emotional distance despite the very real intimacy of their physical relationship.

He didn't know why, and he couldn't identify just what it was about her countenance that made him so sure, but he *knew* she was fighting him.

So he made a characteristically rapid decision. This would be something, he thought, like the time he had accompanied his father on a deep-sea fishing expedition. The objective was to give the fish enough line to make it think it had a fighting chance. Too tight, and the line would break. Too loose, and the fish might squirm away. A strategy of give and take, coupled with patience and strength, was needed to assure victory.

The analogy almost made him laugh out loud. Last night, he'd mentally compared her to the root of a tree. Today, he was looking at her like she was a three hundred and fifty pound marlin. Here he was in what was probably one of the most abstruse moments of his entire life, and the best he could come up with was a fishing story. The woman was doing serious things to his mind.

And he liked all of them.

He liked them so much that he was just about ready to drop to his knees and beg her to keep doing them. But he'd give her, he decided, enough line to keep her from panicking. He could give her time to get used to the idea—days, and the fates willing, nights, to realize that she was meant to belong to him. He wouldn't scare her, he'd nurture her. He wouldn't push, he'd persuade. And before she knew it, he'd have loved her so thoroughly, so completely, that whatever fears she had would have simply evaporated. The very thought made his flesh tingle.

He crossed the kitchen to wrap his arms around her waist from behind. The slight stiffening of her spine made him smile into her hair. Patience and persistence, he reminded himself. He'd built a career on those two principles. He was very, very good at them.

Tipping his head to nuzzle her neck, he whispered, "What are the chances"—he nipped her earlobe— "that I can talk you into canceling your plans for the rest of the day?"

She spread butter on the bagel. "Nil. I've got too much to do."

Her skin tasted like baby powder. He never thought he'd find that so sexy. "Okay."

She tipped her head to give him a surprised look. He took full advantage of the new angle by capturing her lips. When he finally raised his head, her glasses were askew. He straightened them for her. She blinked at him. "Okay?"

He nodded, then scooped up the bagel. "Sure. Whatever you've got to do, I'll do it with you. That way, we'll get it done twice as fast, which leaves more time for," he lifted his eyebrows, "other things." He took a hefty bite of the bagel.

"That wasn't for you," she told him.

Grinning apologetically, he held it to her lips. "Sorry. You eat the rest."

She hesitated, but took a bite. While she chewed, he rubbed the smeared butter from her lips with the pad of his thumb. The shiver that ripped through her made his blood sing. "I could take you out to breakfast," he offered.

She shook her head. "No time. You, uh, slowed me down in the shower."

"Oh really?"

"Yes. It doesn't normally take me thirty-five minutes to take a shower."

His mouth twitched at the corner. "How long does it take?" He pressed the bagel to her mouth again.

"About twenty." She took another bite.

"Me, too. So you see, if we shower together every morning, we're saving five minutes of hot water. I read somewhere that five minutes of hot water equals five thousand recycled aluminum cans. I'm willing to do my part for the environment if you are."

That won a smile. "Who's going to do *my* part for my water bill?"

"We'll split the routine. One week at my place, and one week at yours. We'll both come out ahead, and we'll save the environment."

"You're incorrigible."

"And you're adorable, and I'm totally infatuated."

She slipped from his embrace before he could stop her. "I'm also late. I've really got to go."

"And I really want to go with you."

She gave him a surprised look as she put the bagels and butter back in her refrigerator. "You can't."

"Why not?"

"Because I'm going to see my mother."

"So?"

"So, you can't come."

"Doesn't that place have visiting hours?"

"That's beside the point. She doesn't know you."

"I took you to see my mother."

"Your mother's not a raving lunatic."

He recognized the quip as an effort to put him off. He stood his ground. "You should see her when she's angry."

"Jackson—"

He crossed the room in two quick strides. "Honey, listen." Raising her hand, he pressed a kiss to her fingers. "I am not making fun of you. Please understand that."

She hesitated, but she finally answered him. "I do."

"Thank you. I just want to share this with you."

"I don't—"

"I know you've never done it this way before. I understand that, but I don't want you to keep being alone. You look sad." He pressed a finger to the corner of her eye. "I see it in your eyes, and it hurts me. You helped me with Leo."

"All I did was listen. I didn't even give you decent advice."

"You helped me," he insisted. "If nothing else, you told me it was okay to feel rotten about it."

"Of course it's okay."

"You'd be surprised how many people don't believe that. In the world beyond trained psychiatrists, grief has a timetable."

"I know."

"After a few weeks, sometimes months, the world moves on. It leaves you in the dust, and it moves on.

People don't care that you're still bleeding—they just don't want you to drag them into it.''

"Disassociation," she muttered.

He sensed the battle in her and refrained from pressing. There was something significant in the way she said the word, he was sure of it. He filed it for later as he pressed his thumb to the pulse at her throat. "So, you helped me. And I want to help you."

She studied his face for long, tense seconds. He pressed her hand to his chest. "Let me at least drive you to the hospital. If you don't want me to go in, I won't."

Her expression altered, subtly. "I have to go from the hospital to pick up Amy. Her appointment with Doctor Van Root is this afternoon at George Washington Medical Center."

"Fine. We'll take her together. I need to swing by my place in Georgetown to change clothes, then I'm yours for the day."

"You're making me crazy."

Relief poured through him. He sensed her surrender. "Fair's fair. You've been making me crazy for weeks."

"I've been trying to tell you that since the day I met you."

"And mule that I am, I wouldn't listen."

"I'm not exactly sure why I keep putting up with you."

He snaked an arm around her waist so her body aligned with his. "Aren't you?"

"Contrary to male fantasies, women aren't nearly

as easy as men to manipulate with physical attraction.''

''Want to test that theory?''

''Not this morning.''

He gave her a quick kiss. ''All right. I'll take a rain check.''

''And you're sure I can't talk you out of going with me today?''

''Positive. Unlike you, I happen to be very easy to manipulate with physical attraction.''

''As long as you get your way.''

His grin was shameless. ''I think you're catching on.''

It was a hundred times worse than he'd imagined. Every time Laura Glynn aimed a verbal barb at Cammy, he had to remind himself that the shrew was out of her mind. She wasn't responsible, Cammy would tell him, for the things she said, or for the effect they had. Still, he was having a hard time keeping a rein on his mounting anger. Someone should have told that woman years ago that lunacy didn't give her a license to wound people.

Laura gave him a scathing look. ''I suppose you slept with him?'' she asked Cammy.

Jackson's teeth clenched. Cammy didn't falter. ''I'm not sixteen, Mother. I'm old enough to make choices.''

''Bad ones. You know what will happen if your father finds out.''

''He won't.''

Laura turned her bitter gaze on Jackson. ''He'll kill

you. You might not think so, but he will. He won't hesitate.''

"Is he that protective of his daughter?" he asked.

Laura's laugh sent a shiver through him. "Are you kidding? Durstan doesn't protect anyone but himself. You're a reporter, and Cammy slept with you. God knows what she's told you. He'll never tolerate it.'' She looked at her daughter. "You've really made a mess of things this time, haven't you? You should have stayed with Leslie. At least your father liked Leslie. He'll blame this on me, you know. It'll be my fault for giving you too much freedom.''

"It's no one's fault, Mother.''

"Who's going to tell him that? He'll ignore me for weeks because of this. You know that, don't you? He'll be screwing his mistress just to make me angry.''

"Will it?" Cammy prompted.

"Hah. Do you think I care who he screws? He's a pig. Don't ever think your father is anything but a pig. He hates you, and he hates me.'' Laura wiped a hand over her face. "I keep telling you that, but you're always on his side. You're a fool to trust him.''

"I'm not on anyone's side, Mother.''

"Yes, you are. You believe your father. You think I'm crazy.'' She looked around the room. "You put me here.''

"You were sick. You needed help.''

"So you locked me up with a bunch of crazy people. That must be very convenient for you. Tell me, does Durstan enjoy telling the world they should vote for him because his wife is a lunatic and his daughter is a cripple?''

Jackson wanted to throttle her. He wanted to grab Cammy's hand and get her away from the venomous fury that hung in the room. As if she sensed his unease, Cammy gave him a quick glance that made him hold his tongue. She was assessing him, he realized, making mental notes on how he was handling the situation. He made a conscious effort to ease his tense posture as he gave her a reassuring smile.

She met her mother's gaze once again. ''Mother, do you know that Durstan is dead?''

Only a vacant look registered in Laura Glynn's eyes. Cammy waited several seconds, then leaned closer to the bed. ''Do you know that he's dead?''

Nothing. ''Do you?'' Cammy persisted.

Laura finally looked at her with anger-filled eyes. ''The bastard wouldn't give me the satisfaction,'' she ground out. ''He'd never die and let me be free of him. He's too selfish.''

''He's dead, Mother. He's been dead a long time.''

''You're lying.''

''Why would I?''

''You're taking his side. You always do. Never mind that he treats you like dirt. I don't know why you do it, Cammy.''

She shut her eyes. ''I don't. You know that isn't true.''

''It is. And I want you to leave.''

''I wanted to stay with you a little longer. Has Doctor Philpott been to see you lately?''

Laura turned her head to stare at the pale green

wall. Cammy tried again. "He was going to bring another doctor this week. Did you like him?" Nothing. The silence expanded. "Did he tell you anything?"

Laura still said nothing. Cammy exhaled a long breath and patted her mother's hand. "It's all right. We'll talk about it next time." She rose to go. Jackson couldn't get to her fast enough. He looped his fingers beneath her elbow and walked with her to the door.

When they stepped outside, she refused to meet his gaze. "Was it everything you expected?" she prompted.

He stopped walking. "I hated it."

That got her attention. She turned wounded eyes to his. "Thank you for telling me the truth."

"What am I supposed to say? That it was easy for me to listen to that? It wasn't. I hated hearing it. I hated watching you hear it."

"I warned you."

He closed the small space between them to cradle her face in his hands. "I hated it because you have to live with it. Every day. I hated it because I don't like to think of you listening to all that anger and bitterness. Not now, and especially not as a child."

"It's worse lately."

"I don't care. I hate thinking of you agonizing over it. I hate that your father made you cope with it alone."

"Jackson—"

He gently tightened his hold. "And I hate that you still don't think you can trust me with how it makes you feel."

"You're here, aren't you?"

"Which is more than you've ever given anyone else?"

She hesitated. "Yes."

"Welcome to a shift in thinking. You're not scaring me off."

Before she could respond, someone called her name. "Cammy?"

She turned to face the man making his way down the hall. "Bruce," she said. "How are you?"

"Good. I'm good." Tucking his clipboard under his arm, he greeted her with a warm hug. "It's really good to see you."

"You too. I'm sorry I missed you the other night."

"I'm sorry I had to call you."

She shrugged. "I'm glad you did."

The man's curious gaze turned to Jackson. He extended his hand. "I'm Bruce Philpott. Cammy's mother is my patient."

"Jackson Puller." Shaking the man's hand, he assessed him and the decidedly warm way he looked at Cammy. People, he realized, were naturally drawn to her. She had an uncanny ability to give affection without demanding any in return. What was offered, she rarely accepted. As he reached for her hand, he added that observation to his emerging portrait of the woman he loved. Lacing his fingers through hers, he ignored her not-so-subtle efforts to shake him loose. "Cammy and I were just visiting her mother."

"I'm pleased to meet you. I've admired your work—especially the series you're doing on Cammy."

"Thank you."

"I was on my way in to see Laura," Philpott told them, "but I'm glad I caught you. Have you got a minute to talk, Cammy?"

She nodded. "Of course."

He slid Jackson a curious look. "Do you, uh, want to talk in my office?"

She paused, then shook her head. "No. It's all right if Jackson hears what you have to say."

Philpott nodded. "She's not doing well. You know I had a geriatric specialist over to look at her chart, do a few tests."

"Yes."

"It's bad, Cammy. Her blood toxins are up, her white count is low. Her liver has never been good, but it's gotten significantly worse. Her heart is weakening." He laid a hand on Cammy's shoulder. "She's giving up."

"Is there anything you can do?"

"I don't think so. We've increased her pain medication, and I'm keeping her fairly sedated most of the time."

"I don't want her to be in pain, Bruce."

"No one does. We'll do the best we can to control it."

When Cammy's fingers fluttered in his, Jackson felt it throughout his body. She showed no other signs of distress. "How long do you think she has?"

"I don't know," Philpott conceded, "but not long. If her health continues to deteriorate at this pace, we'll need to think about some serious decisions in the next few weeks."

Cammy nodded. "I understand."

"I'm sorry."

"I know you are, Bruce." Her smile was sad, and it twisted Jackson's heart. "That's why I picked you."

He glanced at Jackson. His eyes seemed to send a silent message that difficult waters lay ahead. "I'll call if there's any change," he said to no one in particular.

"Thanks," Cammy told him.

Philpott nodded at Jackson. "I'm sorry we didn't meet under better circumstances."

"Me too." He released Cammy's hand, then slid an arm around her waist. He sensed the battle she was waging to keep her calm facade firmly in place. As clearly as if she'd said it aloud, he heard her begging him to get her out of there. "We're on our way to another appointment," he told Philpott as he guided Cammy toward the elevator. "Is there anything else we can do here?"

"No. I'm going in to examine Laura, but I don't expect to find any change. The night staff report didn't indicate anything to be concerned about." His gaze met Cammy's. "I can page you if there's a problem."

"I'd appreciate that."

Philpott nodded. "All right, then. I'll talk to you soon, I'm sure."

"Thank you, Bruce," Cammy told him as Jackson nudged her slightly forward.

"My pleasure."

Jackson got her into the elevator before he felt the

storm start to break. Her face was a rigid mask of conflict. When he sandwiched one of her hands between his, her fingers were cold and trembling. "Cammy—"

A slight shake of her head stopped him. "Outside," she said quietly.

He took the cue and waited.

By the time they emerged on the street, she was gasping for breath. She had virtually run the final few steps to the door, fled the inquiring glances at the nurses' station, then bolted onto the sidewalk. She leaned back against the brick wall and sucked in a deep breath of the warm air. "Sorry," she mumbled. "I'm sorry."

He braced one shoulder against the wall and watched her. "You don't have to be sorry."

"I hate that place. Have I ever told you how much I hate that place?"

"No."

"It's like a prison. It suffocates me."

"I'm sure it does."

She didn't seem to hear him. "Every time I come out of there, I feel like I can't breathe—like I barely escape with my life. It's ridiculous, I know. I'm sorry." She pressed her fingertips to her temples.

He resisted the urge, barely, to pull her into his arms. Inside him, a cold knot of anger still twisted when he considered the brutal onslaught of emotional stress that had formed the better part of Cammy's life. He almost wished Durstan Glynn wasn't dead. He'd like to have a whack at him. "Can I help you?" he said quietly.

She shook her head. "No. It's silly. I know it's silly."

"Wrong again, Dr. Glynn." He tapped her head with his knuckle. "There's an awfully good brain in there. Put it to use."

The incredulous look she gave him helped calm his nerves. "What are you talking about?"

"Well, hell, Cammy. Anybody would be rattled by that. I'm rattled, and she's not even my mother. She's cruel to you—" Before she could interrupt, he pressed a finger to her lips. "And I don't give a rat's ass that you don't think she's responsible for what she says. She's out of control, and you have every right to be angry and hurt. Just because you know a lot about what's wrong with her doesn't mean it can't still piss you off."

She stared at him for the space of several heart-beats. "I don't think—"

"For what it's worth, it pisses me off, too. Hell, I wanted to strangle the woman. I almost told Philpott he should go in there and smack her around a little."

"She's ill."

"Yes. She's also bitter and unreasonable and self-ish."

"She can't help it."

"Maybe not, but so what? Where did you get the idea that just because she's got a mental illness means you aren't supposed to resent what she did to you?"

"It wouldn't do any good."

"Sure about that?"

"Of course I'm sure."

"Funny." He braced one hand near her head. "I

know this really brilliant woman psychiatrist. She gives just about the best advice of anyone I've ever known. And she told me that anger is a very healthy, and sometimes necessary, part of the human experience.''

''I did *not* say that.''

''Who says I was talking about you?''

She frowned at him. ''Jerk.''

''Honey, listen to me. You are the smartest woman I know. You can figure this out.''

Her eyes drifted shut. With her head tipped back against the wall, she looked impossibly vulnerable to him. ''Come back to me,'' he said softly.

She met his gaze. ''I'm here.''

''Are you sure?''

She hesitated, then nodded. ''I'm sure.''

''I think that a part of you is still smeared on the wall in her room.''

''Maybe a few stray pieces. Nothing crucial.''

He clasped her upper arms. ''I like all your pieces the way they are. I don't want to misplace any.''

A shadow crossed her gaze. ''Jackson—''

He shook his head. ''It was a joke, honey. Maybe not a good one, but a joke. If you want to talk about this right now, I'm willing to stand here all day.''

''But you'd rather not?''

''I didn't say that. I think there's a storm brewing in you, and it's got to come out sooner or later. I just want you to know I'll lash myself to the mast and weather it with you. I'm not a quitter.''

Some of her mantle of despair seemed to lighten. ''I really love that poetic streak you have.''

"No kidding?"

"No kidding. I've never known a man who liked words as much as you do."

"Then let me give you a few more." He cradled the back of her head in his hand. "I'm acting on instinct here, sweetheart, so I'm not going to push you. I'm still a little giddy from last night, and I'm hoping to hold on to that feeling a little while longer."

Her half-laugh warmed his blood. "Giddy? What happened to the man of steel?"

"Wrong reporter, babe. That's Clark Kent."

Her fingers toyed with the collar of his denim shirt. "I'll bet there's a super hero in here somewhere."

"I'm thrilled you think so."

"Tried leaping a building lately?"

"Tripped over my coffee table last week."

"Hmm." She laid her cheek on his chest. "Faster than a speeding bullet?"

"I can run a forty-five minute mile."

She giggled. Dear God, he loved that sound. "More powerful than a locomotive?"

He quit resisting the urge to gather her close. With her pressed against him, and the feel of her hair tickling his chin, the world seemed to right itself again. "Anytime you're ready," he assured her, "I'm willing to listen."

"What if I'm never ready?"

He considered that for a long minute. "You will be."

"You're sure?"

"I'm sure."

"Why?"

"Because I never thought I'd tell Leo's story to anyone, and you made it happen. When I'm with you, I'm stronger than I am by myself. I'm banking on that being true for you too."

Seconds ticked by. Finally, she nodded. "It is."

His heart swelled. "I'm glad." He tightened his arms. "I'm very, very glad." Savoring the moment, just like she'd taught him, he tucked it away for safe-keeping. "Now, may I make a suggestion?"

"Does it involve going back inside?"

"No." He stroked her back. "Amy's appointment isn't until three-thirty, you said?"

"Yes."

"Why don't we go pick her up and take her to the zoo? I'm sure she's nervous. She could use the distraction." And so could you, he silently added.

"She'd love that."

"I would too."

✧✧ ♡ fourteen

Fighting a wave of sadness, Cammy burrowed deeper into her couch and tried, for the fifth time, to concentrate on the novel she was reading. In disgust, she set it aside to bury her head in her hands. Nothing had helped her shake the gloomy feeling she'd experienced since Jackson had dropped her off that evening.

In fairness, she admitted, it had actually begun early that morning, but she'd managed to ignore it until her apartment's cloak of silence had swallowed her whole. She'd almost invited him in, simply to delay the moment of her emotional reckoning, but, with his usual uncanny intuition, he'd recognized her need for privacy.

"Feeling a little unbalanced?" he'd asked seconds after kissing her senseless just inside her doorway.

She'd managed a slight nod.

"Me too. You do that to me, you know?"

"Jackson—"

"It's okay. I'm learning to like it."

She had known she was clinging to him but couldn't seem to stop. "Thank you for everything you did today."

The trip to the zoo had been a stroke of genius on his part. Amy had enjoyed herself immensely, and the hours had quickly passed until her appointment. Cammy's mind had refused to dwell on the darker events of the morning while surrounded by the warm glow of Jackson's companionship and Amy's uninhibited glee.

By the time they'd reached the medical center, Cammy had managed to conquer the lingering depression she felt from the morning. Dr. Van Root had been professional and encouraging, if not conclusive, in his evaluation. He'd asked to take Amy's test results back to his office for further study before giving them a definitive answer, but Cammy, and, more importantly, Amy felt positive about the experience.

It wasn't until she'd settled into Jackson's car for the ride back to her apartment that the threads of panic began to re-form into a cold knot in her stomach. By the time they'd reached her door, she couldn't decide if she wanted to beg him to stay or demand that he leave. Fortunately, he'd taken the responsibility off her shoulders.

He had seemed to sense her confusion, so he'd kissed her lightly once again, then set her gently away from him. "I'm going to go home," he'd announced. "Unless you want to ask me to stay."

At her hesitation, he'd nodded. "That's what I thought. If you want some space, I'll give it to you. But if you need me, all you have to do is whistle."

She'd glanced at the clock on her mantel. It had been barely after six o'clock. "What are you going to do for the rest of the evening?"

"Are you kidding? I'm going to go home and stare at my phone all night, hoping you'll call me."

"I'm not—"

"Shh." He'd shaken his head. "No explanation necessary."

"Thank you."

"You're very welcome." Hesitating, he'd taken her hand in his to kiss her palm. "Promise me that you'll call if you need anything. It doesn't matter what time."

"I thought I was supposed to whistle."

His lips had twitched at the corner, damn him. He had to know just what kind of effect that had on her. She practically swooned every time it happened. "Whistling works," he'd assured her. "I like the puckering up part best."

"You would."

"You bet." His expression had turned serious again. "I'm not leaving until you promise."

"I promise."

"You're sure."

Nodding, she'd said, "I'm sure."

And he'd slipped through her door, leaving her alone in the cool silence of her home.

For the past three hours, she'd tried to busy herself with something, anything, to take her mind off her confusion. She'd worked on her plans for the Wishing Star fund-raiser. She'd gone over case histories for several new patients. She'd called Macon for a recipe. She'd taken a shower.

And then she'd settled on the couch with the very grim feeling that she should never have allowed things to go so far. She knew that—had even warned herself countless times since the day she'd met him.

But he'd laid bare his soul to her last night. And his vulnerability had battered the walls of her resistance into oblivion. He'd needed her. And she'd needed him. So she'd allowed that night to happen, despite the very high price that came with it.

Now, she felt like they were living on borrowed time. He may not fully understand the ramifications, but she did. She could never be the woman Jackson Puller needed. Watching him with Amy, seeing the easy rapport the two enjoyed, helped reinforce the growing sense of despair she felt when she considered the future. She had only to consider the dreadful strain of her parents' marriage to see the futility of her relationship with Jackson.

He'd argue. She knew that. All that well-intentioned talk of lashing himself to the mast, and waiting until she was ready. Right now, he could probably convince himself that he'd never resent her for the things that lay ahead. But time would take its toll. He'd want children, and she couldn't give them to him. He'd want security, and she couldn't offer it. Sooner or later, he'd condemn her for that. He wouldn't think so now, but she'd seen it happen before. Eventually, he'd realize the sacrifices he'd made. And he would come to resent her.

She'd spent a lifetime enduring resentment. She could never bear it from him.

In her mind, she could see the angry looks and rebukes that had marked the final years of her parents' marriage. Laura Glynn's anger, she knew, was part imbalance, but another part, perhaps even the greater part, came from years of repressed anger and disappointment. Durstan and Laura had destroyed each other. Cammy had witnessed most of that slow descent. For the better part of her life, she'd accepted a generous amount of the responsibility for it.

Years ago she had promised herself that she could never let that happen between her and another person. Yet she'd crossed a very definite line with Jackson, and the longer she allowed things to go on between them, the more damage she'd inflict when she ended it.

The thought depressed her as little else could. Belatedly, she realized that tears had begun to roll down her face. Angry, with herself and at the terrible unfairness of it all, she swiped at them.

And gathering the suit jacket he'd left in her apartment more closely around her, she curled into a tight ball and gave herself permission to cry herself to sleep.

Tomorrow, she promised, she'd be strong again.

The donuts weakened her resistance. She'd always been a sucker for chocolate glazed donuts. His smile didn't hurt any, either. It never did. That smile could probably disarm a terrorist.

Still groggy from her mostly sleepless night on the

couch, she pulled the door open a little wider just to look her fill. ''Hi.''

''Good morning.'' He didn't wait for an invitation before he stepped into her apartment. As usual, he filled the space, overwhelming her. Clad in jeans and a sweatshirt, he had a rumpled look about him that suggested he'd just rolled out of bed. ''I brought donuts. I got everything chocolate that they had.''

She was charmed in spite of herself. ''A man after my own heart.''

''You guessed it, babe.'' He dropped a light kiss on her mouth. ''Sleep well?''

''Yes,'' she lied.

''Is that why you have circles under your eyes?''

''That's rude.''

He rubbed one with the pad of his thumb. ''Sorry. You're teaching me to be more blunt.''

''Lucky me.''

Tilting his head to one side, he studied her closely. ''Tell me that I didn't make a colossal mistake last night by leaving.''

''No. I needed the space. I'm a little over-whelmed.''

He grinned again. ''That's the best news I've had in days.''

''Don't sound so proud of yourself,'' she grumbled as she led the way to her kitchen.

''Are you always cranky in the morning?''

Pulling two clean plates from the dishwasher, she considered the question. ''I don't know.''

''You don't know?''

''No one's ever asked.'' He captured her gaze as a

silent current of understanding passed between them. No one in her life had been interested enough to pursue something as subtle as her moods. She shrugged. "The chocolate will help."

His gaze probed a few seconds more, then shifted to the coffeepot. "You want me to make coffee?"

She wanted to scream. The sheer normalcy of the conversation was wearing her out. Why couldn't he see the impossibility of it all? She was torn between a deep desire to shout at him and an equally intense one to throw herself into his arms. "If you want some."

When his hand covered hers, she started. She hadn't realized he'd moved so close. "What I want," he said, his voice a low rumble in her ear, "is to go back to bed and feed you a donut."

A shiver raced through her. "How can we go back to bed? We weren't in bed."

"Let's pretend." He nuzzled her neck.

Why did he have to make this so hard? "Jackson—"

He lightly bit her earlobe. "I can tell you all the dreams I had about you last night if it will make it more real."

The roaring in her ears drowned out any message her brain might have sent. "I don't think—"

He turned her lightly in his arms, buried his lips in hers. His mouth glided over hers with easy familiarity, shaping and molding the curves of her lips with knee-melting thoroughness. When he finally lifted his head, her glasses fogged. She squinted at him. He gently removed the glasses, then tucked her cochlear earpiece into place. "Come to bed and feed me, Cammy. I'm starved."

Tell him no, her mind urged, but her heart begged for one more day, a few more hours of this unalloyed bliss. She shuddered, torn between fear and desire. "I can't—"

His lips glided over her eyebrow. "Chris called this morning," he mumbled. "I've got to leave for London tonight to cover the summit."

She swallowed. "London?"

"I'll be gone a week. Maybe longer." He kissed the corner of her mouth.

"Longer?"

"Depends on the summit."

Gone. The information eased across her jangled nerves. She'd have room to breathe. Time to think. Oh, Cammy, you coward, she told herself, even as her arms stole around his shoulders. "How many kinds of chocolate did you bring?"

"Six. Two of each."

"Take me. I'm yours."

With a soft laugh, he lifted her into his arms. "I adore you."

She pressed a kiss to his throat. "Show me."

An hour later, she turned into his arms with a soft sigh of contentment. "Still want a donut?" she asked.

His rough chuckle sent a thrill through her. He swept his hand over her bare hip. "I don't think I can move."

"I'll feed it to you," she offered.

His eyebrows lifted. When he'd carried her to bed,

he'd brought the sack of donuts with him. Their morning had begun with Jackson demonstrating just how arousing the act of licking chocolate off an iced donut could be. He'd fed her one of the pastries and intoxicated her with vivid descriptions of just what he planned to do with her afterwards. There were definite advantages, she'd decided, to men with large working vocabularies.

If the look of rough tenderness on his face was any indication, he had been as affected as she by the morning's play. "If you feed it to me," he said, "we'll never leave the bed."

She could live with that, she decided. "Did you have other plans?"

His head dropped against the headboard. "Lord. I've tumbled into paradise."

She ruthlessly squashed the tremor of anxiety his words caused. Just once, she'd force herself to worry less about consequences and more about the moment. How many times had Mike urged her to enjoy the moment, to stop dwelling every instant on what might be, and let herself go? Surely no one, not even the normally unkind fates, would begrudge her these few hours of contentment. "May I come in?"

His gaze narrowed. "That's my line."

She laughed. It felt good. Everything about being with him felt uncommonly good. "Into paradise," she told him as she threaded her fingers through his chest hair.

"Honey," he said as he rolled her to her back, "I hate to break this to you, but in case you haven't figured it out, paradise is anywhere you are."

As he kissed her, caressed her, and finally joined himself to her, she decided paradise wasn't such an elusive thing after all. But now that he'd shown her the way, she thought as she watched in wonder when his head arched backward and his body tightened on the brink of his own surrender, what would she do when the time came to leave?

The web of joy he wove around her lasted for the rest of the day, into the evening, and well past the moment when she kissed him good-bye at the airport. He hesitated before he dashed through the metal detector. "I don't want to go," he said.

She gave him a sad smile. How could she possibly explain the sense of relief she felt at his departure? He wouldn't understand that he was giving her a blessed gift of time, a week to bask in the afterglow of his affection. For one more week, she could pretend that the end wasn't at hand. "I'll miss you."

He wrapped an arm around her waist. "Promise?"

"Sure."

He kissed her again. "I have to go."

"I know."

His gaze probed her, seeking answers. "Cammy—"

At his grim look, she smoothed the crease from his forehead. "If I want you, I'll whistle. I promise."

The final boarding call for his flight crackled on the airport intercom. "Damn it."

She wrapped her arms around him. "It's all right, Jackson. Go save the world."

"I'd rather save you."

Her eyes fluttered shut in exquisite pain. "The world needs you more than I do."

"But *I* need you."

"I'm a phone call away."

"It's not the same."

"We'll make it the same."

He kissed her a final time, then turned to go. He was halfway to the metal detector when he stopped, then turned to face her. "I'm in love with you, Cammy Glynn," he announced. "You'd better start getting used to it."

"Lord." The *following* afternoon, Macon Stratton leaned back in her chair at the Coco Loco restaurant and gave Cammy an incredulous look. "And then he just raced off to London?"

Cammy nodded. "Yes."

"Has he called?"

"Twice."

"So why do you look so gloomy?" Macon stabbed a fork in her empanadas. "Most women spend months trying to get that out of their guy."

"It's different with us. You know that."

"So you say."

"It is. Jackson Puller and I can't possibly have a relationship."

"It's a little late for that, don't you think?"

"A *permanent* relationship."

Macon frowned at her. "Cammy, have you *told* Jackson why you feel this way?"

She shook her head. "It's not the kind of thing that comes up in conversation. I mean, what am I supposed to say? 'By the way, I can't ever give you children.' He loves kids.''

Macon mumbled something under her breath. ''I always find that so terribly unattractive in men.''

Cammy frowned at her. ''He'll want to have some.''

''Maybe he'll want you more.''

''He'll think he will. At first, he'll think he can live with it. He'll think it won't matter, but it will.''

''You can adopt.''

''We could. I wouldn't mind, but he would.''

''And you're basing this conclusion on? . . .''

''I know him. Family is very important to him.''

''So you're going to make the choice for him.''

''I'm making it for both of us, Macon. I can't live the rest of my life knowing that someone resents me for things I can't control. I can't go through that again. I'd end up hating him. I don't want to do that.''

''Have you talked to Mike about this?''

She managed a slight smile. ''It's not like I don't know what he'll say. I took the same classes, you know.''

''But with your mother, and now this. I just think you're under a lot of stress.''

''You could say that.''

''It wouldn't hurt to talk things over with him.''

''He'd get nosy.'' She tilted her head to one side. ''Like you.''

''Cammy—''

''Macon, really, it's all right. I knew what I was doing.''

Macon studied her for long minutes, then shook her

head. "You know, you make me crazy."

"You don't need me for that."

"Very funny. I mean it, Cam. I hate it that you're about to throw this away."

"I never really had it. It wasn't fair to him to let him get so involved without knowing all the facts."

"And you're so afraid to surrender even a little control that you'll toss him aside."

"I think we're a little ahead of ourselves here. I mean, it's not like he begged me to marry him, you know."

"He's going to."

"You don't know that."

"He will." Macon pursed her lips. "I've got more experience with begging men than you do."

Cammy laughed. "The way I heard it, you begged Jacob, not the other way around."

"He's the exception." Her eyes lit as her expression softened. "He was worth begging."

"But if you'd thought, even for a minute, that you were going to hurt him, wouldn't you have let him go?"

"You're not going to trick me into telling you that you're doing the right thing, Cammy."

"Then you're going to have to trust me."

Macon exhaled a sharp breath. "I wish you'd let me help you."

"Liar. You wish I'd do what you want."

"I'm concerned."

"And I appreciate it."

"But you're going to do it anyway?"

"Yes. When he gets back from London, I'll tell

him I think we need to end it. I'm going to try very hard not to hurt him."

"How, exactly, do you plan to manage that?"

"I don't know. I have a week to figure it out, though." She resolutely changed the subject. "I thought we came to lunch today to talk about the media plan for the Wishing Star fund-raiser."

"That was before I realized that the stars in your eyes got there compliments of Jackson Puller."

"I've wished on stars before, Macon. I'm older and wiser now. So just be a friend, and let's talk business. It's easier."

He called her twice a day—once in the late afternoon before she left the office, then again at night. He never mentioned his parting declaration at the airport, for which she was endlessly thankful, but he continued to weave a web of intimacy, and her heart ached within its confines.

On Friday, a different phone call struck at the serenity of that web. She replaced the receiver in its cradle with a deep sense of sorrow. Dr. Van Root had returned from his conference that morning. He'd examined Amy's test results, and called to let Cammy know that he'd concluded the child wouldn't benefit from implant surgery. The source of her deafness was more extensive than he'd first suspected. He was sorry, he'd assured Cammy, but he didn't feel the current technology would suffice, and he was unwilling to risk the surgery without a better chance of success.

The news hit Cammy like a blow to the head. She stared at the receiver, frustrated and grieving. Amy, she knew, would be devastated. Despite Cammy's best efforts to help the child maintain perspective on the procedure, Amy believed a cochlear implant represented the key to her future.

Amy wanted to become a professional dancer, and now, Cammy would have to take away a dream from a child who'd already suffered more than her fair share. She dropped her head in her hands with a soft groan. Tears slipped between her fingers to run down her wrists. A voice that couldn't be quelled reminded her that until Amy had begun attending Cammy's sessions, she'd never known that cochlear implants existed. She'd seen Cammy's implant and what it had done for her. She'd asked questions. Cammy had answered them. Because of her, the child had dared to look ahead. And now, because of her, that dream was going to end in bitter disappointment.

Swamped with guilt, and almost overwhelmed with her sense of loss, she stared out the window at the darkening sky. When the phone rang, she turned her reluctant gaze to it. Jackson, she realized. Right on time.

"Hi."

He sounded out of breath. "Hi. I wasn't sure I'd catch you."

"I waited."

"I'm glad." She heard the shuffling of papers on his end. "Listen, I haven't got much time. I've got an interview in less than five minutes. I just wanted to let you know that I think I'm done here. If this interview goes well, I should be home tomorrow."

"That's sooner than you thought."

"I busted my butt to finish." He exhaled a long breath. "Lord, I'm tired."

"You're not getting enough sleep."

"I get up early to call you."

"I know. You shouldn't."

"I shouldn't—Cammy, is something wrong?"

"Not really." Except that her entire life was splitting apart at the seams. "Well, sort of."

"Honey, what's the matter?"

"You don't have time."

"I have time. I'll always have time. What's going on? How's your mother?"

"No change. That's not the problem." She swiped the tears from her eyes with the back of her hand. "I talked to Dr. Van Root today. He's concluded that Amy's not a good candidate for a cochlear. He won't do the surgery."

Jackson muttered a soft curse. "I'm sorry. Have you told her?"

"Not yet."

"Do you need to tell her right now? Can it wait until I get back?"

"I guess. I hadn't thought about it. He just called."

"I'd like to go with you when you tell her."

"I . . ." Cammy thought about it. Amy loved Jackson. They had developed a rare bond, and she knew that it would make it easier on the girl to have him there. "If you're willing to do that, I think it might make it easier for her."

"I want to do it. I'll be home tomorrow night. Late. We can go on Sunday."

"Do you want me to pick you up at the airport?"

"I won't get in until after midnight. I can take a cab." A buzzer sounded in the background. "Damn. I have to go."

"I know."

"I probably won't get a chance to call you to-night."

"That's all right."

"Are you sure you're all right?"

"I'm sure."

"Honey—" The buzzer sounded again. He swore.

"It's all right, Jackson. Go."

"I wish I were there with you."

She didn't tell him she wished it, too. Instead, she pictured his ruggedly beautiful face, the expression in his eyes when he'd said he loved her. She clung to it for a few fragile seconds. "Don't worry. I haven't forgotten the signal. If I need you, I'll whistle," she quipped.

"Okay. Promise you'll consider yourself kissed un-til I get there."

"That could seriously wreck my equilibrium."

He laughed softly. "I kind of like it when that hap-pens."

As usual, the sound of his voice was having a re-markable effect on her. She'd allow herself, she de-cided, one more memory before she locked the door. She drew a deep breath. "One more thing before you go."

He stopped breathing. She heard it on her end of the phone. "What?"

"I know you'll take a cab, but my apartment is right by the airport. Yours is all the way across town.

You won't have had a decent meal all day, and you'll be exhausted. Come there instead.''

''It'll be late.''

''I don't care.'' She fingered the ear piece of her glasses. ''I'll leave a key with the doorman. Let yourself in. I'll be waiting.''

''Lord, I love you.''

She tucked that close to her heart. ''I'll see you tomorrow.'' The buzzer sounded again. ''Take care of yourself.''

✨♡ fifteen

He dropped the keys on her hall table, then set his suitcase on the floor. Nothing, he realized, had ever felt as good as this moment. She'd left him a key. She'd let him into her life. The significance wasn't lost on him.

He'd scared himself out of his wits when he'd thrown caution to the wind and told her he loved her. He'd been fairly certain that the look of stunned disbelief on her face was not a good sign. As if dropping that bomb on her hadn't been enough, he'd dashed out of the country and left her alone for a week to consider the ramifications. It had probably been one of the stupidest things he'd done in his life. He'd been fairly certain he'd need to spend at least the next two weeks coaxing her back into feeling secure with him.

And then she'd left him a key.

That soft promise had turned his world upside down. His eyes drifted shut as he took long seconds to savor the way he felt. Somewhere down the road, he promised, when he wasn't so tired, and didn't feel this pressing urge to pull her into his arms, he'd take this feeling out and wallow in it.

A memory of the sadness he'd heard in her voice, however, urged him from his reverie. She'd taken the news from Van Root hard, and he couldn't blame her. He swept his gaze over the dimly lit interior of her apartment. An infomercial flickered on the television. Cammy slept soundly on the sofa, wrapped in a cotton blanket. She'd fallen asleep waiting for him. The thought chased away the final shreds of his fatigue. Overwhelmed with tenderness, he made his way across the thick carpet to ease her into his arms. She mumbled something, but tucked her head against his shoulder when he stood.

He set her on the bed, took a minute to strip off his clothes, then slipped in beside her. Pulling the blankets over them both, he pressed a kiss to her forehead as he gathered her in his arms.

She turned toward him. "Are you home?" she mumbled.

Tucking a wayward curl behind her ear, he rubbed his stubbled cheek against the top of her head. She wasn't wearing her transmitter, he realized. So he pressed her hand to his chest. "I'm here," he said. "And I'm staying."

The sound of rain splattering on glass awakened him from a deep sleep. After the pace of the last week, the odd sensation of easing into wakefulness disoriented him. He frowned at the ceiling, then identified the warm presence at his side. With a soft smile, he rolled over to drape an arm across Cammy's waist.

She didn't stir. He nuzzled her ear as he glanced at the clock. Nine-thirty. He could safely assume it wouldn't even be rude to prod her awake—not that it would have mattered. The feel of her soft body pressed to his had effectively chased away every remnant of his fatigue. He'd been too tired last night to accomplish more than a good night kiss and a deep tumble into a dreamless sleep. This morning, he was starved for her.

"Cammy." He swirled his tongue over the shell of her ear. She rolled onto her stomach. He followed her with an unrepentant grin. His gaze landed on her cochlear transmitter, where it sat on her nightstand. She wouldn't be able to hear him, and somehow, that sent an electrifying sensation through him. A writer's first rule, he thought wryly, was show, don't tell. Just thinking of all the things he could show her was having an incredible effect on him. He trailed a caressing hand along her side, then dipped his head to nuzzle her bare shoulder.

He knew the instant she awoke. She tensed slightly, then reached for her transmitter. He covered her hand with his, carried it to his lips. Rolling her gently to her back, he met her gaze with a smile and a slight shake of his head.

"I can't hear," she told him.

"I know," he mouthed.

"I need my transmitter."

He made the sign for *without*.

Understanding dawned in her expression, followed by wariness.

"Trust me, Cammy. Please."

Slowly, she raised her hand to rest it against his face. The sweetness of her surrender almost undid him. He turned his head to kiss her palm. "Trust me," he mouthed against the tender flesh. "I love you."

Cammy's other hand lifted to his shoulder. Arching her back, she raised her head to kiss the corner of his mouth. With a soft groan, Jackson rolled to his back, pulling her with him.

With a slight smile, she settled on him with the softness of a summer rain. Her mouth skimmed his chest. His hands moved over her curves. He used his fingertips to tell her how much he adored touching her.

Her eyes widened in the sweetest kind of awareness when he kissed her secret places. Her fingers took him to the stars and back as they traveled over his skin. With long, leisurely explorations, they studied each other. He felt his mind slipping away, sensed the swell of passion within her as she sought the tenderest places on his body. When he finally eased into her several blissful minutes later, his world splintered. He'd never be complete again, he realized, without this woman in his life. With his eyes, his hands, his mouth, every move of his body, he told her how much he loved her.

Cammy responded with a sweet abandon that sent him all the way into orbit.

By the time they were settled in his car that afternoon, on their way to see Amy, he was telling himself he should be the happiest man alive. But something was wrong.

He couldn't put his finger on it, but something was definitely wrong. Though she was prone to stillness, there was something unmistakably different about her silence this morning. She was anxious about Amy, he knew that, but something more lurked at the edges of her conscience.

Their lovemaking had been uninhibited and abandoned. The experience had outstripped any previous event in his life. He had tried in every way imaginable to show her that every fool who had ever questioned her worth was without the sense to look beneath the surface. She'd trusted him. He sensed how much it had cost her to let him make love to her without the benefit of her transmitter. She'd really left herself open for him.

And unless he missed his guess, she was trying to tell him something. Something he wasn't going to like. Something that scared the wits out of him.

Unable to stand the slightly tense silence, he cleared his throat. "How are you feeling?"

She pulled her gaze from the window. "Fine. Do you have jet lag?"

Rattled enough, he thought, to have lost her touch for subtle shifts in conversation. "You cured me."

She didn't respond to the quip. Several seconds passed while he fought down a wave of frustration. "Cammy, is something bothering you?"

A sad expression ghosted in her eyes. "Not really. Why?"

"You're quiet."

That won a slight smile. "It's an old habit."

She opened her eyes to study the picture he made as he conversed in a combination of signs and words with Amy. The sight made her heart ache. He'd caught her off guard, and she'd fallen right for him.

Belatedly, she realized Amy had asked her a question. She pulled herself from her reverie and focused her gaze on the girl. "I'm sorry," she said. "I wasn't paying attention."

"I can't ever have an implant, can I?"

Cammy carefully considered her answer. "I don't know," she said. "Dr. Van Root doesn't believe a cochlear will help you, but that doesn't mean something else won't help later."

Jackson nodded. "When Cammy was your age," he told her, "there were no implants."

"I was eighteen," Cammy confirmed, "when cochlear implants became an option. Just because this procedure isn't right for you doesn't mean nothing else will be either."

"What if there isn't anything else?"

Cammy nodded. "Then we'll be disappointed and angry and we'll cry about it together."

"I wanted to hear."

"I know." Cammy nodded. "I wanted it for you. But there's so much you can do. You don't have to hear to do all the things you love. Being deaf doesn't have to limit you."

Amy frowned. "I don't mind being deaf," she finally said.

"I know," Cammy nodded.

"I mind living here." She jabbed an angry finger at various spots in the room. "I want to live in a house, like normal kids. I want a mother and a father, not a volunteer who has to drive me around. I don't fit in here. None of the other kids are deaf. I don't have friends.''

"You have Trevor,'' Cammy pointed out. "And your friends from my group.''

"Not here.'' She shook her head. "I want to go to school with normal kids.''

"We'll work on that, then. Trevor is going to a public school next year. Maybe you could go, too.''

"I want to dance.'' She tapped the spot behind her ear. "Now, I can't.''

Jackson shifted his chair closer. "Yes, you can.''

Amy shook her head. "No. Not without the transmitter.''

"That's not true.'' He glanced at Cammy, then focused on Amy. "You danced at the recital.'' At her dubious look, he nodded. "You can do it again.''

Tears filled her eyes again. "Not forever.''

"Why not?''

She gave him an incredulous look. "I can't.''

"If you want to,'' he assured her. "You can. Lynette showed you how.''

Amy's signs became more exaggerated, larger. "I can't dance if I can't hear the music.''

"You'll count,'' he insisted. He took one of her small hands in his. "Ever heard of Beethoven? He *wrote* music and he was deaf. If he could write it, you could dance to it.''

Her brow wrinkled in confusion. "How?'' she signed.

Jackson tapped her forehead. "You use your brain.

It's better than your ears anyway. And your eyes. You watch the other dancers, and you count. Just like you did for Lynette.''

Amy looked at him, her expression intent. She wanted to believe him, Cammy realized.

''You can do it,'' Jackson signed. ''Whatever you decide to do, I believe you can do it.''

Cammy swallowed. The look of cautious hope on Amy's face was very likely mirrored in her own eyes. She recognized the symptoms of a person who desperately wanted to believe whatever Jackson Puller was saying.

By Monday morning, however, the small hope she'd been cherishing promptly fled. She set Jackson's final story on Wishing Star aside with a sinking sense of dread. He'd done a beautiful job. She couldn't have asked for more. Even his last piece, which he'd written the previous afternoon and submitted as the paper was going to press, offered a poignant but compassionate picture of Amy's disappointment, her courage, and her dreams.

And in its wake, a firestorm had begun. Jackson's articles had sparked national interest. She'd already fielded three calls that morning from reporters who now felt the right to question the effectiveness and methodology of her sessions with the children. Earlier in the series, his verbal portrait of her had generated an unprecedented number of information requests and Wishing Star donations. She'd denied interview requests from several news organizations, and only successfully shielded Amy from the pressing demands by hiding her behind her age and her innocence.

Backlash followed his final column, however, and Cammy seriously doubted she'd be able to contain it. Jackson's readers had wanted a happy ending, and his failure to provide it evoked a national sense of outrage. A sharp knock on her door drew her attention.

Mike, looking harried and frustrated, waved a stack of pink message slips at her. "They're piling up out here, Cam."

"I know."

He flipped through them. "There's one in here from Congresswoman Meyerson. Her administrative assistant says the congresswoman has some serious concerns."

"I'm not surprised."

Mike dropped into the chair across from her desk. "Damn Jackson Puller. I never thought he'd do this."

"It wasn't his fault, Mike."

His eyebrows lifted. "Excuse me?"

"It's not his fault. He told the truth, and nobody wanted to hear it."

"Cammy, his last piece suggested that you raised Amy's expectations about the possibility of the implant."

"Maybe I did."

He swore, succinct and to the point. "Good God, Cam. Don't tell me you think this is your fault."

"I don't think it's anyone's fault." The jarring ring of the telephone interrupted her. She waited until her voice mail picked up the call. "I think a little girl is bitterly disappointed. I think that if she had never gotten involved in my sessions, she might not be suffering that disappointment right now.''

"She also wouldn't have learned to dance, or how to make sounds, or the value of friendship, or that there are people in the world worth trusting.''

"She might be better off.''

He frowned at her. "I can't believe you're saying this.''

"You didn't see her face yesterday when I told her. You didn't have to sit down with her and explain that she's being permanently denied a technology which has helped millions.''

"Cammy—''

"And you didn't have to take responsibility for raising her hopes in the first place.''

"All right.'' He glared at her. "I've had enough of this. You know I hate what happened to Amy. It sucks. It's unfair, and I resent it as much as you do, but you're not doing anybody any good by sitting here telling me this is your fault. You're smarter than that.''

The phone rang again. She glared at it. "Congresswoman Meyerson doesn't think so.''

"Congresswoman Meyerson is an idiot. And I'll say that for the record. Damn it, Cammy, the hounds of hell are at your heels and it's Jackson Puller's fault.''

"No kidding.'' Jackson's voice sounded from the doorway.

Cammy swung her gaze to his. "Hi.''

"Hi.'' He looked exhausted, and rumpled, and

much better than she thought he should. "How bad
has it been?"

Mike glared at him. "Like hell, only worse."

"I had no idea, Cam. You have to believe me—"

"You didn't cause this."

"I've been chasing down these jerks all day." He
waved a newspaper at her. "I don't suppose you've
seen the afternoon edition of the *Star* yet, have you?"

"Do I want to?"

He shook his head. "Can I at least preface this by
telling you that I think their editor-in-chief is the scum
of the earth?"

Mike growled. "What's that muckraking SOB got
to say?"

Jackson kept his eyes trained on Cammy as he laid
the newspaper on her desk. It fell open to a picture
of her and Jackson leaving St. Elizabeth's mental hospital. The caption read, "Deaf shrink crazy too?" A
brief summary of her methodology, a description of
the Wishing Star program, and a suggestive comment
about her relationship with Jackson followed. She
groaned and slapped the paper shut. "Great."

Mike snatched it from her hand. Jackson leaned one
hip on the edge of her desk. "Lord, Cam, I'm sorry.
I know how you feel about this."

Cammy pressed the palms of her hands to her eyes.
"Do you?"

Mike swore beneath his breath. Cammy didn't look
at him. Jackson's hand landed on her shoulder. "Listen to me," he urged. "I'll fix this. I promise you, I
will fix this."

"Tell that to Congresswoman Meyerson."

"I already did. I stopped by her office on the way over."

"I'm sure she agreed to call off the hunt."

"I haven't even thrown my first punch yet. Give me a little credit, will you?"

"For what?" Mike said angrily. "Making her life miserable?"

Jackson winced. Cammy gave Mike a chastising glance. "Mike, it's okay. Really." He frowned. She nodded. "Really." She glanced at Jackson. "What are you doing here, anyway?"

"Besides groveling?" He glanced at her and looked quickly away. "I'm on a mercy mission. I called a friend of mine and got three tickets to the ballet tonight. I thought you and I could take Amy. It might help."

Cammy swallowed. "I think maybe we should talk first."

He probed her with an intent stare but said nothing as Mike stomped out of the room. When Costas shut the door behind him, Jackson rounded the desk. He took both of Cammy's hands in his. "How mad are you?"

She gave him a sad smile. "I'm not mad."

He studied her face. "You're sure?"

"I'm sure." Pushing away from her desk, she freed her hands from his grasp and crossed to the window. "I hadn't counted on this, I'll admit, but it's not your fault."

"I had no idea that series would generate this kind of interest."

She glanced at him over her shoulder. "You really didn't, did you?"

He shook his head. "I'm not usually even in the country when a story hits." He shrugged helplessly. "Amy was so—engaging. People fell in love with her. They wanted to help her. And she was right here. Leo, and the others, they were in distant countries. People responded to them, but they didn't feel compelled to do anything with that response."

"I've heard it said that you're partially responsible for the current interest in foreign adoptions."

He frowned. "That sounds a little far-fetched. I'm not that good a writer. Why are we talking about this?"

"Because I have something I need to say to you, and I'm stalling for time."

He surged off the edge of her desk and crossed the room in three quick strides. Placing his hands on her shoulders, he gently kneaded the tense muscles. "Honey, what's wrong?"

She drew a settling breath. "It's about us."

"That's becoming my favorite topic."

Meeting his gaze in the window, she shook her head. "That's what I wanted to tell you. I—I don't think it's a good idea for us to see each other any more."

He went perfectly still. "Excuse me?"

She plunged ahead before she lost her nerve. "What happened this morning should have told you something."

"It did. What happened this morning is that I woke up alone, and I didn't like it. I hated it. I hated it so much that I decided that, if I could help it, I never wanted to do it again.''

''Jackson, don't.''

''I told you that I'm a better person with you than I am without you, and that I want to keep being that person.'' He looked at her narrowly. ''For the rest of my life.''

''You don't understand.''

''I want a huge wedding, where I can tell every person in this city that I'm in love with you.''

''I can't.''

''Then we'll have a small wedding, but either way—''

She shoved his hands away. ''Stop it.'' Drawing a sharp breath, she pushed away from him. ''I'm serious.''

''Honey—''

''No.'' Cammy briefly clenched her eyes shut. When she opened them again, she saw the stubborn set of his face. ''Listen to me. Just shut up and listen.''

''I'm afraid of what I'll hear.''

She ignored him. ''This—thing.'' She waved a hand at her desk. ''All these reporters calling. The next few weeks are going to be chaos for me. Not only do I have the fund-raiser coming up, but now I've got inquiries into my methods and ethics in dealing with these kids. I'm going to have to take a hard and very public look at who I am, and what I'm doing.''

''You didn't—''

''Please let me finish.''

His expression turned mutinous, but he nodded.

Cammy exhaled a long breath. "On top of that, my mother's health is steadily declining. There's every chance she won't live much longer. Bruce says things don't look good."

"Let me help you."

"You've done enough," she snapped, without really knowing why.

His eyebrows lifted. "You are mad."

"I am not mad. Quit telling me what I feel. I happen to be an expert in what I feel."

"You think so?"

"Yes."

"Then tell me you're not in love with me."

"Damn it, that's exactly what I'm talking about." She pressed the heels of her hands to her temples. "Can you even imagine the kind of pressure I'm under right now?"

Before she realized he'd crossed the room, his hands were covering hers. "Yes."

"I don't think so," she argued, but didn't pull away when he eased her into his arms. "I swore to myself a long time ago that I'd never again get manipulated into trying to meet other people's expectations. It never occurred to me that I'd fail to meet my own."

"Cammy, you have got to listen to me. What happened to Amy is no more your fault than what happened to Leo was mine."

She tilted her head back to look at him. "At least I taught you a thing or two."

"You taught me more than you can possibly imagine." He smoothed her hair off her forehead. "You showed Amy how to dream, and you're helping her find the tools to make those dreams come true. Just because she's faced a setback does not mean she has to give up those dreams. It also doesn't mean you were reckless to give them to her.''

"A lot of people think I was.''

"Then a lot of people are wrong.'' His hands moved up and down her spine. "Lord, Cam, don't you think I know what you're going through? I went through this when Leo died. The self-doubt is worse than anything anyone else hurls at you. It will eat you alive.''

Her fingers twisted in the soft fabric of his shirt as she gathered her courage. "It's more than that, Jackson. I spent a lifetime feeling I'd disappointed the people I loved. I can't go through that again. I *won't* go through that again.''

He was silent a long moment. "Sweetheart.'' His voice sounded wary. "Are you worried that you're going to disappoint me?''

The words sliced at her already lacerated heart. "You don't understand. There are things I haven't told you. Things I should have told you. You can't get involved with me.''

"If I get any more involved with you, I'll have to have your name tattooed on my forehead.''

She used what was left of her resistance to push away from him again. "Then it's my fault for letting things go too far. I thought—I hoped—that it wouldn't come to this. I never intended for this to happen. You weren't supposed to fall in love with me.''

"It has been my unfortunate experience that you don't get to plan something like that. If people only loved when they were supposed to, most of the world's problems would disappear."

She ignored him. "I should have been up front with you from the start. I don't know how I let it get away from me."

He leaned against her desk again. "Tell me now," he said quietly.

Once again, she walked to the window. The story was easier when she couldn't see that tender look in his eyes. "Years ago I made the decision that I could never marry."

"After Leslie?" he probed.

"Yes. My father pointed out some hard facts to me that I had to accept." She thought she heard him swear, but she didn't turn around. "Facts like, there's a better than average chance that I could have inherited my mother's predisposition to mental disorder. That in a few months, or few years, I could start sliding into that same pit. And when I did, I'd take whoever I could with me. It destroyed my parents' marriage. In some ways, it destroyed their lives. It would be irresponsible and selfish for me to expose someone else to that kind of risk."

"Cammy—"

"There's more," she interrupted. "Because of that reality, this is really more of a blessing than a curse. At the time, I didn't think so, but I've come to recognize the truth of it." She drew a deep breath. "I can never have children." Finally, she turned from the window to face him. "I'm sterile. I couldn't give you children." With a brief shake of her head, she continued. "That wouldn't be fair to you, Jackson."

He watched her for long seconds. She could see him turning the information over in his head. "So because of this," he said cautiously, "you've made the decision that you have to be fair to me."

"Don't you see? I know what you're thinking. You're thinking that you can live with it. But you can't. Even if I never end up as ill as my mother, you love children. You want children. You *deserve* children. I've never known a man who'd make a better father than you."

"I'd be lying if I told you I didn't see that in my future, but hell, Cam, there are other—"

"No. No matter what you think now, you couldn't live with it for thirty years. I saw what it did to my parents."

"I am not your father." His voice had taken on an edge.

"I know. You're a better man than he was. But it'll take its toll, Jackson. Infertility is one of the leading causes of divorce."

"I don't give a damn about some statistic you read in a professional journal, or whatever poison that bastard who fathered you pumped into your head."

"I didn't expect you to understand."

"Did you expect me to argue?"

"Yes."

"And had you already decided that nothing I could say would change your mind?"

"Yes."

"Then I can't win, can I?"

"I didn't mean—"

"Cammy, I am not going to stand here all day and try to argue with you when I know damn good and well I'm not going to change your mind." He raked a hand over his face in frustration. "But I am not walking away from you either. So you might as well get that through your thick head."

"You've got to listen to me," she urged him. "I've had more time to think about this than you have."

"You've had thirty years to obsess over it is what you mean. I hate to break this to you, Dr. Glynn, but you don't get to tell me what I do and do not want."

"It's a pattern—"

"You analyze minds, you don't read them."

"You're angry."

"Hell, yes, I'm angry. You're trying to throw me out of your life over something that may or may not even happen. Damn it, Cammy. If you can't have children, we'll deal with it. As for the other, your mother is a bitter, angry woman who has filled your head with a lot of misconceptions about the way love should be. Maybe you've never had the advantage of seeing how love really works, but in my experience, you don't choose it. Love isn't some well-ordered organized emotion that you can steer around. It chooses you. And I can't just grow a new heart because you've decided that you get to tell me how I should live my life."

"I'm not trying to do that."

He bit off a curse. "Look, this is going nowhere."

Her phone rang again. They both stared at it. When it finally stopped, she raised stricken eyes to his. "I'm sorry. I can't do this."

"Well, I'm sorry, too, because I can't not do it. I'm not giving up, Cammy."

"You will."

"Don't bet on it." He watched her through narrowed eyes. "Look, I came by here to apologize for what's going on, let you know I'm doing my best to squash it, and find out what time I should pick you up for the ballet tonight. The show's at seven. Do you want me to get you before, or after, I pick up Amy?"

"Have you listened to a word I've said?"

"Yep. I heard all of them, and I'm ignoring all of them. Are you going with us tonight or not?"

"I don't think it would be—"

"Yes or no, Cam. That's all I want to know."

She drew a deep breath. The outing, she knew, would be immeasurably beneficial to Amy. That seemed to matter more than forcing her point with Jackson right now. "Fine. I'll meet you here at six."

He nodded. "Okay, we'll pick up Amy on the way to the Kennedy Center."

The tight sound in his voice made Cammy wince. "Jackson—"

He held up his hand. "Forget it. If we argue about this any more, I'm probably going to say something I regret. Think about it all you want, Cammy, but you are not getting rid of me until you come up with a better reason.'' He pressed a short, hard kiss to her lips. ''Sorry, babe. If you wanted a quitter, you're dealing with the wrong guy.''

He strode from the room before she could respond.

✨♡ sixteen

The following afternoon, Jackson walked into Mike Costas's office and slammed the door. "What the hell am I going to do?" he demanded.

Mike raised his eyebrows. "Nice to see you, too, Puller. I wasn't aware you had an appointment."

"I don't." He dropped into the chair across from Mike's desk. "I need help."

"I've been saying that for weeks."

"Do you mind keeping the snide remarks to a minimum? I'm a little short on patience today."

"Cammy," Mike said quietly.

Jackson nodded. "You've got to tell me what to do."

"How much has she told you?"

"Everything."

"And you're still here?" Mike nodded approvingly. "I had a feeling about you from the start, you know."

Jackson ignored that. "She's scared. I know that. I

understand it. I scared myself when I admitted so much to her.''

"Cammy has some very unusual ideas about relationships.''

"I know. And I almost wish her father wasn't dead. I'd kind of like to strangle the bastard.''

"Durstan isn't the only reason she's afraid of what's happening between the two of you.''

Jackson frowned. "Children. She thinks I can't handle not having children.'' He wiped a hand through his hair. He'd been processing that piece of information since yesterday afternoon. "We don't have to have children. There are other options.''

"And she's afraid you'll resent her the same way her father resented her mother.''

"The guy's dead. How do I get past that?''

"I don't know.''

Jackson glared at Mike. "Thanks.''

A ghost of a smile played at the corner of Costas's mouth. "There's not an easy answer to this, Puller. It's not like prescribing antibiotics for an infection.'' He shrugged. "Cammy's under tremendous pressure. She's taking this business with Amy Patterson very hard. I've never seen her doubt herself before.''

"It wasn't her fault. We saw the child last night. As far as I can tell, she's coping fine. She's sad, but hardly desolate.''

"Did you happen to catch the report on CNN last night?''

He'd been at the ballet, brooding about Cammy, who'd sat two seats down from him and barely met his gaze all evening. "No.''

"Ever hear the name Jeffrey Herrington?"

"From Cammy. He's that activist who is so opposed to cochlear procedures, isn't he?"

"He's been at odds with Cammy and Wishing Star for the past couple of years. He lost two or three legislative battles, as well as some grant funding that went to Cammy's foundation. This little episode was all the bait he needed for a full-blown media event. He's lobbying Meyerson for hearings."

Jackson swore. "That's ridiculous."

"You're right, and nothing may come of it, but it depends on whether or not the public outcry dies down. Seems that Herrington thinks the fact that Cammy's been working with federally subsidized programs, and the kids who benefit from those programs, opens her up to additional scrutiny. I think the precise quote was, 'Our tax dollars shouldn't be squandered on programs whose goal seems to be the emotional devastation of young children like Amy Patterson.' "

Jackson swore again. Costas nodded. "My thoughts exactly. To make matters worse, it's no secret that President Stratton's grandson is deaf, nor that Stratton's been one of Cammy's biggest supporters. Rumors are starting to surface that some of the federal grant money Cammy's received may be less than legitimate, and that certain elected officials have used Wishing Star as a political platform to earn the president's support."

"She's going to have to grant some interviews. If she ignores them, it'll get worse."

"She's got Macon Stratton handling her response."

Jackson drummed his fingers on the arm of the

chair. "Macon's good, but no one can defend Cammy as well as she can herself. If Macon continues to speak for her, it's going to begin to look like she's hiding something."

"I doubt she'll do it. You know how she feels about that. She rarely speaks in public, and then it's prepared speeches only. Never Q&A."

Jackson's frustration mounted. "Damn it to hell, I ought to wring Meyerson's neck. You know why she's doing this, don't you?"

"I can imagine it's some fairly self-interested reason."

"She's planning to run for the presidency, even if she doesn't have a snowball's chance in hell, and she's hoping to use Cammy to make the administration look bad."

"Brilliant deduction, Puller."

Jackson glared at Costas. "In case it has escaped your attention, I'm not exactly in a joking mood. She won't take my phone calls, and I wanted your perspective on this. You've known her longer than I have."

Mike nodded. "Sorry. I wasn't trying to make light of it. You know I want what's best for her."

"That would be me."

"Your ego's intact, I see."

"Not for long. Not if I can't work this out."

Mike thought it over for a few seconds as he tapped a ballpoint pen on the surface of his desk. "If you want my professional opinion, I think what's really going on here is Cammy's inability to face the truth about her mother."

Jackson lowered his eyebrows. "What are you talking about?"

"Cammy has spent a lot of years resenting her mother, and an equal number of years either denying that resentment or feeling guilty for it."

"Anyone would resent that woman. Have you heard the way she talks to Cammy?"

Mike held up his hand. "I'm not saying Cammy doesn't have a right to her feelings. Believe me, I think Laura Glynn's parenting skills left much to be desired. Even before she grew seriously ill, she used Cammy as a tool against Durstan. It's possible, I'd even say it's probable, that Laura's anger at Durstan had more to do with the unrest in Cammy's childhood than her mental illness. I don't know when she crossed the line from cold and bitter to bitter and delusional, but that didn't happen until years later. She was seriously underequipped to deal with the needs of a child like Cammy, and so was Durstan. The fact that Cammy couldn't actually *hear* them arguing probably made it more frightening and confusing, rather than less."

"And now that her mother is seriously ill?"

"Laura's probably going to die soon. If Bruce Philpott is to be believed, it could be any day. The thought is somewhere in Cammy's head that if she doesn't make peace with Laura before she dies, then she'll never resolve her own anger. She also thinks that anger is what drove her mother to insanity. It's natural that Cammy would fear the same consequences."

Mike made an ineffectual gesture with his hands. "For years, Cammy was the focus of Durstan's resentment of Laura, and Laura's resentment of Durstan. The idea that she might have to endure that from you, or from anyone for that matter, scares her to death. She's got all the anger she can cope with, and she doesn't want any more."

"Has she talked to you about this?"

"Bits and pieces. Cammy's a very private person, even with the people she loves. I think she has probably opened up to you more than anyone."

"And that's why she's pushing me out of her life."

Mike nodded. "She's made herself vulnerable to you, and now she's afraid to trust you."

"Is there *anything* I can do?"

"Don't give up. Durstan was a quitter. So was Laura, for that matter. If you get the chance, try to encourage Cammy to forgive her mother." He looked at him through narrowed eyes. "And pray a lot."

"I'm here, Mother," Cammy told Laura.

Laura Glynn looked at her with an angry, vacant stare. "Go away. I want your father."

"He can't come." Cammy frowned at the pallor of her mother's skin.

"I want your father. Where's your father?"

"He's not coming, Mother. He can't be here."

"Durstan? Durstan, it's not my fault. I didn't do anything. I couldn't help her. She needed help and I couldn't help her."

Cammy's eyes drifted shut as her mother continued to babble incoherently. She clenched them tight, and, though she willed herself not to, thought of Jackson. In the glow of his undivided attention, Amy's spirits had risen visibly by the end of last evening. She seemed to be mostly unaware of the firestorm surrounding her, and though she remained disappointed about the implant procedure, she had responded with characteristic resilience. Jackson's unqualified support hadn't hurt.

Cammy had barely made it through the performance intact. With Amy seated between them, and the occasional resolute looks Jackson sent her way sending tremors through her blood, she'd been reminded of similar events from her childhood. On a few occasions, generally for some political reason, she'd accompanied her parents to a public event. Generally, they kept her physically and emotionally between them as a buffer for their anger. By the time they returned home, both were spoiling for an argument. She would sit on the stairs and watch through the wooden balusters as they vented their frustrations.

Always, she'd been left feeling confused and frightened by the fury she sensed in them both.

"Get him here, Cameo," Laura insisted. "I want him to see me. He should see me."

Cammy blinked. "What, Mother?"

"Durstan did this. He should see me. He blames me, but it's his fault. It's all his fault. He should be here. He should help me."

"Mother," Cammy drew a deep breath. "Daddy is dead. He's not coming."

Her mother thrashed in the bed. "That bastard. He wouldn't die. He wouldn't. He's with *her*."

Cammy reached for her mother's hand. Her chilled skin felt as thin as paper. "Mother, listen to me.

Daddy is dead. You know he's dead. He's been dead for years.''

Again, that vacant stare met hers. ''I want him.''

''I know.''

''He doesn't understand how much I want him. That's all I wanted. I just wanted him. He didn't know. He can't die without knowing.''

Cammy swallowed. ''I'm sure he knows, Mother.''

She shook her head. ''I tried. I tried so hard. He never listened.''

''I know.''

The door opened slightly, and Bruce Philpott stuck his head in the room. ''Cammy?''

She glanced at him. ''Hi, Bruce.''

''May I see you for a minute?''

She gave Laura's hand a squeeze, then laid it back on the sheets. ''I'll be back later, Mother.''

Laura shook her head. ''You won't. You're like him. You're not coming back.''

Cammy slipped from the room without comment. Bruce gave her an apologetic smile. ''Sorry.''

''It's okay. She barely knows I'm there most of the time.''

''Maybe we should go to my office and talk.''

''Is it that bad?''

He nodded slightly. ''It's bad, Cammy.'' Linking a hand beneath her elbow, he started walking down the dim corridor. ''I have the reports back from Dr. Marche.''

Roland Marche was the geriatric specialist Bruce had brought in to examine Laura. ''There's not much time, is there?'' Cammy wondered if Bruce would notice the lack of emotion in her voice. For perhaps the first time in her adult life, she had no idea what she was feeling. A block of ice seemed to have settled itself firmly in her heart.

Bruce pushed open the door to his office. "I don't think so," he confirmed. "Why don't we sit down."

Cammy settled herself in one of the leather chairs near his desk. Bruce handed her a manila folder. "That's Marche's report. Do you want me to hit the highlights for you?"

"Please." She flipped open the folder, quickly scanned the cover sheet.

"Most of Laura's systems are in failure. Her liver is barely functioning. Her pulmonary and cardiac systems are in distress. We've run some tests and discovered high concentrations of toxins in her urine and blood. Dr. Marche thinks it's a matter of days before her body simply stops working."

"Is she in pain?"

"Not that I can tell. I've left instructions to give her as much morphine as she needs to stay comfortable."

"Which is going to contribute to her disorientation."

"Yes. I'd like your permission to take her off her anti-delusional meds. I think they could be contributing to her agitation, and, at this stage, I'd rather see her comfortable."

Cammy thought it over, then nodded. "So would I."

Bruce's expression softened. "Cammy, it's going to get rough. I can keep her sedated most of the time, probably will, in fact, but that's not going to change what's happening in her mind. When she's cognizant, I can't give you any indication of what she'll be like.''

"I realize that.''

Bruce drew a deep breath. "I'm not sure I like the idea of you facing this by yourself. I think Costas should know, and I think maybe you should limit how much time you spend here.''

"Look, Bruce, she's my mother.''

"Hell, Cammy, I'd be lying if I told you that I didn't have some serious professional concerns about what this could do to you. Normally, I'd recommend counseling.'' At her sharp look, he held up his hand. "But I know you'd refuse. I want you to take care of yourself. We'll take care of your mother.''

"I'll need to make some arrangements.''

"We can handle that for you, if you like.''

She hesitated, then nodded. "I would.''

"Cammy—'' He laid a hand on her shoulder. "I know there's nothing that can make this easier. Just about anything I would say would sound trite. But I want you to know I'm here for you. I know Mike is, too. You don't have to do this alone.''

Jackson's image popped into her head once more, and she had to momentarily shut her eyes to keep the pain from overwhelming her. "Is there anything I can do for her?'' she finally asked.

"I think it helps more than you know to have you here. I know it's not easy, but she's generally calmer after your visits. I'd like you to come once a day, if you can, but don't stay long. It's not good for either of you.''

"I don't want her to suffer."

"Neither do I. You've already taken care of all the necessary paperwork. We'll do whatever we can for her."

"All right." Cammy handed him the folder. "I'll come back tomorrow. You'll keep me informed?"

"Of course."

"Thanks, Bruce." She left his office with the unmistakable feeling that a storm lay on the horizon. She didn't know when, or how, or even how severely, but soon, it would overtake her.

And the idea that she might not be ready for whatever happened scared her to death.

When she let herself into her apartment that night, her phone was ringing. She frowned at it. The afternoon had been worse than the morning. She'd been hounded all day by reporters who wanted interviews, politicians who wanted dirt, and lawyers who wanted blood. Jeffrey Herrington had announced that he was filing a joint suit with the ACLU against Wishing Star, and Congresswoman Meyerson had scheduled congressional hearings into the issue for a week from Monday. The press coverage had dropped from bad to terrible, and despite Macon's best efforts, the situation looked increasingly grim.

This afternoon, a story had surfaced that Cammy had used her connection to Gordon Stratton to bypass the application procedure for grant money—which she hadn't—and that she'd used that grant money to fund additional research into the speech development of children who received cochlear implants well into their formative years—which she had. Herrington had immediately argued that the research study was proof of Cammy's continued pressure on the deaf children she treated to undergo the implant procedure, while Meyerson's office had issued a statement calling for congressional support for a full legal inquiry.

The phone rang a fifth time, and the answering machine picked it up. "Cammy?" It was Macon's voice. "Hon, I don't know if you're there, but if you get this, you'd better turn on the news. And then you'd better call me. Tonight. I know you don't want to do it, but I think you're going to have to respond to this publicly. We'll talk about it."

Macon hung up. Cammy reached immediately for the remote control to her TV. She found the network station, then dropped onto the couch at the sight of Jeffrey Herrington, flanked by Congresswoman Meyerson and a host of other political activists, announcing the terms of his lawsuit against her. Phrases like "inappropriate conduct," "unethical practices," "abuse of power," and "negligent behavior," floated through her mind in a blur. Rage and something else, something she strongly suspected was disappointment, roiled around in her mind. She shut her eyes in exhaustion.

When the phone rang, Herrington was still performing for the cameras. Cammy lifted a weary hand to answer it. "Macon?"

A long breath preceded the deep voice that said, "No. It's me."

Her heart rate accelerated. Jackson. "Oh."

"I was afraid you wouldn't take my call."

"I'm trying to end my relationship with you, not act like a thirteen-year-old."

"I called you several times today."

"I was out of the office." When he didn't respond, she insisted. "I was. Didn't Mike tell you?"

"Yes."

"And you didn't believe him?"

His soft chuckle warmed her. "I guess I'm the one who's acting thirteen."

She didn't think it should feel so good just to have him on the other end of her phone line, but decided not to fight it. She tucked her feet beneath her and sank lower into the couch. "Did you want something?" she asked him.

"Besides you, you mean?"

"Jackson—"

"Don't bother. I didn't call you to argue." He paused. "Did you catch Herrington's press conference?"

"I'm watching it now—or at least the network highlights."

"The real thing was worse."

"That's comforting. Did you go?"

"I got someone to go for me. I was afraid that my presence would make things more difficult."

"Probably."

"Cammy, listen, I know you're exhausted, so I'm not going to keep you. Mike told me your mother isn't doing well at all."

"She's not."

"Did you see her today?"

"Yes."

"You okay with that?"

The sting of tears surprised her. Jackson was probably the most tender man she knew, and it never failed to get to her. "Yes," she told him, though her voice sounded rough.

He hesitated. She could almost hear him wondering if he should push. "I'll take your word for it."

"Okay."

She heard him mumble something. "I wish you'd let me come over there."

"You can't."

"You're driving me crazy."

"Join the club," she managed to quip.

His sharp exhalation of breath seemed to crackle between them. "All right. I'll let you win this round, but I want my objection noted for the record."

"Deal."

"Now, I just wanted to make sure you knew two things before you went to bed tonight. First, things aren't as bleak as they appear. I've got another meeting with Meyerson in the morning. I think I'm about to have her convinced that this isn't in her best political interest."

Cammy's gaze flicked to the TV. "She looks pretty rabid in this press conference."

"That was before I talked to her this evening."

A sudden chill had her reaching for a cotton blanket. "You don't have to do this."

"You've got no idea, do you?"

"What?"

"You have no idea how many people are on your side. Did you know that the woman who runs Amy's foster facility is ready to testify that all the children you've treated have shown remarkable improvement, that some have even been able to make the transition to public school because of you?''

She frowned. ''She is?''

''Yes. Or that the parents of some of your Wishing Star kids have been burning up my phone lines since the story hit this afternoon? Everyone wants to help you, Cam.'' He paused. ''Let them.''

She watched the parade of anger across her TV screen a few seconds longer. Pulling the blanket closer around her, she said, ''What was the other thing?''

''What?''

''The other thing. You said you had two things to tell me.''

''Oh. You know, you're losing your ability to shift a conversation subtly.''

''I'm tired.''

''I know.'' His voice dropped softly. ''I'm really worried about you.''

''I'll be all right.''

''I wish you'd let me help you.''

''You'd help me if you'd think about what I told you yesterday.''

''Honey, I've done nothing but think about what you told me.''

''You have a very thick head.''

''Then I'm in excellent company.''

''I guess.'' She pinched the bridge of her nose with her thumb and forefinger. ''I really want to go to bed,

Jackson. Are you going to tell me the other thing or not, because I'm hanging up soon.''

"Oh. That. I just wanted to make sure you heard me tell you I love you before the day is over." He sighed. "I love you, Cammy. Try to get some sleep."

And he hung up. She held the receiver to her ear until she heard the dial tone, then slowly placed it back in its cradle. Weary to the bone, she punched the remote to turn off the TV. The dark feeling that she was staring professional ruin in the face suddenly seemed to pale in comparison to the fact that this extraordinary man said he loved her. It would be a comfort tonight, anyway, though she knew she would have to push it away in the morning.

Jackson drummed his fingers on the receiver of the phone in his office as he stared into the night. She had sounded terrible. He hadn't bothered to tell her that Bruce Philpott had called that afternoon to give him an update on Laura's condition. She wouldn't have appreciated that, he suspected. He hated the idea of her sitting alone in her apartment. If he told himself the truth, he hated the idea of her sitting alone anywhere. Behind him, he heard the buzz of the always busy newsroom, but it failed to draw his attention as it normally did.

His phone rang, and he snatched it up with a wild kind of hope in his heart. "Yeah?"

"Jackson?" He recognized his sister Karen.

"Oh, hi."

"You sound distracted. Is this a bad time?"

"No." He frowned at the clock on his desk. "How did you know you'd find me here?"

She laughed. "Are you kidding? There's a big story unfolding that involves a woman you brought home to meet us. I didn't even try your house first. I knew you'd be there banging your head against a wall."

"Good guess."

"So what's going on?"

He rubbed a hand over his face. The two-day stubble of his beard scratched his palm. "It's political, mostly. Meyerson and Herrington are hoping that Cammy's demise will gain them some votes. Cammy's had unqualified support from the president for a long time. That can make a person a target. She got caught in the middle of some political posturing, and my series of stories added fuel to the inferno."

"What's going to happen?"

"I'm going to get her out of it."

"You sound sure."

"I'm sure," he said tightly. "She didn't do anything wrong."

"How's the child?"

"Amy? She's okay. She's disappointed, but it's nothing like the press is making it out to be. Van Root has already called me today to check on her. I saw her last night. She's coping."

"It looks bad from out here."

"The members of my noble profession have a way of doing that. We're bored. There's not much going on, so we're making a mountain out of a molehill."

"How's Cammy holding up?"

He wished he knew. "I'm not sure. It seems bad."

Karen paused. "Is she, are the two of you—"

"You're doing a really poor job asking about my love life."

"Okay. How is it?"

"Depends."

"On?"

"On what you mean. If you mean—how's my love life in the sense that is there a woman I'm completely and irrevocably enamored of, who I want to marry and spend the rest of my life with—then the answer is: my love life is great."

"Where's the catch?"

"She's hardly speaking to me."

"Because of the articles?" Karen sounded surprised.

"It's more complicated than that. I'd explain it, but I'm not sure I fully understand it myself."

"Don't give up on her, Jackson."

"You're about the fourth person who's given me that advice today."

"Must be a sign. Listen, I know you're busy, and I don't want to keep you. I just wanted to see how you were doing."

"I feel like hell."

Karen laughed. "Must be love."

"The worst kind."

"Before you go, Andy wants to talk to you. Do you have a minute?"

"Always." He listened as Karen instructed his niece not to babble.

"Hi, Uncle Jackson."

As always, the sound of her voice warmed him. "Hey, Peanut. How are you?"

"Good. I lost a tooth today."

He did some mental arithmetic. Andy was a little young to be losing her teeth. "No kidding? Did it get loose and fall out?"

"No. Willie Wickerson knocked it out on the playground."

He laughed. "Did he knock it out on purpose, or by accident?"

"Accident. The tooth fairy's gonna bring me a dollar."

"A whole dollar? What are you going to do with it?"

"Buy gum," she said in a pained voice that suggested his intellect had failed to impress her.

"Oh."

"Uncle Jackson?"

"Yes?"

"Are you and Miss Cammy fighting?"

He pulled in a breath. "What makes you think that?"

"Mama said you got Miss Cammy in trouble."

He thought that over. "I did. Sort of."

"Don't you like her anymore?"

"I like her a lot."

"You gotta 'pologize, Uncle Jackson."

He smiled a sad smile. "You think that will help?"

"Uh-huh. Once last year, I got my friend Annie in trouble because I told on her when she really didn't do anything wrong. My teacher made me 'pologize in front of the whole class. I told everyone that Annie didn't do it, that I just thought she did it, and that I wanted to be her friend again.''

"Did it work?" he asked quietly.

"She invited me to her sleep over."

He'd willingly tear his own heart out if Cammy would invite him to a sleep over, he mused. "I'm glad."

"It would work for you, too, Uncle Jackson. I like her."

"Me too."

"She likes you."

"What makes you think so?"

"She looks at you the same way Mama looks at Daddy."

"What way?" He glanced up when Krista Swenlin, a look of triumph on her face, burst into his office.

"Gooey."

He laughed. Krista set a stack of photos in front of him. He flipped through them, searching with a practiced eye. "I love you, Peanut."

"I love you, too, Uncle Jackson."

"And thanks for the advice." He met Krista's gaze when he pulled a photo from the stack. Elation stirred through him as he studied the image. "I think I'll take it."

Karen prompted Andy in the background. "Good night, Uncle Jackson."

"Good night, Peanut. Tell the tooth fairy I said hello."

She giggled as she hung up the phone. Jackson dropped the receiver in its cradle. "Where did you get it?" he asked Krista.

"Congressional Research Service Archive. And don't ask me to do that again, Jack. They got suspicious. Photographers don't generally do a lot of research down there."

He rubbed his thumb over the picture. "I know. Thanks."

"I did it because I really like Dr. Glynn." She leaned over his desk to look at the photo. "Do you think this is really going to work?"

This, he thought, and a few other things. His gaze narrowed on the picture. Anita Meyerson, then a candidate for public office, flanked by Jeffrey Herrington and an assorted group of lobbyists and foreign financiers, stared angrily at the camera. A Georgetown University academic building towered behind them. Meyerson and Herrington, he'd learned today, had both attended the private university. Despite Herrington's vocal support of the deaf community and its needs, he'd opted to attend the upper-crust Georgetown over the deaf college, Gallaudet. That fact wasn't going to play well with his target audience.

But even better, Jackson thought as he studied the picture, Meyerson was deep in conversation with one of the financiers. She had narrowly won her congressional race with the help of several independent expenditures, funded by foreign interests who had suffered at the hands of her opponent's prominent position on the House Appropriations Committee.

The hours he'd spent at the Federal Election Commission that afternoon had yielded a wealth of information about Meyerson's campaign finances and, unless he missed his guess, her less than legal solicitation of foreign money. Her campaign staff had managed to hide the funds behind political action committees and special interests, but Jackson knew enough about the system to believe that the word *collusion* would drain the color from Anita Meyerson's face.

He'd sent Krista to the Congressional Research Service on a hunch. And she'd struck gold. If Congresswoman Meyerson hoped to be president, she probably wouldn't want to explain this photograph to the voters. Nor, he suspected, would she want to weather a series of articles, under his byline, on the strange history of lawmakers who broke laws on their way to becoming presidential hopefuls.

He looked at Krista with a slow grin of satisfaction and whispered, "Gotcha."

❄☆
♡ *seventeen*

Startled from a deep sleep by the flashing of her bedside lamp, Cammy sat straight up in bed at 1 A.M. the following morning. Disoriented, she glanced at the lamp for several seconds before she realized her phone was ringing. Reaching for her transmitter, she fumbled with the earpiece, then picked up the receiver. "Hello?"

"Cammy? It's Bruce Philpott."

"Bruce? Something's wrong." It wasn't a question.

"I'm sorry. I think you'd better come down here. Your mother's asking for you, and I think she may not make it through the night."

"I'll be there in twenty minutes."

"Cammy—" His voice stopped her from slamming down the receiver.

"Yes?"

"Mike called earlier to check on Laura. I let him know things don't look good. Would you like me to call him for you? I'm sure he'd want to be here."

She hesitated, the aching sense of loss she felt compounded by the reality that she'd walk this road alone. At her father's funeral, hundreds of well-wishers had crowded the memorial service. She'd been alone then, too, she realized, but this felt more real, more tragic somehow. After sixty-two years of life, when her mother died, the likelihood was better than average that only Cammy would be present at the graveside. She exhaled a long breath. "No, it's okay, Bruce."

"You're sure?"

"I'm sure."

"All right. I'll meet you here at the hospital. Be careful driving."

"I will."

She hurried into her clothes, wondering a little frantically what she was going to do. She tugged a fleecy sweatshirt over her head, then stopped short when she heard the knock on her door. Firm. Insistent. Jackson.

She knew it before she pulled the door open. He looked tired, she noted. And wonderful. "What are you doing here?"

"I'm driving you. I don't think you should do this alone. You may not want me, but I'm not giving you much of a choice, either." He tipped his head to one side. "Say yes now, and I'll let you yell at me later."

She frowned at him. "How did you know?"

"I have spies everywhere. Are you ready?"

Hesitating, she studied him in the dim evening light. "You don't have to do this."

"Yes, I do. You just haven't figured that out yet." He held out a hand. "Are you ready, or do you need a few minutes?"

She decided against arguing with him. She didn't have the energy, and there was a strange sense of rightness in having him there. Tonight, he'd see the situation at its worst. He'd experience exactly how devastating Laura's long illness had been, and see the ravaging effects Cammy had been trying to explain to him. If he wasn't smart enough to spare himself, she didn't have the strength to argue with him. "Let me get my shoes."

Twenty minutes later, they walked down the near-deserted hall of the hospital. Jackson had barely spoken to her on the short drive. Bruce intercepted them in the corridor. The look that passed between Jackson and Philpott told Cammy all she needed to know about Jackson's unexpected arrival at her apartment. "How is she, Bruce?" she asked.

"Slipping." He laid a sympathetic hand on her shoulder. "Fast. Marche was here earlier. We've got her as comfortable as possible, but her internal systems are shutting down."

Jackson's hand glided around Cammy's waist. "Is there anything we can do?"

Philpott shook his head. "Occasionally, she asks for Cammy, but I've taken her off her regular meds. Marche and I agreed there was no point in adding additional physical stress with too much medication. Her mind is just about gone." He glanced at Cammy. "She may not recognize you."

"I understand." Her gaze fixed on the door to her mother's room. In the back of her mind played a scene. When she'd been fifteen, she'd first discovered the extent of her mother's illness. She'd gone into her father's bedroom to find her mother yelling accusations at the closet door. The wild look in Laura's eyes had frightened her, then. Cammy had fled the house in confused fear, only to face her father's anger later. She'd gone to a friend's house to wait. Durstan had reprimanded her that night for telling her friend's family what she'd seen. No one, he'd said, must know the extent of Laura's deterioration.

She gave herself a mental shake as she started toward the door. She was not fifteen, and she understood precisely what was happening on the other side of that door. This time, there would be no lectures from Durstan, no bitter looks from Laura when the episode passed. She squared her shoulders and slipped free of Jackson's embrace. Pushing open the door, she stepped into the dim interior of her own personal view of hell.

"Hello, Mother."

Laura groaned. Cammy crossed to the bed to take her hand. "I'm here."

Vacant eyes met hers. Her mother mumbled a few incoherent sentences and thrashed in the tangled covers. Cammy smoothed the sheets and straightened the pillows. "Can I get you anything?" she asked. The shaft of light that fell across the semi-darkened room told her Jackson had let himself inside. Without looking, she knew he stood just inside the door, one shoulder braced against the wall, watching.

She drew a deep breath. Monitoring equipment beeped a monotonous cadence of ominous warning. "Do you want some water?"

Laura twitched. "Water. Yes."

Cammy held the straw to her lips. Laura took several greedy sips, then grabbed Cammy's forearms with a surprisingly strong grip. "Cameo?"

"Yes."

"You're here."

"Yes."

"I didn't think you'd come."

She set the water glass on the bed stand. "Of course I came." Curious, she studied the look in her mother's eyes. Laura looked alert, lucid, perhaps more lucid than Cammy had seen her in years. "You don't feel well, do you?"

"I'm dying."

Cammy didn't ask how she knew. "Yes."

Laura nodded. "It's a good thing. I don't want to live like this anymore."

Cammy sat on the edge of the bed. "I'm sorry, Mother."

Laura's hands tightened their grip. "Don't leave me. I don't want you to leave me."

"I won't."

"I want you to tell Durstan that it's not my fault. I didn't mean to fail him. You'll tell him?"

"Yes," Cammy promised.

"He won't believe you."

"Maybe he will."

Laura shook her head. "No. He blamed me for all of it. For you. He blamed me for you."

"I know."

Laura began to weep. "He wanted everything. I couldn't give it to him. He always wanted more. No matter what I had, he wanted more.'' Her breathing accelerated as she kicked at the sheets. ''You have to tell him. You have to make him understand.''

''I will.'' Cammy pressed her hands to her mother's shoulders, trying to still her nervous motions. ''Don't worry.''

Long seconds passed. ''He's not coming,'' Laura finally said.

''No.''

''He's dead.''

Cammy hesitated. ''Yes.''

Laura began weeping again. ''I never got to tell him. I couldn't tell him. I didn't want it to be like this.'' The words trailed into incoherence.

Cammy's eyes wandered as she listened to the mumbling. She sensed Jackson's presence at the edge of the room, but she didn't dare look at him.

The minutes stretched into an hour, then more. Cammy lost track of time as she watched Laura glide in and out of consciousness. Through the hours of the night, attendants would come to monitor her vital signs, administer medication, but the close confines of the room remained eerily still. Her ranting became less and less coherent as she slipped closer to the end. Jackson had taken a seat on the far side of the room, where he sat in silence. The first streaks of dawn were beginning to push their way into the night sky when Laura's gaze fixed on Cammy's. ''Cameo?'' she whispered.

''Yes, Mother.''

Laura's hands reached for her. ''I'm sorry. I'm sorry.''

Cammy felt a tightening in her throat. "You don't need to be sorry."

"I failed him. I failed you. I couldn't do it. I wanted to."

"I know you did."

"I wanted to be a good mother." Her face twisted into a grimace as a shaft of pain streaked through her. "It hurts," she moaned. "Oh, it hurts."

Cammy tightened her grip on Laura's hands. "I'm sorry."

Laura moaned again. Tears glided down her cheeks as her body trembled from the force of her sobbing. "I don't want to be alone. I'm afraid. I'm so afraid."

Watching her anguished expression, Cammy felt a knot of anxiety begin to untwist in her soul. She smoothed a lock of silver hair off her mother's forehead. For years, she realized, she'd feared this moment, but she'd never stopped to wonder how much, or how deeply, Laura feared it.

The confusion, Cammy knew from experience, was terrifying.

Countless nights during her childhood, she'd lain in her own bed confused, alone, terrified. As her parents' relationship had declined into a hellish pit of bitterness and resentment, her fear of abandonment and desolation had exponentially increased. She'd spent hours curled up in her bed, sobbing into a pillow. Then, she'd have given anything for a comforting touch, or the soothing stroke of her mother's hand.

Unbidden, a memory slid its way past her grief. She'd been very young. In the memory, she was in her bedroom in the small house they lived in before her father's election to the Senate. She could not have been older than three or four. She was ill. It seemed like she'd been ill forever. She awakened, late in the night, to find Laura sitting on the bed with her, reading a story. Cammy wasn't able to hear the story, but the vibrations of her mother's voice comforted her. The cool feel of Laura's hand on her heated flesh eased the torment of her fever. When she awakened in the morning, Laura was gone.

Cammy replayed the memory, wondering why it should have stayed with her, or why its impact seemed so profound. It was the only time that she remembered Laura offering her comfort. And, she realized, she'd never forgiven her for that. Now, Laura faced the last hours of her life, and Cammy feared she would carry to her grave the knowledge that first Durstan, and then Cammy, had never forgiven her for her inability to be what they wanted. The idea filled her with a bone-deep regret.

Laura's weeping tore at Cammy's heart as she considered with unfathomable sadness all that they had lost. And in her anger, she'd refused to offer her mother what small solace she could. With an aching heart and trembling hands, Cammy shifted slightly in the bed so she could ease her mother's frail figure into her arms. Laura sobbed uncontrollably. Cammy felt the glide of tears on her own face. "I'm sorry, Mother," she whispered. "I'm so sorry."

She waited long moments. Laura moaned several times, but seemed to quiet. Cammy brushed the damp tendrils of hair from her face. "It's going to be all right," she told her. "I'm going to stay here with you."

"I don't want to die," Laura said.

"I know."

"Promise you won't leave."

"I promise."

Laura exhaled a tortured breath. "I'm afraid."

"Don't be. I'll stay with you." Cammy drew a deep breath. "I'll tell you a story."

And from the corner of her eye, she saw Jackson's eyes drift shut as he leaned his head back against the window frame.

"Now you know," she told him two hours later as she left her mother's room for the last time.

He studied her drawn features with concern. "Let me take you home, Cammy. Philpott can handle this from here."

She shook her head. "I'll take a cab."

"Like hell." If she thought he was going to let her get away with that, she was deranged. She looked exhausted, mentally and physically, and he had the distinct feeling that they'd reached a turning point this morning. "I'm not letting you leave here alone."

"I'll be fine."

"I know you'll be fine, Cam." He linked his fingers beneath her elbow. "That's not the point."

"There's nothing else you can do, now."

"I can be with you. I can listen to you." He looked at her through narrow eyes. "I can love you."

Cammy shook her head. The sadness in her gaze threatened to overwhelm him. "No. You can't."

"Cammy—"

She pressed a hand to his mouth. "You've seen it all now, Jackson. You saw what happened in there."

He kissed her palm, then enfolded her hand in his. "What I saw was an extraordinary woman doing an extraordinary thing. Do you have any idea how much I admire you?"

"Then let me handle this my way."

"Alone?"

"It's the only way I know."

He scrutinized every aspect of her expression. How could he love her so much and be so inept at reading her moods? He wondered if it would always be like this. Would she always catch him a little off balance, keep him slightly off guard? "Honey—"

"I mean it, Jackson. I need time. This was a lot for me."

"Are you telling me the truth?"

"Yes."

She wasn't. He could see it in the careful way she averted her gaze. "I don't want to leave you."

"You have to."

He heard the double meaning implicit in the phrase. "If I give you your way right now, are you going to understand that it's just for today?"

"You're relentless, aren't you?"

"And you're in no shape to be making major life choices." He dragged a hand over his face. "I was there, too." He indicated her mother's room with a tilt of his head. "I saw what went on."

"Then you should understand."

"Yeah, well, I'm a little thickheaded in that department." They reached the elevator.

She punched the down button, then lifted a weary hand to straighten her glasses. "You don't say."

Frustrated, he pinned her to the wall with a hand on either side of her face. "Honey, I do not want to argue with you."

"Then let me go home."

"I think that's a mistake."

Her eyes drifted shut. "Please."

He exhaled a long breath. "All right. This time. Do you want me to drive you?"

She shook her head.

He glided painfully gentle fingertips over the planes of her face. "Do you want me to call anyone? Macon, maybe?"

"No." Her voice was just above a whisper.

Jackson pressed a soft kiss to her forehead. The elevator doors slid open. He guided her inside, where he pulled her into his arms. He was having a terrible time keeping his panic at bay. She was slipping away from him—he sensed it as surely as he sensed the ironlike grip she had on her self-control. Frustrated and angry at his helplessness, he held her close to him, wishing he could simply absorb her.

When the elevator reached the ground floor, she stepped away from him. "Thank you for coming," she said in the same detached tone a stranger would use in a receiving line.

He resisted, barely, the urge to swear. Instead, he pressed a hand to her back and guided her toward the door. "I'll call you a cab," he promised.

"Okay."

"I'll call you later this afternoon."

"You don't have to."

He couldn't resist any longer. He turned her into his arms and buried his mouth on hers. She stood, motionless, within the circle of his embrace. His hands cradled her face. His lips glided over hers as he drank, desperately, of the taste and feel of her. "I won't lose you," he whispered when he raised his head.

She pulled away from him. "Not tonight," she told him. "Please not tonight."

He hesitated a second longer, then nodded. "All right. But if you want me—"

"I know. I know. Whistle. You told me."

He hailed her a cab. She slid into the rear seat with a mumbled "thank you." The door shut between them, and Jackson stared, dismally, at the window. He couldn't fight the feeling this was wrong, but he didn't have a better plan, either. Feeling unaccustomedly lost, and ripped bare, he raised his fingers in the sign for "I love you."

Cammy didn't acknowledge him as the cab sped away.

Macon laid another stack of papers in front of her the following afternoon. "And this is the series of press releases I plan to issue tomorrow." She leaned back against the edge of her desk. "Cammy, are you sure you feel up to this today?"

Cammy nodded absently. "Yes. It's fine."

Macon hesitated, then slapped the folder shut. "No,

it's not. This is ludicrous. I don't give a rip what Anita Meyerson says, or how effective she thinks this is going to be for her campaign. You don't need this right now.''

''It's not just about me, Macon. Gordon's not going to come out of this unscathed, either.''

Macon made a frustrated noise in the back of her throat. ''Yes, he is. You both are. Look, why don't you let Jacob and me go with you today? You could come home with us afterward. We'll have dinner. Trevor and Natalie would love to see you.''

Cammy shook her head. ''It's really okay, Macon. It's not as if I'm having a funeral for her. My father is buried at Arlington Cemetery, and since she can't be interred there—well, this seemed better.'' At Bruce Philpott's recommendation, she'd agreed to have her mother's ashes interred at the Memorial Garden. There had seemed little point in holding a funeral. The woman her mother had been, Cammy had realized, had really died years before. ''I think she would have wanted it this way.''

''Did anyone tell Jackson?''

She shook her head. ''He doesn't need to know.''

''Cammy—''

She met Macon's gaze. ''Please. You can start lecturing me tomorrow, but not today. Please not today.''

''He'd want to be there for you.''

''He was there,'' she whispered.

Macon's eyes widened. ''When she died?''

''Yes.''

''You didn't tell me.''

''I didn't tell anyone.''

Macon studied her for a minute. "Why can't I fig- ure out what's going on in your head? I've known you for five years, and I don't have a clue how to read you, sometimes."

"Join the club of people I frustrate to death. Jack- son Puller is the honorary chairman."

"Do you want him, Cammy?"

She frowned. "Want him to what?"

"Do you *want* him?"

"Oh." She carefully considered the question. "I haven't thought about it. I can't think about it."

Macon's expression turned stubborn. "You know, for the most part, I try to keep my mouth shut about this."

"But today's the exception?"

"I think you're throwing away the best thing in your life."

"When did you join Jackson Puller's fan club?"

"I didn't. I joined Cammy Glynn's fan club, and I don't want to see one of my best friends toss away a chance at happiness."

"It's complicated."

"And you are probably the single most stubborn person I've ever known."

Cammy flashed her a slight smile. "Next to you?"

"Next to me."

"Then you haven't really known Jackson Puller for long. He's worse."

"Good. More evidence that the two of you deserve each other."

With a weary sigh, Cammy leaned back in her chair. "I don't know, Macon. I don't think I'm in the best possible position to be objective about this."

"Love is like that. Jacob turned me into a complete wreck."

The picture made Cammy smile. Macon was one of those women who managed to look perfect despite high humidity, hurricane-force winds, or drenching rains. "I doubt you were ever a wreck."

Macon laughed. "You have no idea. I cried for days. I had stooped to pining over a picture of him I cut out of the newspaper. It got ugly."

"What did you do?"

"I quit listening to my head for once. Cammy," she squeezed her hand, "nobody has *ever* been more concerned about risk management than I was. I threw Jacob out of my life because he couldn't offer me a sure thing. I just wasn't going to step out on a ledge unless I knew, for sure, that I couldn't fall."

"But you changed your mind?"

"Don't you have some professional nomenclature for that?"

"Changing your mind? It's called flakiness, I think."

"Is that a technical term?"

"Sure."

Macon shook her head. "That's not what I meant, and you know it. I mean, isn't there some psychological principle about people who can't commit to relationships because of fear?"

"Chronic disassociation," Cammy said quietly.

"That's it. I had that. I didn't let anyone get close to me. I was too afraid of getting hurt again."

"It's not like a cold, Macon. You don't get it, and

then just decide not to let it bother you anymore.''

"I didn't. Don't get me wrong. The thought of losing Jacob scares me to death. I'm not sure how I'd handle it.''

Cammy frowned. "Then why—''

"Because I figured out one day that I was more afraid of not having him in my life at all than I was of eventually losing him.'' She tilted her head to one side. "Jacob's a demanding kind of guy. Puller reminds me a lot of him. Jacob wasn't going to settle for half of me. It was an all or nothing kind of deal.''

"But you weren't entering into the relationship with the same kind of baggage I am. I'd be asking Jackson to carry an unbearable burden.''

"I don't think you can decide that for him. He's the only one who can make that call.'' She hesitated. "Have you told him you can't have children?''

"Yes.''

"And he said? . . .''

"What I thought he would. He was disappointed, but he thinks he'll get over it—that we'd work it out.''

"And you don't trust him.''

"Forever is a long time.''

"Sure is. Do you want to think about the consequences of spending forever without him in it?''

Cammy frowned. "It feels selfish to want so much. Somehow, I can't get past that. I've known for years that my father believed our lives were supposed to revolve around his.''

Macon shook her head. "Durstan was a very effective and powerful man. I can admire a lot of what he did while he was in the Senate, but what he did to you, well, that's another story."

"He was angry. He saw my mother's illness as a political liability. That's a big enough character flaw alone to put the man in the jerk hall of fame." She flashed Macon a slight smile. "Believe me, I know that."

"I've never understood politicians who aren't willing to simply tell the truth. They're human. They have flaws. Their families have flaws. They're better people if they can simply admit that."

"My father worried that my mother might embarrass him in public."

Macon shrugged. "What if she did?"

"He didn't think his political career could survive. I've never understood that. If she were epileptic and had a seizure, would anyone be embarrassed? Or if she had a heart problem and suffered an attack during some fund-raising banquet, do you think anyone would have condemned my father for that? I know people have a harder time accepting mental disability than physical disability, but my father had the chance to raise the bar." She had a brief memory of Laura calling for Durstan during the final hours of her life. "Instead, he hid behind his own cowardice and weakness."

Macon made a disgusted sound in the back of her throat. "And, unfortunately, he vented that anger and frustration on you." She narrowed her gaze. "Are you going to keep paying for that forever?"

"That doesn't mean—" The insistent ring of Macon's beeper interrupted Cammy's sentence. They both looked at the small black box on Macon's belt.

She switched it off. "Jacob," she explained.

Cammy indicated the phone with a wave of her hand. "Call him."

"It can wait."

"No. Really, call him."

Macon reached for the phone. "I'm not through talking about this."

"I didn't even dare to hope that you were."

She stared thoughtfully at the stack of phone messages on her desk while Macon spoke to her husband. Most pertained to Jeffrey Herrington's hot pursuit of her professional reputation. How in the world, she wondered, had she let things become such a mess?

"You're kidding?" Macon said. "All right, I'll tell her." She paused. "No later than six. Okay. Thanks." She hung up the phone, then looked at Cammy. "Turn on the TV. Jacob said there's something we should see."

Cammy reached for the remote. She kept the TV in her office for use during the sessions she held with her Wishing Star children. "What channel?"

"Pick a network. It's a press conference."

"Is Anita Meyerson announcing my public execution?" She punched the button. "I'm not sure I want to watch this."

"No. It's something else."

"You mean the press has found something else to talk about besides the way I'm—?" She found the station, then froze.

Jackson stood in front of a bank of microphones. The sight of him made her heart ache. He looked like a sea of calm in the midst of a hurricane. He had on a green shirt and the same suspenders he'd worn the day she'd met him. With his dark hair and intent eyes, he still had that slightly old-fashioned look that made him look like the most trustworthy man alive.

He was glaring at a room full of reporters—his colleagues—and speaking in a clipped tone as he told them in no uncertain terms what he thought of them.

"For years," he was saying, "I believed that you and I belonged to one of the most honorable professions in the world. We were responsible for ensuring public attention on key issues, things that affect lives and change history. We are charged with telling the truth, even when we don't like it, and putting the good of the whole above the good of our careers and personal lives."

He drew a deep breath. "It wasn't until several weeks ago that I even began to question whether or not I'd gotten so caught up in keeping my job that I'd forgotten to *do* my job. There's not a person in this room who is unaware of what happened to me in Bosnia while I was pursuing a story. The death of Leo Svetlani was a tragedy in every sense of the word.

"And the truth is, I probably couldn't have prevented Leo's death, but neither did I have to profit from it. Did the story of Leo's death really need to be told? Was anyone's interest but my own advanced because I wrote the last chapter of that story? I don't think so. I don't think Leo's mother felt better knowing I'd shared her grief with the rest of the world, or that Leo's life meant more because I thrust him into the public eye.

"He wanted to grow up and join the Beatles. He hadn't planned on being a superstar because of his death."

Jackson looked directly at the camera, and Cammy's heart skipped a beat. "Then, as if to make sure I knew it was all right with all of you, you offered to give me an award for the noble deed of exploiting the tragedy of Leo's life." He shook his head. "And fool that I was, even that didn't help me find the truth." His voice had turned raw.

"I didn't really see what was happening here until five weeks ago, when I walked into the office of Dr. Cameo Glynn."

Cammy swallowed. Macon's eyebrows lifted. "Wow." Cammy continued to stare at the screen. Jackson glared at the camera. "It was a remarkable experience," he was saying.

Macon made an exultant noise. "I couldn't have written this better myself. Maybe we should go over there."

"We can't," Cammy told her, transfixed. "I want to see the rest."

"We could listen to it in the car."

She shook her head. "I want to *see* it. What I can see is the best part of listening for me."

Jackson was talking about the meeting they'd had in Mike's office. Cammy looked first at the TV, then at Macon, then back at Jackson's beloved face. How in the world, she mused, had she failed to realize how much she loved this man?

He'd looked at her with that same rough tenderness when he'd finally acceded to her wishes at the hospital last night. She'd first seen it, she realized, the morning he'd made love to her without the benefit of her transmitter. He'd been trying to tell her, even then, how much he valued her, flaws and all.

For an expert in nonverbal communication, she mused, she certainly had managed to make a mess of listening to him. Like an idiot, she'd ignored every sign he'd ever given her, set him up to disappoint her, and then judged him wanting without evidence or reason to support her decision. She'd stake her life on the fact that he was trying, now, with his words and his actions, to reach her.

A vision of her mother weeping over Durstan, clinging to her hand, popped into Cammy's mind. What had destroyed her parents' marriage was a stack of unreasonable expectations, compounded by an unwillingness to forgive one another's faults. Surely, if Jackson could forgive himself for Leo's death, he could forgive her, just once more, for being a blind fool.

Her fingers tapped a nervous rhythm on her desktop. "Do you know where he is?"

"National Press Club. Third-floor briefing room. I recognize the wallpaper. Sure you don't want to go?"

A final look at his face as he explained how Cammy had berated him that morning gave her the courage to take the final leap. "No," she told Macon. "I want to watch the rest of this. Then I want you to schedule that press conference you've been pressuring me to hold."

"You're sure?"

"I'm sure. He shouldn't be the only one out there on that limb."

"While you're in this agreeable mood, can I convince you to let Jacob and me go with you to the memorial garden today?"

Cammy hesitated. "I think I'd like that."

"May I call Jackson and tell him to meet us there?"

"Don't push your luck."

✧✧ ♡ eighteen

"I pursued the story," Jackson continued to explain, "against Dr. Glynn's wishes. She feared that with our usual rabid attention to the spectacular and our reckless disregard for lives, we might exploit some of the children she treats."

He paused. The tension in the room was palpable. Chris Harris would probably have his head for this, but it didn't matter. About the only thing that really mattered in his life right now was convincing Cammy that he'd go the distance with her. He'd lain awake most of the night wondering how in the hell he was supposed to get past the fortress she'd built around herself, and knowing that his life wouldn't be worth living if he couldn't.

Somewhere around three or four o'clock in the morning, he'd begun to remember all the things she'd ever said to him about journalists, and their selfish motives and selfish tactics. He'd taken a long look at himself and not liked what he'd found. Was it any wonder, he'd asked himself as he'd crawled out of bed and begun to write the statement he was now making, that she doubted him?

"She was right about all of it," he said aloud. "Without any concern for the consequences, we, the media, latched on to Amy Patterson, and her personal struggle, and made it a quixotic crusade that involves everything from Congresswoman Meyerson's political aspirations to Jeffrey Herrington's personal ambition. And I am just as guilty as every one of you."

He took a deep breath. "Well, things are going to change. Starting now. First, I want to go on record as saying that I have personally observed Dr. Glynn's methods with the children she treats, and find her to be both deeply committed to their welfare and personally concerned about their individual development.

"Amy Patterson suffered a great disappointment, and Dr. Glynn shared her grief. To any extent that I failed to properly represent that to you, I ask your forgiveness. I fully understand why the public found themselves engaged by that child. She has more spirit and courage than most of us—certainly more than I have shown in recent weeks. In that, she has an excellent role model in Dr. Glynn. Dr. Glynn is responsive to the needs of her patients, honest, generous and ethical.

"Which is more," he said firmly, "than I can say for the lot of us. People trust us to be truthful and thorough. They read what we write, or watch us on television, and believe that we have the right to give them that information—that we've researched it, studied it, and are relaying only what we know to be true.

I, for one, am willing to admit that I have betrayed that trust."

He held up the file he'd been working on since late yesterday afternoon. "For the past two weeks, we have relied on the information both Jeffrey Herrington and Anita Meyerson have provided to attack Dr. Glynn, exploit Amy Patterson's story, and sell papers and air time. America wanted more. We gave it to them. Unfortunately, on our way to high ratings, we turned a blind eye to the facts.

"In the briefing folders you received when you came in is all the information you and I both should have been looking at all along. I think you'll find that not only do dozens of experts agree that Dr. Glynn's methods and programs are above reproach but that evidence suggests that Dr. Glynn's detractors are motivated by greed and ambition, not their concern for her patients, or for the public good."

Now for the hard part, he mused. If he got through this without his heart breaking in a million pieces, it would be a small miracle. "I want to interject one personal note, and then I'll take questions. Most of you are aware of the rumors about my relationship with Dr. Glynn. In my experience, Dr. Cameo Glynn is a remarkably gifted woman with a deep capacity for caring. If the world had more people in it like her, and less people in it like us, we might be out of a job. Chances are, there'd be no muck for us to rake. As regards any personal relationship Dr. Glynn and I may have, I would only say that I should be so fortunate, and that if Anita Meyerson and Jeffrey Herrington are looking for a schoolyard fight, they'd better stick with me. Cameo Glynn is way out of their league.''

A week later, he slipped his hand into his tuxedo pocket and fingered the engraved invitation with a vague sense of hope. He stepped off the elevator and glanced at the large ballroom full of people. Cammy's fund-raiser, it seemed, was a rousing success.

In the days since his press conference, he'd barely heard from her. He'd heard from Costas that he'd missed her mother's interment. That had almost killed him. He'd tried, several times, to call her, but he had missed her. He'd finally ended up sending her flowers with a note begging her to contact him. She'd sent him a note in return, thanking him for the flowers and his defense. He'd carried it around in his wallet like a lovesick fool. The next afternoon, he'd sat quietly in the audience and watched her handle herself like a seasoned pro at a press conference of her own. She'd met his gaze just once, her expression unreadable.

The fallout from his public diatribe hadn't been as bad as he'd expected. Chris Harris had been almost pleased with the way the public had responded. No one had gotten fired, which Jackson considered to be a very good sign. As he'd hoped, Meyerson and Herrington had begun to face enormous pressure to justify their attacks on the Wishing Star Foundation. Jackson had written an article citing the views of experts, parents, doctors, scientists, and, perhaps most persuasively, the patients that Cammy had treated. Response had been swift and overwhelming.

The day after Jackson's press conference, President Stratton had ended a Q&A session with a public announcement of his support for Cammy and the foundation. Chris had authorized the release of the Meyerson story, with its allegations of foreign campaign contributions and misconduct. In the days since the story broke, several key members of the House Ethics Committee had called for hearings into the matter.

Anita Meyerson had been the first to see the light, and she'd called off her investigation of Cammy and the foundation. It had taken Jackson, several of his colleagues, and Gordon Stratton to convince her that Herrington had suckered her, but she'd finally given in.

When she turned the full force of her anger on Jeffrey Herrington, the little bastard had squirmed. While Jackson had guessed, rightly, that Anita Meyerson was somewhat misguided but capable of doing the right thing, he didn't hesitate to level Herrington, who represented everything Jackson despised about politics. Releasing all the information he had and making sure it got into the right hands, Jackson had brought coals of fire down on Herrington's head. With Meyerson's help, Jackson had ensured that Herrington would have to choose between backing down and political ruin.

For the rest of the week, every news agency in town carried the story of Cammy's amazing grace under pressure. In the multiple appearances she made, appearances Jackson knew were personally difficult for her, she never wavered. She came across as the gem

that she was. Long ago, Jackson realized that in a
world filled with fakes and forgeries, Cameo Glynn
represented the genuine article. He loved her for it.
And now, the world loved her too.

As a result of her meteoric rise to fame and her
unrelenting charm, the Wishing Star Foundation fund-
raiser had become the talk of the town. With the
White House announcement that the president himself would attend, invitations became scarcer than
snow in July. Every reporter he knew was begging
for a press pass, and he'd seen Cammy on the evening news, talking about the incredible outpouring of
research support and corporate sponsorships for the
foundation.

To Jackson's delight, the executive board of the
Associated Wire Service had voted to give Amy Patterson a complete dance scholarship to the Duke El-
lington School for the Performing Arts.

By all accounts, he should be ecstatic. Things could
not have worked out any better.

But the one thing that really mattered, his relationship with Cammy, remained in a quagmire of doubt.

And now as he stared at the open archway into the
ballroom, he had the unmistakable feeling that his future lay inside. His thumb stroked the invitation again.
Had Cammy not couriered it to his office this afternoon, he might not have mustered the courage to attend. He was a coward, he was beginning to realize,
when it came to her. The thought that he might lose
her absolutely scared the wits out of him.

His heart had almost exploded when he'd removed
the invitation from its vellum envelope. Cammy had

scrawled one word across the raised print of the invitation: WHISTLE.

If you want me, just whistle. He'd jokingly tossed off that statement a half-dozen times, never realizing that it would come to have such significance. Dragging in a deep breath, he headed for the door.

He spotted her almost immediately. She stood near the dais, wearing that black dress she'd worn the night of their "date" at the observatory. A good sign, he hoped, despite his very irrational surge of jealousy at the looks of masculine appreciation she was receiving.

As if she sensed his presence, she glanced across the room to meet his gaze. He couldn't read the expression in her eyes, couldn't decipher the way her lips parted, or the slightly nervous sweep of her hand when she tucked a tendril of hair behind her ear. Frustrated, he began the torturous process of making his way through the dense crowd. Every couple of steps, someone stopped him to comment on his press conference, congratulate him on his Pulitzer nomination, or make small talk. He managed, he hoped, to avoid being rude, but he wasn't willing to bet on it.

He was within thirty feet of the dais when he saw Macon give Cammy a silent cue. Cammy glanced at him once more, then broke free of the group she was in to make her way to the platform. He froze, riveted by the look of promise he'd seen in her eyes.

She walked gracefully to the podium, with the poise of a queen. He had come to recognize her picture-perfect calm as a mask for her nervousness. She stepped up to the microphone, placed two fingers between her lips, and gave a shrill whistle. Jackson's heart stopped beating.

A startled crowd fell suddenly silent. Every eye in the room turned to the platform. With a slight smile, Cammy apologized. "I'm sorry for the racket. My father was always telling me to act more like a lady, and I've had the insatiable urge to do that for years. Besides," she said with a shrug, "it's my party."

The crowd laughed. Everyone, Jackson noted, except for him and Cammy. She found his gaze. Her expression softened and he felt the blood begin to move in his veins again. "And that particular whistle," she went on, "has a special significance I'll explain later."

He watched her carefully begin to disarm the crowd with her indefinable charm, and his heart swelled with love for her. One smile, and she had them eating out of her hand.

"Many of you know," she was saying, "that the journey to tonight's event has been more than a little tumultuous. For those of you who supported the foundation during its darker hours, I offer you my eternal thanks." A devilish smile played at the corner of her lips. "For those of you who've finally seen the light, I'll let you know now that generous donations go a long way toward easing my wrath." The crowd laughed again.

She continued, "Before I introduce President Stratton, whom I know you'd all rather hear than me, I did have one item of personal business I wanted to address."

She met Jackson's gaze again. "Several weeks ago,

a man came into my office and turned my life upside down. I wasn't even remotely prepared for what he was going to do to me. I'd never relished living in the spotlight, and I didn't exactly know what to do when he cast it on me.

"At first, I didn't want to trust him. Reporters, in my experience, and I wish I could say present company excluded . . ." That won her a collective laugh. Jackson almost didn't hear it over the roaring in his ears. This woman who had stolen his heart and taken him captive, who hated speaking in public, was about to save him from a lifetime of misery. Cammy waited for the murmur to die down. ". . . are generally more interested in stories than in people.

"But this reporter was startlingly different. He took an interest not only in the children I work with but in me personally." She drew a deep breath. "And I unfairly tried to decide for him what he should and should not want."

She was looking right at him now. The crowd, he knew, was hanging on her every word. "I believed," she continued softly, "that I was in a better position than he to make decisions about the future. That I knew more about the risks, and that I could more adequately decide how to manage those risks. But then he taught me something.

"Jackson Puller taught me that men of honor and character are willing to go to extraordinary lengths for the sake of justice and compassion. I'm hoping," her head tilted to one side, "that he's also willing to go to great lengths for the sake of a foolish woman who should have known what love looked like when she saw it.''

Holding his gaze for a few breathless seconds, she silently pleaded with him. A nudge at his left shoulder had him pushing his way forward again. He barely had time to glance back and send Jacob Blackfort an appreciative look for the shove.

''He used to tell me that if I ever wanted him, all I had to do was whistle.'' She paused as he neared the stage. ''I'm whistling. I hope he's listening.''

''He's listening,'' Jackson said. He strode onto the platform, grabbed her hand, and edged her away from the microphone. ''If you'll excuse us,'' he told their now rapt audience, ''Dr. Glynn and I have something to discuss.'' In his peripheral vision, he saw Gordon Stratton waiting near the stairs to the dais. ''Besides, the president's here. I'm sure he's got a speech ready.''

Without giving Cammy a chance to respond, afraid he'd lose her if he did, he pulled on her hand until she followed him off the platform. He shouldered his way through the crowd toward a door at the back of the ballroom. Vaguely, he heard the president say, ''Well, that'll be a hard act to follow,'' but the ringing in his ears had turned into a full-blown carillon.

He shoved open the door and tugged Cammy into the close confines of the supply closet. Surrounded by stacks of linens and dishes and stemware, he pulled her into his arms and kissed her soundly. Starving, he realized. He was absolutely starving. His hands roamed over her. He couldn't get close enough. His breathing came in harsh pants. "I told you once," he said, "that I love to listen to you."

In the dim light, he saw a tremulous smile touch her lips. "Even when I say really stupid things?"

"About the only thing you ever said that I didn't listen to is that you wanted to get rid of me." In the ballroom, the crowd burst into laughter. Jackson eased her closer.

"I meant it at the time."

"No, you didn't," he countered. "I've learned that about you. You're a rotten liar."

"Then are you going to believe me when I say I'm sorry?"

"I've got no choice." He cupped her face in his hand. "You're holding my destiny in your hands, Cammy. I want you."

"Flaws and all?"

"If you didn't have any flaws, you'd be impossible to live with. I've never been able to stand perfect women."

"And I positively loathe perfect men." She was smiling now, and his universe was starting to right itself.

"Are you telling me you're ready to believe I can go the distance with you?"

"Yes," she nodded.

"What changed your mind?" He had to know, couldn't risk going through this again.

"Watching you tell a room full of people that you'd forgiven yourself for what happened to Leo."

That made him pause. "Really?"

"Yes. The way I see it, if you'd forgive yourself

for that, then surely you'd forgive me, too.''

"So, the rest of the public apology wasn't necessary?''

"No, I guess not.''

"Well, damn. I wish you'd told me that *before* I made a jerk of myself.'' The crowd's response to the president seemed farther away this time.

"You didn't make a jerk of yourself. I thought it was kind of heroic.''

He heard the crowd laugh again. The harsh intrusion might have irritated him if he weren't feeling so euphoric. "Were you impressed enough to let me have the full package?''

"All of me, you mean?''

"The whole thing, honey. I'm not the type to settle for less.''

"Macon told me you wouldn't be.''

"She was right.''

He saw the fear in her eyes, but she held his gaze. And he adored her for it. "All right.''

"Can we get one thing straight first?''

"There's more?''

"Honey, there's a ton more.'' He paused when he heard the president call his name. "But there are two thousand people waiting for us to come out of this closet, and when I'm ready to tell you the rest, I don't want an audience.''

"Then what did you want?''

"I would like to adopt four children.''

Surprise, then a tender kind of warmth that threatened to melt him into the floor, filled her eyes. "Four?''

"Yes."

"I guess that would be all right."

He heard his name again. The president was beginning to sound edgy. "There's a catch."

Her eyebrows lifted. "Another one?"

"Yep. Didn't you know I'd be hard to live with?"

"The thought did occur to me." She tapped her fingers on his chest. "All right. What else do you want?"

"At least three of the four children we adopt have to be deaf. And one of them has to be Amy Patterson."

Cammy made a slight sound in the back of her throat, threw her arms around his neck. "Oh, Jackson. Did I ever tell you that you've made every wish I had come true?"

"I love you, too," he muttered as he surrendered to her kiss.

When he heard his name the third time, he finally gave in. Without breaking the kiss, he nudged open the door with his foot. Vaguely, he heard the muttered approval of the crowd. As he felt Cammy begin to pull away from him, he slipped his hand around to switch off her transmitter so she wouldn't be distracted from her exploration of his mouth. She'd kill him for this later, he guessed, but he didn't care.

"Mr. Puller," he heard Gordon Stratton say, "I suppose this means everything has turned out okay."

He gave the president a thumbs-up, tuned out the applause of the audience, and pulled Cammy back into the closet. As the door swung shut, he saw Jacob Blackfort move into position in front of the closet. No one was going to climb onto their corner of paradise. With a soft sigh and his heart filled to bursting, Jackson wrapped both arms around the woman he loved, made a mental note to thank Jacob later, and let Cammy take him all the way to heaven.

✨♡ *epilogue*

Cammy reached for the phone with a slight yawn. One thing she'd learned in two years of marriage—Jackson had never mastered the concept of time zones. "It's three in the morning," she told him.

"I know. Sorry."

"Are you still in Romania?"

"No, I'm at JFK."

She laughed at that. "So you really did know how late it is. Did you wake me up on purpose?"

"I woke you up because I was dying to hear your voice."

"Okay. You're forgiven."

"Thanks." He exhaled a weary breath. "How are things?"

"Great. The kids are so happy you're going to make it home for Christmas."

"So am I. Is Amy ready for opening night?"

A smile played on the corner of her mouth. Amy was dancing in the Nutcracker at the Kennedy Center. Jackson, she knew, had moved heaven and earth to make it home in time for the opening. "Yes. She's got jitters, but she's ready. Lynette says she'll knock their socks off."

"I'm sure she will," he said with his typical fatherly confidence. "I never doubted it."

"And I adore you for that." She shifted in the bed.

"Is Peter over his cold?" he asked, referring to the five-year-old son they'd recently adopted.

Her life, she thought, not for the first time, was richly blessed. "Yes. He's better." Since that day on the stage at the Wishing Star fund-raiser, Jackson had found a thousand ways to show her that he loved her. Daily, it seemed, her love for him grew and blossomed in ways she could never have imagined.

"I'm glad. I know it's been hard on you taking care of him by yourself." In the background, she heard the airport loudspeaker.

"We managed." She yawned again. "Are they calling your flight?"

"Yes. I should be home around six or so."

"Hmm. I can't wait to see you."

"I can't wait to see you either." He hesitated. "Uh, Cammy—"

She smiled. She knew exactly what was coming. "Before you start, I think there's something you should know."

"You do."

"Yes. You know that leather jacket you wanted for Christmas?"

"Yes."

"I bought it for you."

"Oh." He sounded confused.

"I also returned it today. I figured those fifteen Romanian orphans you're bringing to our house for Christmas morning needed presents more than you needed that jacket."

His laugh warmed her. "How did you know?"

"Because I love you. I saw your report last night, and the minute you said you'd made arrangements to get those kids to the States, I just knew."

"You are incredible."

"I'm glad you recognize that."

"Are you sure you're all right with this?"

"I'd be disappointed if you didn't show up with a vanload. Besides, who else is going to eat all the candy I bought?"

"I never thought I'd see the day when you were worried about getting rid of chocolate."

"You haven't seen what I bought yet."

"Am I going to have to return your Christmas present, too?"

"Don't worry. I don't think I broke the bank."

The loudspeaker crackled again. "That's my flight."

"I'll be waiting for you."

"No kidding?"

"Would it surprise you to know that I think I've been waiting for you my entire life?" Tears stung her eyes.

"Ah, Cammy." She heard the emotion in his voice. "Promise you'll never quit talking to me."

"I don't think I could if I wanted to."

"Have I told you today how much I love you?"

"In a dozen different ways," she assured him.

"Sometimes, I still can't believe it took me so long to interpret the signs."

"Good thing we've got the rest of our lives for you to figure them all out." The final boarding call sounded for his flight. "I've got to go, babe."

"Fly safely," she told him. "And if you happen to see my wishing star when you're up there, tell it I said thanks."

*Celebrate the Millennium
with another irresistible
romance from the pen of
Susan Elizabeth Phillips!*

The beautiful young widow of the President
of the United States is on the run, crossing
America on a journey to find herself. She
plans to travel alone, and she's chosen the
perfect disguise. Well, almost perfect...and
not exactly alone...

FIRST LADY
by Susan Elizabeth Phillips

Coming from Avon Books February 2000

Discover Contemporary Romances
at Their Sizzling Hot Best
from Avon Books

WIFE FOR A DAY   *by Patti Berg*
80735-1/$5.99 US/$7.99 Can

PILLOW TALK   *by Hailey North*
80519-7/$5.99 US/$7.99 Can

HER MAN FRIDAY   *by Elizabeth Bevarly*
80020-9/$5.99 US/$7.99 Can

SECOND STAR TO THE RIGHT *by Mary Alice Kruesi*
79887-5/$5.99 US/$7.99 Can

A CHANCE ON LOVIN' YOU   *by Eboni Snoe*
79563-9/$5.99 US/$7.99 Can

ALL NIGHT LONG   *by Michelle Jerott*
81066-2/$5.99 US/$7.99 Can

SLEEPLESS IN MONTANA   *by Cait London*
80038-1/$5.99 US/$7.99 Can

Dear Reader,

You loved *How to Marry a Marquis* by Julia Quinn, and you're going to simply adore *The Duke and I*, her latest delightful, sensuous Avon Romantic Treasure. Simon Basset, the Duke of Hastings, must marry and produce an heir, even though he has vowed never to marry. But he made that vow before he met Daphne Bridgerton, the eldest daughter of eight children. And when Daphne is compromised, society dictates that she must marry her reluctant duke—but that's only the beginning!

Sue Civil-Brown is so well known for her delightful, playful contemporary love stories, and *Catching Kelly* is no exception. Kelly Burke left home at 18 and has never looked back. After all, she's much too sensible for that crowd of harmless, but frustrating, eccentrics. Then she gets word that a sexy interloper has taken her place in the family, so she hurries home—never expecting that he'd take his place in her heart!

Next, it's off to Scotland in Lois Greiman's *Highland Hawk*, a tie-in to her successful *Highland Brides* series. Lovely Catriona is on a mission—one that brings her directly in conflict with Haydan MacGowan, captain of the king's guard. This seductive Scotsman knows Catriona is up to something—and he's determined to use every bit of his wiles to learn what that is!

Maureen McKade's western romances are simply delicious, and with *Mail-Order Bride*, she creates one of her most memorable stories yet! Kate Murphy arrives in Colorado expecting to marry one man...but she ends up wed to another. "Trev" Trevelyan needs a mother to his children, and a wife in his bed. But can Kate find love with this improper stranger?

Enjoy!

Lucia Macro
Lucia Macro
Senior Editor

ael 1299